ACCLAIM FOR *SOUL'S GATE*

"Powerful storytelling. Rubart writes with a depth of understanding about a realm most of us never investigate, let alone delve into. A deep and mystical journey that will leave you thinking long after you finish the book."

—TED DEKKER, *NEW YORK TIMES* BEST-SELLING AUTHOR OF
THE CIRCLE SERIES AND *FORBIDDEN* (WITH TOSCA LEE)

"Tight, boiled-down writing and an intriguing premise that will make you reconsider what you think you know about the spiritual realm."

—STEVEN JAMES, NATIONAL BESTSELLING AUTHOR
OF *PLACEBO* AND *OPENING MOVES*

"*Soul's Gate* takes readers on a wild flight of fantasy into the spiritual realm, where we find the battle for our souls is even wilder than we imagined—and very, very real. With vividly drawn characters, startling imagery, and the power of a spiritual air-raid siren, the story is at once entertaining and breathtakingly enlightening. James L. Rubart has crafted a stunning piece of work, a call to arms for everyone who yearns for the freedom of the abundant life Christ promises us—and is willing to fight for it. Rubart knocks it out of the park with this one."

—ROBERT LIPARULO, AUTHOR OF *THE 13TH
TRIBE* AND *COMES A HORSEMAN*

"Don't read this unless you're ready to see with new eyes. Through evocative prose and masterful storytelling, Rubart transports you to the spiritual realm—a realm of vision, mystery, healing and power. A deep and thoughtful—and jet-propelled—spiritual journey of a book."

—TOSCA LEE, *NEW YORK TIMES* BEST-SELLING AUTHOR OF THE BOOKS
OF MORTALS SERIES WITH TED DEKKER AND *DEMON: A MEMOIR*

ACCLAIM FOR *ROOMS*

"Suspenseful . . . compelling."
— *Publishers Weekly*

"Rubart's novel takes an amazing, unique look at God."
— *Romantic Times* TOP PICK

"*Rooms* is one of the best books I've read in the past year. If you liked *The Shack*, I think you'll like *Rooms*. If you didn't like *The Shack*, I bet you'll love *Rooms*."
— Randy Ingermanson, author of *Oxygen*

"A profound spiritual tale spun with imaginative flair."
— James Scott Bell, author of *Angels Flight* (with Tracie Peterson)

ACCLAIM FOR *BOOK OF DAYS*

". . . Rubart has created a page turner."
— *Publishers Weekly*

"Rubart has again created a unique and amazingly thought provoking novel."
— *Romantic Times*

"Rubart combines scripture with legend to create an engaging tale of self-discovery . . ."
— *Christian Retailing*

"Well crafted and full of plot twists and turns . . . will appeal to fans of Ted Dekker."

—LIBRARY JOURNAL

"Rubart is one of my favorite new authors . . . a master storyteller with his second release as good as or better than *Rooms*."

—EXAMINER.COM

"James L. Rubart is a storyteller who pricks the heart of our generation and causes us to think about where we've been and where we're going. *Book of Days* is a must read."

—RACHEL HAUCK, BEST-SELLING AUTHOR OF *THE WEDDING DRESS*

"*Book of Days* is a great read, why people buy novels."

—DAN WALSH, AWARD-WINNING AUTHOR OF *THE UNFINISHED GIFT*

"[In *Book of Days*] Rubart crafts a terrific story that is equal parts fast-paced thriller, thought-provoking allegory, and moving drama."

—RICK ACKER, AUTHOR OF *WHEN THE DEVIL WHISTLES*

ACCLAIM FOR *THE CHAIR*

"James Rubart is one of my new favorite authors. *The Chair* has the same depth and creativity as *Rooms*, and it was impossible for me to think of anything else until I finished it. I can't wait for his next book!"

—TERRI BLACKSTOCK, BEST-SELLING AUTHOR
OF *INTERVENTION* AND *VICIOUS CYCLE*

"Romance, mystery, danger, betrayal . . . and most of all, a message of healing and restoration. Taking readers far beneath the surface, Rubart masterfully paints a picture of God's depth of love and longing for relationship with even those who are running away from Him as fast as they can. A tale of unimaginable sacrifice and unconditional love that will tug at your heart long after you've completed the last page."

—KATHI MACIAS, AWARD-WINNING AUTHOR
OF *DELIVER ME FROM EVIL*

"Rubart has a stellar ability to communicate spiritual truth through a highly original, well-told story . . . a compulsively readable tale."

—*ROMANTIC TIMES*

SOUL'S GATE

Soul's GATE

A WELL SPRING NOVEL: BOOK 1

JAMES L. RUBART

Thomas Nelson
Since 1798

NASHVILLE   DALLAS   MEXICO CITY   RIO DE JANEIRO

Published in Nashville, Tennessee, by Thomas Nelson. Thomas Nelson is a registered trademark of Thomas Nelson, Inc.

The author is represented by the literary agency of Alive Communications, Inc., 7680 Goddard Street, Suite 200, Colorado Springs, CO 80920. www .alivecommunications.com.

Thomas Nelson, Inc., titles may be purchased in bulk for educational, business, fund-raising, or sales promotional use. For information, please e-mail SpecialMarkets@ThomasNelson.com.

Publisher's Note: This novel is a work of fiction. Names, characters, places, and incidents are either products of the author's imagination or used fictitiously. All characters are fictional, and any similarity to people living or dead is purely coincidental.

Scripture quotations are taken from HOLY BIBLE: NEW INTERNATIONAL VERSION®. Copyright © 1973, 1978, 1984, 2011 by Biblica, Inc. ™ Used by permission. All rights reserved worldwide. NEW AMERICAN STANDARD BIBLE®, © The Lockman Foundation 1960, 1962, 1963, 1968, 1971, 1972, 1973, 1975, 1977, 1995. Used by permission. *Holy Bible, New Living Translation.* © 1996. Used by permission of Tyndale House Publishers, Inc., Wheaton, Illinois 60189. All rights reserved. THE ENGLISH STANDARD VERSION. © 2001 by Crossway Bibles, a division of Good News Publishers. *The Message* by Eugene H. Peterson. © 1993, 1994, 1995, 1996, 2000. Used by permission of NavPress Publishing Group. All rights reserved. HOLY BIBLE: NEW INTERNATIONAL READER'S VERSION®. Copyright © 1996, 1998 Biblica. All rights reserved throughout the world. Used by permission of Biblica.

ISBN 978-1-4016-8785-4 (SE)

Library of Congress Cataloging-in-Publication Data

Rubart, James L.
   Soul's gate / James L. Rubart.
      p. cm.
   ISBN 978-1-4016-8605-5 (trade paper)
   1. Christian fiction. I. Title.
PS3618.U2326S68 2012
813'.6--dc23

2012035205

Printed in the United States of America

12 13 14 15 16 QG 6 5 4 3 2 1

FOR HALL, FOR MAKING MY
DREAMS COME TRUE

"Our fight is not against human beings. It is against the rulers, the authorities and the powers of this dark world. It is against the spiritual forces of evil in the heavenly world."

PAUL OF TARSUS TO THE EPHESIANS, AD 62

"There are two equal and opposite errors into which our race can fall about the devils. One is to disbelieve in their existence. The other is to believe, and to feel an excessive and unhealthy interest in them. They themselves are equally pleased by both errors."

C. S. LEWIS

"We are locked in a battle. This is not a friendly gentlemen's discussion. It is a life and death conflict between the spiritual hosts of wickedness and those who claim the name of Christ."

FRANCIS A. SCHAEFFER

O∩E

REECE ROTH SPUN AT THE SOUND—A DULL SCRAPE LIKE
log on log. But there was nothing behind him except a small pile of
driftwood worn white by years of ocean rain and wind. A shadow
flitted in the corner of his eye, but as he turned farther to his left,
the darkness vanished.

His heart pumped faster as he took another quarter turn to complete the circle. His feet dug into the russet sand, his gaze darting
from ground to sky, taking in everything—seeing nothing unusual.

Only waves and seagulls and an endless beach stretching beyond
his sight both north and south. But the sensation that skittered up
and down his back didn't come from his imagination. Reece forced
himself to breathe slower as he brushed his thick graying hair back
from his forehead and squinted at the orange sun sinking below the
horizon.

Calm. Abba's peace. Embrace it. He needed to be here.

To get comfortable with doing this again after so many years away.
You killed them.

The thought slammed into Reece's mind like a fist to his temple.

*Admit it. It was your arrogance. Your pride. Just like you're going to
kill the four of the prophecy. You will fail again.*

"No." Reece squeezed his eyes shut. It wasn't the truth. *Take
every thought captive. Every idea.*

He prayed against the attack and a few moments later the

thoughts melted away. The power inside him was more than enough to counter any kind of assault. Without question Reece's head knew it was true. If only his heart could believe with the strength it used to.

He looked up the beach to his right. A hundred yards away two men in tan pants and white T-shirts seemed to materialize out of the dusk. They strolled toward him, glancing between the waves and the rocky cliffs to their left. A blast of wind shrieked into Reece's ears and kicked sand into his eyes. He slammed his eyes shut and covered his face.

When he lowered his hands and opened his eyes, the two men stood ten feet away. Smiling.

Reece's heart rate spiked.

"Good evening, Reece." The man on the right flicked his finger toward the orange-and-red-smeared clouds and the sky turned dark. He motioned again and the thundering waves froze in place as if they'd been doused in liquid nitrogen. "You don't mind, do you? Always nice to set an appropriate mood, you know?"

"Greater is he that is in me." Reece riveted his gaze on the two men.

"Yes, we're familiar with that sentiment. Thanks for bringing it up."

Reece stumbled back a step. "Jesus."

The man on the left smiled wider and pointed in back of Reece. The wood-on-wood sound filled the air again and Reece glanced behind him. What was a pile of driftwood minutes earlier had morphed into a sort of hut, maybe three feet tall and four feet wide.

He turned back to the men. "You have no power over me."

"Really?" The man on the left pointed behind him again. "You might want to look out, old man."

Something heavy slammed into his upper back and Reece lurched to his hands and knees and gasped for air. A moment later the hut thudded down around him. A driftwood cage.

"Comfortable?" The first man sauntered through the sand toward Reece and the other man followed.

Reece shoved his huge six-foot-five-inch frame hard against the driftwood logs that made up the ceiling and grunted. Nothing. The structure was like concrete bolted to the ground.

"Don't exhaust yourself. You won't escape."

"You can't stop me." Reece reached out and wrenched on the wood in front of him, but it didn't budge.

"Of course we can." The man laughed as he bent down, his face inches from the wood, and stared into Reece's eyes. "If you try, we'll take you out again. Like last time so long ago. You think you're ready to train them? You're not even close. You know that. So do we. Consider this a friendly warning, for old time's sake. Stay away from the four. Drop the idea of taking them to Well Spring. Cancel the trip. If you do, we won't go after them and we'll leave you alone. All those concerned will be much happier."

"In the name of Jesus get out of—"

"Good-bye, Reece. Please believe us, it will be extremely unprofitable for you—and for the four—if you attempt to go through the gateway into someone's soul ever again. Consider what is about to happen in the next few seconds an example as to what would come your way if you do."

The second man winked at Reece, then swirled his toe in the sand in a tight circle. As he did, the ground under Reece's knees and palms gave way and he was sucked down into the sand.

Grains poured over his head and forced their way into his mouth, covering his tongue and scraping down his throat. He choked, his head jerking forward, his lips parting, allowing more sand to jam its way into his mouth. He tried to suck in a breath through his nose but the sand filled it. The sand around his body thickened, pressing Reece's arms against his hips, pressing the remaining air out of his lungs. The darkness surrounding him grew and seemed to fill his mind.

No. Fight this. Have to get out of here!

The pressure on his body increased and the blackness swallowed him.

Your blood, Jesus, your power, now!

TWO·

AN INSTANT LATER THE SAND AROUND REECE VANISHED. Early morning sun shot through the maple trees in his backyard and spilled over him. He heaved forward in his chair, huge coughs racking his body and filling the Pacific Northwest air. He blinked and gasped, his hands clenching the arms of his teak chair. How long had he been . . . ? His watch said seven fifteen. He'd been inside for an hour and a half. Too long. He shouldn't have pushed it that far.

Reece stared at the fire pit in front of him. The flames had died out but the coals still burned red, throwing off enough heat to warm his hands. He let the warmth seep into his palms for a moment, then rubbed them against his face and over his head.

He shivered in spite of the fire. The sweat that soaked through his Beatles T-shirt made the cool late spring morning colder. He slipped onto his knees on the stamped concrete that surrounded the fire pit and leaned forward, hands on his legs.

"I can't do this, Lord. I'm not ready."

It's time. And there is little time left for you to do what must be done.

"You saw what happened in there."

Yes.

"And I'm supposed to train them to do what I *didn't* just do?"

Silence.

"You heard what they told me, Lord."

Nothing. Reece stayed on his knees for another five minutes, allowing his emotions to settle. Finally he rose to his feet, grabbed the thick, gnarled stick next to the ring of large stones that made up his fire pit, and spread out the coals. No chance of a spark lighting anything on fire even if it did escape, but it couldn't hurt to be safe.

He stared at the embers as he moved the stick through them in a slow circle. Should he postpone the trip? Get more prepared? Going in this morning should have been simple. The soul he'd entered should have been a safe place to practice. It made no sense.

It was meant to be a straightforward exercise, a test to make sure he still knew how to go in and get back out safely. To build his confidence for when he taught the four how to do it. To make sure he could protect them. But he'd blown it. They were leaving for Colorado in five days. He should have practiced every day since he embraced his destiny to train them. Why had he waited so long?

Simple. Fear hounded him. He was scared of being back on the front lines. Scared that it would turn out exactly as it had just now. Scared that the nameless ones were right and he would only usher in more death.

He glanced at his watch again. Seven twenty-five. In a little over thirty-two hours he'd head for Snoqualmie Falls, introduce the four to each other, and give them a few final thoughts before heading for Well Spring. And what would those thoughts be? He didn't know.

Reece set his fire stick down next to the pit, closed his eyes, and shook his head. He should call it off. He couldn't train them in his current spiritual condition.

I am in this. I will walk with you, every step.

"You were in that? Just now? Where?"

Again, silence. He picked up his old beat-up tan Stetson, put it on, and stood. As he stepped the one hudred yards from the fire pit to the back door of his two-story log cabin twenty miles northeast of Seattle, Reece again mulled over what he would tell the four tomorrow at the falls.

They needed inspiration. They needed to believe, erase any doubts about going. Reece pushed away the fear that continued to lap at the edges of his mind. He needed inspiration. He needed to believe. Reece pulled out his cell phone with shaking fingers.

"Hello?"

"I have to talk, Doug." Reece clomped up the stairs to his back deck and sat rigid in one of his polished wooden chairs, his body still twitching.

"About?"

"Well Spring. The prophecy. All of it."

"You were attacked when you were inside."

"You're not surprised."

"Something felt wrong when I was praying for you."

Reece pushed his hat back and rubbed his forehead. "Something was definitely wrong."

"I apologize, friend. I cannot chat at the moment. I have a call on the other line and the rest of my day is absurdly full, but I can chat late tonight or anytime tomorrow from midmorning on."

"I'm seeing all of them tomorrow afternoon. I want them to be introduced to each other at least once here before we head for the ranch together. What if I were to call you on the way, say around three thirty?"

"That will be fine. In the meantime remember, courage is not the absence of fear, it is action in the face of fear."

Reece hung up the phone and stared at it. Doug's words were true. It was enough. For the moment. But even if it wasn't, did Reece have an option? If the Spirit was in this and the prophecy was true, the only choice was to step into the battle and swing his sword till there was no breath left within him.

Reece pulled a yellowed paper folded in quarters from his back pocket. Had it really been thirty years since Doug had stood in front of him and spoken the words? He opened the paper and smoothed it out on his knee.

There will come a day when you will train them—they will be four. The song, the teacher, the leader, the temple. Keep your eyes open to see, your ears open to listen, your heart open to feel, and your mind open to discern.

When the time comes, the Spirit will reveal each of them to you. You will teach them the wonders of my power they can't yet imagine. And instruct these warriors how to go far inside the soul and marrow.

They will rise up and fight for the hearts of others. They will demolish strongholds in the heavens and grind their enemies to dust. Their victories will spread across the nations. You will pour out your life for them and lead them to freedom, and they will turn and bring healing to the broken and set the hearts of others free.

And when the wolf rises, the four must war against him and bring about his destruction.

Only they have hope of victory.

And for one, their vision will grow clear,

And for one, the darkness of choice will rain on them,

And for one, the other world will become more real than this one,

And for one, death will come before the appointed time.

He folded the paper and put it back in his pocket. Five days from now Reece would explain to Brandon, Dana, Marcus, and Tamera that they were the four. And pray like mad they believed him.

THREE

BRANDON SCOTT HELD THE LAST CHORD ON HIS MARTIN twelve-string till its amplified sound was smothered by the roar of more than four thousand fans crowding the SDSU Open Air Theatre in San Diego.

Seeing the audience with raised arms, pouring themselves out to Jesus, used to be an ocean of bliss pouring over him. These days? He didn't feel anything.

Where are you, Lord?

Brandon shuddered and let his head drop to his chest. The ache inside seemed to burn through his dark blue T-shirt. So many people right in front of him wanting hope, wanting joy, longing for life, and all he could offer was a formula he'd pumped out seven times this month alone on stages across the country.

As his head remained down, a smattering of applause floated toward him. They probably thought he was praying for them. He should be. The words of the song he'd just sung were strong and true and eloquent. Many would be moved by them. But to him they'd turned into words he'd sung too many times for too many years.

Where had the old days gone when the Spirit flowed and it didn't even feel like he was playing? The days when there was no set song list, when he played whatever God told him to play at that moment? The days when he'd stop in the middle of a song and pray for someone in the audience God told him to pray for? Vanished. That's where those days were. One more song. One more and the concert would be over. *Grind it out. Come on. Let's go.*

8

"You okay?"

"What?"

"Wake up, bro. One more, right?" His bass player, Anthony, bumped his shoulder into Brandon's. "You with us?"

Brandon raised his head and forced a smile. "Just pausing for dramatic effect."

Anthony laughed, which always made his ultralean frame shake like a lopsided blender. Brandon glanced at the rest of his band and started the count for the last song, "One, two, three, four!"

The band kicked into his signature closing song, "Run Wild, Run Free," and they played it flawlessly. At least Brandon hoped they did. His mind was on his meeting tomorrow. Was he really going on that retreat thing? Sure, why wouldn't he?

Three minutes and forty-two seconds later, Brandon held his guitar high in the air and pointed at the sky as thundering applause filled the arena.

"He is King! He is Lord!" Brandon waved to the crowd—flashing a big fake smile—then darted off the stage and down the stairs that led to the dressing rooms. The praise from the crowd seemed to follow him through the corridor, its sound reverberating around him but leaving a metallic taste in his mouth.

Because it was all a lie. He was a lie. Didn't used to be. But for the past three years? Yep. Going through the motions. Was God still part of it? Were people still being reached? Probably. He hoped so.

Hard shoes clicked on the floor behind him. Brandon didn't bother to turn around. It would be Kevin Kaison. Why was the guy managing him? All the girls Brandon knew said Kevin should be modeling. He had the look—five foot nine, brown hair, lean build. He had the vibe, people liked him immediately, and he was smart.

Brandon wasn't going to push Kevin away—he made life on the road and in his marketing and everywhere else run like a finely tuned Jaguar, but managing him couldn't be the end of Kevin's desires. Two more clicks and Kevin was beside him, matching Brandon's swift stride.

"Sweet show, pal. They love you here. Of course, they love you everywhere."

"Thanks."

"What song are you doing for an encore tonight?"

Brandon shook his head. "No."

"You don't have a song named that." Kevin whirled and walked backward in front of Brandon.

"I'm not doing an encore tonight."

"You're not?"

"No."

"What?"

"No." Brandon picked up his stride.

"I heard you the first two times."

"Then why'd you ask again?"

"It was a rhetorical *what*." Kevin smacked his hands together. "We need an encore."

"My *no* wasn't rhetorical."

"Stop."

Brandon stuttered to a stop and folded his arms. "Yeah?"

Kevin adjusted his Kangol glasses and pointed back down the hallway. "They're expecting an encore. I'm sure you must have an excellent reason why you're not doing one."

"I'm wiped out." Brandon pressed the tips of his forefingers into his eyes until stars appeared.

"Look at me, Brandon."

"Okay." He offered Kevin a half smile and leaned forward. "I'm seeing you."

"Who am I?"

"Who are you?" Brandon chuckled.

"Yeah."

Brandon folded his arms again and leaned back against the light gray concrete wall to the side of him. "I'm sure you have a point to this."

"I'm guessing 'I'm tired' works wonders with other people, but

I've been your manager for six years and your friend even longer. You're at the breaking point."

"I'm fine. Just tired. We've only had three days off in the last five weeks."

Kevin waved his hand back down the hall toward the stage again. "This is the fourth city in a row that has gone crazy asking for an encore, and the fourth city in a row where you've refused."

"Really. The fourth? I thought it was only the fourth."

"That's hilarious."

"Thanks." Brandon made a half turn and wiggled his thumb toward his dressing room. "Can I go now?"

"What's going on with you?"

"Like I said, I'm tired. I just need some sleep. A few days off the road and I'll be back to normal."

"You haven't been normal for a long time." Kevin looked up and down the hallway. "You need this getaway with Reece."

"You barely know the man."

"True, but I know he cares about you. I know he can't play the drums but thinks he can."

Brandon laughed. "He wasn't that bad, and the band had a good time with him sitting in for a couple of songs."

"And I know him enough to know you need to go."

Brandon shrugged. "Yeah, maybe."

"That doesn't sound convincing."

"I know, but I'm not exactly in the greatest place spiritually these days."

"Do I need to say it?"

"That's exactly why I have to go."

Kevin tapped his nose. "And, uh, do you think God's telling you to go on this thing?"

"Yeah."

"You're sure?"

"Yeah."

"Checkmate."

Brandon threw his arm around Kevin's neck and yanked his manager to his chest. "You're good for me, bro. I promise, I'm going to Colorado. I need to go. I can't go on like this much longer."

He released Kevin and eased down the hallway toward his dressing room. His manager's voice called out from behind him, "You're doing an encore in Phoenix."

"I'll do two there to make up for tonight."

Brandon stepped through his dressing room door and shut it behind him. Tomorrow he would meet the others going with him to Well Spring and find out why Reece had refused to tell him ahead of time who the other three were.

FOUR

REECE NEEDED A SERIOUS INJECTION OF BELIEF. AS HE pulled onto Paradise Lake Road on the way to Snoqualmie Falls Tuesday afternoon, he grabbed his phone and called Doug Lundeen to finish their conversation from the day before—hoping his friend would somehow resurrect Reece's faith in a quest that now felt foolish.

"How are you feeling?" Doug's soft voice floated through the phone, and immediately part of the tension that had burrowed into Reece's shoulders lifted.

"I'm not sure we should still go."

"You're going to Well Spring. You don't have a choice. You've put it off as long as you dare. The wolf is rising. It is gaining significant influence in the Kingdom and it has to be stopped. More than stopped. The wolf must be destroyed. Soon. Before it grows too powerful. And you cannot do it without the four."

"I realize that, but I'm not ready to take them through the gate."

"Do you want to describe what happened yesterday morning inside?"

Reece told Doug what happened, and his friend listened without comment. When he finished, Doug was silent.

"What happened to me? What went wrong?"

"Whose soul were you in?"

"Cline's."

"How long did you remain inside?"

Reece sighed. "Too long. But I needed to get acclima—"

"Which gave them enough time to sense you were inside and come through the gate."

"Yes."

"Was Cline the best choice to practice on?"

"He's solid. You know that."

"He is a good man, yes, but he was not the best choice. He has become an infrequent participant in our gatherings out here and his path has been shrouded in shadows for the past few years."

"You should have told me that."

"You should have asked."

Reece glanced at his speedometer and tapped on his brakes. "True."

"And how much prayer did you engage in before entry?"

"Not enough."

"Well now, even though the encounter was unpleasant, lessons have been learned and I imagine you're taking the confrontation inside as significant encouragement."

"Encouragement?" Reece gripped his brown leather steering wheel harder. "I got my backside dented in."

"Precisely. Which means you're worrying the enemy. You knew it wouldn't be easy when you came out of spiritual retirement."

"I haven't been retired."

"What would you call it?"

Reece slowed to a stop and stared at the red light hanging above Woodinville-Duvall Road as he waited to turn left. Yes, maybe he'd been at a stoplight spiritually for a while, but then again maybe the light had never turned green. Not true. It might have been green, but he'd stopped looking at it ages ago. "I'd describe it as having spent a few years not as engaged as I could have been."

"You have not truly been in the game for over twenty-five years. To others it probably looks like you're a pillar of the body, but a number of us know the truth."

Doug was right. He'd kept his foot in the water at best. Maybe not even that. Maybe just a couple of toes. It hadn't been close to enough. For so long he'd longed to dive in deep and wash off the dirt and grime that came from living on the fringes. To quench the thirst in his throat and heart. The past had kept him on the shore, but now the prophecy and Doug's persistence had pulled him back in. Reece just hoped he could keep his head from going under.

"I concede," Reece said.

"Are all four of them set to go?"

"Yes."

"Are you worried about any of them?"

"No. They're all committed." Reece slid on sunglasses against the light slicing through the clouds over the fields west of Duvall. "I still say it would be powerful to have you there with me."

"But it wouldn't be right."

"I know."

"This is your battle, friend. Your destiny. You have to lead with a confidence you won't always feel, release the power that has long lain dormant, and live in the faith of the old days. You must be strong. You can go through the gate again. I believe it. I know it. When the time comes you'll be ready."

Doug's words seeped into Reece's soul, and peace started to push back the trepidation lodged inside. "Thank you."

"And I will be there with you by interceding in the heavens. All of your old allies out here will be."

As Reece hung up, he turned right on Snoqualmie Valley Road and listened for the voice of the Spirit. As the lush spring growth on the trees and in the fields rushed by on his right, the Spirit spoke and Reece knew what he would tell the four of the prophecy. He would use this final day of May to explain how God would unveil the miraculous if they chose to step into it.

Thirty minutes later Reece sat in his Chevy Avalanche in the parking lot of Snoqualmie Falls waiting for Marcus Amber, Dana Raine, Brandon Scott, and Tamera Miller to arrive—praying they would catch the vision of the revolution that could happen at Well Spring, praying they connected with each other. He asked for strength to fight against the fear that lingered in his mind like a low-lying cloud. He prayed for Doug's words to take root. Reece prayed for wisdom as he stumbled down a path he hadn't been on for thirty years, and prayed for a machete to clear the overgrowth clogging the trail.

Marcus arrived first in his Jeep. The professor got out of his car, threw on a purple University of Washington sweatshirt over his thinning head of dark hair, and glanced around the parking lot.

Marcus sauntered toward the small gift shop at the north end of the lot. The shop was full of posters and trinkets based on the falls designed to capture a memory and separate the tourists from their coins of the realm. The bells on the shop door echoed over the asphalt and through Reece's open window as Marcus stepped inside.

A few minutes later Brandon pulled into the lot in his old Toyota Tundra. He'd had the car as long as Reece had known him. With the kind of money Brandon made, Reece thought it would have been replaced eons ago. That Brandon hadn't was one of the many reasons he loved the kid.

As the musician got out of the Toyota, Reece stepped from his car. "Brandon!"

A big smile on his face, the singer turned and ambled toward Reece. Brandon's longish dirty-blond hair waved in the breeze like he was in a music video. If he'd grown up in the sixties, Brandon would have been a perfect addition to the Beach Boys—and he would have been the best looking of the bunch.

"Thanks for coming."

"No problem." Brandon turned a slow circle, gazing at the trees, the Salish Lodge, and the paths that would take them out to the viewpoint. "I haven't been up here in years. My dad used to bring me here on Saturdays when I was a kid. This place holds some good memories."

"Such as?"

"Spending time with my dad. Getting away from my stepmom for a few hours."

Reece gazed at Brandon, waiting for him to offer more on his history. He didn't take the opportunity. Over the years the musician had always said he'd describe his past when the time was right, but the right time had never arrived. The pain on his face when they touched on the subject said it never would be right. Another reason Brandon needed Well Spring.

"What's kept you from coming back?"

"Life snatches you up, and the days fly by, bro." Brandon punched Reece playfully in the arm. "Am I the first to get here?"

Reece pointed over Brandon's shoulder at the gift shop. "See the man coming out the door?"

Brandon turned and nodded.

"He's another one of the four going to Well Spring. The other two haven't arrived yet."

Marcus spotted them, waved, and loped over.

"Marcus Amber, meet Brandon Scott."

Marcus grabbed Brandon's hand. "Brandon Scott, like the musician?"

"Yeah, like the musician."

"You're serious."

Brandon put on a mock frown. "I avoid being serious as much as possible these days. It depresses me."

"Fascinating. The temptation to call my wife and daughters right now is almost overwhelming." Marcus tilted his head back and gave it a slight shake. "How do I convey the following sentiment without looking like a somewhat obsessed fan? Actually, it's inconsequential. I've devoured your music for years."

Brandon grinned at him. "And you're Marcus Amber, like the brilliant physicist?"

"Exactly like him, excluding the brilliant section of your assessment." Marcus returned Brandon's smile.

"No kidding. The one who wrote *Time Holes: The Portals Around Every Corner*?"

"Do you mean to say you actually ingested that tome?" Marcus cocked his head.

"I did. Every word. Loved it."

"Finally, a conundrum solved. I now know what happened to the one copy that was purchased." Marcus laughed and tapped his fist against his head. "Do you have an affinity for quantum mechanics and all the surrounding machinations?"

"Yeah, bro. I started out watching every time-travel movie I could find, and then I graduated to books like yours."

"Then it appears we have elements in common." Marcus rocked on the balls of his Pumas on the parking lot.

"You don't mind if I pick your brain on the multiverse, do you?"

"Instruct me on how to perform three of your songs and we have a deal." Marcus motioned as if he were strumming a guitar.

"Do you play?"

"Not yet." The professor laughed.

"Okay, then we might need to know each other for a while." Brandon clapped Marcus on the shoulder and smiled, then glanced around the lot. "Any sign of the other two?"

Before Reece could answer, Tamera pulled up and leaped out of her Volkswagen Bug wearing black sweats that were in stark contrast to her fair skin and short blond hair.

Reece pointed her direction. "Here's one of them now."

She spotted him and jogged over to the three of them. "Hey, Reece, how are you?" She yanked lightly on the cords of her hoodie sweatshirt and smiled.

"I'm good. And you?"

"Excellent." She glanced at Marcus and Brandon. "You must be the other recruits."

Reece lifted an upturned palm and introduced everyone.

Marcus held out his hand and Tamera took it and smiled. "You're kinda cute."

The professor frowned. "I'm married."

"Well, he's cute too." She winked at Brandon.

"Nice to meet you, Tamera," Brandon said.

"Likewise."

Reece cleared his throat. "Marcus is a professor at the UW

and Brandon is a musician. Why don't you tell them a little about yourself, Tamera."

"I'm a personal trainer."

"Rock on," Brandon said. "In clubs or are you independent?"

"Independent, training private clients at the moment, until a TV show comes through."

Marcus took a half step back. "Is that a serious pursuit?"

"Very. It's my dream. I want to be on TV, reaching out to people, helping them get into better condition. We all need to take care of the temple, you know?" She motioned up and down her body, then held up a finger. "And it's more than a dream. I got an agent a few months back, and we've had a number of serious conversations with some producers down in LA, so it's a real possibility."

"I don't think I want to be your friend." Brandon laughed. "You'd make me work out more."

"Ah, you're in fine shape. I can tell." She turned to Marcus. "And you look like a runner."

Reece glanced at his watch as the three chatted. Dana was now ten minutes late—which wasn't like her. "Excuse me a moment." As soon as he was out of earshot of the others, he dialed her number. She picked up on the fourth ring.

"Dana, where—?"

"I am so sorry, Reece. I was just about to call you. I should be there right now, I know. But work is the *Titanic* at the moment, and I'm the only one bailing."

"This is a critical meeting. You need to be introduced to the others before we head to Well Spring."

"I know, I know, but it's not going to work. I'll have to meet them another time."

"You need to meet them now."

"I understand that. And in a perfect world, I'd be standing beside you at this moment. You know me, Reece. It's not like me to miss this, but if I'm thinking about being on that plane with you on Sunday, I have to get these projections finished."

He didn't respond.

"Reece? Are you there?"

"I'm here. With my feet in the spot your feet should be in as well."

"If you want me to apologize again, I will. Because I do regret not being there, but believe me, I don't have a choice."

"All right, Dana. You'll meet two of the others at the airport and the last of the team at the ranch."

"Yeah . . . yeah, sure. I think."

"Are you still committed to coming?"

"I don't know, Reece. Being around people I don't know isn't really my—"

"We've talked about this. What did God tell you?"

"With my work right now, he's saying stay home."

"It's your choice," Reece said. "I only request you ask God for the answer."

"I will."

"I hope to see you Sunday morning."

Reece hung up and clenched his fist. Not a good start. He stared at Brandon, Tamera, and Marcus. The Spirit would have to do some heavy lifting with Dana once they arrived in Colorado. If she even came. He trudged back over to them.

Reece motioned toward the falls with his thumb. "Let's head over to the viewpoint and talk for a few minutes about what I think the Spirit is saying."

They meandered down the pathway lined with Douglas fir trees, their shoes scuffing on the gray concrete pathway. Brandon whapped Reece's shoulder with the back of his fingers as they strolled along. "So is the last member of our tribe coming?"

"She is not."

"Why?"

Reece turned right at the end of the path and spoke over his shoulder. "Work."

"I still don't understand why you wouldn't tell us about each other until today."

Reece didn't answer.

"Okay, Mr. Conversation, can you at least give us some high-lights on this lady?"

"No."

"What?"

"You're not ready to hear about her yet." Reece stopped and faced Brandon.

The kid pointed to his chest. "Me? Or them too?" He motioned back and forth between Marcus and Tamera and himself.

"You."

"Oh, man, now you've gotta spit it out."

"I will. In time."

Brandon tapped his watch. "I'm thinking now."

"I'm thinking later." Reece stared down at Brandon till he broke eye contact and shrugged.

They stepped onto the deck of the viewpoint overlooking the falls, and Reece walked to the railing and leaned forward on his elbows. The sight of thousands of gallons of water pouring over the lip of the falls and thundering 268 feet down never failed to inspire. Taller than Niagara. He closed his eyes as mist rising up from the roar in front of him settled on his face. After a few minutes Reece opened his eyes and glanced around the platform and the trails leading to it. The four of them were alone. Good.

"For the Snoqualmie people, these falls have been central to their faith and spirituality for centuries. They say prayers are 'carried up to the Creator by great mists that rise from the powerful flow.' And that 'the mists rising from the base of the waterfall are said to serve to connect heaven and earth.'

"I like those images." Reece motioned toward the falls. "Consider the force of the water pouring over the edge of that cliff in front of you. It is an ideal picture of the Spirit. Living water. Unending. And if harnessed, able to do things far outside the imagination of the common man. And the common follower of Jesus.

"I want you to lock an image of these falls into your mind. I want you to consider it every time you press into the Spirit."

Reece stooped and picked up a leaf lying on the platform, held it up, and pointed to a drop of dew that hung from the end. "This is the amount of water most people who follow Jesus tap into. But that"— Reece pointed at the falls—"is the kind of power available when we fully tap into the Spirit. You look at Snoqualmie Falls and realize the force it contains. Inside you lives the God who created it. The God who made the oceans and a universe so vast we measure the distance across it in light-years. The God who says you will do greater things on earth than he did.

"And tapping into and wielding that power is what I'm going to teach the four of you to do at Well Spring."

"I've been meaning to ask you about that," Brandon said. "The three of us and this other gal live in Seattle, right?"

Reece nodded.

"Then wouldn't it make a lot more sense to hang out around here for our getaway?"

"No."

"Why not?"

"Because." Reece glanced back at the falls behind him. Did he really have to get into the why right now? Probably. "Because of the atmosphere there."

"Care to expand on that a little?" Brandon rested his elbows on the railing of the observation platform and gazed at the falls.

"We need a place where the distractions are minimized. Where you're out of your routine. Where you're jolted out of your assumptions and traditions."

"Okay, I get that. But there are a lot of retreat centers around here."

"The ranch is a place where I've found the curtain to be thinner."

"Describe this curtain for us." Marcus stared at Reece with inquisitive eyes. "What is it?"

"The veil between us and the spiritual world that surrounds us. The curtain between us and God."

Brandon laughed. "You know, Reece, when I read those sci-fi and fantasy books, I realize they're fiction. Probably the same with the prof and Tamera."

"Marcus?" Reece turned to the professor, who stood in profile staring at the falls. "Do you think they're fiction?"

"Not all of it." He looked at Reece and smiled. "My mind is unlocked and ready to consider myriad possibilities."

"Did Tamera and I miss an inside joke?" Brandon said.

Reece shook his head. "No, but over the past three years, Marcus and I have often discussed the idea that the magic is real."

"Magic?"

"Things in the Bible that most followers of Jesus would dismiss as magic. Truths more real than the things in this world—mysteries you've not imagined but that few explore."

"Like?" Tamera said.

"Don't worry. We will look into a number of them at Well Spring and in the days that follow."

"You're not going to try to jack us into *The Twilight Zone* out there in Colorado, are you?" Brandon said.

"We're going beyond *The Twilight Zone*. Way beyond."

"Hmm." Brandon kicked a small stone off the edge of the observation deck and watched it float down into the side of the cliff. "Why is the curtain thinner there?"

"The entire purpose and focus of Well Spring Ranch is to bring healing and freedom to the warriors of the kingdom. To show them Jesus in a way he hasn't been seen before. It's a place for restoration and training and revelation. There are warriors who will be praying for our time there. They pray back the soldiers of the kingdom of darkness and bring in the kingdom of heaven in all its power and glory."

Brandon wiggled his fingers. "So you go in for all that woo-woo demons and angels stuff? I mean, hey, I believe that stuff too, but it sounds like you've bought the farm when it comes to the supernatural."

"Probably every farm in the country." Reece glanced at them. "It's time to go." He pushed himself off the railing, turned, and tromped off the platform and toward the parking lot.

Brandon called after him, "Care to expand on that a little?"

"Don't worry, expansion on that topic will come. Probably to a far greater degree than you're comfortable with."

When they reached the parking lot, Reece folded his arms and glanced at the three of them. "We meet up at Well Spring in four days. Between now and then I'd like you to do three things. First, read through the Gospels. Second, read the book of Acts. Third, I want you to watch a movie."

"Which one?" Tamera asked.

"*The Matrix*. Keanu Reeves, Laurence Fishburne. Came out in 1999."

"Done." Brandon made a check mark in the air. "I own it. I've probably seen it seven times."

"Watch it again. Pray before you do that you would have eyes to see and ears to hear."

Brandon swept his hands around in a poor imitation of kung fu. "Wow, now this is what I call a Bible study."

"I'm assuming you've seen it as well, Marcus."

"I have. Nine times, if my memory is serving me accurately." He held out his hand, palm up, and beckoned toward Reece with his fingers. "But it seems apparent you'd liked me to view it again."

"I do."

"What about you, Tamera? Have you seen it?" Marcus asked.

"Once." She pulled her phone out of her pocket and made a note. "Are you going to tell us what *The Matrix* has to do with our little jaunt to Colorado?"

"No."

Tamera tugged on the bottom of her sweat jacket. "I see."

"Stay in prayer. There will be resistance to your coming. It would surprise me if there wasn't. But fight it. This is your destiny."

As Reece wound through the back roads on his way home, Dana settled into his mind and he prayed. He had a feeling the odds against her going were the highest.

FIVE

DANA RAINE CRUNCHED THE NUMBERS IN HER EXCEL spreadsheet for the third time, and for the third time, they crunched back. She sighed, pushed her reading glasses on top of her head, and slumped back in her leather chair. How could it be the end of the month already?

There was no way she'd hit budget for third quarter. Not at the pace they'd been setting. She should have at least 60 percent of their revenue locked in by now, and at the moment they were barely over 45. Yes, they'd made budget for first quarter, but those projections were the lowest of the year. And with only nineteen days to go in the second quarter, she'd be lucky to finish at 85 percent of that goal.

Two down quarters in a row would not make for wide smiles at corporate. They didn't care that the station's ratings were down. Didn't care that spending on broadcast radio was flat. Didn't care that Internet radio and social media and online discount sites were chewing up local ad budgets like locusts.

Dana stood and stared through her floor-to-ceiling windows at the Space Needle in the distance and then down to the stream of red taillights inching along Mercer Street toward I-5, most likely headed to homes with more than one person in them.

A home with someone other than a Pekingese to talk to about overwhelming days and weeks and months. Must be nice. She blew out a long breath and watched it fog the window in front of her. Two and a half million dollars to go. Piece of cake with buttercream frosting on top.

She rubbed her eyes and sighed. And she was supposed to leave in four days for Colorado? And stay there for four days while her boss and her boss's boss wondered why the station's general sales manager had left in the midst of the fourth straight month of declining revenues?

Dana's cell phone rang and she glanced at the caller ID. Perry. She smiled and the knots in her shoulders softened a bit. Finalizing plans for Saturday night would take her mind off the budgets. She tapped her Bluetooth.

"Hey, you. You're definitely a welcome distraction at the moment."

"Okay."

"So what time on Saturday?" She gazed at his picture on the screen of her phone. Dana liked this guy a lot. Going on eight months and so far the sailing had been silky. Getting some time together before she headed east would be a great send-off.

"I'm thinking Saturday is not going to work."

The hesitation in his voice sent a chill down Dana's back. "What's wrong?"

Perry puffed out a breath. "Wow."

"Wow what?"

"I'm a clod-o-la. I should be doing this in person."

No. Dana slid back into her chair. He couldn't be. "Doing what in person?" Why did she even ask the question? The ice skittering down her back grew colder and wrapped itself around her chest. "Doing what, Perry?"

No, don't say it.

"You know. Us."

Her chest tightened. "We've been great."

"No, you think we've been great. Yes, we've had fun and I love being with you, but at a certain point, it makes sense to move on from fun to something deeper."

"You're breaking up with me on the phone?" She closed her eyes. Wasn't it supposed to be the other way around? Wasn't the woman supposed to want to go deeper? Weren't guys looking for a woman who didn't push for commitment? Why couldn't he wait till she was ready?

"Like I said, I should have done it in person, but I need to get it over with so we can both get on with our lives."

She swallowed and stared at the framed photo on her desk of them at Alki Beach together. "I don't want to get on with my life. I want us to be together."

"No, you don't, Dana."

"Yes, I do."

"No, you don't!" A sigh surged through the phone. "Your words say that, but your actions disagree. Every time I try to get through that shell you've got wrapped around yourself, you build another layer."

"I can go deeper. I can."

"That's what you said the last three times we talked about it. Remember—"

"Don't give up on me, Perry. I'm trying."

Not again. Please, no.

"I don't want to be a jerk about this, but remember last month when I said things needed to change or we'd have to go different directions? I meant it and nothing has changed. Maybe down the road it can work out between us, but not now. I'm sorry, Dana. I do think you're an amazing person. I gotta go. Please take care of yourself."

Her phone went dead. Dana closed her eyes, let her head fall back on her chair, and tried to slow her breathing. She wouldn't cry. Not this time. But moments later the sales awards on the shelves high on her office wall blurred, and she couldn't stop the sobs from pressing their way out into her silent office. Why couldn't she let anyone inside? It happened three years ago. Why couldn't she get over it?

She wiped her eyes and looked at the photo of her and her grandfather, his head tilted back slightly, his mouth wide open as a barrage of laughter poured out. Dana reached out and touched the frame. It was cool, so unlike her pappy who had been such an amazing dad to her after her own father abandoned her by dying far too young.

"I miss you so much, Pappy. You'd make this all better." She slumped back in her chair. "I know you'd at least try to."

Dana blinked and puffed out a quick breath, turned back to her computer, and pushed Perry out of her mind. But he kept returning. And he brought his friends with him: Clint, whom she'd gone on three dates with a year back, and all he wanted to talk about were their pasts and what their childhoods were like. Ugh. Let the past stay there. And Glen, who'd suggested they go to counseling after only dating for four months. Why couldn't she pick a guy who just wanted to have fun?

Dana went to the corner of her office and huddled in the barrel chair there and stared out the window. Why couldn't she open up? Simple. Because every time she did the person had vanished from her life. Her parents' divorce. Then her best friend in eighth grade dumping her to get into the popular group. Then her dad dying on her from consumption of too many adult refreshments. Then her mom getting throat cancer and leaving too. Then three years ago her fiancé breaking up with her three months before the wedding.

By the time her tears dried, she admitted Perry was right. She was an emotional paraplegic, and maybe that was the reason she'd accepted Reece's invitation to Well Spring. She admired the man and liked him from the moment he joined their home group. When he spoke—which wasn't often—the words were worth listening to. And something about his eyes reminded her of Pappy.

He'd approached her four months ago about going. A chance to get away. A chance to see another side of God. But also a chance to turn from a way of thinking that only led to sorrow. He'd called her out, said following Jesus meant she was part of a body, and that meant depth in relationships. Opening her heart.

Of course it did. She knew she had to open up again if she didn't want to live the rest of her life alone. But how was she supposed to throw wide the door when the room she'd created in her soul didn't have one?

She would get over it. She always did. Dana rose, walked back over to her desk, and fiddled with the spreadsheet. There had to be an answer somewhere. Ten minutes later she jerked up at the sound of a voice in her office doorway.

"Hey, girl! Let's go. We need to do some serious calorie burning."

Toni, the station's promotions director, stood in the doorway pumping her arm up and down as if she held a barbell. She grinned, her brilliant smile in sharp contrast with her mocha-colored skin.

Perry flitted back into her mind. "I'm not up for a workout at the moment." *Stay strong. Don't cry.* Never finding anyone didn't mean she had to be alone. She could always move in with Toni and her husband someday. "And I don't have time anyway."

"What are you talking you don't have time? It's almost seven o'clock." Toni strode over to Dana's laptop, wiggled the mouse, and clicked Shut Down.

"I have work. I can't lose this job."

"Lose your job? No way. They love you."

Did they? Up till a few weeks ago Dana would have agreed. But through the grapevine she'd heard corporate was conducting a full evaluation of all of their Seattle station managers, and a rumor swirled of a headhunter looking for a seasoned sales manager for one of the stations.

Love her? Yes, they would love her madly right up till the second she started missing her goals. And that second was here.

Toni grabbed her sleeve and tugged on it. "And I promise work will still be here when the sun shoots up outta the east tomorrow."

"I have to figure out a way to hit these budgets to keep our beloved GM from bringing serious heat down on my salespeople."

"Let them take the heat for once. Why are you always protecting them?"

"I have to finish running these projections."

"More blood to the brain will smarten you up." Toni ran in place and poked Dana's head. "Besides, you do not want that slice of strawberry cheesecake you had for lunch today to take up permanent residence on your hips."

"Maybe I do." Dana tried to smile and reached to turn her laptop back on.

"Nuh-uh." Toni grabbed Dana's hand. "You don't. Let's go."

As they shuffled across Dana's office, Toni stopped and pointed to the picture on her wall of an ancient-looking train trestle. "Nice photo, lady." She smiled. "You took this, right?"

Dana nodded.

"You getting back into snapping pics?"

"A little. Not much."

But with no distracting dates on the weekends, she'd have more time if she wanted to take it. She checked the time on her phone and sighed at the wallpaper on it. As soon as she had a chance, she would change the picture from Perry to anything else. A shot of her Pekingese or her neighbor's overly friendly cat. Something she could love that wouldn't add another layer of pain to her heart.

When they got to the elevator, Toni pushed the button, then tapped Dana on the shoulder. "How's things with the kinda new boyfriend whose name I can't ever remember?"

Dana blinked and swallowed. *Keep it in.* "It didn't work out."

"When did you split?"

"Recently."

"What does 'it didn't work out' mean?"

"That it didn't work out." The elevator doors opened, they shuffled in, and Dana pushed the lobby button.

"What happened this time?"

"He broke up with me."

"Details?"

"That's all I can share at the moment. It's time to go to a commercial break." A few tears slid down her cheek.

Toni rubbed her back. "I'm sorry, girl."

"It'll be okay."

"You're beautiful, funny, smart—"

"I'm not beautiful. I'm one of those women guys describe as 'natural' looking, which means ordinary. Plain."

"You look like an older version of Emma Stone. That's beautiful."

"Right. I look exactly like her except for the gorgeous hair, eyes, face, and figure."

"You must be looking in the wrong mirror."

The elevator door opened and the click of their shoes echoed through the lobby.

"I'm old."

Toni frowned. "Old?" She pushed the door to the street open and held it for Dana. "You think your thirty-five years qualifies you as old? If you're old, then my forty-four years makes me ancient."

Dana strode through the front door of the building and brushed her light brown hair back from her face. "When your left ring finger still has nothing weighing it down, thirty-five is ancient."

"Maybe you're dating the wrong men."

"Maybe."

"Or maybe God wants to bring you someone else." Toni shifted her workout bag on her shoulder and stared at Dana.

"That's hilarious." She picked up her pace on the sidewalk.

"I'm serious, girl."

"You don't believe in God."

"True." Toni tapped her cheek and it made a hollow echoing sound. "And while he and I don't have much of a relationship, it doesn't mean I don't believe in something out there that helps us. And I know you're into all that so I'm trying to talk your language."

"Thanks."

"You want to know the real reason guys keep disappearing?"

"No."

"Because you keep a sixty-foot pole between you and them.

With a spiked tip. And every time they try to get to fifty-nine feet, you stab them with it."

Dana sighed. "I know."

"What ever happened with that guy from long ago and far away when it got serious?"

Dana slowed and kicked at an empty gum wrapper. "What?"

"Before you came to work at the station. You said you dated a basketball player or an artist—somethin' like that. Three or four years ago. Weren't you engaged or close to it?"

"It doesn't matter."

"Sure it does."

"Can we drop this, Toni?"

"I was just asking."

"Stop asking."

As they stood on the corner waiting for the little white man with no hands or feet in the black box to tell them it was okay to cross the street, Dana glanced at the Tully's Coffee on the opposite corner.

A man sat in the corner of the shop where the windows came together . . . Was he staring at her? She glanced at the red hand across the street telling her to keep waiting, then back to the man. He was still looking her direction. Midthirties?

Kind of cute. Dark hair. Confident eyes bordering on cocky. The kind of guy she would have been dying to date in her early twenties. The kind of guy she had avoided in her late twenties—but still would have been tempted to date. Now? Perry was the last. She would swear off dating forever. All it brought was pain. The man didn't break eye contact. Neither did she. If he wanted a stare-down, she'd give it to him.

A man jostled her from behind and she turned. The light had changed. As they clipped across the intersection, she looked at the man in the coffee shop again. He was studying a magazine that obscured the bottom half of his face, but she could see his eyes. Alluring.

"Dana? You there, girl?"

"Yeah, I'm fine."

"What or who were you staring at?"

"A guy sitting in Tully's."

"Oh really?" Toni did a little jig. "See, God's bringing you someone new already."

She groaned. "Stop it. I'm going to become a nun."

Dana glanced back at the man. Something shimmered across the window. A grayness or . . . a kind of haze. What was that? Then a feeling sped across her mind. He didn't belong here. An instant later a dull pressure began in the front of her skull and started to spread.

No, not now. She didn't need this on top of everything else.

"Dana, wake up." Toni pulled her sleeve.

"What?"

"I just asked you about your trip coming up on Sunday."

"Sorry. I think I have one of my world-famous migraines coming on. What about the trip?"

Toni laughed. "You're not seriously telling me you have a headache, are you? You think that will let you escape the workout?"

"I'm not trying to get out of it. I'll be fine." She squinted against the now-harsh sunlight angling into her eyes.

"Then back to my question, are you still going on this crazy spiritual quest, follow the guru thing in Colorado?"

"I don't know." Dana picked up her pace. "Why would I want to put myself in a cabin for four days with people I don't know except for Reece?"

"What!" Toni whacked Dana's shoulder. "You have to go."

"Why?"

"You know you're closed off. This will be a chance to open up. Plus, you told me the Holy Spirit guy told you to go."

"Once again, since you—"

"Hey, don't give me that 'I don't believe in God so I can't speak about it' gar-baj. When you told me, there was no doubt in your mind you were supposed to go. Just be sure now that you're bagging out because the Spirit changed his mind rather than you changing yours."

They reached the club and stepped through the glass doors of Burn It Up Fitness. "I think I hate you, Toni."

She laughed. "Nah, you love me. Always have, always will."

Dana yanked her Bluetooth off her ear and shoved it into a pocket in her workout bag and pulled out a bottle of Aleve and a bottle of water. She popped three caplets into her mouth, took a swig of water, and swallowed. If she didn't knock this migraine out now, it would rule her entire night.

"You and the guru and two guys at the ranch, right?" Toni swiped her card at the front desk and Dana did the same.

"There's another woman coming. If she wasn't, God would definitely be changing his mind."

Ten minutes later, as sweat trickled down Dana's neck, she turned to Toni. "Don't worry, I'm going."

"Good. You know that sixty-foot pole? Maybe God has some plans to break it."

SIX

"ARE YOU EXCITED ABOUT TOMORROW?"

Marcus turned from the packed suitcase resting on his bed toward the doorway of his bedroom. Kat leaned against the door frame smiling, auburn bangs spilling over her brown eyes, an ever-present smile on her face.

He couldn't imagine life without her. Sure he could. Single. Miserable. Maybe not living in a tent, but a home not much better.

"The needle on my anticipation meter is quite high. Reece has dangled a significant amount of questions that have my mind whirring as if a cyclotron is attached to it."

"You're forgetting there are little brains in the room." She smiled.

"My apologies." He knocked on the side of his head and grinned. "A cyclotron is used to accelerate charged particles."

"So that's what's inside your skull? Particles?" Kat sashayed over to Marcus and grabbed the collar of his polo shirt. "God is going to get you on this little retreat."

"Is that so?"

"Yes." She pulled him down and kissed him lightly on the lips. "I've been praying about this, and I think changes are coming— good changes inside you. Big changes. Plus you'll probably get a chance to continue your ongoing discussion with Reece about time travel being more than theoretically possible."

"After hearing his presentation up at Snoqualmie Falls, I get the distinct impression he believes in more than time travel. I've never heard him talk that way."

"Then you should have a wonderful time, my love."

"You haven't felt any hesitation about me participating in the retreat?"

"No." Kat looked down, a frown passing across her face.

His stomach churned. He knew that look. "What?"

She pulled away and walked to their bedroom's picture window and gazed out at the hemlock trees in their small Seattle backyard near the University of Washington.

"What aren't you telling me?"

Kat slid a finger along the windowsill, then moved back toward the door and waved her hand. "Nothing."

"What aren't you saying?"

Her tone went flat. "It's not important."

"I don't believe you."

Kat stepped partway through the door and stopped but didn't turn back toward him. "Abbie's soccer game. The championship has been rescheduled."

"What?"

She turned. "They moved it up."

Marcus pressed his fingers into his eyebrows. "To when?" He didn't need to ask. The look in Kat's eyes told him if he went to Well Spring, he would miss the game. This couldn't be happening.

"Wednesday evening."

He grabbed the bedpost and slid his grip down it as he slumped onto the bed. "Congratulations, Professor, you've just failed the test."

Kat eased back into the room and walked over to him.

"But making the correct choice isn't a complex problem." He turned to Kat. "I'm not going to Colorado."

"You're right, it is an easy choice. Yes, you are going."

"I'm calling Reece." He fished his cell phone out of his pocket.

"Wait." Kat sat next to him on the bed.

"For what purpose? I will not break my word. When I made that promise I meant it. There were too many years of—"

"You've been to every one of Abbie's and Jayla's games, every one of the girls' events for the past year and a half. You've been fully present on vacations. Do you realize how many memories you've created? The kids know you've changed. They've seen it. I've seen it. Abbie will understand."

How could she understand? How does a thirteen-year-old understand breaking a promise like the one he'd made?

I will never miss one of your games again. Ever. For any reason. You have my word and I will not break it.

"Have you told her yet?"

"No, but I will."

"That won't be necessary." Marcus stood. "I'm not going."

"You told Reece you would long before they changed the date. There's no way you could have known the game would be moved. And like I said, God is in this. She'll understand."

"It's not just a game but the championship. Those don't come around like the second hand on a clock."

"She'll understand."

"Why did they move it?" Marcus clenched his teeth.

"I don't know." Kat shook her head. "It doesn't make sense. It was totally out of the blue and they didn't even give a good reason."

"Why didn't you tell me this earlier?"

Kat reached over and touched his cell phone. "Because you would have called Reece and told him you weren't coming."

Marcus rubbed his face and groaned. "You weren't going to tell me at all, were you?"

"Not a chance." Kat folded her arms.

"Your feeling about my going contains that much strength?"

Kat's eyes grew moist and she nodded. "Are you going to go?"

"I don't know. I need to have a conversation with Abbie." He snatched his suitcase off the bed and tossed it to the floor. "Thanks, Lord. I appreciate the support."

+ + +

"Abbie?" Marcus tapped on his daughter's door with the tips of his fingers.

A muffled reply floated through the wood. "What?"

"Can I come in?"

"Whatever."

Marcus turned the knob and stepped through the door. Music pulsed through the speakers on the corners of her desk. The only light in the room came from a tiny lamp to her left and the laptop Marcus bought for her six months back. His daughter pecked at the keyboard, her face awash in the light from the screen.

He reached for the light switch next to the door. "Do you mind if I bring a bit more illumination to the room?"

"Yes."

He eased up beside her desk and crouched down. "Can we talk?"

"Uh-huh." Abbie continued to glance back and forth between her screen and a piece of paper to her left.

"Will you look at me, Abbs?"

"Sure." She spun in her chair, folded her hands in her lap, and looked at him, her bright gray eyes questioning.

"Mom has informed me that your game has been moved to a day when I'm scheduled to be out of—"

"It's not a big deal." She brushed back her long red hair and glanced at her laptop. "Don't stay home because of me."

"That's precisely why I will remain home. The championship is not a game I'm going to miss."

"Don't sweat it. It's not like you really come to my games anyway."

"What are you talking about?" Marcus stood and squinted. "I've come to every game for the last eighteen months."

"I suppose."

"You suppose?"

"No, I mean, yeah, I guess you have." She glanced up at him.

"You have. I know you've changed and everything, like, I mean you got totally different when your friend's daughter died and all that, so it's all good."

But it wasn't good. Kat said Abbie would understand his going on the trip, not that she wouldn't care if he went. Yes, he'd changed, but what good had it done? Wasn't it yesterday she begged him to come to her games? She wouldn't be doing that ever again. His stomach tightened as he searched for the right words.

"I've gotta get this homework done, okay?" Abbie turned back to her laptop.

"Abbie? I—"

"Really, Dad. I have soooo much studying to do, it's driving me nuts."

"Yes. All right." He walked to the door, then turned and stared at the back of her head. So clichéd to say it, but so true—in moments he'd be staring at the back of her head in a church as she stepped into another life with another man. What good would his regrets do him on that day? "I'm sorry, Abbie."

She didn't turn. "No worries, Dad. Really. You're good."

He shut her door, marched to his den, and slammed the door behind him. Beautiful shelves and beautiful books and his beautifully framed doctorate surrounded him, mocking him. Marcus strode to the far wall and yanked the framed certificate off the wall, flung it to the ground, and dug his heel into the back of it. The sound of crunching glass seemed to reverberate off the walls.

He had degrees, tenure, the respect of his peers, countless papers written, and three published books. But pages had been ripped out of his life he would never get the chance to read. And he was the one who'd torn them out and tossed them on the fire.

Should he go to Well Spring? Or stay and see the game? As Marcus drifted into a fitful sleep that night, he still wasn't sure which path he would choose.

SEVEN

"NO COMPLICATIONS, PLEASE."

On Sunday morning at six fifteen, Reece pulled out of his gravel driveway, headed for the airport, and continued to pray that the five of them would get to Sea-Tac and into the sky without any obstacles being hurled their direction. No car troubles, no plane delays, no lost luggage, and no turbulence once they were in the clouds. Reece hated turbulence.

When he reached Highway 522 a few minutes later, he pulled out his cell phone and called Doug Lundeen. *Be there, friend.*

"Hello?"

"It's Reece."

"How's your heart?"

"I'm good."

"Your tone of voice contradicts your words."

"Every emotion inside is screaming to turn around and head back home."

"Good. The nest of hornets has awakened."

"That I believe."

"On that note, I must tell you I was praying this morning and had the distinct impression you're going to hit a snag."

"Which is?"

"That was all I received. However, it certainly is feasible it was a bad selection of roast from last night talking." Doug chuckled.

Reece turned on his windshield wipers to push away the light mist landing on his window. "I don't need snags."

"Are you looking forward to seeing the place again?"

An image of Well Spring Ranch filled Reece's mind. "That I am. It's been six months since I've been out there, which is far too long."

"Do they know how Well Spring came to be?"

"No."

"Do any of them know of your financial situation?"

"It's never come up," Reece said.

"You've known them for years."

"It's not a secret. But I don't want them to get distracted by it."

"I see." Doug cleared his throat. "What time do you fly out?"

"In a few hours. I'm on my way to the airport right now."

"How have the last few days been?"

Reece turned the speed of his wipers up a notch as the mist turned heavy. "Better. But still wrestling with uncertainty. Still worrying about going in with them."

"When I spoke the prophecy over you many years ago, did you believe it?"

"Yes."

"After you and I and the rest of the group prayed over it and tested it, did you believe more strongly?" Doug asked.

"Yes, but—"

"And when the Spirit revealed the four to you, did you doubt then?"

"No, but—"

"The prophecy and your part in it are true regardless of your emotions. God's protection is true regardless of how you feel. The freedom you will introduce to the four is true regardless of what the enemy tries to assault you with."

Reece peered through the thickening rain at the red taillights ahead of him and flipped on his own lights. "And if I take them in and something goes wrong? What about my feelings then?"

"Yes," Doug said, then went silent.

"Yes, what?"

"Yes, something could go wrong. This is war. In war casualties occur. But your job isn't to worry about that possibility. Your job is to step into your destiny and lead them. They have chosen to come. You will give them the choice to step into the training or hold back."

"So be it."

"By the way, have you considered this journey you're now on isn't only about their freedom but about your own?"

"Not really," Reece said.

"How can you lead them into freedom if you yourself aren't free?"

"Those who can't do, teach."

"I'm serious."

Reece rubbed the steering wheel with his thumb and stared at Home Depot off to his right. This wasn't supposed to be about building him up, it was about building them up.

"Reece?"

"I'm not thinking about me."

"That sounds noble, but it's not. Do not miss what the Spirit has for *you* during this time."

"I'll keep my eyes open." Reece took the ramp onto 405 and joined the flow of early morning cars headed south.

"Anything else, friend?"

"Last night I think the Spirit told me to come see you on Tuesday."

"That would be an excellent idea. But I have to ask how you plan to come to Denver, spend time with me, and arrive back at Well Spring without commandeering the entire day to accomplish it. What are you planning to have the four do at the ranch while you are off gallivanting with me?"

Reece didn't answer and Doug laughed. "You really are going to traipse back into the old days, aren't you?"

"All the way."

"Well, good for you, son. Good for them. You do realize if you use that mode of transportation, one of them is liable to discover what you've done."

"I hope so. I'm counting on it."

Doug chuckled again. "Whenever you arrive here is fine. I'll be ready."

Fifteen minutes later his cell phone rang. "Reece here."

"It's Tamera."

Good, he could get his mind off of himself. "Hello, Tamera. Are you at the airport already?"

"No."

"Are you almost there?"

"No."

Not good. Reece turned the wipers on high to battle the onslaught of rain pelting his windshield. "Don't tell me you got a flat in this downpour. That would be a little too cliché."

It took her three seconds to respond. "I can't fly out till tomorrow."

"What?"

"I'll have to fly out to Denver tomorrow and meet you guys at Well Spring on Monday night late."

"What's going on?" Reece's stomach churned. The prophecy was four, not three; they all needed to be there.

"My agent set up a meeting in LA for this afternoon. Last-minute thing, but the opportunity opened up and it's a can't-miss-it kinda deal. I'll fly down there, do the meeting, fly back late tonight, then get on a plane to Colorado tomorrow morning." She paused. "First thing."

The Mount Baker Tunnel loomed in front of Reece. "I might lose you when I go through the tunnel. Hang on."

His Avalanche entered the tunnel and Reece glanced at his phone. One bar. "Can you still hear me?"

His Bluetooth beeped three times and the call dropped. "Don't let this happen, Lord. Get her to the airport now. Break through this. Break it down."

As he exited the tunnel his phone lit up. "Hello."

"This is a chance I can't pass up, Reece. This is my show. But I'll only miss one day of the retreat."

"It doesn't work that way."

"What do you mean?"

"It's all the way or nothing. You need to be there from the start to the finish. Halfway in won't work."

"But it's not halfway. I'll only miss a quarter."

"I'm sorry."

"What if I flew from LA to Denver and got in late tonight?"

"Did God tell you to come with us to Well Spring?"

Tamera released a heavy sigh. "Yes."

"Then you need to go. Not tomorrow, not tonight. You need to join us now."

"I need a few minutes to think about this."

"No." Reece glanced at his watch. "If you're coming you'll need to leave immediately."

"I . . . I don't know what to do."

"Yes, you do." Reece took the ramp that would spill him onto I-5 south. "The plane lifts off at eight thirty. I am praying you're on it with us."

"I can't. I have to do this."

"I see."

She went silent and didn't speak again for several seconds. "Do you still like me?"

"Of course, Tamera. It doesn't change my care for you one iota. And I won't stop praying for you."

Reece hung up and tossed his cell phone onto the passenger seat. She'd never hesitated about coming like the others had. She was locked in from the start. No worries, no concerns, very few questions. Brandon? Dana? The professor? None of them bagging out would have surprised him. Which was why he should have seen it coming with Tamera. Prayed harder. Prayed with more precision against the attack. Done something.

Twelve minutes later he pulled into the Shuttle Park 2 parking lot a mile east of the airport and sat and stared through his windshield at nothing. Score one for the opposition. He punched the dashboard. The war had begun and he'd lost the first skirmish.

EİGHT

DANA SPRANG OFF THE TOP OF A SILVER ESCALATOR AT 7:23 a.m., stared at the Alaska Airlines sign to her left, and tried to figure out why she felt so good. She'd been up till midnight, and since morning wasn't her favorite time of day, she should have been more than a mite sleepy. Not to mention getting up at five.

But she wasn't tired. Probably because of her anticipation of what might happen at Well Spring. Reece said she'd find renewal, and hope, and healing. Bring it. She'd needed all three in abundance—ever since she tossed her engagement ring into the Snohomish River three years ago.

"Are you ready?" a voice off to her right asked.

Reece stood ten yards away, a red Osprey Talon daypack slung over one shoulder, a dark green hiking coat thrown over the other. They didn't come close to matching. And his dark tan, ancient-looking Stetson Muzzle Hat didn't help the mix.

She smiled at him and strolled over. "Very."

"Excellent."

The word he spoke was right, but something in his tone wasn't. The big man frowned and turned away. "What's wrong?"

"Nothing."

"Yeah there is, I saw it in your eyes."

Reece responded with a glance at his watch, then pulled out his cell phone and talked more to himself than to her. "Where is Marcus?"

46

He stared out the glass windows of Sea-Tac Airport probably at the cars and shuttles dropping travelers off for departure.

"He should be here by now." He glanced at Dana, then back out the windows. "Marcus?" Reece shifted the phone to his other ear. "I'm fine. Where are you? We have a plane to catch."

Concern was etched into his face. Dana looked over his shoulder at a tall, lean man loping toward them who seemed like he was in his late thirties or early forties. Dark hair, thinning a bit, with a complexion that looked like it had rarely seen the sun.

He smiled at her, pointed at himself, then to her, then at Reece's back. He held a finger to his lips. He stopped ten yards away. It had to be Marcus Amber.

"How soon is soon?" Reece said into his phone as Marcus took three silent steps toward Reece's back. Funny. Nice to know Marcus had a sense of humor.

"Define *very*." Reece scowled.

Marcus said something into his phone, too soft for her to hear, then turned it off and dropped it into the pocket of his light green jacket. Then he took three more steps in their direction till he stood inches from Reece's back. Reece listened a moment, then dropped his hand and phone to his side and stared at Dana. "He hung up on me." He glanced at his watch again. "We need to get going if we're going to make that plane."

Dana stifled the laughter forcing its way out of her mouth. "Maybe he lost his signal."

"Boo." Marcus spoke the words an inch from Reece's ear.

"Wow!" Reece jumped to his right and raised his fists.

"Just in case your consciousness hadn't fully woken yet this morning." Marcus laughed, his eyes bright behind silver wire-rimmed glasses.

Reece nodded and slowed his breathing. "I'm seeing another side to Marcus Amber."

"We academics at the U-Dub are allowed a sense of humor."

"Thanks for the almost heart attack."

"My pleasure." Marcus grinned.

Reece wagged his finger back and forth between her and Marcus. "Marcus, this is Dana. Dana, Marcus." He turned and strode toward the security line. "Let's move."

"I like you already." She shook Marcus's hand as they followed Reece. "It was all I could do to keep a straight face until you, uh, greeted our host."

Marcus grinned again. "I could not pass up the opportunity. In addition, it seems Reece would benefit from a stiff injection of humor into his life."

Reece turned but didn't smile. Come to think of it, Dana couldn't ever recall seeing him smile. "I agree." They picked up their pace to keep up with their leader. "Reece told me a few days ago that you're a physics professor at the University of Washington."

"Guilty." Marcus shifted his briefcase to his other hand. "And he tells me you work in the broadcasting industry—in radio. But you aren't on the air."

"Nope." She switched her rolling suitcase to the other hand. "Remember that old Billy Crystal movie *City Slickers*? Where he 'sells air'? I'm in charge of the people who sell the air."

"Do you enjoy it?"

"I need it."

She didn't offer the reason why and Marcus didn't ask. They continued to chat as they wound back and forth through the cordoned-off lanes and passed through security to the other side. Thankfully she didn't have to stand in the little booth, lift her hands over her head, and have some stranger give her the X-ray vision treatment.

After she put her shoes back on and slid her laptop back into her briefcase, she glanced around for the others. Reece stood fifteen yards to her left, Marcus waited for her just a few feet away. She pushed her hair behind her ear. "Do you know the other—?"

Oh no. Her face went hot.

"What's wrong?" Marcus frowned.

Her throat tightened and she strode toward Reece. When she reached him, she released her rolling bag and put her hands on her hips. "Aren't we missing someone?"

"No."

"Is the other gal—this Tamera—is she meeting us at the gate?"

"No." Reece pushed his hat back on his head and stared at her.

"Why isn't she here, Reece?"

"She's not coming."

"She's what?"

"I'm sorry, Dana. She called me on the way to the airport. I just found out."

Dana spun to her left and stared at the white airport ceiling. "I don't believe this."

"Neither do I."

She yanked her arms tight across her chest. "How would you feel if I reduced the number going with you to two?"

Reece looked at her with compassion. "That would be your choice."

Dana unfolded her arms, tapped her cell phone, and looked at the time. Seven forty. She was tempted to ask for the number and call Tamera, but it wouldn't change anything. If she wasn't already working her way through security, she wouldn't make the plane. But going to Well Spring as the only woman? No way.

Dana glanced back the way they'd come. Reece was right. It was her choice. She didn't have to go. And right now she wanted to choose home.

"You said I wouldn't be the only woman there."

"That was the plan." Reece turned and strode toward their gate. "Let's make sure we're there in time."

"I need a few minutes to think about this."

"Same thing Tamera said, so I'll give you a similar answer. If you're coming, you need to decide now."

Why are you doing this to me, God?

Dana shut her eyes and ground her teeth. Unbelievable. She

blamed Tamera, blamed Reece, blamed God, blamed herself. But she was already here and Toni was probably right. She needed this trip. Dana opened her eyes and glared at Reece. She had been an island all of her life. Why should she expect anything different now?

Dana grabbed her suitcase and slogged after Reece as the fatigue she should have been feeling earlier showed up in full force.

As they stood at the gate waiting to board, Reece motioned them both closer. "I am truly sorry, Dana. I thought Tamera would be the last one to cancel. But the enemy does not like what we're about to do. Did you have any second thoughts about coming? Anything thrown at you to keep you home?"

Other than what had just happened? Yes. Her budgets. The possibility her job was hanging on a weakening string. Still stinging from another guy breaking up with her. But not enough to keep her from coming. "A few things."

He looked at Marcus. "You, Professor?"

"Yes." Marcus nodded as his face clouded over. "This morning my wife, Kat, talked me into coming. I've been a picosecond away from canceling for the past eleven hours."

"A what?" Dana said.

"Excuse me. A trillionth of a second."

Reece didn't question why Marcus almost hadn't come, and Dana didn't know him well enough to ask.

"I would have been surprised if you hadn't bumped up against resistance."

"But not you, right, Reece?" She was half serious.

The look on his face said his battle ran deeper than she could imagine. So she wasn't the only one with issues. And he probably wasn't any happier about Tamera canceling than she was. Maybe it didn't matter what Tamera did. Maybe the only choice Dana needed to consult the mirror about was her own.

Ten minutes later they boarded their Boeing 707 and sat in 2A, 2B, and 2C. Marcus patted his armrests and looked at Reece. "Thanks for the seats."

Reece downed a glass of apple juice the flight attendant had given him and turned to Marcus across the aisle. "At my size, flying in coach is not easy for me or the people around me. So I always fly first class."

Always? Fascinating. Nothing about Reece had ever reflected the ability to always fly first class. Not his car, not his watch, certainly not his clothes. Even though she'd known Reece for over a year, she had no idea what he did for a living. It had never come up and she'd never asked.

As the plane climbed its way to thirty-five thousand feet, Dana turned to Reece. "Would you like to tell me about the other guy who's coming?"

Reece accepted a refill of apple juice from the flight attendant. "He'll join us later this afternoon. He's wrapping up a business commitment in Denver and should arrive at Well Spring shortly after we do."

"That's not what I asked."

"You'll meet him when the time is right."

"I don't like that you haven't told me who this guy is or anything about him." She stared out her window at the rapidly shrinking ground below. "Just tell me his name."

Reece downed his juice, leaned back in his seat, and closed his eyes. "Take a good look at Seattle."

"Why is that?" Marcus asked.

"Because next time you're here, you'll be seeing things differently."

"Do you care to expand on that?"

Reece pulled his hat over his eyes. "Please wake me up ten minutes before we touch down."

Marcus leaned over to Dana and whispered, "Have you noticed how evasive he is when you inquire of him?"

"Yes. If he wasn't so big, I'd strangle him." She pulled the in-flight magazine out of the seat pocket in front of her. "Did he tell you what we'd be doing at Well Spring?"

"It's likely he didn't reveal much more than you already know. We're to explore a Christianity most followers of Jesus aren't acquainted with. One we're not acquainted with."

Marcus was right. That part she'd heard. "Anything else?"

"That we'll find more freedom and heal some emotional wounds by delving into our pasts."

Great. Sharing her wounds and shortcomings with total strangers. *Thanks, Lord. This will be a blast.* Especially if the third guy wasn't as approachable as Reece and Marcus.

Dana leaned closer to Marcus. "Do you know who the other guy is?"

"We were introduced last week."

"Who is it?"

"I apologize." Marcus squinted and shook his head. "But I assume you know Reece has asked me to stay silent on that matter."

Dana slumped back in her seat, her stomach knotting as an image floated into her mind of arriving at Well Spring and being shoved inside the lions' den.

NINE

As Reece, Marcus, and Dana bounced along a dirt road three hours southwest of Denver, she tried to rid her mind of the pictures battering her imagination. Alone for four days. With three guys. One whom she'd never met. Exactly the scenario she'd promised herself she wouldn't get into. Yes, Marcus seemed fine. But Reece wasn't the type of guy who was entertained by small talk. This retreat wouldn't be about cute and cuddly Christianity. He would want everyone to go deep and open up. Not her strong suit.

You're right. You shouldn't have come.

The thought simmered in her mind and she latched onto it.

He's not safe.

Who?

But Dana knew the answer.

You've seen it in some of the meetings you've been in with him. He's on the fringe.

She stared out the window at the mountains rising far to her left as perspiration broke out on her forehead. Her stomach churned as the feelings of isolation and caution intensified. Dana couldn't shake the feeling she was walking into an emotional minefield, or ignore the voice telling her to be on guard against Reece.

Yes. Be careful. He's not stable. Reece is not of the Truth as he's pretended to be.

She wiped her hands on her pants, but the moisture worked its way out of her skin with such persistence, she finally gave up and rested them on the seat next to her. Dana closed her eyes and tried to ignore the thoughts that filled her mind like a dark mist—it wasn't true about Reece. He was solid. Loved God. Had tremendous wisdom. Was respected by all the people in their home group—but the images continued to pound her imagination.

It didn't help that the headache that had started when they landed in Denver had slowly morphed into a full-blown eight point five on the Richter migraine scale. The three Aleve she'd taken half an hour ago hadn't put even the hint of a fingerprint on it, and hitting a rut in the road every few seconds didn't help the pressure squeezing her brain like a grape at winepress time.

A minute later Reece made the situation worse. "You have to take those thoughts captive, Dana."

"Wha . . . what are you talking about?" She opened her eyes and lurched forward.

"When you get hammered with thoughts from the enemy like you are right now about me, about coming to Well Spring, you have to fight them, but you can't do it without the Spirit's power. Your own strength and own thoughts won't win. And I don't think that migraine is from natural causes. I think it's an attack. But I could be wrong."

Her breathing grew shallow and rapid. "How do you know what is going on in my head?"

"Just an impression."

"That came from . . . from where?" Dana strained against the seat belt as if she were strapped to a gurney in a hospital struggling to sit up. "How do you know about my thoughts? How did you know about my migraine?" Her whole body went hot. How had Reece gotten inside her head? He knew what she was thinking?

Reece looked at her in the rearview mirror. His eyes were soft. It was the most tender she'd seen them. "I apologize. My intent was not to scare you but to give you a way out of what you're dealing with right now."

"Who are you?"

"The same guy you've gotten to know over the past year. I'm just showing you a little more of who I am."

"How do you have that kind of power?"

"It's not my power." Reece shook his head. "I'm just a man who has learned to hear the voice of the Spirit."

Reece slowed the car and brought it to a stop on the side of the road. Then he turned and reached for her hand. She hesitated, then placed hers in his. It was warm, his touch gentle.

"Sometimes I'm wrong about what I hear from the Spirit. Sometimes I think I've heard God's voice and I haven't. But Jesus said his sheep would hear him. That the Spirit would speak to them. That's all. So no fear, Dana. Don't let any other lies in about me, or about you being here."

She glanced at Marcus. The look on his face told her she wasn't alone in her surprise at Reece's mind-reading ability.

"God is for you. So am I. So is Marcus. It is all for good. That's one of the reasons you're here. To learn to hear his voice as well as I do. Maybe better."

"Okay." Dana's breathing slowed. "But the thoughts are still there, my head is about to explode with this migraine, and I can't say your freaking me out just now helped the anxiety sloshing around my brain."

"Let's take care of those things right now. Marcus?"

He looked at Reece. "Yes?"

"Will you join me in warring for Dana?"

"Uh, certainly." Marcus shifted in his seat so he faced Dana. "What will the nature of this battle look like?"

"Prayer."

"Right. Yes, of course."

Marcus shut his eyes and bowed his head. Reece didn't. He looked just above Dana's eyes and spoke with intensity. "We come against the attack on Dana's thoughts by the blood, power, and authority of Jesus Christ, our Master and King. And we come against her migraine and break its power. Go. Now. Leave her. Bring peace, Jesus. Bring more of you."

Reece turned around, threw the rented Nissan Xterra into drive, and pulled back onto the dirt road.

"That's it?" Marcus said.

"Yes." Reece glanced back at her in the rearview mirror. "What's going on now, Dana?"

"I don't understand." She blinked and massaged her temples. "This can't be happening."

"What are you feeling?"

She looked up at his reflection in the mirror, then at Marcus to Reece's right. "How did you . . . I don't . . . it's gone." It was impossible. Her migraines never just vanished. Never. Twenty years of gutting through them had conditioned her for at least a three- or four-hour battle every time. She rubbed her temples again and tried to feel a wisp of pain. "My migraine is completely gone."

"What else? What about the thoughts?"

Right. The thoughts. She tried to access them, but it was like trying to find fog after a summer sun had burnt off an early morning cloud cover. They had vanished as well.

"All I can think about is peace." She shook her head. "My mind is . . . clear. It's clear now."

"Good. That's Jesus. That's his heart, the way he feels about you in action."

"That prayer didn't have a great deal of length to it," Marcus said.

Reece glanced at him. "Was it supposed to?"

"I . . ." Marcus stopped.

"I know, I understand. The longer we pray, the more God is obligated to answer our prayer, right? I slip into that way of thinking from time to time. But that's religion, earning the right for our prayers to be answered." Reece adjusted his hat. "Don't get me wrong. Sometimes prayer takes hours and fierceness and perseverance to find breakthrough. But sometimes it doesn't."

"What gives indication of the kind of prayer that will be necessary?"

"You listen to the Spirit."

"What are the inner workings of the listening?"

Dana slumped back in her seat and only listened to fragments of Reece and Marcus's continuing conversation. She was still reeling from what just happened. All questions about Reece being the real deal and her needing to come to Well Spring turned to vapor. But if this was only the beginning, what was in store for her over the next four days? The thought was exhilarating and unnerving at the same time.

They rode for the next twenty minutes in silence. Part of Dana wanted to pepper Reece with all kinds of questions. Another part asked why? It was obvious what had happened. They prayed for healing and God healed her. Why was that so tough? She'd heard God's healing power preached in church for years. She'd prayed for others to get healed. But she never believed it would really happen. And it hadn't. Not like this.

It had always been so distant. Like looking at a snowcapped mountain through binoculars turned the wrong way—not ever really knowing if her prayers made a difference. Yes, sometimes people got better, but whether they did or didn't, it never diminished or increased her faith.

What had just happened was on the spiritual field of battle in a close-up-and-very-personal way and had already taken her faith to another stratosphere. What was it Marcus had told her on the plane? That Reece said the magic is real? At least for the moment that was very, very true.

Marcus was the first to break the silence. "I'd like to pose a question, Reece."

"Sure."

"Who is the proprietor of Well Spring Ranch?"

"The owner chooses to remain anonymous. They hire a man to manage the place, coordinate renting it out, but the person who built it stays in the shadows."

"You haven't met him or her?"

"I have." Reece hesitated and adjusted his grip on the steering wheel. "But I'll leave it at that."

The silence returned for another ten minutes. Dana broke it this time.

"How remote is Well Spring?"

"Very. The nearest house is fifteen miles away."

"How much farther?"

"We're getting there, making good time. I'm guessing—"

"Hey, my phone just dropped to one bar." Dana tapped on her phone. "How is the coverage at the ranch?"

"Now that's a picture," Reece said.

"What's a picture?"

"I was imagining a picture of your face when your cell phone shows no bars." Reece pointed out the window of the vehicle with his forefinger. "Not much longer till that happens."

"Hold on. Are you saying we won't have cell service up here?" Dana's head snapped forward.

"You've always been sharp, Dana. I can see why God chose you as one of the four." He winked at her in the mirror.

"What about Wi-Fi?"

Reece shook his head.

"I'm not going to be able to get to the Internet on my laptop?"

"Correct."

"Then we have a major problem. You didn't say anything about no Internet and no cell service."

"You didn't ask."

"I didn't think I needed to." Dana ground her fingernails into her thigh.

"You assumed."

"I have to be in contact with my station. They have to be able to reach me. I need to be able to reach them."

"They won't have that opportunity for the next four days."

"They have to," Dana said.

"Who says?"

"Just stop the car, Reece, and turn it around."

"Drive you back? Drop you off at the airport?"

"That will be fine."

"I thought you were going to stop listening to the voices, Dana." Reece kept driving.

"Stop the car!"

Reece glanced out the window. "My guess is we have about six more miles before we reach the ranch. That means we've come forty-four miles since we last saw any signs of significant civilization. If you'd like, you can get out of the car right now and hike back to Buena Vista, rent a car, and drive to the airport."

Dana slumped back in her seat and muttered, "I'm going to get fired."

"I believe they will survive without you. My prediction is the station will still be standing when you emerge out of the wilderness."

"That's *so* reassuring."

The SUV hit a pothole that rattled her joints. Reece didn't seem to notice. "At sixty-two I'm old enough to remember when cell phones were not in every pocket of every pair of pants in the entire universe. But somehow mankind survived. Technology is an amazing gift from the human race. The lack thereof at Well Spring Ranch is a gift from God. It's a place to unplug from the matrix."

"The matrix?"

"Yes."

"So that's one of the reasons you wanted me to watch that weird movie."

"Yes, one of them."

Reece turned to Marcus. "It doesn't seem like the lack of cell coverage is bothering you."

His face was white. "The lack of cell coverage isn't a gift, it's a nightmare."

At least she wasn't the only one who would be suffering withdrawal.

Reece glanced at Marcus again. "Why does it bother you?"

"I need to be able to reach my family."

"Why? They can't go a few days without hearing from you?"

The professor sighed, ran his fingers through his dark hair, turned to his window, and didn't respond.

Dana stared out her backseat window at the gathering storm clouds. Isolated from the outside world completely. Wonderful. Perspiration returned to her palms. The next four days would be really good or really bad. Probably some of both.

TEN

When Dana, Reece, and he arrived at the ranch, Marcus's first thought was that Reece's description of Well Spring didn't come close to capturing the splendor of the place. Its sprawling beauty rushed into his head and heart and he grinned. The surging river far in front of them, the aspen trees full of emerald leaves along its banks, the chalk cliffs rising on the other side of the water all gave promise of sanctuary and revelation. Then there was the main cabin. Two thousand square feet he guessed, and it looked like it should be on a postcard.

Reece gave them a tour, describing the detail that went into construction of the place.

"The main cabin is made from an old barn built in the late 1890s that came from Gray Rock Ranch ten miles south of the town of Eagle. The barn was going to be torn down and destroyed. It was thought worthless.

"The builders of Well Spring disagreed." Reece gazed around the inside of the cabin, nodding slightly. "The rest of the cabin was added on a year later." He strolled over to the main hallway and ran his fingertips along the wall. "Look at the wood."

"It's gorgeous," Dana said.

"It comes from trees destroyed by the pine beetle. They've decimated many trees around here, but wood that was discarded and thought only good for fires was taken and restored into something beautiful."

Reece didn't need to mention the symbolism. It was obvious. God restoring the broken and inviting them into glory.

Marcus studied the wood, then let his gaze roam to the photos hanging every few feet along the length of the hallway. Pictures of the river outside lit up like gold in a late afternoon sun, a close-up of a radiant aspen leaf full of spring green, a shot looking down on the cabin that must have been taken from the mountains above the ranch. Each of the photos was captivating in its artistry and color.

Dana wandered over and smiled as she studied each photo. When she reached the end of the hallway she turned. "These photos are magnificent. Really, really stunning."

Marcus studied the look on her face. "Is photography an interest of yours?"

"No, not really." She shook her head. "Well, sort of. It's a hobby I don't take much time for. But I did bring my camera on this trip. And I'll definitely be taking some shots." She glanced once more at the photos and walked back down the hall to join Reece and him.

Next Reece led them outside where a covered porch protected a fireplace that looked well used. A pile of kindling sat next to the fireplace, and a huge pile of split logs was stacked between two of the log posts that held up the awning. From there Reece led them down fourteen steps made from railroad ties onto a long walkway. He pointed at the white path. "These stones are French limestone. They were purchased for a dime on the dollar."

The path led to a circular patio with a fire pit in the center of it, which overlooked the river thirty feet below. Marcus glanced up and down the steep descent to the riverbank, looking for stairs. There were none. But he did see worn paths and thick ropes streaming out from a few of the trees growing out of the bank. It was evident climbing down to the river was common among the visitors to Well Spring Ranch. For some reason it seemed appropriate there were no stairs.

Reece motioned at the circular patio they stood on. "This is the listening post. My favorite spot of the entire ranch. It's where the Spirit has spoken to me over the years I've been coming here and where I suspect God will talk to you. It's where he seems to talk to most people who gather at the ranch. But maybe your spot will be down by the river."

Reece motioned toward the cliffs rising on the other side of the valley. "Or maybe at the base of the mountains. Or maybe high up in the hills."

"How do you know he'll speak to us?" Dana said.

"Remember what I said on the way here about Jesus saying his sheep will hear his voice? He will speak. That's not the question. The question is if you'll listen. The question is if you'll choose to believe what he says."

Reece looked at each of them for a long time as if to punctuate his comment. "The third member of our band won't arrive for another"—he pulled back his sleeve and glanced at his watch—"two hours, so I'd like to suggest you start in on your journals."

"What journals?"

Reece pulled two small black leather journals out of his satchel and handed one to Dana and one to Marcus. "A life worth living is a life worth recording. And I believe the life you're going to live over these next few days, and the months and years after that, will be well worth documenting."

Marcus ran his fingers over the leather. Like silk. His name was etched into the front of the journal. He glanced at Dana's. Her name graced the cover as well.

"Thank you, Reece," he said.

Marcus smiled as he pondered Kat's last words before he left this morning. *"No regrets about missing Abbie's game. No regrets about anything in the past. You can't change it, but dwelling on the past can mar the future. So step into the future with everything God has for you."*

God willing, he would. No regrets. Not anymore—if only it were that easy.

Dana smiled at Reece. "Yes, thank you."

"You're welcome." Reece started to say something else, then stopped.

"Were you going to add something?" Dana asked.

Reece shielded his eyes from the sun. "This has been a long time coming. I'm glad both of you are here."

Marcus didn't touch the statement and neither did Dana. Pain glazed the man's eyes as well as longing, fear, and a hint of regret. Reece hid it, but Marcus knew that look too well through personal experience.

"And I'd also spend some time in prayer. We're going into battle and we'll all need to be fully stocked up."

"When does the battle begin?" Dana said.

"It already has."

ELEVEN

BRANDON STARED AT KEVIN AND FANTASIZED ABOUT strangling his manager. They had taken another wrong turn on the way to Well Spring Ranch, yanking them another twenty minutes off schedule. Kevin was the navigator and his skills were not pinging the bell.

"Do you want to drive and I'll tell you where to turn?" Brandon opened his bag of sunflower seeds and popped a few in his mouth.

"The GPS on my phone keeps screwing up." Kevin smacked his cell phone and stared at the screen. "The blue dot, which is us, keeps disappearing. But we're on the right path now. Pretty sure. Kinda sure."

"Let's stop at a house and ask."

"Other than the fact that guys aren't allowed to even consider asking for directions, there hasn't been a home for the past three miles." Kevin tapped his phone again.

"I sure hope you're right, Columbus. I'm guessing we've only got a few more miles before you lose service."

"What?"

"Reece said cell coverage is almost nonexistent out here."

"But you'll have Internet and cell service at the ranch, right? Satellite?"

"Nope. I'll be off the grid."

"No way, uh-uh." Kevin frowned and shook his head. "That can't happen. You have to have cell coverage."

"Don't think that's going to be the case, pal." Brandon grinned.

"What if I need to reach you? And you know I'll need to. We have to be able to communicate."

"Do me a favor while I'm here. Find out what people did before cell phones and the Internet and e-mail. See how they survived."

"That's hysterical. My gut has busted and spilled out on the floor."

A snake slithered across the road ten yards in front of them. "Did you see that?" Brandon jabbed his finger at the road. "That thing was huge. It was like a sewer pipe crawling across the road. Probably a rattler."

"Great. No coverage and you're going to die of a snakebite." Kevin slid his cell phone into his pocket and pulled out the map sitting on the dashboard.

A half hour later their Ford Escape bounced from rut to rut on a narrow dirt road, bouncing them as well, their seat belts the only thing keeping their heads from slamming off the ceiling like pinballs.

"Glad you rented an SUV," Kevin said.

"Reece recommended it highly. He said I would hate him if I didn't."

"I'm hating him even with the SUV. How far out is this place?"

"He said it was remote."

"He must be the bard of understatement."

A gulley in the road jerked them to the left and Brandon yanked on the wheel to get them back to the center of the road—and calling it a road was a generous description.

"How long have you known Reece?"

"About three years. Don't you remember? He came to a couple of my concerts and we hit it off. Now he offers perspective on life." Brandon propped his elbow on the edge of the window and stared at the gathering rain clouds.

"And you think you need some."

"Hey, don't play dumb. I'm not the only one who thinks that." Brandon glanced at Kevin. "You're thrilled I'm going."

"All right, I admit it. You've been off lately, and I think some counseling could be good for you."

"This isn't counseling. The way he was talking up at Snoqualmie Falls, I'm about to learn the ways of the force. Help me, Kevin K. Kenobi, you're my only hope."

"The gospel according to George Lucas." Kevin smiled. "But you'll also get into how you were all hurt by your fathers, won't you?"

Brandon sighed. "My father was okay. He loved me. There're really good memories there. I just wish he'd stood up to my stepmom every now and then. Always made me feel a little undervalued."

For the next fifteen minutes they rode with rough cuts from Brandon's next album providing the sound track for their cross-country trek. Brandon flicked off the power and glanced at Kevin. "I suck."

"What are you talking about?"

He wasn't saying it to make Kevin tell him the music was great. Brandon really did think the new songs were weak. Yes, he said that about every album and felt it to be true at the time the songs were made. But this time it really was true. Sure, he could rework the songs—speed up the tempo or slow it down, slide in a guitar solo or another layer of backup vocals—but it wouldn't do much good. Without God's spark, the album would tank. Brandon sighed. If Well Spring didn't provide an answer, he had no idea what would.

Kevin broke his downward mental spiral a few minutes later. "Remind me, who else is going on this retreat?"

Brandon blinked and gripped the wheel tighter. "There're four of us, plus Reece. One's a physics professor from U-Dub, one's a personal trainer, and the third works in downtown Seattle."

"You've met all of them?"

Brandon slid on his sunglasses and shifted in his seat away from Kevin. "I met the prof and the trainer up at Snoqualmie Falls last week, the other gal couldn't make it."

But she'd be there at the ranch ready to rock both their worlds.

Now he understood why Reece hadn't told him who it was till last night. If he'd had more time to think about it, he might not have come.

Brandon shook out another handful of seeds into his hand and popped them in his mouth.

Kevin laughed. "I don't know how you can shell those things inside your mouth and not choke on them."

"Talented teeth and tongue." He slowed for a series of five-inch-deep potholes.

"You're sure Reece is legit?"

"What are you talking about? Just last week you were telling me I should go on this thing. Now you're telling me to watch out?"

"I'm just saying you better be looking for cameras in that place when you get inside to make sure you don't wind up on some reality TV show. It's my job to worry about you."

"He's the real deal. Trust me, K2."

Kevin folded his arms. "There's nothing wrong with keeping your eyes open."

"For what?"

"A handout. You told me how he dresses."

"Just because his clothes are old doesn't mean he's going to hit me up for cash."

"Not yet. But once he puts his guru spin on everything, he'll be asking you to donate fifty thousand dollars so he can advance his cause."

"I'll put him in touch with you if he asks." Brandon grinned.

"That's what I'm afraid of." Kevin glanced at the map. "I think we should be there pretty soon." He tossed the map onto the car floor. Ten minutes later they crested a rise in the road and Well Spring appeared in front of them.

"Wow." Kevin rolled down his window and the scent of pine filled the car. "Reece must have some sizable donors to his cause to get you all into this place for free."

Brandon stared at the ranch. Stunning. He parked next to what must be Reece's rental car, exited the SUV, and grabbed his back-pack. "You want to come in and meet everyone?"

Kevin came around the front of the vehicle and got comfortable in the driver's seat. "No thanks." He looked at his cell phone. "Zero bars. No service." Then he squinted at Brandon. "I guess I'll be talk-ing to you in four days. I'll be praying for you."

"Thanks, bud." Brandon stared at the cabin as the crunch of the SUV's tires driving away faded into the afternoon. This next part wouldn't be easy. He tramped down the path to the cabin, lugging his backpack over one shoulder, each step bringing him closer to the fuse he couldn't stop from lighting.

TWELVE

DANA DRIED HER HANDS OFF ON THE THICK BROWN HAND towel that hung from a brass ring on the wall of the cabin bathroom, checked her hair in the mirror, and paused before opening the door and again asked the question stuck in her mind like a bad advertising jingle. "What am I doing here?"

Three against one. She should have seen it coming. Tamera coming was too good to be true. Yes, the healing Dana had experienced on the way here was real. Yes, she believed God wanted her here, but she wasn't sure she was ready to dive into Reece's world of spiritual Olympics with people she barely knew.

She would be fine. She functioned quite capably among the men in the radio industry and could handle this, but still, why couldn't Tamera be here to temper the testosterone? Dana needed to let it go. Trust God in this. So easily said, so hard to live.

Reece still hadn't told her anything about the third member of their group, even after they arrived. Which was certainly not a good sign. Why would he keep the mystery going till the last possible second? Why couldn't she know anything about him but Marcus could?

This wasn't just a recipe for disaster, this dish had already been baked and served with a nice hot chili-pepper sauce on top. She sighed, pulled the bathroom door open, and shuffled down the hall and around the corner into the great room.

"Okay, any bets on when the third member of our little tribe is going to show—?" The last word didn't just stick in her throat. It filled her stomach and made her want to retch.

It couldn't be him. Not here. But it was him, standing fifteen feet from her, a stupid smile mashed all over his face as if it were four years ago and they were looking for something dumb to do on a Saturday night and succeeding more often than not.

Brandon. What had Reece done? She hadn't seen him in three years. Not a phone call. Not an e-mail. Not a Christmas card. Nothing. But what had she expected? When Brandon broke it off, she made him promise to get out of her life entirely. No contact whatsoever. He had abided by her request. And she'd successfully buried the part of her that wished he hadn't honored her demand.

"Hi, Dana." He shifted his weight back and forth on his Converse All Stars, black denim jeans hanging loosely, dark blond hair styled like he was ready to step onstage at Creation Fest and whip his adoring fans into a frenzy.

"Brandon Scott." She widened her legs slightly and clenched her jaw tight. There was no way she'd show surprise or any other kind of emotion. She took another step into the living room and slowly folded her arms across her chest.

"Yeah." He shoved his hands into the front pockets of his jeans. "From the look on your face, you didn't know I was coming."

No kidding, cowboy. She blinked. "What are you—?" The words stuck again.

"Doing here?" Brandon pulled his hands from his pockets and popped his fists together and looked at Reece. "You want to tackle this one?"

Dana glared at Reece with her best "I want to kill you" stare, but he didn't flinch and stayed silent. She spun back to Brandon. "You don't look surprised to see me."

"Not entirely. Reece told me last night you'd be here."

She glanced at Reece, then back to Brandon. "Then why in God's green and blue and purple and gold universe did you still come?"

Brandon sputtered a few unintelligible words.

"And you." She took two strides toward Reece and pointed at him. "Why didn't you tell me? And don't give me some flippant 'You didn't ask' type answer. I did ask."

Reece's face was stone. "If you had come to the meeting at Snoqualmie Falls, you would have discovered then that Brandon is one of the four and would have been able to choose whether or not to come to Well Spring."

Her face went hot. "You could have told me in the airport or on the plane or on the phone."

Reece bent and picked up the hatchet resting on the ledge of the fireplace and split a piece of pine into kindling. "No, it wasn't something to do on the phone. And it wasn't something to do without both of you here. That day at the falls was the only time both your schedules would allow you to address the issue in person. I told you the meeting was critical. And you chose not to come."

"I'm leaving." Dana spun on her heel and marched out of the room into the hallway.

"The considerable distance to the next town that we discussed on the way here has not changed."

"I'll take your rental car." Dana stopped at the front door, yanked it open, and shouted back toward the great room, "When I come back, don't be here, Brandon." She slammed the door as hard as she could and stumbled outside, her shoes kicking up small clouds of dust.

✦✦✦

"Hand me some of that newspaper, Brandon." Reece pointed to a wicker basket next to the couch.

"Sure." Brandon grabbed a handful of paper and walked it over to Reece. He wanted to hand him his resignation papers. He should be the one to leave, not her. Did he expect Dana to be upset? Of course. But not this bad. He'd known he'd hurt her, but it had been three years and . . . the reality was he didn't know anything. He looked up. Marcus was staring at him.

"She and I, uh, have some history together."

"It was not a challenge to surmise that." The professor adjusted his glasses. "I assume the severing of the relationship was difficult."

"Very." Brandon turned to Reece, who knelt at the fireplace crumpling the paper and laying kindling on top of it. "By the way, thanks for giving me all that warning about Dana not knowing I would be here."

Reece turned to him slowly. "Do you miss her?"

"What?"

"You heard me." Reece turned back to building his fire.

Wow. Brandon gave his eyes a quick squeeze with his thumb and forefinger. Did he? He hadn't let that question surface for a long time. Because he didn't want to face the answer. That can of worms was buried in the vault inside the vault inside the vault. Because if it was yes—he missed her—then he'd blown it by breaking up with her.

If it was no, then he should have given her a better answer than he did for why he ended things. Who was he kidding? He should have given her a better answer in either case. And he would have, if he knew what it was.

"I don't know."

"I think you do know." Reece stood. "I'm going to go talk to Dana."

As the sliding glass door closed behind Reece, Brandon admitted the truth. He missed her deeply.

✦✦✦

Dana dug her fingers into the palm of her hand as she stumbled toward the river. No tears. No way. He'd been the cause of a reservoir full three years back. He'd already taken his allotment—and far more than he was worth. But her heart didn't agree with her head, and tears spilled onto her cheeks a minute later. She walked down the long walkway to the listening post, sat, and stared at the stream, lit like a river of diamonds by the late afternoon sun.

"What are you doing to me, God? This makes no sense."

She held out her ring finger and massaged it with her right index finger. Brandon's ring had fit there like finger and ring were one. Now it seemed the finger would stay empty the rest of her life. He'd stepped through her front door on that early May afternoon three years ago, and it had taken a millionth of a second to know something was wrong.

"Hey, handsome." She sat up in her chair and smiled.

"Hey." Brandon closed her front door and stood just inside it, his eyes blinking as his gaze darted everywhere in the room except at her.

"What is it?"

"Nothing."

She motioned him over and set her book on the end table next to her overstuffed light green chair. He sat and Dana took his hands.

"Talk to me. Did something fall through with our honeymoon?"

Brandon shook his head.

"Tell me."

He pulled his hands out of hers, pressed his palms against his temples, and leaned his head back. "We're not supposed to be together anymore."

Her throat constricted and a dull tingling sensation smothered her. "Wha . . . what?"

"I'm sorry."

The room blurred and everything seemed to slow down. Except for her breathing. She sucked in rapid breaths. "I don't . . ." No more words came.

"I'm so sorry."

"Why, Brandon? What are you doing?"

"I don't know, I just know it's right."

This was impossible. Three months before the wedding and he's breaking up with her? "There has to be a reason."

"I know, I know . . . you're totally right, but I just . . . can't put it into words—"

"You mean you know why you're doing this but don't know how to say it, or you don't know why you're doing it?"

"I don't know."

"You have to know!"

Brandon stood and shouted back, "I don't know." He paced on her tan carpet. "If I knew I would tell you."

"Have you prayed about this?"

"Yes, of course. I—"

She stood and pulled at her white blouse. "It's nerves, Brandon. That's all. It happens."

"It's not nerves. It's just right."

"How can it be right if you don't even know why you're doing it?"

"It's not that I don't love you, I do, but—"

"If you love me, then what is it?"

"Forgive me, but this is what I have to do."

They'd talked on and on, never getting any closer to the center—to the reason he was leaving.

The door had closed behind him an hour later, and Dana sat in the room till night came and tears came no more.

When her eyes fluttered open early the next morning, the memory of what happened the night before smashed against her heart and the tears came again. Finally she stirred and her head flopped to her right. She glanced at the open Bible on the bottom of the end table. A verse was highlighted in faded yellow. She lifted the Bible to her lap and stared at the words: "Weeping may last for the night, but a shout of joy comes in the morning."

A bitter laugh spilled out of her mouth. How ironic. Her weeping had certainly lasted the night, but she wouldn't be shouting for joy this morning. Two years and thirteen months of mornings had come and gone, and she was still waiting for the joy.

"Why did you put me through that, Lord?" She looked up at the mountains. "Why am I still going through it?"

A response came so fast Dana blinked.

I'm in this.

The sound of shuffling feet spun Dana around. Head tilted down, hands behind his back, Reece stood ten yards behind her.

"You feel I've betrayed you."

"It's not a feeling, it's a fact."

"May I join you?"

Dana shrugged.

Hands shoved into the front pockets of his jeans, Reece strolled up and stopped a few paces from the wooden lounge chair she sat on.

"When you break a bone, you often scrape up the skin at the spot where the break occurs. If you went to the doctor and he treated the scrape and did nothing about the break, you'd sue him for malpractice."

"What's your point?"

"You've been treating the scrape, Dana." Reece took a step closer. "It's time to mend the break. Set it right. Give it a chance to heal."

"Is that the only reason I'm here? So I can face the fact that Brandon Scott is a colossal jerk? I already know that."

"Far from it."

"I'm all ears."

"It's your destiny to be here, Dana."

"Oh really. How nice. Is it Brandon's destiny to be here too?"

"Yep."

"How interesting that my supposed destiny is intricately tied to the one person in the world I never want to see again. The one person who ripped out my heart and stuck it in a blender."

"It is interesting. Because I don't think God plays dice with our lives."

"Einstein. But he said, 'God does not play dice with the universe.'"

"Very good. I'd have expected Marcus to know that quote, but not you or Brandon."

"I'm so thrilled I could surprise you." She leaned back and released a heavy breath.

He took two more steps and sat next to her on the long wooden lounge chair. "If you want to go home, you can. You can take the car. But before you make a decision, sit here and ask the Spirit what he wants.

"This is going to sound harsh, but I don't know any other way to say it. And I apologize ahead of time for being a man. But these next four days aren't all about you. It's about the Spirit and what he wants to accomplish inside all three of you, which will train you to do so much for others. This small little group is a body and you need each other. Marcus and Brandon need you. You need them. For whatever reason, God chose the three of you, and no one else can take your place."

"I can't stay, Reece."

"The enemy took Tamera out. Don't let him take you out as well."

"If I'd known Brandon would be here, I wouldn't have come."

"Don't you think God knows that? Which might be one of the reasons you didn't come to that meeting at Snoqualmie Falls."

"I still want to kill both of you."

"God and me, or Brandon and me?"

A smile slipped to the surface of her face.

Reece leaned forward. "I don't blame you, but don't let the emotion of the moment steal what Jesus has here for you."

He stood and walked back toward the cabin. Dana watched the undulations in the water, wishing she could get in the current and float away. But Reece, as harsh as he was, was right. God had told her to come. There was no doubt about that. So why would Brandon's being here change that?

Because it just did. It changed everything. She screamed into the mountains. Again. And again. Then slid off the chair and sank down till she sat crisscrossed, her head folded forward.

"Lord, are you in this?" She looked up at the aspen trees. "You say you are, but how can you be in something I can't do?"

Stay.

She continued to stare at the river. Finally she stood, turned, and gazed at the cabin a hundred yards away. "I'm yours. You know that. But while we're here, if you could give Brandon a serious case of poison ivy or poison oak or whatever kind of poison is in these parts, I'd greatly appreciate it."

✦✦✦

Thirty minutes later Dana walked through the sliding glass door and eased into the living room. "I'm staying."

The closest thing she'd seen to a smile instantly appeared on Reece's face and vanished just as quickly. "That is excellent news."

"I'm pleased, Dana," Marcus said.

"Thanks."

She didn't look at Brandon and he didn't say anything. At some point they'd talk. But not yet. Maybe not at all. She knew that wouldn't be the case, but she could still hope for it.

Reece motioned Dana over and as she gazed into those deep liquid blue eyes, a joy washed over her. For all his gruffness, she saw in his eyes a depth of compassion and love she hadn't known since Pappy died.

When she reached him she wrapped her arms around his chest and leaned into his massive body. He wrapped her up in his long arms and squeezed so tight, she thought she might burst and wished he would squeeze even tighter. Something broke inside her, but a good kind of breaking. And it wasn't Reece holding her . . . it was her pappy in the days before he grew weak and succumbed to the leukemia. The moment only lasted a few seconds but it also lasted for centuries, and somehow she knew the healing of her heart had begun.

Reece gently released her. "Okay. Now that introductions are finished, it's time for us to meet in a more organized way. Let's take ten minutes to get settled, and then we'll meet out at the listening post and talk about what's going to happen for the next few days."

"Are there any accoutrements you'd like us to bring?"

"Accoutrements?" Brandon snorted. "My dear professor, I'll have to start carrying around a dictionary to have any hope of understanding you."

"Um, paraphernalia, supplies, accessories—things we might need while we're gathered."

"An excellent question," Reece said. "Yes, bring an attitude that is ready and willing to explore a Christianity you've never known before. And bring a heart that is willing to an even greater degree." Reece gazed at each of them for a few seconds. "We're about to boldly go where few men and women have gone before."

"You need to get out of the sixties, Reece." Brandon grinned.

"*Star Trek* is forever, pal." Reece tilted his head. "And I'm hoping you soon find out how true that statement is."

THIRTEEN

WHEN BRANDON STEPPED THROUGH THE SLIDING GLASS door that led outside ten minutes later, something told him Reece was right—they were about to go places few others had gone. As he'd done a quick unpacking, Marcus told him about Dana's healing in the car, and Brandon caught the professor's excitement about what could happen during this retreat. If it was real.

The problem with being a performer at his level of fame was he'd been backstage. He'd heard the comments after shows where all the promoters cared about was the gate, people were just dollar signs. He'd seen fake tears spill down the faces of other musicians and pastors and preachers that turned to faces of stone as soon as the curtain closed.

And the old cliché about one finger pointed at others means three pointed back at you was true. For the past three years he'd been the one smiling onstage, and once he stepped off, he often wore a face only appropriate in a morgue.

Brandon tightened his grip on the journal Reece had given him and stared at the rest of the group already sitting at the listening post around a fire that crackled in the pit in the center of the patio.

Reece stood on the edge of the terrace overlooking the river, his broad back seeming to fill the space in between the aspen trees that bordered the circular patio of French limestone. Marcus and Dana sat in teakwood chairs a few yards behind him, both of them writing in journals that looked like his.

As he settled into a chair next to Marcus, Reece turned and nodded at Brandon, then the others. "Welcome to Well Spring Ranch. Welcome to the war."

Reece paused to look into each of their eyes. "My friends, we are not in the garden, and as much as I like John Lennon, love is not all we need. We are living in the midst of an epic battle that will not end till the new heaven and the new earth are revealed. There are no neutral zones; there is no Switzerland in this fight. And sticking our heads in the sand is not an option. We need to be equipped.

"We have an enemy whose goal is simple: steal, kill, destroy. God has a destiny for you. But so does Satan. God wants the fullness of life for us. Joy. Healing. Freedom. The desires of our hearts to be realized. But this kind of life doesn't roll off the assembly line. It's opposed by a demonic host with a hatred of mankind so fierce, the only thing that can stand against it is the risen Christ. But we have been called to stand in the gap. To raise our swords and fight. To bring freedom and healing and hope to the captives."

Reece dropped his head and paused again, probably to let the words sink in. When he raised his head, his countenance had lightened.

"The next four days will be the first phase of your training. The second part will start when we return to Seattle at the end of this week. The journey you're about to embark on is one of risk. But a life without risk is a life without faith. As Annie Dillard says, 'You have to jump off cliffs all the time and build your wings on the way down.' We are going to be jumping off cliffs together.

"Let's pray. You can bow your heads, you can keep your eyes open, shut them, whatever you want to do. All I ask is you join me with all the strength you have."

Reece raised his head to the sky. "You are life. We need it. You are freedom. We long for it. You are truth. We have to have it. Come now, Spirit of God. Come now, Jesus. Come, Abba. We invite you in to do what you would do. So be it."

Reece stood again and turned toward the river. "Every now and then we get a break from reality. A glimpse into the other world that is more real than the reality we live in 99 percent of our days." Reece spun back around and squatted in front of them.

"The Bible is about a world of demons and angels and great evil and even greater glory. A world the prophets saw; the world Enoch, and Elijah, and Paul, and John the apostle all saw. A world that is all around us in every moment if we would have eyes to see it and ears to hear it.

"But we don't see it. We close our eyes and have created a box within the box. And the church calls men like me—who believe there are no boundaries—a mystic."

Reece pointed at the flames that leapt out of the fire pit. "Can you explain what you're seeing?" He looked at Marcus. "Maybe you can, Professor. But you can't touch it, taste it, or contain it."

He picked up a small log and tossed it into the center of the pit, sending sparks skyward. "Yet its power is unmistakable.

"At Pentecost it was tongues of fire. The Spirit is described as a consuming fire. Fire is what consumed the prophets of Baal.

"And the fire of the Spirit is what will refine and restore and set us free. During our time here, my belief is the Trinity will speak to each of you specifically, go deep into your soul, and begin a work of restoration. I pray you will allow that fire to burn bright."

Reece sat down again, closed his eyes, and didn't speak for so long Brandon glanced at the others. Their eyes held the same question his likely did. Should they say something? A few seconds later Reece sat forward and glanced at Dana and him. "Now, before we go further, I need to make sure you"—Reece pointed at Dana, then him—"and you will not be affected in the present by what happened in your past."

"No, I won't," Brandon said.

"Dana?" Reece asked.

"I'm fine."

"That doesn't answer my question."

"No, it won't affect anything."

"Good. That answer segues perfectly into the first rule. Speak truth. You both just tossed out falsehoods for Marcus's and my consumption and apparently expected us to swallow them without question."

Dana's eyes widened and Brandon suspected there was a look of surprise on his face similar to the one on hers. Reece's gaze darted back and forth between them. "Of course your past is going to affect your being here. That's one of the reasons I believe the Spirit put you two together in this confined area."

"I can't wait." Dana shifted in the teak chair and tightened her arms across her chest.

"Neither can I," Brandon said. Getting back to Seattle couldn't come fast enough.

"Good to hear that." Reece leaned forward, elbows on his knees. "As I just said, the first rule of your training is to speak what is true. If you choose not to say anything, fine. But anything that does come out of your mouth will be the truth. We will be authentic with each other. Are we clear?"

He waited till each of them nodded. "That holds for when the four of us are together and when you are one-on-one." He glanced at each of them. "Do any of you have a problem with that?"

"Yes," Dana said.

"What's the issue?" Reece stared at her.

"You want me to be honest?" Dana waggled her thumb toward Brandon. "Being authentic in front of him might mean wrapping a towel around his neck and strangling him."

"That sounds abundantly forthcoming to admit that."

"What I mean is, I don't know if I'll ever be able to tell what I'm really feeling deep down—"

"In other words you'll take option one and stay silent." Reece raised an eyebrow.

"I suppose so."

"Now"—Reece looked at Brandon—"why are we here?"

Brandon laughed and glanced at the others. "I think that's our line."

Reece turned to his left. "Why did you come, Dana? Why did you accept my invitation?"

"Because I thought I was supposed to."

"Not enough. What's the deeper reason?"

"There's nothing more than that. I just thought—"

"What is the first rule?"

"Not right now." Dana shifted in her chair and rubbed the spot in between her eyebrows. "Not yet."

"No problem." Reece shifted his gaze between Marcus and Brandon. "Next?"

"Because I'm tired," Brandon said.

"Of?"

"Going through the motions. Of not feeling things anymore. I want my heart back."

"When did you start losing it? Do you know?"

Did he know? Yeah. Precisely. The slide from alive to half dead started the instant he broke up with Dana. He'd always known there was a connection. It was blindingly obvious the two events were fused together. He'd just never let himself admit it for more than a second. That would force him to face why he'd broken up with her in the first place. Not a concert hall he was willing to play in at the moment.

Brandon gave a single nod. "I have a pretty good idea when it started."

"Do you want to tell us about it?"

"Not at the moment."

Reece glanced at Dana's chair on the edge of the patio, then faced Marcus. "Why did you accept my invitation?"

"Because you indicated the magic was real and I want to see if that statement is correct."

"What's the deeper reason?"

Marcus stared at the white stones at his feet. "I exist in a world of regret and guilt for what I have not done, which prevents me from living fully in the present. I live in a world of could-have and should-have. If the magic truly is real, my dream is it will bring about the disintegration of those regrets and cause them to vanish."

"Marcus?" Reece waited till the professor met his gaze. "Thank you."

Reece opened his satchel and pulled out an ancient-looking notebook. "Do you want to know why I think you're here?" He held the notebook like it was glass and stared at it for a long moment. "I think you're here because of this."

He opened the cover as if it were a priceless ancient scroll, then turned to the middle of the journal and pulled out a piece of paper. Reece laid it on his knee and ran the tips of his fingers over the surface. The sheet was yellowed, the ink faded.

"As I read this, close your eyes and listen to the Spirit and see if what I say is true." Reece cleared his throat, and when he spoke his voice had softened. "This was a prophecy spoken over me by my spiritual leader when I was younger than all of you. He and I have prayed over it ever since." Reece took a deep breath, then read.

There will come a day when you will train them—they will be four. The song, the teacher, the leader, the temple. Keep your eyes open to see, your ears open to listen, your heart open to feel, and your mind open to discern.

When the time comes, the Spirit will reveal each of them to you. You will teach them wonders of my power they can't yet imagine. And instruct these warriors how to go far inside the soul and marrow.

They will rise up and fight for the hearts of others. They will demolish strongholds in the heavens and grind their enemies to dust. Their victories will spread across the nations. You will pour out your life for them and lead them to freedom, and they will turn and bring healing to the broken and set the hearts of others free.

And when the wolf rises, the four must war against him and bring about his destruction.

Only they have hope of victory.

And for one, their vision will grow clear,
And for one, the darkness of choice will rain on them,
And for one, the other world will become more real than
this one,
And for one, death will come before the appointed time.

The prophecy was about them? Obviously. As Reece spoke the words, a shot of adrenaline had coursed through Brandon. The words were electric. Reece wanted truth? This felt truer than anything Brandon had touched in the past thirty-six months. And more unsettling.

"We are three of the four." Marcus said the words more to himself than to them. "Everything in my mind says your conclusion is preposterous, yet every indication from my heart asserts it is true."

"The Spirit has revealed that to you."

"How do you know it's us?" Dana said. "Not to be a skeptic. I mean, I think I'm sensing the same thing Marcus is, but still."

Reece stood and rubbed his chin. "With you, Dana, I knew—"

"Excuse me? Before we get to the history, which I'm sure will be fascinating, can we talk about that last line?" Brandon pointed his finger at his temple as if it were a gun. "One of us is going to die?"

"I don't know." Reece scuffed his boot. "My spiritual leader and I have discussed that many times without a firm conclusion. It could be the death of a dream, death of a career . . ."

"Or perhaps the obvious conclusion is simply difficult to acknowledge," Marcus said, "especially when you're attempting to convince people they're part of a prophecy and you'd rather they not reject the idea."

"Maybe." Reece stared at Marcus. "But even if it is a physical death, 'appointed time' doesn't mean one of you would die young."

Dana waved her hands. "Can we get back to why you think it's us? Before I buy in fully, I need a little more evidence. I suppose I'm the leader, but really? I manage a few salespeople. I'm not that much of a leader. Plus, there are thousands of people who could fit those four descriptions. Millions."

"I don't think we've even started to see the kind of leader you can be." Reece clasped his hands behind his back. "And how did I know? With you, Dana, I knew after we met in our home group— what was that, a year ago? The Spirit said, 'That's her,' the moment I saw you. But like you, I needed more convincing.

"With each of you, the Spirit gave me clues to look for over the years. For example, with Dana, one of the clues was a picture that kept appearing in my mind of an upright wooden radio from the thirties. So when I found out you were in radio, it was a significant piece in the puzzle among others.

"One clue with you, Marcus, was what I sensed when I read each of your books, as well as what I heard as you grew up."

"Grew up?" The professor frowned. "Explain."

"Your dad and I weren't close, but we were acquaintances. Don't fret, I'll tell you more about that in the days to come and why it's taken till now to tell you this. For the moment, suffice it to say when he would talk of you and your exploits, a curiosity stirred inside me and I wondered if you were the teacher. Then when I read your first book and called you five years ago, and we started having coffee together, and I heard your ideas and passions, I was almost certain."

Reece turned to Brandon. "You were the easiest. Not long after the prophecy was spoken, I had a vision where I was shown a poem and told the song would have something to do with what I'd seen. I wrote the words down and tucked them in the back of my Bible. On a fall day three years ago, as I drove along Alki in West Seattle, I popped in your CD *Go Higher*. When the third tune came on with the exact words the Lord had given me in the vision, I had little doubt you were the song. So I came to one of your concerts and you know the rest."

"Little doubt? Meaning you still had some?"

Reece nodded and looked at each of them. "The final confirmation was your agreement to come on this trip to Well Spring."

"So where does that leave Tamera?" Dana said.

"I'm not sure. But I'm praying about it, asking for an answer." Reece rocked forward and slapped his hands on his hips. "I think that's enough to stew on for the moment. Pray about the prophecy. See what the Spirit reveals."

"What is this wolf rising thing?" Dana asked. "We're supposed to destroy whatever it is?"

"When the time comes, yes. I believe it's an organization here in the US and we'll discuss it further at some point—I don't know when. But it's why you're here. The ultimate reason for your training."

He glanced at his watch. "It's six o'clock now. I'm going to start cooking dinner; we'll eat at seven thirty and then—"

"One more moment, please." Marcus held up his forefinger. "I'd like to know more about this organization. Who they are, what they do, why you believe they're dangerous."

"In time, Professor, but not for a while. First the three of you need to be trained, then you'll be ready to hear about the full scope of the war."

Reece took a step toward the cabin, then turned. "Before we eat I want you to take time alone. To pray. To think. To listen to what God has for you here. Explore the grounds. Get down to the river. Or sit here at the post and take in the cliffs."

Brandon tapped his feet on the stones and the tips of his fingers together. "Before we break, what does 'go far inside the soul and marrow' mean?"

"We'll get to that. Probably tomorrow. And I pray your spiritual ears will be wide open. They'll need to be."

FOURTEEN

AFTER BREAKFAST ON MONDAY MORNING, REECE STOOD, walked to the coatrack, slipped into his green North Face jacket, and put on his beat-up Stetson. "I'm going out. Your training will start when I return."

He waved his hand at the bookshelves on either side of the fireplace. "While I'm gone you might want to choose a book and read a few chapters."

Brandon glanced at the shelves, then at Marcus and Dana. They both shrugged. Brandon scowled. Read? Reece brought them up here to read? At the door he paused as if he'd heard Brandon's thoughts. "You might enjoy it, Brandon."

"Where are you going?"

The door shut without an answer from Reece.

Brandon rose, jogged to the front door, and yanked it open. He watched the big man stride up the slight incline on the narrow path that cut through the sparse underbrush opposite the road they'd come in on, dust rising a few inches with each footstep.

"Bring me back a latte!" Brandon called after him.

Reece didn't turn but lifted his arm and flashed a thumbs-up. When Brandon went back inside, Marcus and Dana were already perusing the bookshelves.

"What was his destination?" Marcus said.

"No idea. Off into the woods somewhere." Brandon walked up to the bookshelves and folded his arms.

Marcus pulled G. K. Chesterton's *Orthodoxy* off the shelf and turned it to the back cover.

"Since you've known Reece the longest, Professor, what do you think so far?" Brandon asked.

"I've already seen multiple sides of him that have not previously surfaced."

Brandon pulled down a large coffee-table book on rock bands from the sixties. "Like the whole mystic vibe."

"That's one of the sides." Marcus pulled another three books off the lower shelf to the right.

Dana studied the books on the other side of the fireplace. "I want to know more about his past."

"That desire might go unfulfilled. I don't think he communicates anything he doesn't want to reveal, and for me his past has always been Fort Knox times a googolplex." Marcus moved a rich russet throw pillow to the armrest of the couch and lay out, his stocking feet propped up on the armrest at the other end. "What rises to the surface of your mind when you think about us being an element of this prophecy?"

"*Part* of the prophecy?" Dana turned and stared at Marcus. "According to Reece we *are* the prophecy."

✦✦✦

Dana sat in the wicker couch in front of the outside fireplace, struggling to get through the first chapter of Pascal's *Pensées*. Between the river song behind and below her, Brandon's presence, and Reece's cryptic statements last night, her brain wasn't willing to take on any new data.

The door to the left of the fireplace swung open and Marcus walked through and waved his thumb back at the cabin. "Is there anything from inside I might bring you?"

"No, but thanks." She shifted on the couch. "Are you done reading?"

"No, I'm just taking a short break." He pulled off his glasses and rubbed his eyes. "I'm practicing a productivity method called the Pomodoro Technique. Essentially you study or write or work intensely for twenty-five minutes, then take a break, then proceed again for another twenty-five."

"Does it work?"

"Not yet." Marcus smiled. "But it's too soon to quantify the results."

"Keep me posted."

"I will do so." The professor motioned to his right. "I'm going to take a short walk before engaging again with my book. My hope is whatever you read will be scintillating."

"You as well."

She watched Marcus meander off, then glanced to her right to find Brandon leaning against the edge of the cabin thirty feet away, his face questioning. He pointed at himself, then at her, and back at himself. Great. Did she want him to come over? No. This would be the first conversation with just the two of them since they'd arrived. The first since he snapped her heart in two. But it would have to happen at some point. She might as well get it over with. She put her heart in full lockdown mode, motioned him over, and grabbed a thick piece of kindling to hold on to.

When he reached her he said, "Are you going to bash me over the head with that?" Brandon stood next to one of the wicker chairs, hands jammed in the back of his pants.

"If you get close enough."

He smiled. "So you're really okay if I join you for a bit, Day?"

Day? Unbelievable. The guy was a caveman.

"You do not call me Day. Ever again."

"But I used to—"

"That's right. You used to. Past tense. Waaaaay in the past." She shook her head and glared at him. "Wake up, Brandon."

"Sorry." He shifted his weight back and forth. "Can I still—?"

"Fine." She flicked her hand toward the chair he stood next to. "Whatever."

He settled into the chair and held his palms out to warm them from the fire, then reached into his pocket and pulled out a bag of sunflower seeds and held it out to her. "You want some?"

"I see you're still sucking on those things."

"I'll take that as a no." He shook a handful out of the bag and popped them in his mouth.

"What do you want?" Dana frowned.

"Just to talk."

"About what?"

"Anything."

"I don't believe this." Dana reached down and tossed another piece of wood onto the fire.

"Believe what?" Brandon set his bag of seeds on his armrest.

"Come on, are you kidding me? Really?"

Brandon patted his chest, then the front pockets of his jeans. "Oh no. It looks like I forgot my woman-speak code breaker at home, so do you mind helping me out with a little translation on what I'm missing?"

"Don't be a jerk."

"I'm sorry. But I honestly don't know what you're driving at."

"You just want to have a little chat? Wonderful! That sounds great. Let's compare our journals, okay?" Dana glared at him. "I don't hear a peep from you for three years, then you show up here and suddenly want to chat? Am I supposed to welcome you with open arms?"

Brandon gripped the back of his neck and stared up at the chalk cliffs across the river. "You are a piece of work, you know that?"

"Thank you. I try. And you're being a jerk again." She pushed herself into the back of the couch and yanked her arms tight against her chest.

Brandon rose to his feet and strode away. "Wonderful talking to you," he called over his shoulder.

"You too. I hope we do it again in about a million years."

Dana blinked. No way. She wouldn't let tears come. Steel. Her heart was hardened steel. But there was a fire burning on the outside and the metal had started to melt.

FIFTEEN

THE SCRAPE OF THE CABIN'S FRONT DOOR PULLED MARCUS out of the world he'd lost himself in. He rolled over on the couch and looked up. Reece was back. His breathing was slow and rhythmic, but something in Reece's face made the big man look like he'd just sprinted one hundred meters. It was flushed. He held what looked like a *USA TODAY* and a white coffee cup in one hand, the other held an old piece of wood, bleached almost pure white by the seasons.

"Welcome back." Marcus sat up and set down his book.

Reece nodded at him.

"Was your excursion enjoyable?"

"It was good." Reece set the newspaper and cup on the kitchen counter and peeled off his coat. "Time well spent."

"You appear winded."

Reece stared at Marcus for five seconds before answering. "I'm not." He turned the piece of wood over in his hands and rubbed its surface. "Where are Dana and Brandon?"

"They confiscated your SUV and set out for Denver."

The hint of a smile passed over Reece's eyes, but his mouth stayed stoic. "Wonderful. They wanted to spend a little alone time together? That's good. We need a team that's unified."

Marcus stared at Reece as the man spread honey on a slice of wheat bread, then took it and a glass of milk to the small round oak table near the windows. Something in the equation of the moment was off. And it felt like it should be obvious as to what it was.

The thought niggled at the back of Marcus's mind, so he waited. After years of studying anomalies in the world of physics and trying to find answers where the questions hadn't been formed yet, he'd learned to trust his brain and give it time to unearth answers.

That's it!

The newspaper. Where had Reece gotten the newspaper? Marcus rose from the couch, walked over to the kitchen counter, opened the paper, and glanced at the date, then at Reece, then back to the paper. Impossible.

"May I inquire as to where you were?"

"I already told you." Reece tilted his head forward and stared at Marcus from under his eyebrows. "Out."

"Where?"

"I had to do something."

"And what was that something?"

"Drop the verbal ping-pong, Marcus, it grows tedious quickly. If you feel you've discovered something and want to ask me about it, say it. Clearly."

Marcus pointed to the newspaper. "The date says June 6."

Reece took off his hat and tossed it across the room onto the couch. "And that's a problem why?"

"Unless you've discovered a method of rearranging the laws of physics, that cannot be today's newspaper."

"Explain." Reece cocked his head.

"Your SUV has remained in the same spot since you left, and the distance between us and the nearest town is thirty-seven miles." Marcus folded his arms. "It would fascinate me to understand how you covered seventy miles in the past hour and a half, unless you were given transportation from here to Buena Vista and back by the Blue Angels. And I didn't hear any F/A-18 fighters taking off."

"Well done, Marcus." Reece slapped the top of the table and the hint of a smile returned. "If anyone would notice, it would be you."

"Well done what?"

"Find the others. Then gather them at the listening post." Reece stuck the last of his bread into his mouth and chewed slowly. "Bring your Bible. Tell Dana and Brandon to do the same."

"What for?"

Reece took a long drink of milk. "Let's do it now, shall we?"

+ + +

When Brandon reached the listening post, Reece was already there sitting down. His eyes were bright as he handed Brandon a cup of coffee.

"It's vanilla. I had to heat it again. I hope you don't mind."

"Where did you get this?" Brandon stared at the cup.

"That's what we're going to talk about right now."

Brandon took a sip of the coffee. Not bad. He hadn't seen an espresso machine in the cabin. Reece must have one up in one of the smaller cabins.

"I was kidding about the latte. I didn't know you had a machine around here."

"It was no effort." Reece lifted the Bible from his side onto his knees.

A few seconds later Dana and Marcus arrived. Once they were settled, Reece lifted his head. "Holy Spirit, I invite you into this. Give them ears to hear and a heart to understand."

He glanced around the circle, his blue eyes on fire. "It's time for your first lesson, thanks to the eye for detail the professor has as part of his unique makeup." Reece opened his Bible. "But first I need to ask each of you something. Do you think the Bible is from the mouth of God?"

They nodded.

"Do you think the stories in it are real? That they happened?"

They nodded again.

"Excellent. Then this should be simple." He turned a few more pages in the Bible on his knees. "Turn to Acts chapter 8. Read verses

26 through 40. Come get me when you're finished and we'll talk about it. It should be very stimulating." He stood and walked the fifty yards down the stone path back toward the cabin and sat in a chair right outside the nine-foot sliding glass door. For a few moments the only sound was the river racing around and over the boulders and stones that covered the stream bed.

"He seems pretty pumped up about this," Brandon said a few minutes later.

"Almost animated." Dana looked at Marcus. "Did you do this to him?"

"All I did was notice he had today's paper."

"That got him all excited?"

Marcus nodded. "His explanation should be mesmerizing."

"Why does he have to explain having a newspaper? There are other times in recent recorded history when people have had a newspaper," Brandon said.

"This is either an extraordinary newspaper or our leader has a very remarkable talent."

"Can you just spit it out, Prof?" Brandon said.

Marcus pointed to Reece's SUV and then to the dirt road leading toward Buena Vista and raised his eyebrows. "It's *today's* paper. Consider the implications for a moment."

"Why can't he have today's paper?" Brandon asked.

"Duh." Dana tapped the side of her head. "There was no time to get to Buena Vista and back. And we would have heard his SUV fire up."

"Precisely." Marcus crossed his legs and wrapped his hand around his knee.

"So how'd he get the paper?" Brandon glanced at them.

"Exactly."

Brandon opened his Bible. After he finished the section in Acts, he looked at Dana. "Why has your face turned a whiter shade of pale?"

Dana blinked, closed her Bible, and let it slide from her hands into her lap. "Because I think I know what Reece's explanation will be when we call him back over here."

"I think I know as well." Marcus smiled.

Brandon continued to stare at Dana. "And that's freaking you out?"

"Yeah, a little."

"Because?"

She massaged her lower lip with her thumb and forefinger. "If I'm right, we're either dealing with a man who has an extremely serious connection with God, or a religious lunatic who has misplaced his brain and wants us to do the same."

SIXTEEN

"You guys ready?" Brandon glanced at Marcus and Dana.

They nodded.

"All right then, let's get this circus started." Brandon waved his hand. "Reece! The clowns are ready."

Reece made his way back to the fire pit and sat with his back to the cabin. "Marcus, would you lead us in asking the Spirit for wisdom in these next moments?"

"Yes." Marcus bowed his head. "Open our eyes, help our vision extend past ourselves, and reveal our limiting beliefs. Show us the truth, Lord. Amen."

"Thank you." Reece cocked his head. "Here we go. Read the passage out loud, Brandon."

Brandon leaned down and chided himself for the fourth time in the past two hours for not bringing his reading glasses. Criminal that at thirty-five he had to deal with them, but at least he wasn't at the point where he had to do the daily wrestling match with contacts.

"'But an angel of the Lord spoke to Philip saying, "Get up and go south to the road that descends from Jerusalem to Gaza." So he got up and went; and there was an Ethiopian eunuch, a court official of Candace, queen of the Ethiopians, who was in charge of all her treasure; and he had come to Jerusalem to worship, and he was returning and sitting in his chariot, and was reading the prophet Isaiah. Then the Spirit said to Philip, "Go up and join this chariot." Philip ran up and heard him reading Isaiah the prophet, and said, "Do you understand what you are reading?" And he said, "Well, how could I, unless someone guides me?" And he invited Philip to come up and sit with him. Now the passage of Scripture which he was reading was this:

"' "He was led as a sheep to slaughter; and as a lamb before its shearer is silent, so he does not open his mouth. In humiliation his judgment was taken away; who will relate his generation? For his life is removed from the earth."

"'The eunuch answered Philip and said, "Please tell me, of whom does the prophet say this? Of himself or of someone else?" Then Philip opened his mouth, and beginning from this Scripture he preached Jesus to him. As they went along the road they came to some water; and the eunuch said, "Look! Water! What prevents me from being baptized?" And Philip said, "If you believe with all your heart, you may." And he answered and said, "I believe that Jesus Christ is the Son of God." And he ordered the chariot to stop; and they both went down into the water, Philip as well as the eunuch, and he baptized him. When they came up out of the water, the Spirit of the Lord snatched Philip away; and the eunuch no longer saw him, but went on his way rejoicing. But Philip found himself at Azotus, and as he passed through he kept preaching the gospel to all the cities until he came to Caesarea.'"

Brandon looked up and heat washed through him. Reece couldn't be serious. The big man tapped the pages of his Bible. "Read the first six words of verse 40 again."

"'But Philip found himself at Azotus . . .'"

"Does that seem strange to any of you?" Reece glanced at each of them. "The distance between Jerusalem and Azotus is sixty-six kilometers, or forty-four miles." He shut his Bible and looked at each of the three again. "Questions?"

Brandon held up his Bible. "You're not actually saying—"

"I am." Reece snapped his Bible back open. "'The Spirit of the Lord snatched Philip away . . . Philip found himself at Azotus.'"

Marcus, Dana, and Brandon glanced at each other.

"You're saying this"—Brandon stabbed at the chapter in Acts with his forefinger—"is actually possible today? That you've got some sort of spiritual *Star Trek* beam-me-up-Scotty machine tucked away in the woods?"

Reece stared back at Brandon as the corner of the big man's mouth raised almost imperceptibly.

"You are." Brandon laughed and slumped back in his chair. "You are for sure crazy. If last night left any doubt, it has now been erased. Zippo. Gone. Ladies and gentlemen, Reece has left the universe."

Dana frowned, shut her eyes, and opened them a moment later. "You really expect us to believe you zapped yourself into Colorado Springs or Denver or wherever and back?"

Reece looked toward the chalk cliffs that rose to two thousand feet on the other side of the river. "I wasn't expecting to talk to you about this till later. Marcus figured it out quicker than I expected him to."

"That wasn't a no," Dana said.

"True."

"You're saying the Spirit of God picked you up, transported you instantly to another part of the state, and while there you picked up a paper and a vanilla latte for Brandon, then traveled back here just like Philip was teleported after talking to the Ethiopian." Dana whirled her finger around her head to indicate how crazy Reece was.

"Philip didn't take a *USA TODAY* or coffee with him." Reece rubbed his neck. "How's the coffee, by the way, Brandon?"

"It's excellent. I guess it didn't lose its flavor in the beaming process."

"Good to hear that. Sometimes it gets lost in transportation."

Dana stared at Reece. He was clearly enjoying the interplay between the four of them. "Next thing out of your mouth is going to be that we can do that too."

"It might be."

"You are crazy. Brandon is right. There has to be a logical explanation." Dana turned to Marcus. "What do you think of all this?"

"I'm keeping my mind open."

"You're a physics professor. You should be the least swayed by this fantasy."

"No, that's probably why I'm more receptive."

"Do you care to explain that?" Brandon said.

"At some point. I'm still contemplating a number of hypotheses."

"Didn't you all tell me in one of our early conversations that you'd read the New Testament?" Reece placed his hands behind his head.

"I have read the New Testament." Dana drew out her words.

"And the Old?"

"I've read that too." Dana frowned at Reece.

"Excellent."

Brandon crossed his legs and leaned back. "What's your point?"

"If you've read them, when are you going to start believing what they say? I thought you said at the start of this conversation you believed the Bible was God's book and the things in it were true."

Dana started to speak, then stopped. Brandon stepped in. "Maybe something like that did happen once, but I haven't heard a heck of a lot of it happening lately."

"So the Bible is a book of exceptions?" Reece leaned forward, elbows on his knees. "Just because you haven't heard of it happening in modern times, it hasn't happened? That verse about God being the same yesterday, today, and forever is simply poetic license?"

Brandon stood and held his arms at shoulder height and wiggled his hands. "Watch!" He froze in position for a few seconds, then let his arms fall to his sides. "Whew! I made it. I'm back."

Dana and Marcus laughed. Brandon shook his head. "Sorry. I'm not buying it."

Marcus stared at his Bible, then looked at Reece. "Isn't it possible the scholars who translated the verse out of the Greek were incorrect? That 'snatched Philip away' and 'found himself' meant something different than instantaneous transportation?"

"Yes, I think we have to consider that." Reece thumbed through his Bible. "But what about the other times? Were those mistranslations too?"

"Other times?" Marcus asked.

"Where from?" Brandon said. "The book of Reece?"

Reece stopped turning pages. "Let's see what Jesus' buddy John has to say about it." He scanned the pages with his finger. "Here we are. John, chapter 6, starting at verse 16."

He stood and lumbered back and forth across the edge of the patio as he read. "'When evening came, his disciples went down to the lake, where they got into a boat and set off across the lake for Capernaum. By now it was dark, and Jesus had not yet joined them. A strong wind was blowing and the waters grew rough. When they had rowed about three or four miles, they saw Jesus approaching the boat, walking on the water; and they were frightened. But he said to them, "It is I; don't be afraid." Then they were willing to take him into the boat, and immediately the boat reached the shore where they were heading.'

"Anyone want to explain that one to me? Is that another mistranslation? That the boat 'immediately reached the shore where they were heading'? The Sea of Galilee is about eight miles across. The boys had been rowing against a strong headwind and were about halfway across. So even if you want to say the meaning of the story is they 'got there quickly,' I'm not thinking they covered four more miles 'immediately.'"

Reece dropped his Bible on the concrete ring of the fire pit in front of them. "My friends, you're not in Sunday school anymore, and we're not dealing with a nice, neat little flannel graph Jesus that fits easily into the shoe box when the class is over.

"You're going to have to accept the fact that this Jesus and the Spirit all three of you have followed most of your lives isn't one that will stay locked up in a westernized translation of Christianity.

"Remember Snoqualmie Falls, Brandon? Marcus? And the power we saw there?" Reece turned and looked at the river. "If you believe there is a spiritual realm, I suggest you further your exploration of it. If you believe there is a spiritual realm, then it's time to master its secrets. I think God meant it when he said, 'And I will give you treasures hidden in the darkness—secret riches.' But most people don't like exploring without all the lights on. And if you say you believe the Word of God, it's time to start acting like it."

Reece picked up his Bible and ambled across the patio. "I'm going to give you some time to think about this and talk about it with each other. Just one suggestion: pray about it. Because I guarantee you, the enemy of your souls does not want you discovering a Christianity of the truly miraculous that leaps off the pages and becomes active in the real world."

He turned to leave. "Oh, and if you think the idea of teleportation is intriguing, I think you'll enjoy tomorrow's discussion as well. Maybe even more so." The heels of his boots made muted clicks on the walkway as he strode off.

SEVENTEEN

BRANDON STOOD AND TRIED TO WRAP HIS BRAIN AROUND Reece's explanation of where he'd been. It wouldn't wrap. Dana's headache getting healed? Sure. Even a prophecy about the three of them was possible. But teleportation? Right.

"Our host is certainly not boring." Brandon set his Bible on the stones next to his feet.

"I think we should hike down to the river to talk about this," Dana said.

"Good call. I don't want him overhearing our escape plan." Brandon motioned with his hands like he was driving a car and Marcus smiled.

They walked off the patio and up the bank till they found a crude path that led down to the river. Brandon offered his hand to Dana and she refused it. No surprise there. There was probably a greater chance Reece had actually beamed across Colorado and back than the ice between them would ever thaw. Yes, Brandon had blown it. Broken her heart. Betrayed her. Whatever you wanted to call it. He was wrong. But how long would he have to pay for that? Forever and three days most likely. Whatever. It was her issue, not his.

And then God arranged for her to be part of some prophecy one of Reece's mystic pals spoke over him, which Brandon wasn't sure he believed in, and *boom*—they're in this Well Spring wackiness together.

Thank you, Lord, very exciting to be here with her.

But it *was* his issue. And he had a feeling God wouldn't let it go. When they reached the river, Brandon said, "Upstream or downstream?"

"Up," Marcus said. "It was the direction Reece walked this morning, yes?"

"Yep."

"Do you believe Reece?" Marcus asked.

"That he really beamed back and forth like a ray of light?" Brandon tossed a stick into the water and watched it swirl downstream. "No. You?"

"We must take into consideration the physical evidence."

"The paper," Dana said.

"Yes." The professor nodded.

"C'mon, are you serious? That paper isn't evidence," Brandon said.

"Why not?" Dana picked up a stick of her own and tossed it in the river.

"You know how long it would take to mock up a fake *USA TODAY*? For someone with even a sliver of graphics experience? A few hours."

Dana grabbed another stick. "And the coffee?"

"Have any of us been in all of the seven smaller cabins? Have we been in even one of them? No, we haven't. There's probably an espresso machine in each of them."

Dana shrugged. "Okay, let's say he did mock up a fake paper and made your coffee in one of the cabins. Then the question becomes why?"

"How should I know? Probably the whole thing is a lesson to get us thinking outside our cloistered Americanized Christianity— bigger world out there, believe God for big miracles, to consider that people in third-world nations who aren't all caught up in the westernized way of thinking are probably walking on water, doing healings every minute, and casting out demons, all that sort of thing."

"That's not him," Dana said. "He wouldn't play those kinds of games."

"Not him?" Brandon raised his palms. "Didn't we say he's been different here than we ever saw him back home?"

Dana twirled her branch like a baton, then ran her fingers over its surface as she trekked up the riverbank. It looked like a snake and she gave it a funny look before tossing it into the river. As she did, a shiver ran down Brandon's spine. Darkness seemed to swirl around the stick. Great. Apparently being around Reece had him seeing demons under every rock.

Dana stopped to watch the stick float away. "I think he believes every word he's telling us. Maybe he's crazy, but he's not a liar."

"I'm not convinced. I think he's been setting this game up since we all agreed to come, and this is his move up from pawns to rooks," Brandon said.

"My conclusion is the same as Dana's," Marcus said. "Reece's personality teeters on the brink of eighty grit at times, but I do not believe he's a fraud."

"Eighty grit?" Brandon asked.

"His personality is sometimes like eighty-grit sandpaper."

Brandon grinned. "Maybe that's what we should call him. Everyone likes a good nickname."

"Can we stay on topic?" Dana said.

Marcus poked a rock at his feet. "If he's not playing games and not lying, we are left with a single alternative."

"Come again, Professor?" Dana said.

Marcus bent down and picked up a small stone. "Over the years, Reece and I have discussed the fact that Einstein's theory of relativity can be used to prove the possibility of time travel. For instance, wormholes are solutions of general relativity that allow for it. So what is the hindrance to Reece's teleportation idea being possible as well? It would be a type of time travel."

"Go on," Dana said.

Marcus moved the stone in his hand from one side of his body to the other. "Since God isn't limited by space and time, why couldn't he create a wormhole to instantly transport an individual from one location to another?"

"That's interesting and maybe we should look for a logical explanation." Dana shrugged. "But ultimately I don't think this is about science. It's about faith. Let's throw out the newspaper, say it's a fake. Let's say the coffee came from one of the cabins. There's still the story in Acts about Philip making his trip. Did that happen? Or was that made up? Did Jesus instantly transport that boat four miles across the Sea of Galilee, or was that made up too?"

Brandon rubbed his face, picked up another stick, and broke it into three pieces. "I suppose I'd say those things truly happened."

"So can they still happen today?"

"I don't know."

Dana glanced back and forth between Marcus and him. "I think at a certain point we have to decide if we're in on this journey God has us on—crazy as it might seem—or we're out."

Marcus tossed his stone toward the river. "I'm in."

"Me too." Dana turned to Brandon. "And you?"

Brandon stared at Dana and the professor. Was he in? Probably. But probably wouldn't cut it. With Reece or with God. Deep down he knew his resistance wasn't as much about belief as it was about fear of facing the reason he broke up with Dana. But that song would probably be sung no matter what. And part of him wanted it to be sung. "I'm in."

As they climbed back up the bank, Marcus asked, "Have you two been considering the prophecy?"

"Which part?" Dana asked.

"All of it, but in particular the part about going into the soul and marrow."

"You have an idea what that means, don't you?" Dana said.

The professor pushed his glasses up on his nose. "I do, and I believe it will cause Reece's teleportation idea to look like a minor stretch of the imagination in comparison."

EIGHTEEN

Monday evening after dinner, Reece sat with the three around the fire pit at the listening post trying to figure out how to best introduce the idea that would either make or break their time together at Well Spring. He'd prayed for their eyes to be open, for their ears to hear, but this would take spiritual contact lenses and hearing aids of great sensitivity. As it turned out, he didn't need to come up with an intro. Marcus offered him one.

"I would like to further our discussion of the prophecy. Specifically the part about us going into the soul and marrow. You indicated we would chat about it."

Reece shifted in his seat and stared into the fire. *Here we go, Jesus. Grant me the right words.*

"We're going to enter into people's souls and war for their hearts and set them free."

"What?" Brandon cupped his hand around his ear. "Once more, please, for the hardly hearing?"

"I'm going to teach you how powerful intercessory prayer can be. I'm going to teach you not only how to war for a friend's soul with the power of prayer but how to go inside."

"Inside another person's soul," Dana said.

"Yes." Reece poked the fire and sent a plume of red sparks into the darkening sky.

Dana stared at him as if he'd told them Santa Claus really did live at the North Pole with Rudolph and the Easter Bunny. Marcus looked amused but intrigued.

"Come again?" Dana said.

"Hello? Anybody home?" Brandon rapped his head with his knuckles. "We're going to what?"

"Unless your ears gave out in the past thirty seconds, I think all of you heard me."

"Check, please." Brandon held up his hand and snapped his fingers. "Tell me what you want us to donate to your cause, and then we can all get in your car and get back to reality."

Marcus folded his hands. "Assuming you are serious, and I think you are, what are the particulars surrounding the entrance into another's soul?"

"Good question," Brandon said. "I missed that sermon in church."

"You're going to find out."

"Before I leap, or rather teleport myself to any conclusions, I want to make sure I'm hearing you clearly." Dana steepled her fingers in front of her face. "Are you saying we're going to sit with people and pray for their souls and hearts, or that we're going to physically enter their souls?"

"Not physically enter. Spiritually."

Dana fell back in her chair and blew out a long breath. "That's pretty clear."

Reece tapped his finger in the center of his outstretched palm. "Demons enter people's souls, don't they?"

None of them answered.

"It's clear from the Gospels this happened with a high frequency. Go to any third-world country and they'll tell you all about it happening today. Even most of the churches in America will admit it happens, even if begrudgingly. So if demons can do it as spiritual beings, why can't we?"

"Because we're human beings," Dana said.

"No. As Pierre Teilhard de Chardin succinctly said, 'We are not human beings having a spiritual experience; we are spiritual beings having a human experience.'"

"Next thing out of your mouth will be that astral projection is real," Brandon said.

"Every spiritual idea we see floating around the world is a counterfeit of something God has already created. Satan can create nothing. He can only take and spin what God has created or keep us from seeing what God has given us."

"I'm willing to listen, Reece, but this is beyond the pale and straight into the nether regions of the multiverse." Marcus tapped his pen against his journal. "How exactly is this supposed to work?"

"Exactly? I don't know. I don't know how prayer works either. But I do know that our spirits can separate from our bodies."

"How?"

"Because I've done it."

Marcus scribbled something in his journal. "I would imagine those of a more conservative nature would want scriptural evidence to verify your claim."

Reece grabbed his Bible off the patio next to his chair, flipped to the back, and pointed to the middle of the page. "Paul went to heaven and said he didn't know if he was still in his body or not, which implies the ability to go places with his spirit his body didn't."

Pages whirred and Reece jabbed his finger again. "In Revelation John says he was 'in the Spirit' when he heard a voice like a trumpet behind him. Read the rest of the chapter. It doesn't sound like he was there in body."

He shut his Bible, his voice rising with passion. "Think to the time when you've been in deep, deep prayer for another. Time seems to vanish, you can feel your spirit in harmony with God's Spirit, and all outside distractions melt away. You have a sense of how to pray. It's like you're touching that person's heart, your spirit is touching theirs. Do you know what I'm saying? Have you had those times of intercession?"

Reece didn't wait for an answer. "We all have. That's what going into a soul is like. It's taking that experience, but going further. Much further."

Dana crossed her legs. "Have you done this type of teaching before? Have you really gone into souls yourself? Or are we an experiment?"

Reece poked at the coals in the heart of the fire. Yes, in a sense they were an experiment. After all these years they were a massive experiment of faith, of believing that what the Spirit had spoken to him through the prophecy, through Doug, was true. That it was time once again to go into the souls of others and fight to set them free.

"Did you hear me? Do you have experience doing it? Taught others how?"

Reece nodded. "A long, long time ago."

"So are any of your trainees still around?"

"Yes. Three are."

"How many did you start with?"

"Five."

"What happened to the other two?"

What should he tell them? He had two alternatives. Stay silent. Tell the truth. And the first choice wasn't an option. But revealing the fear pounding at the outer shell of his heart was not required.

"They died."

"They *what*?" Brandon lurched forward.

"Are you kidding?" Dana said. "Because of something you did? Or didn't do?"

Reece stood and the breath he'd been holding whooshed out like a slashed tire.

"You have to tell us what happened," Dana said.

"I made a mistake. One I will never make again. One I won't let you make." Reece strode toward the cabin. "Sleep well. There's much to be done tomorrow."

✦✦✦

Brandon turned to Marcus and Dana. They both had to be questioning Reece's sanity after the speech he'd just given them. "Am I the only one who has Mexican jumping beans dancing in his brain? Who is asking how long till this guy takes a swan dive off the deep end and tries to melt our minds?"

Dana shrugged. "I think he's just a bit dramatic."

"A bit?" Brandon opened his eyes wide. "He's talking about traveling into other people's souls and that's a little splash of drama? People died and that's dramatic?"

"To Reece 'die' could mean a walking away from the faith. I doubt he means physical death," Dana said.

Brandon kicked the pile of kindling that sat next to the fire pit. "The 'people died' thing is hyperbole? Hmm."

"You've been pretty quiet, Professor," Dana said. "Any thoughts on the subject?"

"Not with regard to people expiring." Marcus leaned in. "But I have been considering the quantum mechanics that would make the entrance into a soul possible."

"I'm still trying to get my head around the teleportation thing." Brandon sat back and folded his arms.

"Fine. That first. Let's see, how can I explain this?" Marcus glanced around the fire pit till his gaze rested on Brandon's journal. "Might I appropriate that for a moment?"

Brandon handed Marcus the journal and he opened the pages. "If this were a story, the characters in it would start here"—he flipped to the front of Brandon's journal, held it open, and pointed at the first page—"and end here." He flipped through the journal till he came to the last page.

"They would move in a linear fashion from start to finish. They would not possess the ability to exist outside the pages, correct?

"But God is the author of the story. He exists outside the book. We are finite looking out. God is the infinite looking in. He can progress to the front, the middle, the end whenever he desires. There are no restrictions upon him. He can enter the characters' lives wherever and whenever he wants to. As the author, when he's composing the story, he can remove a character from one spot and insert him hundreds of pages later. To the characters it would seem miraculous, but to the author? Simple."

"I want to know why Reece isn't crazy saying we can go into another person's soul," Dana said.

Marcus rubbed his chin and Brandon knew exactly what he looked like when he lectured at U-Dub. "Would you subscribe to the belief that God is so far beyond our comprehension, we can't even start to ascertain it?"

"Of course."

Light seemed to fill the professor's eyes and he rushed his words. "Think of, of . . . Calvin and Hobbes or Charlie Brown and Snoopy. They live in a two-dimensional world. They're not free to explore the third dimension.

"If we entered into their world, what would it look like to them? Say we could extend our hand down into their universe. They would see a being appear out of nowhere, then vanish just as quickly when we pulled our hand out."

Marcus placed his hand on the pages of the journal. "Since they can't comprehend the dimension we live in, our appearance would seem to be magic. Just as to us, exploring the fourth dimension and beyond would seem like magic.

"Now, what dimension do angels and demons live in? Certainly not on the physical plane. But we believe they exist. And they enter into our world from time to time.

"However, we are trapped in three dimensions just as Calvin and Hobbes are trapped in two dimensions. God created the dimensions, whether there are four or eleven or hundreds. And this is where he exists—outside all the dimensions. Ultimate freedom."

Marcus squeezed his thumb and forefinger together and held them up. "The shortest possible distance between two objects is 1.6×10^{-35} meters. It's called Planck length. Any shorter and it is not possible for quantum mechanics to distinguish between here and there. The shortest possible time we can record is 10^{-43} seconds." Marcus snapped his fingers.

"It's called Planck time. Any shorter and we can't tell if the events happen simultaneously.

"Since God exists everywhere, he exists in those moments we can't measure. He is outside of time, he's outside of distance. He can transverse from one point in the universe to the other with no time having passed because he's already there."

Marcus looked toward the cliffs across the river and opened his arms. "If we can believe that, if we can grab hold of the faith to step into that . . ." The professor trailed off and held out his hands to them. "I believe there is a dimension . . . multiple dimensions of wonder and freedom that are far beyond our ability to fully fathom.

"And since our souls exist on a different metaphysical plane, I say God is powerful enough to transport us into this other dimension."

Dana looked into the fire. "'No eye has seen, no ear has heard, and no mind has imagined . . .'"

"Yes, Dana, yes! Through prayer, through faith and the power of the Spirit, we can go parsecs beyond our myopic vision. We are dealing with the infinite God, friends."

Brandon stirred the fire. "Okay, you're persuasive, Professor, but I still think Reece is trying to play in the two-hundredth dimension, and something about 'people died' doesn't make my stomach feel all warm and fuzzy."

"If we thrust aside our emotional reactions to Reece's statements, we can easily conclude he is not insane. We also know he loves God with tremendous passion. Consequently, for the moment, I think our choice must be to trust him. More crucial is we trust God. Stay with this."

"But keep our eyes open," Dana said.

Brandon stood and nodded. "Wide open."

✦✦✦

When they reached the cabin five minutes later, Brandon stopped just inside the sliding glass door and watched Reece shove a stack of papers into his black leather satchel.

"You're not residing in the main cabin with us tonight?" Marcus said.

"No. That will give the three of you a chance to talk about me without the chance of my overhearing your conversation." Reece stared at them. "Don't look surprised. Of course you're going to debrief on the lunatic who brought you up here and the insane ideas he's trying to push on you."

The three let out stifled laughs.

"We just had that conversation," Dana said. "We don't think you're insane anymore. Possibly delusional, but Marcus has persuaded us to keep our minds open."

"Good to hear." Reece tipped his hat and strode to the front door.

"Where are you going to sack out?" Brandon said. "Since you don't have to work in the morning, are you going to crawl off to sleep in the bath?"

"John Lennon, 1965. Side one, second song on *Rubber Soul*."

"I'm impressed!" Brandon laughed. "That would go over most people's heads."

"Went over mine," Dana said.

"You have to remember, Brandon, I'm slightly older than you three. I was alive when 'Norwegian Wood' came out." Reece stepped through the front door. "If you do need me for any reason, I'll be sleeping in one of the seven cabins. In the one called Piñon Bothy, named courtesy of Doug Lundeen."

"What is the origin of the name?" Marcus asked.

A hint of a smile surfaced on Reece's face, then vanished an instant later. "Piñon is the name of the small pine trees dotting this area. They give shelter, food in the form of pine nuts, and they grow strong in difficult environments. They also make great firewood. The tantalizing aroma you've smelled during our fire comes from the piñon.

"Bothys are small cottages in Scotland you would find along the shores of the ocean and in the mountains. If a traveler found one and needed shelter, they were welcome. They were left unlocked and full of provisions."

Reece opened the door and turned to go. "Don't stay up too late. And if you don't sleep well tonight, don't worry—tomorrow night you most assuredly will."

NINETEEN

DANA WENT OUTSIDE TO THE FIREPLACE ON THE NORTH side of the cabin to start a fire and mull over the things Reece had said. Six minutes later the fire crackled like popcorn, and she slipped off her shoes and held up her blue stockinged feet to let the flames make them toasty warm.

"Do you mind if I join you?" Marcus stood in the doorway.

"Not a bit." She motioned to the chairs on her right. "I'd enjoy it."

Marcus settled into a tan wicker chair.

Dana adjusted her sweatshirt. "What's the toughest thing about being here for you?"

"Being absent from my wife and daughters. Fighting the feeling I should be with them right now instead of here." A shadow flitted over the professor's ruddy complexion.

He wasn't attractive in the classic sense. His ears were a bit too big for his face, his head a bit too small for his body, but his countenance was full of trust. And that was attractive. He would have been a wonderful older brother.

"Their names?"

"Kat is my wife, Abbie is my older daughter, and Jayla is the younger." Marcus pulled a photo out of his back pocket and stared at the picture for at least ten seconds before handing it to her. Kat had auburn hair and a radiant smile, as did the girls. She guessed his daughters' ages at ten and twelve.

"They're beautiful." She handed the photo back to him. "You're the only testosterone in the house, huh?"

"That wasn't always the situation." Marcus sighed, grabbed a piece of wood, tossed it into the fire, and stared at the flames. "But it is now."

Whoops. Everyone had their hidden sorrows. "I'm sorry, I didn't mean to pry—"

"Don't be. What indication have I given you that you might know?" He glanced at her with sad eyes. "There is no harm in asking. But I'll reserve the right to tell you about it till another day. What about for you? What's the toughest part?"

Dana sighed. "Having Brandon here, as you might imagine. Regardless of whether it's part of some divine plan, it's still a sizable sliver in my heart. No one will ever be able to tell me God doesn't have a sense of humor."

"Because of your past together?" Marcus shifted the logs and sat back in his chair, gazing at the river.

"Uh, yeah."

"Do you care to share your story?"

Dana shook her head. It was the last thing she wanted to do. But in seconds the feeling changed. Maybe it was being at Well Spring. Maybe it was because seeing Brandon had stirred everything up again, and she needed to talk to someone about it. Maybe it was because there was something about the professor that made him trustworthy. Should she? The silence stretched to a minute.

"I worked at Spirit 105.3—"

"Really? My wife listens to that station with great frequency. You were employed there?"

"For seven years. Then three years ago I took a job to manage the sales department of another station in Seattle."

"Was that a beneficial move?"

"I'm not sure. I know it was the right move. But I miss the people at Spirit. I still have a lot of friends there."

"What caused your departure?"

"Personal reasons." Dana pointed toward the cabin.

"I see." Marcus leaned forward and tossed another log on the fire. "He was involved with the station?"

She pulled her legs onto the chair and sat crisscrossed as the memory swelled up in her mind. Her assistant, Rebecca, had rushed into her office that day five years ago waving her hands like she was on a parade float with her arms programmed at quadruple speed.

"He just pulled into the parking lot! Our parking lot!"

"Who?" Dana asked.

"Brandon Scott. He's doing a private set for the air staff and programming and anyone else in the station who wants to come."

"That's right, I was going to try to make that. I like his music."

"Try?" Rebecca grabbed Dana's hands and pulled her into the hallway. "No, no, no, you must do."

Dana slid into a chair in the back just after Brandon started his set. He was cute. And she liked his laugh as he bantered with the group. After his third song, he set his hands on top of his guitar and glanced at the twenty or thirty of them and smiled. "You guys rock. Truly. This is so fun for me. Thanks for the invite." His gaze settled on Dana and stayed there longer than on the others. Quite a bit longer.

He launched into a song about running the wilds together, and something inside her stirred. If she were still in her teens, she would have called it a crush. Now she wasn't sure how to define it. As Brandon sang he continued to glance at her and the feeling inside her grew.

As he played the rest of his songs, she fell in love with his music. When she shook his hand before he left the station, she had the distinct impression she would be falling in love with him.

She sighed, folded her hands, and stared at Marcus. "The next day at work I got a rose from Brandon with an invitation to have lunch. That turned into dinner, which turned into beach walks and movies and eventually a diamond on my finger. Then one day six months later, three months before the wedding day, he showed up at my home and shredded my heart, and here we are."

"That's why you left Spirit 105.3?"

"I couldn't handle hearing his music all the time and walking past that signed poster of him in the hallway every day."

"What were his reasons for ending the engagement?"

"You'd have to ask him."

Marcus frowned and stared at her. "An explanation for his actions wasn't given?"

"Nothing more than he was sorry, please forgive him, and this was 'what he had to do.'" Dana tossed the book she'd had in her lap onto the chair to her right. "I asked him six more times why, and six times he answered, 'I just know I have to.'"

"I'm sorry."

"Me too."

They sat in silence watching the fire die down.

"It's interesting to observe the way he looks at you," Marcus said.

"How?"

"Like a man who has lost his greatest treasure."

Dana shook her head. "You need to get those glasses of yours replaced with ones that help you see more clearly."

"I realize that sentiment might be a challenge to hear, but it's true." Marcus stood and gave her shoulder a quick squeeze. "I'm going inside to attempt to get more of the slumber I didn't get last night. Thanks for revealing part of your story to me."

Dana stayed at the fire for another twenty minutes, trying to ignore Marcus's comment about the way Brandon looked at her. She found more failure than success. But even if Brandon did still have feelings for her, it didn't matter. She would never let him back into her heart. She would never let anyone back in ever again. Being abandoned was her calling in life, and she'd learned to live with it.

Dana stood and stirred the fire, then tried to squash the feeling of despair sloshing around her mind and heart as she walked toward her bedroom. She should be thrilled. She was seeing parts of God she'd never imagined. She was in a stunning setting. But her heart ached.

You are so alone.

She let the thought spread through her soul. Because it was true. *You will always be alone.*

She flopped down on the bed and stared at the knots in the pine wood on the wall to her right. Part of her wanted to stay. Step further in. See if God would or could bring healing. Another part dreaded the idea because it would mean opening up. And she couldn't do that.

You don't belong here. He tricked you. He can't be trusted. You know that now.

Reece. Some friend. No, he hadn't lied to her. But he'd deceived her. He could have told her Brandon would be here. And she had to make budget. Had to!

They'll fire you.

No. It wouldn't happen. She would develop a promotion that would loosen the purse strings. Write a package advertisers would snatch up by the hundreds of thousands of dollars. But it needed to be in motion today. Not next Monday. Now.

She pulled out her cell phone and checked her e-mail out of habit. A message flashed: No SERVICE, COULD NOT CONNECT TO THE INTERNET. Tomorrow she would borrow Reece's car. Drive out, write the promotion, and get it to the station. She'd be there and back in two or three hours easy. Then she could breathe. Then she could open herself up to what God had for her at Well Spring.

Dana sat up and squinted at the window. A small square envelope was taped to the top right corner. She slipped off the bed, pulled the note off the window, and opened it in the wicker chair in the corner of the room.

Dana,

I've never been talented with words, so I won't try to make this note one of eloquence. And I've never had an overabundance of tact or subtlety, so forgive my bluntness.

You're screaming to get out of here. Every emotion you have is telling you to flee. But you must not leave. Stay in the wound. It's the only way to find healing.

The enemy is likely throwing thoughts your way that are not your own. Fight it.

And Brandon is not your enemy.

Give it time, please?

Put everything from home out of your mind—including your radio station. Do not let the temporal distract you as you're delving into the eternal.

The issue causing your stress at the moment isn't that the station needs you—it's that you need the station. It has become your idol, the thing you turn to for assurance, for worth, for your joys and even your sorrows. And it keeps you from feeling totally alone.

Now you are in an environment where you are stripped of the caffeine-like shots of e-mail. There's no promotions director or client or salesperson needing your immediate attention. Here you are not needed at all. But you are wanted. You are valued. You are desired by God himself.

And you are not alone.

Breakthrough is coming. I promise.

Reece

For a man who supposedly didn't have a way with words, Reece did quite well. She let the note fall to her lap. She wasn't sure whether to hate the man for reading her mind once again, or like him for telling the truth.

TWENTY

Reece woke at six on Tuesday morning and grimaced. Too late. His alarm hadn't gone off. He wanted to be up by five. This day needed to be slathered in prayer, and now he'd have less than half the time he wanted before waking the others. He wanted to be on the trail by eight o'clock because he wasn't positive what kind of shape the three of them were in. Yes, he wanted them gasping for air most of the way up, but he didn't want to kill them.

By seven fifteen he had a breakfast of biscuits, scrambled eggs, and sausage sitting on the kitchen counter for whoever wanted it. Marcus sat in the big chair next to the fireplace. Dana was in the kitchen putting together a bowl of fruit, some yogurt, and making toast. Now they just needed Brandon.

A minute later the musician bounded down the stairs two at a time from the upstairs bedrooms. "Good morning, all. Great to be alive today, wouldn't you agree, Dana?"

She glanced at Brandon with a disgusted look and turned back to her food. Reece gave a slight nod. Good. Better to have them sparring than to have complete silence. There was hope for détente yet.

"Gentlemen, grab some eggs, biscuits, and sausage if you like, or create your own breakfast like Dana is doing. Just be done in fifteen minutes or less."

Brandon grabbed a plate and piled it with eggs and two biscuits. Close behind Brandon was Marcus. No eggs. Just one sausage, a biscuit, and a banana.

"Eat well," Reece said. "This day could be a bit strenuous."

"Spiritually or physically?" Marcus asked.

"Both. We're going on a little hike."

Dana carried her breakfast to the table and sat with her back to them. "Define little."

"Less than ten miles round trip."

"That's not little." Dana took a spoonful of yogurt.

"If you're in shape it is."

"I already worked out this morning," Brandon said.

Reece ignored the comment and picked up a jar of salsa. "Do you want some of this for your eggs, Brandon?"

He shook his head. Reece grabbed a drinking glass and poured the entire contents of the jar into it, then stood and walked to the window and toasted the trail they'd be on in fifteen minutes. "To a day that resounds with life to the full, much joy, and much freedom."

He lifted the glass of salsa to his lips and drained half of it in one gulp.

"What do you think you're doing?"

Reece spun to see Brandon standing right behind him, shaking his head and squinting.

"Having breakfast."

"That's salsa."

"It's breakfast. It's low calorie, high in nutrients, and with the heat that's in this, it cleans out the system at the same time." Reece flicked the glass with his fingernail and the noise rang out through the cabin.

"You and Stallone." Brandon laughed. "You're the Rocky Balboa for the spiritual set."

Reece glanced at his watch, drained the rest of the salsa, and turned back to them. "All right." He raised his voice. "We'll meet at the rise just beyond the archery range in ten minutes. At eight o'clock we leave. Don't be late."

"Yes, sir, Drill Sergeant, sir!" Brandon gave an exaggerated salute and stood with his chest out, stomach in, chin up.

Reece stared at him and felt a smile rise inside. It almost made it to his face. He loved this kid. He looked at each of the three and prayed. They needed God to come through when they reached the lake.

Be there, Jesus.

✦✦✦

Dana breathed deep as she stood with the others in a tight circle and guessed it was the aroma of piñon trees that filled her senses. Reece had predicted a breakthrough for her today. A hope rose inside that he was right.

Reece scuffed his hiking boots in the dirt and cleared his throat. "A couple of quick things before we start. First, it's uphill all the way to our destination. In a few places it will be steep. Very steep. Second, the pace I'm going to set will likely irritate you at first, and by the time we take our first break, I'm guessing you'll be ticked off at me. I don't care. This isn't summer camp. It's boot camp. Third, if you feel like you're going to keel over, let me know. Any questions?"

"What's our destination?" Brandon asked, hands on hips.

His dark blue sunglasses and red bandanna took Dana back to a hike they'd taken together soon after they started dating. The hike where he'd first kissed her. *So soft, so tender.* She pushed the memory from her mind. *Stop it.*

"Our destination?" Reece replied. "Up."

"What's the point of the hike?" Marcus added.

Brandon stretched his arms over his head. "I'm guessing we'll find out when we get there, right, Reece?"

He stared at Brandon. "That's right, guitar man."

A look passed over Brandon's face that said he liked the name.

"Are you ready?" Reece hiked up the strap on his daypack and glanced at each of them.

Marcus and she nodded.

Brandon said, "No."

"Good. Let's roll."

The pace Reece set wasn't a jog. At least for him. With legs seven feet long he probably thought he was taking a leisurely stroll through the Colorado backcountry, but for Dana it was close to a jog.

"Hey . . . are you trying . . . to kill me?" Dana panted out as she shifted her daypack higher on her shoulders. When it settled down, it squished her sweaty T-shirt into her back. Good thing she'd brought an extra shirt.

"Yes."

"I don't see the humor in that statement."

Reece didn't slow his pace. "It wasn't meant to be funny."

Two hours into the hike Reece stopped. "Lunch break."

There was little talk while they ate. It was enough to eat and recover from the hike so far.

The drought of conversation continued after they set out again on the trail. Dana supposed Brandon and Marcus felt the same as she did. Spent. Body maxing out. But a part of her—her spirit maybe—was exhilarated, which seemed to give her a reservoir of endurance.

The things Reece spoke of about a relationship with God were far beyond what she'd ever imagined. At the same time it felt like she was crossing a suspension bridge three hundred feet above a raging river with slats missing every few feet.

The trail now wound alongside the river, sometimes hiding the stream, other times giving them unobstructed views. But there wasn't time to savor the beauty at the pace Reece continued to set. After an hour of steady hiking, Reece called out from his position in front. "Everyone doing okay?" He stopped and looked at Brandon. "How are you holding up?"

"I'm having a fabulous time." Brandon leaned forward, hands on his knees, drops of sweat dripping off his thick blond hair, sucking in breaths like he was a Kirby vacuum cleaner.

"Thank you for the sarcasm, Mr. Scott. It tells me you haven't hit your exhaustion point yet." Reece glanced back at her. "What's your condition, Dana?"

"Fine." She wiped the sweat off of her forehead.

"Are you lying?"

"Maybe."

But she would survive. She would faint before she'd let Brandon outhike her.

"Talk to me, Marcus."

"You're a thoroughbred."

Marcus panted but looked the least winded of the three of them. Who knew the prof would turn out to be a mountain man?

"Let's take a break," Reece said.

"I thought my condition would handle this hike with more aplomb." Marcus set his daypack at his feet. "But it isn't. At least not compared to you."

"Every summer I climb a fourteener—one of Colorado's fourteen-thousand-foot peaks. Now that's a workout."

"How many have you done?"

"Twenty-seven. Only twenty-six to go."

"You want to do them all before you die?" Dana took a long drink of water.

"Who says I'm going to die?" Reece lifted the bottom of his T-shirt to wipe off his forehead. The guy had the abs of a thirty-year-old.

"Are you not?" Marcus said.

"I don't know. John the apostle didn't die. Enoch didn't die. Why should I have to?"

A cloud seemed to pass over Reece, but as she glanced at Brandon and Marcus, it seemed they didn't notice it.

"What do you mean John didn't die?" Marcus asked.

"Some people think he's still walking around the earth based on Jesus saying, 'If I want him to remain alive until I return, what is that to you?'"

"Do you think he's still alive?"

"No, that would be crazy."

The promise of a smile once again flitted across Reece's eyes but vanished an instant later. The man had to have a history of pain and had probably built a steel wall around his heart three feet thick and fifty feet high. Kind of like she had done for her own.

Brandon poured half a bottle of water on his head, then slicked back his hair. She hated when he did that. Made him look far too appealing.

"I suppose you're going to float off into the clouds when your time comes," Brandon said.

"Maybe." Reece took a long drink of his Tropical Mango Gatorade. "I believe that Bible stuff." He winked at them.

Two minutes later they were off again. The air was thick with the scent of pine, and a breeze wicked away the midday heat that would have made the trek unbearable without it.

"We're almost there."

Apparently "almost there" meant another grueling quarter mile. Fifteen minutes later the trail flattened. Five minutes after that, flashes of a sea-green lake showed through the pine trees. After fifty more yards the trail took a ninety-degree turn and led them down a narrow path straight to a small lake.

The water was like glass except for the far end where the river poured into it from a waterfall thirty feet above. So pure. The bottom of the pond looked like it was two inches down and twenty feet deep at the same time. Dana panted for what felt like ten minutes before she could breathe normally. "The curtain might not be thinner up here "—she sucked in a deep breath—"but the air certainly is."

✦✦✦

Reece studied them. The ones of the prophecy. The ones who would change the world. Would they? Did it matter that Tamera wasn't with them? He'd asked the Spirit about that again, but again there had been no answer.

No one spoke for three or four more minutes. Reece was grateful for the reprieve to soak in the peace of the place. He hadn't been up here in years. The trees were certainly taller. And the lake seemed even more crystal clear than the last time he'd made the trek. Fifteen years. He blew out a long breath. Had it been that long? Yes. It had been on the tenth anniversary of their deaths.

You killed them.

No.

"Jesus." He pushed the memory and the voice of the enemy from his mind.

He would live in this moment, not the ones from his past, no matter how vivid they might be. *Live in the past and you allow the past to control the future.* He closed his eyes and soaked in the overwhelming love of the Spirit. Of Abba. Of Jesus. There was forgiveness for what he'd done. Someday it would reach his heart. And now with these three, a chance for redemption.

He opened his eyes and glanced at them. Marcus was almost laughing—eyes closed, arms raised, and what seemed like a conversation with God pouring out of his mouth. The professor's spiritual sensitivity was increasing almost by the hour. It surprised Reece. He expected the man of science to be the last to open himself up and tune in to the spiritual world Reece was showing them. It was Brandon, the artist, whom he'd expected to tap into the spiritual the fastest, but he seemed to be resisting the most. Reece watched Dana spin in a slow circle, taking in every view. The smile that filled her face took a year of stress and two years of age off her.

Brandon sat at the edge of the lake. He'd taken his shoes and socks off and lay back in the silky sand—arms spread wide, a soft smile on his face. The beauty of the place had captured all of them.

After ten minutes Reece called them together. "I'm tempted to simply let you soak in the peace and beauty of this spot . . ." He took a long look at the lake and the mountain that rose behind it. "But I want to give you enough time."

When each of them had settled into a circle, Reece said, "Okay, let's get started. Gather round and get comfortable."

He waited till the three sat, Marcus and Dana on a fallen log, Brandon leaning against a small flat boulder near the lake.

"The next hour or so will be one of the most critical parts of your training," Reece said, "so listen closely.

"In Revelation it says, 'He who has an ear, let him hear what the Spirit says to the churches. To him who overcomes, I will give some of the hidden manna. I will also give him a white stone with a new name written on it, known only to him who receives it.'"

Reece stood and glanced at them. "There is great power in a name. To heal. Or to destroy. And something so sacred about the name Jesus will give us when we get to heaven that no one else will know what it is."

He went to the lake and stood with his back to them, arms held out to his sides. "I believe the God who created this lake and waterfall and sky and trees wants to give you names right now."

"I think our parents took care of that for us at birth," Brandon said.

Reece spun around and pointed at Brandon. "Did you hear what was done recently in India? How young girls rejected the names they were given at birth and received new names?"

"No," Brandon said.

"Did you?" He looked at Marcus and Dana.

They shook their heads.

"I believe it will transform the lives of these young women."

"What happened?" Dana asked.

"Officials in Mumbai gathered hundreds of girls who had been given names that God would never have given them. Names like Nakusa, which means 'unwanted' in Hindi."

Reece squatted down, picked up a thin stick, and wrote *worthless* in the brown sand.

"In a public ceremony these girls were given the right to rename themselves. Some girls named themselves after Bollywood stars like Aishwarya, or Hindu goddesses like Savitri. Some just wanted a traditional name, such as Vaishali, which means 'prosperous, beautiful, and good.'

"A fifteen-year-old girl was in tears as she told how her grandfather gave her a name that means 'unwanted' when she was born and that she will now be called Ashmita, which means 'very tough' or 'rock hard' in Hindi."

Reece swiped his hand across the sand, erasing *worthless*, then wrote in the grains a second time: *Tough. Hard. Unbreakable.*

"They received certificates officially changing their names. You think that won't make a difference in their lives? I believe that one act of choosing a new name has the power to shatter the past."

Reece wiped the sand off his hands and strode to his daypack. He reached in and pulled out a stack of blank note cards, three pens, and three boxes of matches.

"Now we're going to do the same thing. Take two cards and a pen. Only you're not going to name yourself. Jesus is going to name you, just like he did with people in the Bible."

Reece pointed to his left, then his right. "I'm going to send you off to spend time alone. To sit in the silence and ask the Spirit for a new name."

"My comprehension is lacking, Reece." Marcus turned the card over and looked at the blank side. "What do you mean Jesus is going to give us a name?"

Reece looked at Brandon and Dana. Their blank stares said they had no idea either.

"Marcus, did you have any nicknames growing up?"

He nodded.

Reece lifted his hand and wiggled his fingers toward himself. "Care to share with the rest of the class?"

"Not really." He scraped the heel of his boot into the ground. "But I will."

"Thank you."

"In high school my nickname was Brainiac." Marcus's face flushed.

"Like from the Superman comics." Brandon struck a Superman pose, arm and fist thrust high. "The guy who had super intelligence."

"Yes."

"But your face says the name wasn't a compliment."

"No." Marcus looked away. "It wasn't."

"Explain," Reece said.

"It's not important."

"You're right. It's not important. It's critical."

Marcus tilted his head back and sighed. "I was the brain in school. Tests showed an IQ of 150 by the time I hit seventh grade. The other kids resented me because studying wasn't necessary, and the teachers did as well since I was smarter than they."

Marcus stared at the dirt. "However, I preferred Brainiac over Runt. Skipping a grade was bad enough, but when my classmates grew and I remained the same size . . . not achieving puberty till my late teens was not beneficial to my social life."

"How long did you carry that name around in your head?"

Marcus turned and stared at the lake and hesitated before he answered. "I still carry it."

Brandon took a gulp of water from his bottle and leaned forward on his rock. "How can you still carry it? What are you? Six one, six two?"

"Six one." Marcus turned back and tried to laugh, but the sound sputtered out of his mouth and fell to the ground. "The reasons still aren't clear in my own mind, but I decided to attend my ten-year high school reunion." He laughed and this time the sound rang true. "I walked in and people stared at my wife, trying to recall her from high school. They assumed she was their classmate as no one recognized me due to the six inches of growth and fifty pounds I put on since graduation."

"Sweet." Brandon gave a fist pump. "So you put a stunned look on their faces and buried the name."

"Wouldn't it be wonderful if it worked that way? Yes, they indicated how well I looked. But somehow having them say that didn't make the memories vanish and the scars heal."

"The files still play, don't they?" Reece said.

No one answered. No one needed to. Reece knew he'd just pressed Play on all of their mental digital players.

"Dana?"

She shook her head and waved her hand. "I'm standing on the fifth."

"Okay." Reece turned to Brandon. "Nicknames?"

"I'm standing on the fifth as well."

"Sorry, that defense has already been taken."

"Fine." Brandon glared at Reece. "I had more than a few."

"What was the first one that came to mind?"

"Why are you going for the throat, Reece?"

"Because the throat is where we swallow things. Good and bad. And I think you've been swallowing lies. Out with it. What's the name?"

"One I've tried to forget my whole life." Brandon tossed a rock into the water. "Thanks for dragging it out of the dungeon."

"You're welcome. Are you going to tell us?"

"No." Brandon threw another rock into the lake.

Reece stayed silent. Marcus and Dana took his cue and said nothing.

"X-Cree."

"X-Cree? What's that, like a comic book character? We seem to have a superhero theme going here," Marcus said.

"Not exactly." Brandon shifted to his left so his face was turned from the three of them. "As I kid I loved comic books. Devoured them. But for whatever reason my stepmom didn't like me reading them. She was always tossing them in the trash, and my dad never stood up to her. One day she forbade me from reading any more.

"So I snuck them into the house and read them with a flashlight in the back of my closet after she and my dad went to bed.

"One night the closet door flies open and smacks against the wall. I can't move. I'm sitting there with a flashlight in one hand and an issue of the Green Arrow in the other.

"She rips the comic out of my hand, shreds it into quarters, and throws the pieces up in the air. As they're floating down on my head, she says, 'You want to be a superhero? Fine. I'm going to call you X-Cree, short for *excrement*, because that's what you are and always will be.'

"My dad tried to get her to stop, and she finally did—three years later—but wonder of wonders, somehow that name still bounces around my mind from time to time." Brandon tossed a third stone into the lake. "All the time."

No one spoke. Brandon stood and moved away along the west side of the lake, then slowly came back.

Reece folded his hands. "As I already said, words are powerful. Names are powerful, as we've just seen. Sticks and stones can break my bones, but words will never hurt me?" He broke a branch over his leg. "It's a lie from the pit. That's why we're here. We're going to do something about it. Now.

"Throughout your life you've been given names by the people who surround you. You might have been given names of affection or names of deep pain as we saw with Marcus and Brandon.

"So the first thing I want you to do is bring those names to mind. It will be painful. But don't back down. Those names have been weights around your necks long enough. Write down every one of them. Then you're going to burn those names and break the power you've given them to control your life and your destiny.

"I want you write down every name that has been an arrow into your soul. Ugly, stupid, fat, manipulator, lazy, X-Cree, Braniac . . . whatever they are.

"When you're finished and every foul name from hell has been written down, I want you to pray over those names, bring the blood of Jesus over them, renounce them, destroy them, burn them. Then I want you to ask God for a new name. The names that are the true you. The real you. The ones God destined from before time for you. Abram became Abraham. Saul became Paul. Jesus nicknamed Peter The Rock. James and John were nicknamed The Sons of Thunder.

"This"—Reece raised his arms again and turned in a circle—
"is a place where you can hear from God. Where you can be alone.
Where you can pour your heart out to him without any fear of inter-
ruption or distraction. Are you ready?"

The three nodded.

"Good." Reece pointed to his right. "Brandon, I want you to go
in the opposite direction of the way you wandered a few minutes
ago. Yes, of course that is a symbolic move. Dana, I want you to
hike up to the top of the falls and find a place there. That leaves
you, Marcus, to go in the way Brandon went earlier. I want all of
you to hike away from here for at least ten minutes. I want you to be
completely alone. Any questions?"

They each stayed silent. Reece reached in his pack and grabbed
three Ziploc bags and tossed them onto the ground. "You might
want to take one of those as well."

Brandon bent down and picked up one of the bags. "Kleenex?"

Reece winked. "I've heard it can get awfully dusty out there.
Even for guys."

✦✦✦

Brandon hesitated, then reached down, grabbed one of the plastic
bags, and stuck it in his back pants pocket. Reece was right—at least
when it came to him. Tapping into his deep emotions was one of the
things that helped him write songs that changed people.

Or used to help him. Nowadays the well was bone dry at the
bottom. But he felt it. Lingering not far below the surface was his
heart. He wanted it back. And this would be the moment God would
speak a name to him, and his heart would return.

"One more thing." Reece held up his forefinger. "There is no
time limit on this exercise. If you're ready to come back in three
minutes, fine. If you need three hours, take three hours. But I would
be surprised if you came back in three minutes. Do not rush this
process. Take the time you need to hear the Spirit speak to you. And

don't listen for the answer in your mind. The mind gets in the way of the Spirit. Listen for it in your heart."

✦✦✦

Two hours later Brandon stepped to the edge of the trees at the edge of the waterfall and stared down one hundred yards below at the spot he'd set out from. Light laughter bounced off the water. Dana's. Then Marcus's low laughter followed. Brandon massaged the left side of his chest with his knuckles as if that would make the ache in his heart vanish.

The bounce in Dana's step as she walked back and forth along the edge of the water picking up stones told him God had given her some kind of name. Obviously a good one. Marcus was almost as animated as she was—gesturing with his hands to Reece, probably telling about the vast number of new names God had bestowed. Brandon wasn't upset about them getting names—he was happy they'd gotten something—but was it so impossible for him to share in the wealth?

Brandon clutched his walking stick and held it up like it was a Louisville Slugger. "Batter up." He swung it against the pine tree to his right. Hard. The stick snapped into three pieces and disappeared into the underbrush. "You're out."

He fell to his knees onto sharp rocks. He didn't care. "Give me a name, Jesus, please," he whispered. Still nothing. He waited another five minutes. Silence.

"Give me a name!" He stood and shouted, then listened to the echo spring back to him.

The others stared up at him from the edge of the lake, but he didn't care. Why hadn't God spoken to him? Given him at least something to take back to the group? Reece said people sometimes got multiple names. Dana and Marcus probably got three each. Brandon would have been happy with one. Even half a name. Should he go back to the spot he'd sat in for an hour and a half and try again?

Brandon looked at the sun. Three, maybe four hours of daylight left. And while the hike down to Well Spring would be faster than coming up, he didn't think any of the others would relish the idea of hiking the last few miles in the dark. Besides, what was the point of staying here? Either he was deaf or God didn't have a name for him. Brandon massaged his eyes with the heels of his hands and let out a sigh. Might as well go down and greet the others.

When he reached them, none spoke. Reece walked up to him and slung one arm around his shoulders. Brandon glanced at the others. "That's cool that God gave you names."

Reece turned him from the others and whispered, "I'm sorry."

"No worries. It's all good."

Dana approached like a spooked doe. Did she care? Or was there a part of her secretly happy he hadn't gotten anything? No, he couldn't think like that. That wasn't her heart and he knew it.

"No names were spoken by God to you?" Marcus said.

Brandon pulled away from Reece, stepped up on a boulder, and threw his head back and his arms out. "That is correct! Marcus Amber wins the Well Spring Ranch State the Obvious award!" He kicked at a small stone sitting on the boulder and sent it whizzing into the lake.

"Do you want to tell us what happened?" Reece said.

"Nothing. That's what happened. Didn't you hear me up there?" Brandon jabbed a finger in the direction he'd come from. "There was a lot of silence. Then more silence. Then I came back. End of story."

"Nothing good came out of your time?"

It was a lie to say there was nothing. There was some good. He stepped off the boulder and glanced at Marcus. "Sorry, Professor."

"It isn't a problem."

"Tell us." Reece's face was as serious as Brandon had ever seen it. "It's important you speak it out."

Brandon grabbed a long stick off the ground and drew a circle in the dirt at his feet, then made lines one under the other. "I wrote down all the names I could think of that I've been called over the years. It was a good-sized list." He continued to draw lines in the dirt.

"After I'd gotten 'em all out, I decided to rank them in order of the pain they caused me. Then I prayed through each one and then burned them."

"Excellent," Reece said. "Anything else?"

"Enough of the self-pity." Brandon looked at Dana and Marcus. "I'd love to hear your new names."

Marcus hesitated, then nodded. "All right. I heard two names. The first was—" He stopped and laughed. "Ebenezer."

"Ebenezer? As in Scrooge?" Dana asked.

"Okay." Brandon snorted. "God is calling you Scrooge. Not exactly the most inspiring name."

"Definitely not at first glance. But I felt God say there is great healing in that name for me, once I acquire the understanding of why he gave it to me. So I'll reserve judgment till I receive the answer."

"And the second name?"

"Restorer."

Reece nodded. "A powerful name. Did he tell you what that one means?"

Marcus shook his head. "Once again, no indication. But as before, I know the meaning will come in time."

Reece nodded again. "Without question it will."

Marcus frowned at Reece. "You know what my names mean, don't you?"

"I have an idea. But it's not for me to say." He turned to his right. "Dana?"

She glanced at him, then looked at Reece. "One name. Arwen. From *The Lord of the Rings*."

Brandon smiled. It was perfect. A warrior. A princess. A leader. A queen. Full of beauty and compassion and fire. "So true."

She met his gaze again, then looked away. "Thanks."

Just before the moment grew awkward, Reece picked up his

daypack and hefted it over his shoulder. "The sun won't wait for us to get back. We should move."

When they reached Well Spring, Reece gathered them in a circle in the spot they'd left from. "I'm proud of all of you. That was not an easy hike. The physical portion was meant to test your character, and you all showed strength and tenacity.

"The spiritual part was up to God and he always comes through. Marcus, Dana, I suggest taking time tonight to journal about what God spoke to you and the deeper meanings of the name or names he gave you. You're right, Marcus, the full meaning might take awhile to come—it might be days, it might be months—but the answer will come.

"The enemy would love to steal what was given to you today. Don't let him. Capture the truth and the emotion on paper while it's still fresh. Do you understand?"

They nodded.

"After that, I want the three of you to relax and get to bed early."

The three moved to go inside.

"Hang on, Brandon." Reece beckoned the musician with his fingers. "Can you join me at the listening post for a few minutes?"

"Sure." He glanced at the paved path leading to the listening post and back to Reece. "Why not?"

"Good. I'm going to suggest a reason why you didn't get a name."

TWENTY-ONE

WHEN THEY REACHED THE FIRE PIT, REECE SAT AND motioned Brandon to sit in the chair next to him. The big man didn't speak and Brandon was grateful. Something about sitting in the silence with Reece gave him hope. They sat for two minutes without speaking, the rush of the river providing a grand score for their combined solitude.

Finally Reece turned to him and broke the silence. "How are you feeling?"

"Great."

Reece scooted his chair closer to Brandon's. "How are you feeling?"

"Fine."

"Am I going to have to ask you three or four times to know the real answer?" Reece leaned in till his head was inches from Brandon's.

"Probably."

Reece settled back in his chair. "I'm going to ask you again how you're doing. And you have two options. Either stay silent and keep your own counsel, which is perfectly acceptable. We'll go inside, join the others, and have a peaceful evening. Or you can tell me about the brutal thoughts you've been sparring with since earlier today that have you almost to a ten count. And you're the one on the mat."

"How do you know I've been sparring?"

"Really?" Reece raised his eyebrows. "Are you kidding? Like

anyone with half a heart couldn't tell the whole name thing ripped you up inside? You put out quite a bit of convincing evidence up at the lake."

"You have a heart, Reece?"

Reece laughed. It startled Brandon so much he laughed himself. It was the first time he'd heard any kind of mirth pour out of the big man's mouth. "I did at one time, son."

"That's good to know." Brandon uncrossed his legs and smiled at him.

The silence returned and this time Brandon spoke first. When he did it was just above a whisper. "I wanted to hear a new name." He glanced into Reece's piercing blue eyes. "So bad. I wanted something to replace the names I burned."

"I know."

"A replacement for the name at the top of my list."

Reece nodded. "What was the name?"

"Worthless. Exactly what you wrote in the sand. It's like you knew."

"Where does it come from?"

A scene flashed into Brandon's mind before he could stop it.

Three years, two months, and fourteen days ago. There he'd sat with his biological mother in the Macaroni Grill in Alderwood Mall, just north of the Seattle city limits, trying to make a connection.

Brandon nibbled on flatbread and poked his spoon into a bowl of pomodorina soup, which the waiter finally took away less than half eaten. His mom picked at a plate of calamari fritti. The mother he'd only seen twice since he was eight years old. Up till the moment his mom walked out the door of their brick rambler, she had been his best friend. She walked out without a reason, without a good-bye—without even a note. He didn't hear from her again for nineteen years, till he started making money and getting famous.

"Your singing career seems to be going well." His mom lobbed out a vanilla statement and Brandon lobbed back.

"Yeah, I'm making it okay." He spread butter on a piece of bread he knew he wouldn't eat. "And you're liking retirement?"

"Yeah, it's good. I'm spending a lot of time making jewelry for fun."

Silence settled over the table. Brandon glanced at his watch. They'd made small talk for twenty minutes already, and it was obvious both were running low on things to say.

He pushed his plate toward the center of the table. "Thanks for coming."

"Yes. Of course."

"Do you want to know why I asked to see you?"

His mom took renewed interest in her calamari. "No."

Here we go. On the high dive now. Take a deep breath and jump. The water will be there. I hope.

"I just want a chance to get to know you. And see if you have any desire to get to know me. We live an hour from each other and we barely know each other. And I need to know why you left me."

His mom's eyes grew moist as Brandon continued.

"If I was your dad and you were my daughter, I'd want to know who you are, what makes you love life, what makes you hate life, what the joys and sorrows of your life have been. Not because of what I've achieved in the world of music, but just because it's me."

Brandon's mom pushed back from the table and rubbed her face with both hands.

"Aren't there questions you want to ask me? I'm a decent person and I'm your son. Don't you want to tell me what happened? Why you walked out without ever letting me know why?"

Tears streamed down his mom's face.

Say it! Tell me it tore your heart out to leave, tell me you've missed me every day for the past twenty-four years, tell me you've been dying to know who I am!

"I don't know what to say." She picked at her pink fingernail polish.

"I want a relationship with you. Not with your husband. Not

with my half brothers. With you. I want you to call me periodically. I want to get an e-mail from you on occasion. I want to hear what's good and what's hard in your life. I want you to know more about my music than what's playing on Spirit 105.3."

His mom wiped her eyes with a napkin, then grabbed another one.

"I'm not asking you to be a mother to me—that day is past. I'm just asking to have a relationship that's not based on me giving you money or you telling your friends your son is famous."

Brandon took a drink of water to buy time to think. "I want to know if I matter to you at all."

Tears continued to spill onto his mom's face—the second napkin was soaked. Brandon was out of words. What more could be said? Had he hurt his mom? The tears meant something, but what? Sorrow? Regret? A breaking that would mean hope for the future?

He leaned in on the table and held his hands out to her. "Grab my hands, Mom."

But she didn't. Brandon slowly slouched back in his chair.

"I'm sorry," she said and continued to stare at the table right in front of him. "So sorry."

Enough. Brandon pulled a piece of paper out of his back pocket and slid it across the table. "That's my e-mail address. And my cell phone. Maybe we could talk every now and then. Get to know each other if you want to. I know I do. It's up to you."

She continued to cry, from what, Brandon couldn't tell. And he didn't ask. He spilled his guts on the table as well as his kidneys, spleen, and certainly his heart. But all his mom could do was glance at him with a face of sorrow.

The meeting ended awkwardly, with Brandon offering to pay for the meal and his mom insisting she pay. In the end they split the bill. Before walking to their cars it looked like his mom was going to reach for him, but her hands stayed at her sides.

She called Brandon one week after their lunch. It was a minute-and-a-half conversation that was forced and awkward. Three weeks after that, an e-mail arrived talking about the weather. Brandon wrote back and that was their last communication.

He clasped his hands together and stared at Reece. Brandon was shocked again, this time to see tears in the man's eyes.

"I'm so sorry, Brandon."

"It's okay."

"No. It most certainly is not."

The rush of the river seemed to grow and Brandon let its song wash over him.

"Do you have any hope she'll call?"

"No. I'm over it."

Thankfully, Reece didn't challenge the lie. The last vestiges of the sun fell behind the cliffs to the west and twilight crept up on them. Neither of them spoke till the river below faded from sight into the shadow of early night.

"Your mom has her own wounds, her own reasons for not pursuing you. Her tears meant something. Maybe a longing to know you but no idea how to start."

"She's not my mom."

"Did you hear anything else I just said?"

"I heard it."

"Try to believe it, son."

"I can believe what you're saying, but I'm tired of making excuses for her."

"I understand. And history has repeated itself." Reece rubbed his hands on his pants. "At least we now know why."

"What are you talking about?"

The big man turned and stared at him. "You don't know?"

An instant later he did know. "Dana."

Reece nodded.

Heat rose into Brandon's face as shame filled his heart. He'd done the exact thing to her that his mom had done to him. Why had he never seen it?

Lord, forgive me.

Lord, forgive me.

Brandon sank forward, head in hands, and let the tears come. "I gotta talk to her."

"Yes."

"When?"

"When the time is right. When the Spirit tells you to."

"I need to tell her now."

"No. Not now. Wait. Tell her when the time is right."

Brandon turned to the sky, pinks and reds mingling across it. Reece tossed a small stick into the fire pit. "Why did you break up with her?"

"I honestly haven't known why." Brandon shook his head. "But now it's obvious."

"Tell me."

"Because if my best friend left me once, she could leave me twice, and when I was eight years old, I vowed I would never, ever allow myself to be put in a position to go through that kind of pain again." Brandon settled his head in his hands for the second time, and again the tears flowed.

"Do you see how this vow shut down your emotions toward your music?"

"No." But a moment later he did. Worship was all about opening one's heart—exposing pain to God's light. Facing the wound and allowing healing to begin.

He looked at Reece. "When I locked Dana out, I locked God out as well."

"Yes." Reece drew close and wrapped his massive arm around Brandon's shoulder. "Maybe you didn't get a name today, but I'd still say there was a huge step toward healing and freedom. It will take time, but it's coming."

A few minutes went by before either spoke. Brandon finally turned and smiled. "I think this will stay with me even longer than the idea of beaming across the country."

"The Father's desire for restoration and truth in the innermost being will always be more powerful than signs and wonders. The signs and wonders only serve to point us to him and his unfathomable love for us."

Brandon glanced toward the cabin, its warm, golden glow inviting him back. "I know we should go in, but before we do, can we shift gears back to the name thing?"

"Of course."

"Why didn't I get one? You said you knew the reason."

"I don't think up there was the way you needed to hear it. The Spirit is rarely on the same schedule we are. But sometimes it's because he wants to give it to us in a way that is completely unexpected. A way that will make more impact. I could be wrong, but that's what I'm sensing will happen with you."

"I believed I would get a name. I had no doubt, and yet I walked off that mountain with the silence of God ringing in my ears like thunder."

"Your name will come, Brandon. Of that I have no doubt. Trust me. Trust the Spirit."

"When?"

"When it's time." Reece stood. "And tonight I promise you'll have an experience that will take your mind off of the subject completely."

"What's that?"

"I've been praying all day about this, and I believe the Spirit is saying it's time."

"Time to . . . ?"

"Go through the gate into someone's soul."

TWENTY-TWO ◉

AT EIGHT O'CLOCK ON TUESDAY, REECE STOOD IN FRONT of them in the main room of the cabin, his eyes darting back and forth in an apparent display of nervousness Marcus hadn't seen before.

"Tonight your training will take a quantum leap forward."

"You're about to escort us into someone's soul," Marcus said.

"Yes."

"The purpose of which is . . . ?"

"To heal the brokenhearted and set the captives free. It's not an instantaneous process. Healing takes time. But being inside a soul often breaks chains that have been wrapped around people for years. Chains they often don't even know they have."

"Can I just say I feel I'm far from ready?" Dana pushed herself deeper back into the dark green cushions of the couch.

Marcus tried to ignore the cold sheen of perspiration running down the middle of his back. He was intimately acquainted with the feeling.

"That's exactly the attitude I want each of you to have." Reece glanced at Brandon and Marcus. "This is not a game. It's not without significant dangers. If God hadn't told me to train you, we would not be doing this right now." A slice of pain and worry flecked Reece's features, but it vanished a second after it appeared.

"Are you nervous, Reece?" Marcus asked.

"Yes. I am. Going into a soul is to be approached with great

147

caution. The fear and reverence of the Lord is the beginning of wisdom. The fear and reverence of entering into another's soul is also wise."

Reece's face hardened. "A few ground rules. First, you never go into a soul without God leading you to do so. Second, you never go into a soul without explicit permission." He paused and stared at each of them. "Is that clear?"

They all nodded.

"There is never an exception to rule number two. Never. Are we abundantly, exceedingly clear on that point?"

They nodded again.

"Number three, when we're inside we stick together. Because not only do you have to go in as a unit, you can't get back out unless everyone is together." Reece folded his arms and stared into the fire that blazed in the hearth behind Dana. "Fourth, never go in without covering yourself with Jesus' blood. And fifth, if at all possible, avoid going in alone."

Marcus finished scribbling in his journal and looked up. "When was the last time you entered into a soul?"

"Yesterday."

"Wait a minute. How did we miss that?" Brandon said.

"That was why I went to Denver—along with getting your coffee, Brandon, and the newspaper. I went to see an old friend, Doug Lundeen, so I could pray with him and practice with him. And it's his soul we're going into tonight with his permission and full support."

"You crossed the threshold into this Doug's soul yesterday?" Marcus asked.

Reece nodded.

Brandon rapped his knuckles together. "I thought you weren't supposed to go in alone."

"There were others who went with me."

"Who?"

"A group of men I used to gather with, pray with, war with. The ones who taught me how to go inside many years ago."

"Their acquaintance is one I'd like to make," Marcus said.

Reece studied his face. "I believe you will someday."

Brandon clapped. "And now that you've had a little practice, you're about to do it again. This time with us along for the ride."

Marcus's hands grew cold. Up till now all Reece's talk had been theory—something he was used to exploring in the classroom. But if what Reece said was true, they would be stepping out of the classroom into a staggering spiritual arena.

Marcus tapped his journal with the end of his pen. "I have to confess, my synapses are firing in a rather odd manner right now."

Brandon stared at him. "Can you translate that for me?"

"He's freaked out," Dana said.

"Not 'freaked out.' I'm full of anticipation. Okay, perhaps I'm hanging over the edge to a slight degree." Marcus rapped out a staccato beat on his journal. "All right, fine. A significant portion of me is hanging over the edge."

"What else do we need to know?" Brandon's knee bounced like a mini jackhammer.

"The first time you go into a soul it is extremely disorienting. But I'll be there, and as you get more experienced, it will grow easier."

Reece paced behind his chair. "Inside a soul there are areas of light and areas of darkness. Don't let the areas of darkness intimidate you. The enemy will entice you to enter the black fortresses inside. Some you'll be ready for. Others are too dangerous. Be on guard. But know also, the darkness is nothing compared to the light and power of the Spirit."

"When you talk of darkness, are you indicating sin within a soul, or a demonic presence inside?" Marcus asked.

"Both."

"Wait," Dana said. "Demons can't be inside a Christian's soul, even if it's only for brief periods."

Reece stopped pacing and leaned on his chair. "Really? How do you know that? Where does it teach that in Scripture?"

"Christ lives in us, so how would Satan or one of his demons be able to be in his presence?"

"Yet he can be in the presence of Jesus when he asks to sift Peter like wheat? He can be in God's presence when he talks to him about Job? There is still sin inside us if you believe Paul in Romans 7, so if there is the darkness of sin still inside us, why couldn't a demon be there as well?"

Brandon squinted at Reece. "Are you talking about demon possession or oppression?"

"I don't know how it all works. I'm not a theologian. I have many more questions on the subject than I do answers. But I'm not interested in debating the subject with anyone. What interests me is seeing people set free, and I've been inside enough Christians' souls to see things there that need to be destroyed in order to bring about that freedom."

Brandon put a piece of wood on the fire. "Can you describe what we'll be seeing inside Doug's soul? I mean, are we going to be standing on clouds or be in some kind of construction of his memories or dreams like in *Inception* or—?"

"It's impossible to know. Even if you went into the same soul one hundred times, it's doubtful you would see the same thing. Each soul on this planet is vast, with a thousand layers to it. Remember, the Spirit is the architect and guide of each journey inside. He takes us in and shows us what we need to see.

"With some people you'll stand at the center of a city. With others you'll be in a wilderness with mountains on every side. I know of a home on the West Coast where each room was a part of a person's soul."

Reece sat and clasped his hands. "When inside, the ground under your feet will feel as solid as the floor beneath you does right now. Your bodies will feel as tangible as they do right now."

"Will fatigue be an issue?"

"Yes."

Dana blinked. "How is that possible if our bodies are still here?"

"The mind and the body and the spirit are woven together so tightly, you cannot exhaust one without tiring the other."

"This is too weird." Brandon laughed. "I see why you wanted us to watch *The Matrix* again. I feel like we'll be jacking in."

"Jacking in?" Dana said.

"Did you get a chance to watch the movie, Dana?" Reece said.

"No."

Reece motioned to Brandon. "Can you give Dana the *Reader's Digest* version of the movie?"

"Sure." He leaned forward. "The Matrix was this computer system that controlled mankind—the machines made humans their slaves in order to harvest their electrical energy. Every person lived in these pods where the machines stimulated their brains to make them think they were living a normal life. They had no idea they were slaves.

"But there was a resistance. People who had been freed from the computer simulation and lived in the real world. And they learned how to jack into the computer world that controlled everyone and set other people free."

Dana rubbed her hands together, then held herself tight. "And let me guess. The machines weren't happy about the resistance."

"Exactly." Brandon talked with his hands as much as his mouth. "The machines created a program inside the Matrix that pitted entities known as agents against those seeking to set others free."

"Demons." Dana nodded. "If we're carrying the analogy into our world."

"Yes," Reece said. "It's why I wanted you to see the movie."

Brandon turned to Reece. "So you agree? We're kind of jacking in?"

"Not kind of. That's exactly what we're doing," Reece said. "With a slight difference."

"Which is?" Marcus said.

"That was a movie. This isn't. This is real. And this is God's Spirit doing the jacking in."

"Plus the script isn't written yet," Marcus said.

"Very good point." Reece sucked in a quick breath. The look Marcus saw earlier passed over his face again. Fear. But again it faded quickly.

Reece clapped twice. "It's time. Grab hands. That will lessen the feeling of vertigo. We won't be in there long. This is just a taste."

Marcus grabbed Dana's hand on one side and Brandon's on the other. Both were damp with perspiration. If what Reece was telling them really was true, quantum mechanics would leap off the page and crash through the wall of theory into flesh-and-blood life.

He smiled at Reece. "Let's launch."

Reece glanced at each of them, then closed his eyes. "Spirit of God. Take us."

Immediately the cabin and the fire vanished and Marcus's stomach felt like he was dropping down the biggest chute on the world's fastest roller coaster. Darkness surrounded them, then flashes of light, and then his feet were on solid ground. Not solid ground. Solid sand. To their right were rolling hills covered with huge oak trees, to their left, an ocean. He looked up. Clear. No clouds to mar the perfection of the blue sky overhead.

"Wow," Brandon coughed out. "What a rush."

"It looks so real." Dana spun in a slow circle, her eyes wide.

Reece did his own spin of their surroundings, his face covered in a thin sheen of sweat. It was the first time Marcus had seen their guide seemingly worried.

"Are we all good?" Reece asked as he glanced up and down the beach.

"Are you good?" Marcus asked.

"I'm fine." The big man's head continued to wag back and forth as he surveyed the sand.

"Are you sure?"

"Positive." Reece stopped turning and looked at Marcus full on, then Brandon, then Dana.

"Doug and I have known each other for years. He's strong in

the Spirit. But that doesn't mean his soul is a safe place. There are dangers. When you're in a soul, you need to think like a scuba diver. No more than ten feet should separate you from those you're with at any time."

Reece dug his feet into the sand. "We have permission to be here and Doug knows we're here."

"Yeah, you mentioned that," Brandon said.

Reece didn't seem to hear him. "You will see things in here so real, you won't be able to tell them from the dimension we normally live in. You'll see colors you didn't know existed."

"But none of it is truly real, right?" Dana asked.

"All of it is real."

"On a spiritual level," Brandon said.

"On every level. It's Western thinking that separates the seen world from the unseen realms, not God. The line is thinner than most people realize."

As the words came out of Reece's mouth, the topography in front of them shifted, and Marcus felt like he was in the middle of a visual hurricane. Images spun around him so fast he couldn't make anything out. When the images settled they stood in a canyon, its walls so high he couldn't see where they stopped. A moment later light spun like water down the craggy brown walls of the canyon as a cloud of gray pressed toward them.

Marcus couldn't tell if the light held the darkness at bay, or the darkness was pulling the light toward it. One second he was positive it was the former, the next second the latter. It was like an optical illusion where the shadow of the cube shifts from one side to another.

"What do you see ahead of us?" Reece glanced back at them. "I want everyone to answer."

Marcus spoke first. "A long narrow canyon, light and darkness swirling inside it."

"Good. Dana?"

"The same."

"Next?"

Brandon frowned. "I see a meadow in late spring or early summer. A few clouds in the sky. A deep black path through the middle of it as if it was recently burned."

"Anything else?"

"Yes." Brandon squinted. "I think there's a man on the far side of the meadow, strolling back and forth."

"Excellent."

As Marcus listened to the others' comments, the canyon faded and he saw what Brandon had described. Dana pulled on Marcus's arm. "Are you still seeing—?"

"No. Now I'm viewing Brandon's scene."

"Me too."

Amazing. Marcus stared at the field—trees surrounding it, the burn mark, the wildflowers peppered through the meadow, and joy spread out from his heart till it filled his body.

Reece's describing what they would see as being beyond their normal color scheme didn't come close to describing what flooded Marcus's eyes. The colors so rich, he could imagine tasting them. The beauty of a human soul was stunning.

Their leader's voice broke through his ponderings. "It's time to go. Join hands. Close your eyes."

As soon as they clasped hands, Marcus was back on the roller coaster and a moment after that was back in the living room of the cabin, staring at the flushed faces across from him.

"I . . . I don't know what to say." Dana blinked and gave a quick whistle.

No one else spoke. Finally Reece broke the silence. "I'm proud of you. You did well."

"It was astonishing." Marcus scribbled more notes in his journal. "Will we go through the gate again? And if yes, do you have an indication when?"

"I believe we'll go into another soul again soon, but not as a dry run like we did with Mr. Lundeen. We'll be on a full-out mission to bring healing and freedom to the soul we go into. Which means battle."

Dana glanced at all of them. "Do you have an idea whose we'll go into?"

"Yes." Reece slowly nodded as he gazed into the fire. "It will be one of yours."

TWENTY-THREE

On Wednesday morning, Marcus felt like he floated down the stairs as if his feet barley touched the wood underneath them. He stopped on the bottom step and gazed around the room, his mouth slightly open.

"Marcus? Are you okay?" Dana said. "What's wrong?"

"I'm in a very passable condition."

"He's more than passable." Reece pointed at him. "That's the look of a man who has just had a profound spiritual experience."

How did Reece know? It didn't matter. He didn't care. After what had just happened nothing could shift his focus from the images still careening through his mind.

Brandon lurched up from his chair. "You all right, pal?"

"I'm fine." Marcus held up his palms. "Really."

"You said that already, but you don't look it," Dana said. "You look spooked. But in a weird way I'd call happily spooked."

"That's probably an apt description of how I appear in this moment." Not to mention how disheveled his smile must appear. He glanced around the room, wanting to tell them about the vision but not sure where to begin.

"What happened?" Dana asked.

Marcus slumped onto the couch, smiled, and looked at each of them. "Unbelievable."

"Are you going to tell us?"

He stood and floated over to the sliding glass door and stared at the mountains across the river, then turned back to the others.

Brandon turned to Reece. "Do you have any clue why the professor is acting like he just came back from a visit to Oz?"

"Because I think he just did." Reece glanced at Marcus, then at the others. "We have one day left here and part of tomorrow morning. I think the Spirit is going to kick off this last full day right with what Marcus is about to tell us. Give him a moment."

A few minutes later Marcus walked back and plopped down on the couch next to Brandon. "I think I just had my first vision."

A hint of a smile played on Reece's face as he pointed at Marcus. "I told you."

"Told him what?" Brandon said.

Marcus grinned and looked at the ground. "The day Reece invited me to come here, he said if I would open my mind to the possibility of seeing visions, that I would start having them. And once they started, I'd have them with increasing frequency."

Dana smiled. "'In the last days, God says, I will pour out my Spirit on all people. Your sons and daughters will prophesy, your young men will see visions, your old men will dream dreams.'"

"Does that mean I'm still young?"

"Quite," Reece said.

"Are you ready to tell us what you saw?" Dana said.

"Yeah, spill it, Prof." Brandon leaned back on the couch, arms spread wide along the back.

Marcus blinked and rubbed his eyes, then sat forward. "Yes. Certainly. I mean, I'll attempt to . . . it was so—"

"Ethereal?" Dana asked.

"No. So real. Like seeing a film but standing inside it at the same time."

"Yak it, brother," Brandon said.

"I was on my knees. Praying. I slowly leaned forward till my head pressed into the carpet. I asked God to show me more of him and more of the reality of the spiritual world. A few seconds later there was a flash, and suddenly it was as if a film was playing. My eyes were closed but the sensation was as if they were open. And the movie was playing on a sixty-foot screen in 3-D.

"I found myself on a narrow road with four others. In front of us, inches off the ground, clouds gathered, rolling in on themselves and growing larger. Black and red sulfurous clouds. We were on a road leading into the heart of the vapors. Sprinting. Full-out on white horses.

"I felt the rhythm of the horses and their muscles strain as they pushed on as hard as they could. It felt as though the four others and I rode as one. There was one rider to my left and two to my right. In front of us was one with the name Warrior. He leaned forward on his horse, so all I saw was the back of his head. But his intensity was obvious from his pace, and his horse rather than acting driven seemed one with its rider.

"As the vision unfolded I knew we were riding against the hordes of hell, and the clouds were a demonic manifestation of evil. The clouds swirled with hate, death, torment, and above all, fear. Great clouds of fear. But there was no fear in our band. We rode like the wind and with fire in our eyes.

"As we rode deeper into the cloud, it parted around us. Like a subway tunnel. It didn't recede much, but enough that we didn't breathe its fumes. The clouds became demons that flew at us and I was aware of it, but there was no fear. We had swords out and we struck with fury, swiftly slicing through the demons' bodies like lightning. But it was only a slight distraction from the laser intent of the ride. To go deeper into the stronghold.

"A demon flew up and grabbed at a chest, either mine or someone near me—that part is cloudy. I can't remember. But the loathing was palpable, the hatred in its voice only a whisper compared to the hatred in its eyes. But as it touched the breastplate that all of us wore, it screamed and pulled back as if its hands had been scorched.

"We continued riding and as we did, a realization swept over me. The torrent that was swirling above and around us was an illusion. The enormous wall of clouds I saw at the start of the vision had descended on us, yes. But the tunnel that we rode through was just that. A tunnel. Only four or five feet thick. As the thought finished in my mind, the tunnel began clearing and soon we were beneath a reddish-gray sky.

"There was no life on the red sand that covered both sides of the road. Soon we reached a point where the way sloped sharply downward, then after a hundred yards or so grew level.

"The Warrior leading us stopped and told us to remain there till he returned. He rode to the bottom of the slope and seemed to be searching for something or someone. Suddenly a man appeared from nowhere, his hands and feet shackled. The Warrior's sword flashed and its razor edge bit into the chains, shredding them into a hundred splinters.

"More men and women appeared, reaching out and crying for him to come to them, all shackled and chained to the ground they lay in. Not on. In. They were buried up to their knees and waists in shame and sorrow.

"Then I looked beyond the valley below and up the other side. The road twisted and turned into cliffs that shot almost straight up. At the top of a column of dark red rock was a fortress. It seemed to radiate dark power.

"The Warrior rode up to the gates of the fortress, dismounted, and strode through its gates and disappeared. I saw him again a moment later on the highest wall of the fortress facing the dark one.

"There were no words. Neither dropped the gaze of the other. The dark one struck the Warrior, and he was cast over the wall where he landed on the rocky ground a hundred feet below. But the triumph of the dark one remained only for an instant.

"The Warrior stood and grew so tall so fast it happened in seconds. His feet were on the ground, his waist even with the high wall of the fortress. He had to be three hundred feet tall. The Warrior reached down to the dark one and plucked him off the wall between his thumb and forefinger. He held the dark one up to his face and spoke with a phrase that surprised me in its simplicity. 'You don't understand, do you?'

"Then the Warrior reached down to the floor of the stronghold and picked up a box. It appeared ancient and heavy looking. And not much bigger than the dark one.

"The Warrior threw the evil one into the box and slammed the lid. Then the Warrior shrank to the size he was when I first saw him. And the box that held the evil one shrank too, so it was smaller than one of the Warrior's fingernails.

"The ground surged under our feet and the red and gray sand grew brown and rich in texture. And the Warrior took the box that held the dark one and tossed it to the ground, where it was swallowed up by a crack in the soil. And in the next instant the soil was swallowed up by a carpet of thick wild grass.

"And the people the Warrior set free gathered round him, shouting and dancing. A moment later the four of us were back at the spot on the road where we had started, the Warrior facing us and our three horses.

"'You have been chosen to ride.'

"His eyes bored into mine with fire and truth and love. I was ten feet from him. He on his horse, me on mine. But in the next instant, he was crushing me with an embrace of acceptance. I wept as his overwhelming love surged through me." Marcus finished and looked up. His cheeks glistened from the moisture on them and his countenance was filled with wonder.

They sat for a moment, digesting Marcus's words. After a few minutes Brandon said, "That fries me."

"Why is that?" Marcus said.

"First, how powerful that is. Second, that you had it." Brandon laughed. "I've never met anyone who had visions. I didn't even know that happened these days."

Marcus looked at them. "Do I need to even say we are the riders?"

"I think we all picked up on that, bro. And I think we've just found the name for our little band." Brandon smiled. "Warriors Riding."

"So be it," Reece said.

✦✦✦

As Reece listened to Brandon and Marcus discuss the message of the vision and how it would play out in their lives, he smiled inside. They were stepping in. The vision would open worlds to them if they embraced it. And they had gone into Doug's soul last night without complication. Knowing Doug and his old allies had been praying and would keep praying, Reece could imagine his confidence growing to where it had been in the old days. Almost.

Reece glanced at Dana and shot up a silent plea to the Spirit. Covering Dana's faded jeans and light green sweatshirt was a translucent white dress that started to shatter. *Bring it, Lord.*

A few minutes later Brandon stopped talking and looked over at Dana, who had her head down. Yes. Brandon had seen it in her as well. Or sensed it. Or the Spirit had told him. Now he just needed to speak it. He saw hesitation in the musician's eyes. *Give him the courage, Jesus.*

Brandon shifted on the couch and gazed at the floor. "Um, Dana, are you okay? You've been pretty quiet since Marcus finished telling us the vision."

Yes. That's it. Go with it, Brandon. Lean in.

"I'm fine." She blinked back tears and rubbed her face.

Reece's gaze darted back and forth between them. *Stay with it, Brandon.*

"Maybe it's me, and it probably is, but I'm feeling like the Spirit is saying . . . I mean, I'm getting the sense you need to—"

Dana's head shot up and she lasered Brandon with her eyes. "It would have to be you that noticed, right?"

Grace now, Brandon. Grace.

"Yeah, it would. Sorry it had to be me." He clasped and unclasped his fingers. "Just wanted you to know we're here if you want us to pray or you want to tell us—"

"Tell you what?"

Don't back down. Speak the truth. But speak it with tenderness.

"Anything inside that might be pounding to get out." He tapped his chest over his heart. "And if the Spirit is telling you to tell us, you need to. Because maybe we need to hear it spoken out loud too."

Yes. Well done, Brandon.

Dana lifted her head and looked at the ceiling, then let it drop back down, chin against her chest. "Talk about going for the throat," she whispered.

The rest of them stayed silent.

✦✦✦

Did she have to tell them? Of course. There was no question the Spirit was leading her to. But would they hear her? And in front of *Brandon*? Dana sighed. God certainly had a sense of humor. But it was right. How to start? She rehearsed an opening line in her mind, and a hint of light seemed to splash on her heart. *Lord.*

Ten seconds later she glanced around the room at each of them. Even Brandon. "All right. I think I'm supposed to—I know I'm supposed to—tell you guys what the cloud is that's been wrapped around me my whole life. When Marcus was describing his vision, the answer struck so hard it was almost physical."

She hugged herself and shifted back on the couch. "And you're exactly right, Marcus. That gray cloud wrapped around me might be in reality only a few feet thick, but it seems like there're miles of it between me and the sun."

"I can relate." The professor leaned forward.

Dana ran her upper teeth over her lower lip and stared into the fireplace. "It happened when I was six."

"You're sure you want to tell us?" Reece said.

She shook her head but started speaking. "My mom and dad divorced when I was five, my mom worked, so I was put in day care after school got out."

Dana shuddered as the scene floated up from her memory.

"Will Mommy come soon?"

The woman sitting cross-legged to Dana's left smiled. "I'm sure she will. She doesn't get off work till after the other moms, so that's why you always get picked up last."

"Okay." Dana picked up a white stuffed kitten and made it jump from knee to knee. "I don't like it here alone."

"I know, I know." The woman patted Dana's knee and glanced at her watch.

"I'm sure your mommy will be here almost instantly." The woman snapped her fingers and Dana smiled.

A few minutes later the door to the room was flung open and another woman rushed through. "There's a phone call for you, Tina."

The woman's face went white. "What's wrong?"

"It's your son."

"Is he okay?"

"Yes, they say he'll be fine, but they want to talk to you."

The woman sprang to her feet, took two steps, then turned back to Dana. "I'll be right back, honey, okay?"

Dana nodded and held the kitten tight to her chest.

"I answered it in the office, so you probably want to take the call in there."

"Okay, thank you." The woman stumbled through the door into the hallway.

The other woman called after her, "I have to go, so I'm sorry, but I can't help you lock up tonight."

"Go, go. I've got it." The woman waved her on, then turned to Dana. "You'll be okay playing by yourself for a few minutes?"

Dana nodded as she rocked back and forth, clutching the kitten, and stared at the back of the door as it closed with a soft click. The only sound was the tick of the big white clock on the wall over the door. Her stomach started to hurt as the sunlight outside the windows faded and dusk turned to night. Where was Mrs. Sander? She said she was going to be right back. And it was so, so quiet.

Finally Dana rose and trundled over to the door of the playroom. It creaked as it opened, but that was the only sound in the day care. "Mrs. Sander?"

Her heart beat like she'd played hopscotch too fast. There was no answer.

"Mrs. Sander!"

Tears spilled onto her face as she wandered through the day care, her sneakers squeaky on the floor of the hallway, her legs wobbly and her stomach aching even more. She finally went back to the playroom, plucked the stuffed kitten off the floor, and huddled in the corner next to the bookshelf.

"Don't worry, kitty. Mommy will be here soon. Very soon." Tears streamed down Dana's cheeks. "Please. Please come now."

But her mom never came that night twenty-nine years ago. It was her dad's turn to pick her up and take her to his home, and he forgot. Her mom called him early the next morning to make sure she'd slept okay and to remind him to get her to school on time.

Dana stared at the fire in the hearth and let the tears come. The men didn't say anything and the silence grew louder. What? They didn't know what to say? They thought it was stupid to be so worked up over some silly childhood memory? They thought she should just grow up? Why did men have to be such men at times like this? Dana grabbed a pillow next to her and buried her head in it. Foolish! Why couldn't she have stayed quiet?

Then a strong arm draped over her shoulders and pulled her close. Had to be Reece. She opened her eyes but it wasn't him. It was Marcus and his eyes were watering.

"Why are you—?"

"Crying?" He glanced at her, then at Reece and Brandon. "This isn't logical; I have no idea where these emotions are emanating from." He looked back at her. "But I'm hurting for you."

"A gift from the Spirit," Reece said.

She closed her eyes. "I've never told anyone about that until now."

Marcus gave her one more tight squeeze and scooted a few inches away. When she opened her eyes, Reece was staring at her. "How do you feel?"

Strange. She felt peace. The memory wasn't as razor sharp. The fear not as deep. "Better. Not so all by myself."

"Yes. That's right, Dana. We've all been broken. Every soul that's ever lived. We're not alone. But the enemy wants us to believe we're alone so we keep our stories hidden inside. When we tell them to others, healing often begins."

She nodded and glanced at Marcus. "Will you pray for me?"

"Of course."

✦✦✦

Freedom filled Reece's heart as he watched peace settle on Dana's face. He would love to have stayed, but it was time to go. Let Marcus and her finish without an audience. He motioned for Brandon to join him and they stepped out onto the patio and meandered down to the listening post. "Well done, friend."

"I thought for sure she wouldn't open up, so I almost didn't say anything."

"I'm glad you did. Our job isn't to worry about the outcome; it's to worry about whether we're willing to step in or not."

"What comes next?"

"Jesus is bringing freedom to Dana right now. I believe Marcus will help bring more as they pray together."

Brandon clasped and unclasped his hands. "She needs to know why she was abandoned another time in her life."

"I agree." He patted Brandon on the shoulder and strolled back toward the cabin. "I'll ask her to come out here and join you when and if she's ready."

TWENTY-FOUR

AN HOUR LATER THE SOUND OF SHUFFLING FEET ON THE white limestone sounded behind Brandon. Dana. He turned. Her eyes were red from the tears, but she was still beautiful. *Arwen.*

"Thanks for coming out."

She sat in the teak chair across the fire pit from him, her legs tight together, her arms wrapped around her body. "Reece said you wanted to talk to me."

Brandon struggled to find the words. The rehearsal had gone fine in his head as he waited, but now, with her sitting in front of him, the perfect sentences melted away.

"Do you have something to say?"

"That was powerful in there." He pointed to the cabin and shifted in his chair.

"Of course it was powerful, but it doesn't mean you and I have to debrief on it together."

"I want healing between us too."

"There's nothing to heal." She stared at him, eyes steely.

"That's a lie."

"I'm not ready to talk about this, Brandon."

Her voice said she wasn't, but her eyes said she was. "Do you ever have feelings for me?"

"No." She turned and stared at the river.

"You never think about us?"

"Is that it?" Dana stood. "Or was there something else?"

He scratched his head and fumbled for the right words. "I'm sorry."

"For?"

"What I did."

"Really."

"Yes." He motioned to her chair. "Can you sit for a few more minutes?"

She sank into the chair and glowered at him.

"I didn't mean to hurt you."

"Then why did you?" She flicked a leaf off the armrest of the chair and watched it float to the patio. "Why couldn't you ever give me a reason?"

"I did give you a reason."

"It wasn't a reason. Not the real one."

"It's a long story."

"I have a long time to listen."

Brandon got up, moved closer to Dana, and sat on the concrete ring of the fire pit. "If we're going to work together in Reece's little band, we'll have to get along."

"I think we've been getting along fine. I learned to live without you. It doesn't mean we have to be friends." She pulled her knees tight to her chest. "I can't get into this right now."

"Why not?"

"I just can't. Drop it."

"How can I drop it? If God has us together on Reece's team, then I can't believe God doesn't want us to be friends."

"There's a difference between being friends with someone and being on a team with them."

It wasn't going as he'd imagined. But what could he expect? No matter the reason, he'd still broken her heart. Enough stalling. "My mom left when I was eight. Walked out and I never knew why. I still don't." Brandon stared at his feet. "And I did the same thing to you." He glanced up at her.

"What does that have to do with not telling me?"

"She was my best friend and it ripped my heart out. I vowed I would never put myself in a position to be hurt like that by a woman ever again. But I didn't know it." He looked down and massaged his fist with his other hand. "I knew it, but I didn't know it. Not till yesterday after the hike. I'd buried it and didn't face it when the wedding date was racing up on us. It was like I couldn't control what I was doing. I didn't want to do it but had to at the same time. Do you understand?"

"I'm sorry about what happened with your mom, but I'm not her."

"I know."

They sat in silence till Dana shifted forward as if she was about to leave.

"Have you forgiven me?"

Dana closed her eyes and sighed. "Yes."

"Truly?"

"Yes, Brandon, I have." She opened her eyes and fixed her gaze on him, then spoke just above a whisper. "But if I went into a lion's cage and he mauled me, I can forgive the lion for what he did. But it doesn't mean I'm going to get back in the cage and hope it doesn't happen again." She slapped her hands on her legs. "Are we done?"

Dana didn't wait for an answer. She rose and clomped back up the path to the main cabin. Brandon stood and scrambled down the bank to the river and walked north. Ice cubes were warmer than her reaction. But what had he expected? Her to wrap her arms around him while the birds sang the "Hallelujah Chorus" and the sun broke through the clouds to illuminate them with a beam of light? But he'd told her. For the moment maybe that was enough.

✦✦✦

Marcus sat at the listening post late that afternoon and pulled out the photo of Kat and the girls he'd shown Dana. Tonight Abbie would cavort down the field without him on the sidelines. He should be there. Right now he should be standing beside Kat and

Jayla, blistering his lungs with shouts of encouragement. Maybe Abbie didn't care if he was there or not. But he cared. And deep down he believed she did too.

Yes, he'd changed. But so many years had been wasted. The moments he'd missed that were gone forever. His girls' first steps. Their first words. T-ball games, Soccer Tots, the award ceremonies in grade school, the school play where they were both tomatoes.

Never building the tree house he'd promised them. The Disney World trip that was always going to happen the next year. Yes, they'd made the excursion last year and it was good, but why didn't he create the time when they were still children and he could have seen the uninhibited wonder on their faces?

He pinched the bridge of his nose and tried to fight the thoughts. Tried to take them captive. Tried to grant himself forgiveness and put the past in the past, tried to tell himself there was nothing that could be done about deeds already done, but it was like attempting to dam up the river below him with two small stones. The thoughts kept coming and surged around his feeble attempts to fight them.

"I must get free of this, Lord. Living in the past creates a barrel of iron that weights down the present with great heft."

Marcus continued to pray but peace eluded him, and he stared at the cabin as the lights inside grew brighter against the darkening sky. The glass door slid open and Reece's huge frame was silhouetted against the light. "You coming in, Marcus?"

"Yes. Soon."

The big man closed the door behind him and eased down the path till he stood at the edge of the patio. He glanced from left to right, then focused his eyes on Marcus and pointed at his head. "Up here you understand there is no profit in dwelling on the past." He pointed to his chest. "But this is where you need to know it to be free."

"I have no understanding of how to create that reality."

"The destruction of your chains is coming, Marcus."

"How do you know?"

"'The Son of God appeared for this purpose, to destroy the

works of the devil.'" Reece held out his hand and Marcus grasped it. "First John 3:8."

The big man pulled him out of his chair and grabbed him in a tight embrace. "And he is ready to war for you. Of this, I have no doubt."

TWENTY-FIVE

WEDNESDAY NIGHT AFTER DINNER REECE GATHERED them around the fire pit at the listening post to talk, and Brandon tried to guess the topic. Probably to talk about what they could expect when they returned to Seattle. He hadn't gotten his name. Tension was still thick between Dana and him. But he'd faced the issue of his mom and uncovered why he hadn't been feeling anything. He still was out of touch with his emotions, but at least now he knew why. And he sensed breakthrough was coming.

After the fire roared to life, Reece said, "We're going to talk about next steps, but first, Brandon, would you be up for leading us in a few songs?"

"Love to." Brandon smiled.

He picked up his guitar and strummed a chord, letting it linger in the air, then launched into "Running Wild in Search of Wonder," a song he'd written when he was sixteen and hadn't played in years. By the time he got to the chorus the second time, the others picked up the words and melody and joined it. Reece sounded like a wounded rhino but he sang with passion, and in that moment it was all Brandon cared about.

Marcus had a nice voice and Dana's lilting alto brought him back to the days they used to sing together. He'd always told her she was good enough to sing backup on his songs—but the timing never worked out to get her into the studio.

And as he played, a sense of the old days crept into his soul. The joy of a song. The sense of Jesus in it. Just a sense, but the hope it offered was a geyser. After the song ended, he stopped and let them soak in the presence of God.

"Into this, Lord. Into this. Invade us. Take us deeper into your unquenchable love."

Two songs later he held his fingers on the frets of his guitar and let the final chord slowly fade into the night.

"That was a treasure, Brandon. Thank you." Reece tossed a stick on the fire, then rested his gaze on each of them in turn.

"You've done well during this first phase. There has been breakthrough for each of you. Your eyes have opened to what is possible with God and the vastness of the spiritual realm. When we get home and start the next part of your training, I believe he'll continue to open your eyes to things around you you've never seen.

"Healing has begun in you. Back in Seattle you'll begin bringing that healing and freedom to those around you." He picked up another stick and smacked it into his palm. "That's the good news."

"And the bad?" Dana asked.

"Even before we got to Well Spring, our quest was noticed by the enemy. He tried to keep each of us from coming. He succeeded with Tamera and she was taken out. His goal going forward will be to take out the rest of you. In subtle ways, in overt ways. We need to be ready."

"Great," Brandon said.

"So be alert. He's prowling. He wants to shred you. Stay strong, stay in prayer, don't let yourself be isolated. You start feeling alone in this"—Reece glanced at Dana—"you call me or one of the others immediately and pray together against it."

Dana nodded.

"I'm proud of all of you." Reece stood. "Try to get some sleep tonight. We leave tomorrow morning at ten."

✦✦✦

Dana wandered down to the horseshoe pit early on Thursday morning, then over to the field ringed by the seven small cabins. She wanted to take one more stroll around the ranch and soak up the solitude. Maybe take a few more photos before doing her final packing for home. She smiled. Her enjoying solitude? The healing had truly begun.

As she sauntered back along the path above the river, she spotted Reece sitting on the edge of the embankment, a camera held up to his eye, a deep red strap draped around his neck. A few yards from him, she snapped a twig and he turned.

"May I join you?"

"Of course." He released the camera against his chest and motioned to a spot on the ground beside him.

"I didn't know you were a photographer." She sat and stretched out her legs.

"I've taken a few shots over the years. How about you?" He motioned to her camera.

"Actually, yes. I've dabbled in it off and on—but never gotten serious." She looked at the river. "I don't want to interrupt your shot."

"The light won't be perfect for at least a few minutes."

"How do you know when it is?"

"I don't. I guess and most of the time I get it wrong. But every so often I get it right." Reece clasped his arms around his legs and took a quick look at the sun.

"Have you ever put any of your shots up for sale?"

He looked at her with a quizzical expression. "I've sold a few over the years."

Dana glanced at his photography bag, did a double take, and stared at the lettering along the side. It couldn't be, could it?

"Where did you get that?" She pointed at the bag.

"Why?"

"You're not really him, are you?"

"Hmm?"

She jabbed her finger at the bag. "Roth Photography. Galleries in exotic locales around the world. Multiple celebrities with Roth photos in their homes. The photography legend with no first name. And no shots of himself anywhere to be found."

"I have the same last name as the guy. Is that what you mean?"

It had to be him. She shook her head in disbelief, leaned back on her hands, and stared up at the mountains across the river. "How did I miss it? In all the time I've known you, I've never really thought about your last name. I've always known you simply as Reece." She turned to him. "It's you, isn't it?"

He stared out over the river. "Guilty."

She'd always wondered what he did for a living. The time she asked when they met he'd said, "I'm in business," and she never pressed for details. It wasn't important. Unbelievable. Reece was Roth Photography.

"You're a legend." Dana turned and sat cross-legged.

"You already said that."

"It's true."

"Only in some people's minds."

"Brandon and Marcus will be floored." Dana glanced at the bag again. "They think you barely make it meal to meal. Marcus keeps trying to figure out how you paid for first-class tickets and how you can afford this place for a week." She motioned at the ranch.

"I own Well Spring, Dana."

"What?" She blinked.

"I thought it was obvious and one of you would have figured it out by now. I had it built a number of years ago."

"Of course you did." She laughed.

"It was to be a training center."

"What happened?"

Darkness passed over Reece's face. "It still will be."

Dana looked toward the main cabin. "I can't wait to tell them."

"Don't. Please. I don't want them thinking I'm somebody I'm not."

"Somebody you're not? You're a world-famous photographer."

"No, I'm not that person anymore. That was a life I walked away from ten years ago."

"You don't own the galleries anymore?"

"No. I sold them for a very fair price."

"A new one just opened in Maui."

"I'd heard that." Reece lifted his camera and turned it on Dana. "Do you mind?"

She shook her head and the shutter fired before she was done.

"Do you miss the business?"

"Not at all. My love was never the shops or the business or the money. It was photos. It's being there live, seeing it, experiencing it, storing the moment in my soul."

Reece pointed to his eyes. "These are the most sophisticated cameras ever designed." He tapped his camera. "This can't come within a light-year of what our eyes experience."

"So that's the best part for you?"

"Without question, the rush comes from capturing an image at that perfect time, when the shadows and the light are at their most ideal. Capturing a moment of God's wasteful, lavish, extravagant artistry that he splashes across the earth every day."

"Wasteful?"

"Think of the most stunning sunset you've ever seen. It's there for a moment, then wiped from the sky minutes later. And he does it again and again and again. Have you ever asked why? Why such staggering beauty? Do we need it to live? To breathe? To eat? No. But he can't help it. It's his nature to pour out on us beauty that stirs our deepest longings and desires." He paused and snapped another shot of her.

"Stop that."

"When I find a captivating subject it's hard to resist." Reece gazed at the river. "It's why I believe God's greatest gift to us is sight. I would miss the smell of piñon wood crackling in the fire pit. I would miss hearing the sparrow's song. I would miss being able to hike through thick groves of Douglas fir or touch the dew on the grass on a summer morning. I would miss not being able to speak, but I would struggle to live without my eyes."

"I feel exactly the same." Dana took her photos for the same reasons. But she'd never heard it expressed so eloquently. Reece said he didn't have a way with words. He was wrong. Dana glanced at his camera again, then at the river and the cliffs and the grounds of the ranch and laughed.

"What's funny?"

"I just realized something. All those photos in the cabin. You took them, didn't you?"

Reece held up his hands. "Guilty once again."

"They're gorgeous."

"Thanks, Dana. My passion has been revealed."

"I'll keep it silent." She stood and pointed at the river. "I think you missed your moment when the light was perfect."

"I have a very strong feeling God will spill his lavish beauty on us all again tomorrow wherever we might be." Reece glanced at his watch. "I need to go. We leave soon and I have to shut down the ranch."

✦✦✦

Reece closed his eyes and tried to sleep as they bumped along at thirty-five thousand feet on the way back to Seattle. He rubbed his face and stared at the thick clouds surrounding the plane. Symbolic. In a few hours the real battle would begin. *Bring your light, Lord.*

The time at the ranch had gone as well as he could have expected. Brandon and Dana seemed to be working together. But there was more work to be done there. Would they choose life when the chance came? The professor had stepped into the magic and embraced it. But the darkness of his regrets still hung over Marcus. Still held him back. And the darkness over Reece's own soul had lifted little.

You killed them.

He pushed the thought out of his mind and sank into a fitful sleep.

After picking up their luggage at baggage claim at Sea-Tac Airport, Reece gathered the three together.

"A final thought before we part." Reece paused to look deep into their eyes. "In C. S. Lewis's story *The Silver Chair,* two children stand at the end of the world in Aslan's country. The Great Lion is about to send them into Narnia to carry out a crucial quest. He gives the girl, Jill, four signs that will guide them. Before he sends them he says, 'Here on the mountain the air is clear and your mind is clear; as you drop down into Narnia the air will thicken. Take great care that it does not confuse your mind.'

"You're coming off the mountain and about to enter into the second phase of your training. Stay strong in prayer. Your spiritual sense is more attuned now, but that means the attack of the nameless ones will also increase. Be on guard." Reece hefted his pack over his shoulder.

"We meet again on Sunday to go to church together?" Marcus said.

"Yes. It's time to immerse ourselves in religion."

"Religion?" Brandon asked.

"It's time for you to observe the greatest enemy of the church firsthand and experience religion in all its glory."

"What does that mean?" Dana pulled her light brown hair back behind her head.

"At this service I suspect at least one of you will experience something you'll never forget."

"Which one of us?" Marcus asked.

"I don't know." Reece pushed his hat down farther onto his head. "For some reason the Spirit doesn't tell me everything." He winked. "But he did say one of you would have your eyes opened so wide, you'll think they've stretched out to the sides of your head."

"I have the sensation it will be me," Marcus said.

"Then get prayed up. If it is you, the curtain is about to be yanked back, and the wizard you'll likely see behind it is a bit more ominous than the one from Oz."

TWENTY-SIX

MARCUS ARRIVED IN THE PARKING LOT OF HILLCREST Creek Community Church fifteen minutes before the service was scheduled, and once again he tried to shake the feeling he was about to see things he wasn't ready for. He tapped the power button on his steering wheel and Brandon stopped singing to him through the car's speakers about living fully alive. Pretty fun to have become allies with a man he'd listened to for years.

Marcus wasn't sure why it rankled him to imagine he would be the one chosen to see deeper into the spiritual world. Maybe because the pace Reece had set for their spiritual discoveries was approaching light speed, and Marcus's brain needed more time to process what they'd found. Yes, part of him wanted to accelerate as fast as Reece, but another part wanted to take the time to analyze what had happened. At the same time the taste of God's magnificence he'd seen so far drew him like he was underwater swimming toward the surface and running out of air. If this morning would bring more of the same, he would be ready.

More cars filled the lot and scads of families got out of their vehicles and traipsed into the church—Mom and Dad pressed and polished, little boys in matching shirts and slacks, and little girls in flowered dresses to complement the rare sun-drenched June morning.

Marcus glanced around the lot. He didn't see any of the others. Wait. There. At the far end of the lot he spotted Reece's beat-up

Avalanche. A moment later he swung the door open and stepped onto the blacktop.

Reece was dressed in his typical jeans and an old sport coat over a Jimi Hendrix T-shirt. At least he wasn't wearing his hat. Marcus got out of his car and ambled toward Reece.

"I'm glad to see you didn't overdress for this morning's service."

"I'm not good at pretending I'm someone I'm not." Reece smoothed his jeans. "Are you ready?"

"For what?"

"For what's going to happen in there. You felt you would be the one to see extraordinary things today."

"What am I supposed to do?"

"Ask the Spirit to show you exactly what he wants you to see. Give him rein over your mind and your heart and your spirit."

Ten minutes later Reece, Brandon, Dana, and he sat in a row toward the back of the church on soft blue chairs. The lighting was muted, big plants anchored each side of the large stage up front, and a huge polished wooden cross hung on the wall at the back of the stage.

At exactly ten o'clock the drummer in the group to the left of the stage smacked his sticks together three times and the band kicked into an instrumental piece most of the 1,200-plus congregation clapped along to. Four women and two men pranced onto the stage, picked up microphones, and launched into a song as blue and red and yellow lights flashed on and off around them.

After twenty minutes of worship and a few announcements about the annual summer picnic and an original play that would be performed a month later, the pastor of the church, dressed in a solid dark blue suit and crisp white shirt, clipped up the four stairs to the stage, set his Bible on the glass podium, and smiled as he glanced over the crowd.

"It is truly wonderful to have all of you here this morning. If you're here for the first time, I'd like to extend a special welcome and encourage you to fill out the visitor card in front of you." The pastor smiled—a warm, genuine smile that filled his face and reached his eyes.

"Before we dive into today's teaching, let me ask you an extremely important question." He paused and held out his arms. "Where does your strength come from?"

No one responded. The pastor grinned. "That was not a rhetorical question. I want to hear it from you. Where does your strength come from?" He opened his arms wide and stepped back and forth across the stage.

"The Lord!" someone a few rows back from the front cried out.

"Yes. That's right." The pastor continued to pace and held his hand up with his thumb and forefinger a few inches apart. "You're almost there, but there's more. Think about it. Where does your strength in the Lord come from? Anyone? Bueller, anyone?"

Some of the congregation chuckled—probably only those in the over-forty crowd or those conversant in Matthew Broderick movies.

"Tell me, I want to hear it now." The pastor put his hand up to his ear and hopped on one leg.

"The joy!" a woman on Marcus's left called out.

"Now we're cooking on high." The pastor pointed toward the woman who had spoken. "That's right, the joy of the Lord. That's our strength. Today my prayer is you receive his joy in abundance." The pastor returned to the podium and opened his Bible. "Can I get an amen on that?"

A smattering of people called out "Amen," and the pastor smiled and nodded. "Let's try that one more time. Can I get an amen?"

This time it seemed "Amen" roared out of every mouth.

"All right." The pastor picked up his Bible and walked out from behind the podium. "Let's dive into God's Word and see what he has for us this morning."

Marcus turned to Reece. "Although the pastor is a bit over the top, at least he isn't lackluster."

"He's a good man trying to follow hard after Jesus. He listens to

God and tries to lead his flock well." Reece sighed and zeroed in on Marcus. "I want you to watch him closely. I think you'll see something in him few ever witness."

Marcus looked back up at the pastor who held his Bible out in front of him with one arm and motioned toward the crowd. "Will you stand with me now as we look into God's Word for guidance and discover truth for our lives?"

The congregation stood and Marcus and the others joined them.

"From the book of James, chapter 1, verse 27. 'Pure and undefiled religion in the sight of our God and Father is this: to visit orphans and widows in their distress, and to keep oneself unstained by the world.'

"Now turn with me to Proverbs, chapter 20, verse 1. There we read, 'Wine is a mocker, strong drink a brawler, and whoever is intoxicated by it is not wise.'"

Both verses flashed up on three massive screens along the back of the church in white letters on a sky-blue background, with the church logo in the lower right corner.

The pastor shut his Bible. "You may be seated."

As the congregation sat, something flashed in Marcus's peripheral vision to his left. In the aisle next to him—as well as in the two others farther to his left—stood three men. He glanced at the two aisles to his right. Same thing. They were evenly spaced. One man at the front of each aisle, one in the middle, and one at the back. They wore dark suits that complemented their thick brown and black hair. Average looking. Average height and weight. Ushers? Their hands were folded, their eyes fixed on the pastor.

Marcus leaned to his right and whispered to Reece, "Did I blink at the wrong moment, or did ushers just instantly appear in the aisles?"

Reece whispered back, "No, you didn't miss anything." He patted Marcus's shoulder. "Well done. Now watch closely. I'm guessing it's about to get interesting." Reece pointed at the pastor.

Marcus turned his attention to the man, who had just apparently delivered a particularly resounding part of his message because the congregation cheered.

"And I challenge you not to go to one R-rated movie the rest of this year!" The pastor slammed his fist against the podium, then turned and clipped back and forth across the stage like a rock star, whipping his audience into a frenzy. "Who is with me?" he shouted.

As Marcus stared at the pastor, something grew on his back. Something made of cloth? No, it was a thick material, colored dark green and red. Then straps grew out of the top of it and around the front of the pastor, over his shoulders, and under his arms.

A moment later Marcus knew exactly what it was. An oversized backpack stuffed so full it was surprising the seams didn't split. The pastor staggered under the weight of the pack but kept his footing as he lurched toward the front of the stage. Then something else materialized around the pastor's neck. Thick ropes—three or four at least—with overflowing bottles of water hanging off the ends. As the bottles materialized, the pastor's head dipped down and he seemed to have trouble breathing.

Heat rushed through Marcus as he realized what he was seeing. He'd prayed for his eyes to be opened; Reece had said it was going to happen. But this?

Marcus closed his eyes and breathed deep. When he opened them the pastor was again bounding across the stage; the backpack and ropes and bottles of water had vanished.

"Will you join me? Will you accept the challenge? Maybe alone you don't think you can do this. But together—if we join together and hold each other accountable—we can!"

He raised his arms high and shook his finger at the sky. "Between him and me and you, we will have victory!

"Now look in front of you. There are special cards in the back of the seats. On them you'll see a line that says *Not One Sip*. Below that line you'll see *Not One Movie*. All you have to do is check the boxes, write your name down, and slip it into the offering basket when it's passed."

The pastor stopped and placed his hands on either side of the podium and lowered his voice. "If you're with me, grab one of those cards now."

Marcus closed his eyes a second time. *Jesus, I am on the far side of comfortable, but I'm willing to go deeper if you want to take me there.*

When he opened them, the backpack had returned and the pastor held on to the podium with both hands, his fingers turning white from the death grip he must have had on it to keep from falling over. An instant later backpacks appeared on the backs of at least half of the people in the room. Some bulged. Some were empty. Some were filled only slightly.

Then a figure shifted in the corner of Marcus's eye. It was one of the ushers. He walked toward a man who had his hand raised and had turned toward the aisle. When he reached the man, the usher held out two stones. The one in his right hand was large, the size of a grapefruit. The one in his left was massive, as big as the biggest watermelon Marcus had ever seen.

The man on the aisle stood and took off his backpack, set it on the chair, and unzipped it. Then he turned back and glanced between the two stones, reached out his hand, and rubbed the surface of both. Finally he grasped the watermelon-sized stone with both hands and hefted it off the usher's palm. His arms jerked downward with the weight of the stone and he staggered forward.

The usher in the dark suit grasped his shoulder with both hands till the man regained his balance. The man said something to the usher. From the movement of his lips it looked like "Thank you."

Marcus pulled his gaze away from this bizarre exchange and glanced around the room. All over the same thing was happening. Men and women choosing stones and placing them into their backpacks or having the ushers do it for them.

The pastor continued to pound out his message. "I challenge you to take not even a *sip* of alcohol for the rest of this year. I know many of you haven't touched alcohol in years. Praise God that you haven't. But many of you sitting here do imbibe on a regular basis.

Every night you're toasting your spouse or your friends with the mocker, the brawler."

More people raised their hands and the ushers moved to them like tigers stalking prey as the pastor continued.

"What good can come of drink? Men, do you really need to have that beer with the game? Because it's not a beer, is it? It's two beers, three beers, four beers. Can you tell me you'd be having those beers if the Lord was sitting watching the game with you? Really? Of course not.

"Am I telling you what to do? No. That's for you and God to decide. But tell me if my words aren't ringing true inside you at this very moment."

The weight in the pastor's pack seemed to increase. Sweat ran in rivulets down his face but his voice didn't waver. He grabbed the sides of the podium and took a few seconds to stare at each section of the congregation.

"Yes. I can see it in your eyes. You're ready. Ready to make a commitment to God." He held his fist up. "No R-rated movies this year."

He slammed his hand on the podium again. "No alcohol." One more slam.

Reece turned to Marcus. "Go."

"Go where?"

"Walk up there, to one of the ushers. You need to see what's happening up close."

"I don't believe this is the kind of pastor who would welcome an approach up the aisle in the middle of his sermon."

"That's very true. Good observation." Reece waved his hand toward the aisle. "Now go."

"I think you missed my point about the pastor. Which is why I can't do what you're suggesting."

"It's not a suggestion." Reece pointed toward the front of the church. "Go."

"He'll see me along with the entire congregation."

"No, he won't."

He stared at Reece. The man's face was like granite.

"Do you trust me, Marcus?"

"Yes, I do, but—"

"Then go. Now."

Marcus flipped his hands palms up and snapped them. "Do you have any counsel on what to say when the pastor asks for a reason for my actions?"

"Yes. Don't quench the Spirit. Stay with the vision. Don't analyze what you're seeing and don't worry about the pastor. If he sees you, what's the worst that can happen? He'll ask you to go back and sit down or ask you to leave. You don't know anyone here, so if it happens why would it matter? Just go."

Marcus glanced at Dana, who frowned, then rose from his chair slower than a hydraulic jack and took a tentative step into the aisle, then one step forward and stopped. He turned to look at Reece. The big man jabbed his finger at the stage.

Marcus heard Brandon whisper, "Where's he going?" Reece told him to stay silent.

The pastor stared directly at him. Marcus froze. But the preacher continued the sweep of his gaze to the far side of the congregation as he rambled on.

"Ladies, do you really need that glass of wine when you get home each night? Do you really need that margarita when you go out with your girlfriends for a night out? No! So join us, won't you?"

How could the guy not have seen him? Was it possible? Marcus took molasses-covered steps forward till he reached the dark-haired usher a few rows from the stage. The man turned with bright eyes and smiled. His teeth had to be professionally whitened. "Can I help you?"

Heat flashed through Marcus's body. He spun to find Reece but he had his head down.

"You can see me?" he whispered to the man.

"Yes. Of course I can." The usher flashed another wide smile. "What can I do for you?"

"But the pastor can't see me. Or the congregation."

"They don't have the eyes you have with which to see."

"What kind of eyes are those?"

"Ones of enlightenment."

"Are you and the rest"—Marcus gestured toward the rest of the dark-suited men dotting the auditorium—"angels?"

"Yes." The man smiled again, even wider this time. "We are."

Marcus stared at the man. Unbelievable. Just like Gideon and Jacob and Mary and all the others—he was seeing them. Talking to one.

"I'm gazing into the spiritual realm. You're doing something for these people that can only be seen in the spirit."

"That's exactly right."

"What is the purpose of the stones? Why weigh people down with them?"

"Excuse me." The usher shoveled another stone the size of a basketball into the backpack of a young woman a few seats closer to the front of the church. "As you can see, I am exceedingly busy at the moment, so this isn't the best time to chat. Can we find some time later? Thanks so much for your understanding."

"Are there more of your kind of angels in other churches?"

"I'm sorry, I just don't have the time at the moment to converse. So I'd be grateful if you'd go back to your chair immediately, okay?" The man smiled and nodded as if that were the end of the conversation. He turned and pulled a stone the size of a grapefruit from out of nowhere and handed it to a middle-aged man to his left.

"Answers would be greatly appreciated."

"As I said, this is not the time or the place. I have work to do." The man offered a baseball-sized stone to a teenager, who looked like a young Mick Jagger. The teen snatched it out of the usher's hand and stuffed it into his pack.

"Enjoy," the usher said to the teen.

The teen nodded three times, then turned back to the pastor, and the usher turned to Marcus. "By the way, it would be best if you put what you've seen today out of your memory forever. Call it a dream, too much coffee this morning, whatever you like. Besides, who would believe you anyway?" The man took two paces down the aisle and pulled three more sizable rocks out of his pocket.

It didn't make sense. There was no way the rocks could have fit in the usher's pockets. It was like watching a magician pull doves out of nowhere. But this wasn't physical; it was spiritual. The usher displayed the stones for a woman who looked to be in her midseventies. The woman squeezed them as if she were trying to find a ripe pear and settled on the one in the middle.

Marcus staggered up to the usher. "I don't understand. How is it no one else can see me except you?"

"You are starting to irritate me, Marcus."

"You know my name."

"I know a great deal about you. And I realize you like to examine every mystery completely as good physics professors do, which is the reason you're persisting in bringing my level of irritation to a point it normally does not reach. But since I like you, I will exercise patience and politely ask you one more time to leave me alone."

"What do the stones represent?"

"Have your buddy Reece explain it to you. Now, please, leave me."

"Why is the pastor—?"

"Hang on for just a moment, Marcus."

The usher shoved the rock the lady had chosen into her backpack, patted it once, then turned, stood straight, and moved his face to within an inch of Marcus's.

"Listen closely." The usher pointed at his lips. "I've tried to be kind. But you obviously don't understand that method of communication." Lightning seemed to flash across the man's eyes. "So let me be extremely clear. If you don't get the hell out of here right now, I will personally bring a nightmare into your dreams tonight that will make every horror movie you've ever seen look like *Sesame Street*, then fry your brain so completely you won't remember how to feed yourself."

A wave of frigid air seemed to pass through Marcus's chest and his heart felt like it was being crushed in a vise. He stumbled backward and bumped the edge of the seat behind the woman. The little girl in the seat glanced into the aisle with a puzzled look on her face.

Marcus jerked backward two more steps, his gaze locked onto the usher—who obviously wasn't an usher. Marcus grabbed his legs hard to try to stop them from shaking, but he probably would have had more luck stopping a jackhammer from moving. After two more steps, he turned and stumbled back to the row Reece, Brandon, and Dana sat in. When he reached them, he lurched forward and caught himself on Brandon's chair at the edge of the aisle.

"Are you okay, bro?" Brandon stared up at him. "Why'd you go up there?"

"He's fine." Reece rose and scooted past Dana and Brandon, grabbed Marcus's arm, and led him to the back of the church where they leaned against the wall.

"How are you holding up?" Reece said in a hushed voice.

"I . . . I . . ." Sweat trickled down his back. "That wasn't real. It wasn't real."

"You know it was real."

"What was he?" Marcus ran his hands up his face and over his head. "What are all of them?"

"I think you know exactly what they are."

"Demons." Marcus clenched his hands so hard his knuckles turned white.

"Yes."

"He said he was an angel."

"Technically demons are angels."

"We have to leave here." Marcus shifted from one foot to the other and glanced to his right at the double glass doors leading to the parking lot.

"It's okay. Greater is he that is in you, yes?"

Marcus sucked in and blew out his breaths in rapid succession.

"How can they be inside a church? There's no . . . it doesn't make sense."

"They love being in church. Church is often the most fertile breeding ground for religion."

Marcus steeled himself and glanced at the aisles. "Demons can't be in a church."

"So Satan can be in the presence of God, but demons can't be in a church? You gotta start reading the Bible, pal. Things will make a lot more sense."

"I do read the Bible."

"Uh-huh."

"You're referring to Job." Marcus slid down the wall and sat on the floor.

"Very good." Reece joined him on the beige carpet and tapped out a slow rhythm on his knees. "Maybe it's not so much a matter of your reading the Bible as it is choosing whether or not to believe what it says."

"But no one can see them. And the rocks the people are taking . . ." Beads of perspiration broke out on his forehead.

"Deep breath, Marcus." Reece demonstrated by pulling in a long breath of air of his own. "On second thought, take two deep breaths, or three."

"Is that an attempt to make me smile so I don't sprain my mind?"

"Something like that."

"I don't understand why the rest of the congregation was unable to see what I saw."

"Don't be so surprised. It's been going on around you all of your forty-two years, but you've never seen it before this morning."

Fifteen minutes later Marcus stood in the parking lot with Reece, Dana, and Brandon, still trying to process what had happened, the bright noon sun a welcome sight after what he'd experienced. A shiver ran down his back. What had Reece said? That his mind would be blown? That was an understatement. But emotions of the incident were fading and his logical mind was taking over. Reece was right. The Bible was peppered with stories like the one that just happened to him. His eyes had been pried open.

Marcus stared at Reece. "We have to tell the pastor what transpired in there."

"If someone had come to you before today with the story of what you just saw, what would you think? How would you respond?"

Marcus shook his head. "I still think we should try."

"Maybe. Maybe someday." Reece patted Marcus's shoulder.

Dana reached over and placed her hand on Marcus's arm. "What did you see?"

Brandon folded his arms. "And what were you doing up toward the front in the middle of the service?"

Marcus rubbed his lips and shook his head again. "I saw a slew of demons. Three in each aisle of that church. And I conversed with one of them."

Dana and Brandon stared at him as if he'd turned into a gigantic, fanged Easter bunny—a mixture of surprise and terror.

"What? During the service?" Brandon said.

"Where were we when all this happened?" Dana asked.

Marcus clasped his hands behind his head and squinted into the sunlit clouds above.

Brandon cocked his head. "You're serious, you really saw them?"

Reece glanced at the people milling around them as they strolled to their cars. "I'm thinking we should talk about this someplace else. Anyone up for a bite to eat?"

"Lunch?" Marcus pointed toward the church doors. "I don't have much of an appetite."

"Good call, I'm starving," Brandon said.

Reece turned to his right. "Dana?"

"Famished."

"Great. How about Mexican? Las Margaritas in Woodinville?"

Brandon and Dana nodded.

Marcus frowned. "I'm not hungry, or did you all miss that?"

"We didn't miss it, Professor." Brandon threw his arm around

Marcus's shoulders. "But since you're the one the adventure happened to, you'll be doing the talking so you won't have time to eat."

As Brandon and Dana walked to their cars, Reece smiled at Marcus. "It's a good idea to debrief, and"—he moved his head in Brandon and Dana's direction—"they need to know what happened."

"All right. That's fine." He and Reece walked across the parking lot to their cars. "I get the whole demon stuff and religion thing and the backpacks and the stones. But please explain to me how the pastor looked right through me."

"With pleasure." Reece clapped him on the back. "We'll talk about that at the restaurant as well."

"Do you want to give me a hint I can mull over on the way there?"

"The professor has found a puzzle he can't solve and wants a clue?"

"Exactly."

They reached Marcus's car and Reece rested a hand on the hood. "Think about *Star Wars Episode IV*. That should get you started."

TWENTY-SEVEN

THE CLINK OF SILVERWARE, THE CLANK OF THICK glasses, and the smell of chimichangas and frying fajitas seemed to calm the professor, Dana decided. The frantic expression he displayed in the church parking lot had been replaced by a look of mixed puzzlement and concentration, as if he was trying to apply Occam's razor to what had happened inside the church. She smiled. Marcus would probably be impressed she knew what Occam's razor was.

After they ordered, Dana tapped her fist lightly on the back of Marcus's hand as it rested on the table. "Ready to regale us with your amazing tale?"

"Yes."

Marcus described what happened and when he finished, questions poured out of Dana's mouth and Brandon joined her.

"You're sure they were demons?"

"The one you talked to. What did he sound like?"

"Did anyone not have a backpack?"

"How did you stop yourself from freaking out?"

When Brandon asked why the pastor hadn't seen Marcus, the professor's eyes lit up and he pointed at Reece. "That's precisely what I want to know. Please explain how I could walk down the middle of that church and have no one see me."

"Mass hypnosis," Brandon said.

Reece took a chip and used it to scoop up a liberal portion of salsa from the small brown bowl in the center of the table. "The Spirit covered his eyes."

"He was blinded?"

"Yep. As well as the rest of the congregation."

"That's impossible."

"Clearly," Brandon said.

Their waiter brought their food and after Reece blessed it, he tapped the tips of his fingers together. "I'm confused. I thought we established that all of you have read the Bible."

"Oh, okay." Brandon spread guacamole and sour cream on his chicken enchiladas. "You mean where it tells us where to pick up our invisibility cloak? I looked up that verse the other day. Second Rowling, chapter 3, verse 16—if memory serves."

"The idea wasn't original with J. K."

"Right, right, it's in the gospel according to Obi-Wan Kenobi?" Brandon smiled. "You're ripping off a page right out of *Star Wars*."

"No. Lucas was ripping off God and didn't even know it."

"How so?"

"As I've already said, everything that has been created came from God. Everything. All Satan can do is imitate and counterfeit."

Dana took a drink of her root beer. "*Star Wars*? I'm lost."

"Don't tell me you've never seen *Star Wars*." Brandon cut off a large bite of his enchilada. "We never watched those together?"

"I saw each movie. One time." She glanced at Brandon. "Yes, with you. That was plenty. So forgive me if I didn't memorize every scene."

Brandon rubbed his hands together. "There's this scene in *Episode IV*—the first movie—where Obi-Wan waves his hand and says, 'These aren't the ones you're looking for,' or something like that, and the soldiers couldn't see Han Solo—"

"Han Solo? Try Luke," Marcus muttered.

"Hmm." Dana raised her eyebrows. "So I'm not the only one without a perfect memory."

Brandon scowled at her. "The point is Obi-Wan confused their minds. They should have seen it was him but they didn't."

Marcus turned to Reece. "Is that what you're saying? You waved your hand, which caused them to no longer see what was right in front of them?"

"The Spirit did it. Not me."

"But you initiated the process and created a scenario where I was rendered undetectable to everyone in that room."

"I think we've already established that."

"I missed that lesson in Sunday school," Brandon said.

"Too bad." Reece took a massive bite of his nachos.

"So are you going to tell us where you think this is in the Bible?" Dana said.

"Ib eeding."

"And talking while you're chewing," Dana said. "That's delightful."

"Look it up on your phone." Reece wiped his mouth. "Luke chapter 4, verses 20 through 30."

Brandon fumbled with his phone and thirty seconds later held it up. "Got it."

"Read." Reece took another bite.

Brandon held his phone close to his face. "'Then he rolled up the scroll, gave it back to the attendant and sat down. The eyes of everyone in the synagogue were fastened on him. He began by saying to them, "Today this scripture is fulfilled in your hearing."

"'All spoke well of him and were amazed at the gracious words that came from his lips. "Isn't this Joseph's son?" they asked.

"'Jesus said to them, "Surely you will quote this proverb to me: 'Physician, heal yourself!' And you will tell me, 'Do here in your hometown what we have heard that you did in Capernaum.'

"'"Truly I tell you," he continued, "no prophet is accepted in his hometown. I assure you that there were many widows in Israel in Elijah's time, when the sky was shut for three and a half years and there was a severe famine throughout the land. Yet Elijah was not sent to any of them, but to a widow in Zarephath in the region of Sidon. And there were many in Israel with leprosy in the time of Elisha the prophet, yet not one of them was cleansed—only Naaman the Syrian."

"'All the people in the synagogue were furious when they heard this. They got up, drove him out of the town, and took him to the brow of the hill on which the town was built, in order to throw him off the cliff. But he walked right through the crowd and went on his way.'"

"Must be the wrong translation. I didn't really pick up on the verse in there where Jesus turns invisible." Brandon set his phone down on the table. "Anything else you want me to look up?"

"No, that covers it." Reece took a long drink of his Dr Pepper and looked at Marcus. "Now do you understand?"

"Not exactly," the professor said.

"I'm still lost as well," Dana said.

"Make that three," Brandon added.

"Read verse 30 again."

Brandon picked up his phone and poked at the screen. "'He walked right through the crowd and went on his way.'"

"Think about it." Reece placed both palms on the table. "How do you think he did that? Are you kidding me? Why didn't they see him? He simply walks away like he's on a stroll through the park?"

Reece grabbed a bottle of hot sauce and spread it on his nachos. "Please explain to me how a crowd of people has a guy cornered on a cliff ready to throw him off of it, and suddenly—*poof!*—he turns around and walks right through the middle of all of them? How did that happen? Did he point at something on the horizon and say, 'Holy cow! What's that?' then race off while they were looking in the other direction?"

Reece took another bite of his nachos, staring at each of them as he chewed. "Here's a man who can make blind men see and you're surprised he can make seeing men blind?"

"Might I view that?" Marcus reached for Brandon's phone and stared at the screen. "They have him on the cliff, ready to push him off, so he must have . . . he had to . . . he must have . . ."

"He must have what? Stay with it. Ignore your mind. What is

your spirit telling you? You just did the same thing in that church service. Tell me, what did Jesus do?"

"He . . ." Marcus shook his head. "I can't believe I'm going to say this."

"Say it."

"He must have made himself unable to be seen somehow."

"Exactly."

"Are you insinuating you can do the same thing?"

"No. Not me. Like I already said, the Spirit does it." Reece pulled his cell phone out of his pocket. "But we can tap into that power, yes."

Reece grabbed another chunk of nachos. "What's the deal with you three? Have you been studying only the boring parts of the Bible?"

"I've read that verse so many times, but have never seen that," Dana said.

"In John's gospel Jesus says, 'Believe me: I am in my Father and my Father is in me. If you can't believe that, believe what you see—these works. The person who trusts me will not only do what I'm doing but even greater things . . .'

"Jesus raises people from the dead, walks on water, walks through walls, keeps Peter, James, and John from recognizing him on that beach after he was resurrected, and he says we'll do the same things he did." Reece pushed his plate away. "I'm thinking we should believe him. Peter did. Remember when he escaped prison in Acts chapter 12? He strolled out of jail right past two guards."

Reece paused and looked at each of them. "The Bible says Jesus isn't the same today as he was yesterday? Is that how the verse goes? Nay. I think not. I think he's the same."

Dana sat stunned. What could she say? What could any of them say to refute Reece's little speech? The look on Brandon's and Marcus's faces and the silence on their lips told her they were jumping through the same flaming mental hoops. But it was impossible. Wasn't it?

"The arrogance of man is that he thinks he can explain the universe. And the church thinks they can explain God." Reece shook his head. "It's comical. Go back and look at the science books from one hundred years ago. Even fifty years ago."

Reece motioned to their waiter for the check, then glanced at the professor. "You know this better than any of us, Marcus. Much of the content is laughable. And people fifty years from now will laugh at many of the things we swallow so, uh, blindly. Go back and look at the things the church has believed through the ages. We don't have it all figured out."

The waiter arrived and Reece handed him a Visa card. "You're all discovering the power of God's Spirit. What it can reveal. How it can heal. How it can bring freedom to your lives. This coming week watch for chances to bring those things to the lives of others."

He put his thumb and forefinger up to his eyelids and stretched them wide. "There are chances in every moment if we have eyes to see."

"When do we meet again?" Dana said.

Brandon tossed his napkin on the table. "I have a couple of concerts this week, so I'm out till next Sunday."

Reece took their bill from the waiter and scrawled his name. "I'm not sure about our next meeting. I'm praying about it. I'll let you know."

As Dana drove home she spun through the faces of the people she worked with at the station and imagined what God might show her about them. But the face that stuck wasn't one of her coworkers. It was an image of Marcus's wife from the photo she'd seen at Well Spring. But Kat's face was no longer smiling. It was full of fear.

TWENTY-EIGHT

KAT AMBER PUSHED HER BLUETOOTH TO ANSWER THE call coming in from Marcus. "How was the church service?"

"Enlightening would be a vast understatement."

"Really?" She pushed her auburn hair back over her shoulders. "Would you like to describe it for me?"

"It was a continuation of the trajectory Reece started for us at Well Spring."

"I'm still not convinced Reece didn't slip something into your drinks out there in Colorado and you're imagining all these things."

"You're not serious."

She smiled. "Of course not, but you have to admit it's out there, even for you."

"But you believe me."

"Yes, but give me a little room for some skepticism, okay? I've only had two days to digest what you've told me."

"Fair enough. And tonight I'll give you all the details of the latest revelation. It was truly a staggering experience."

Kat glanced at the clock on the dashboard of her Toyota. She was going to be late. "Was it good or bad?"

"A little of both."

"What's wrong?"

"Just keep your eyes open," Marcus said, and the words seemed to echo through Kat's Bluetooth.

"What does that mean?" Kat sped down 35th toward the soccer fields and glanced at the clock again.

Marcus started to speak, then stopped. "Our little band of warriors has been delving into areas the enemy cannot be pleased about."

"You hesitated. You were about to say something else."

"I'm just thinking about the girls."

"What about?"

"That the enemy might come after them."

"You're scaring me, Marcus."

"Like I said, keep your eyes open. I'll see you at home this evening."

Kat half jogged, half walked to the soccer field where Abbie would be waiting for her. Kat was only a few minutes late, but she didn't like her thirteen-year-old daughter being alone too long after practice ended. And now, with Marcus's words ringing in her ears, the uneasy feeling in her mind escalated.

Kat scanned the sideline where a few kids and parents milled about, talking to the coaches. Abbie wasn't among them. *Don't panic. She's here.* There, on the other sideline holding two soccer balls and talking to a man with dark brown hair of average height and weight. He wore a dark blue sweatsuit and a whistle around his neck.

"Abbie!"

She waved, said something to the man, and jogged over.

"Who was that?"

"He said he was an assistant coach for the Raptors and came out to scout our team, you know?"

The man strolled toward the far end of the field.

"Said?" Kat stared at the worry darting across Abbie's face. "You don't believe him?"

"I don't remember him . . ." Abbie dropped the soccer balls and nosed one of them with her foot. "And I know all the coaches for the Raptors. We all do. We've played 'em enough times."

"Maybe he's new."

"Maybe."

"What else?"

"It was kinda weird." Abbie shifted her weight and dropped her eyes. "He said knee and ankle injuries happened a lot of times to girl soccer players. And that sometimes accidents happen off the field too. It felt like he was talking about me."

A wave of heat washed over Kat and she laid her hand on Abbie's shoulder. "I want you to hang out here for a few minutes. I'm going to go have a conversation with this supposed coach."

She looked up to where the man had been a moment earlier, but he was gone. Kat glanced around the field and at the parking lot, but the man had vanished. Her breathing quickened.

"Where'd he go?" Abbie stared up at her, gray eyes worried.

"He must have jogged off. Let's go talk to your coach."

"Hey, Kat," the coach said when they reached her. "Abbie's looking good out there."

"Thanks, she's loving this season."

Kat pointed across the field to where the man and Kat had talked. "Coach, do you know the man my daughter was talking to a few minutes ago?"

"I was going to ask Abbie the same question." The coach bent over, picked up one of the ball bags at her feet, and opened it, and Abbie tossed her soccer balls inside.

"He said he was an assistant coach for the Raptors."

"Then he's lying." The coach glanced over to where the man had stood with Abbie. "There are creeps everywhere, Kat. I'll be keeping my eyes wide open. I'm thinking you and Abbie should do the same."

TWENTY-NINE

DANA STEPPED THROUGH THE STATION'S GLASS DOORS at seventy thirty on Monday morning and sent a silent prayer skyward as she clipped past the front desk toward her office. *Give me eyes to see today.* She repeated the prayer at nine. And eleven. And again at one. Nothing.

An ordinary day slid by with ordinary rate negotiations and ordinary clients and ordinary salespeople brainstorming on the same problems they brainstormed every day. And miracle of miracles, her budget deficit had shrunk while she was gone—far from enough—but enough that she would sleep better tonight than she had in a while. Maybe this was God's plan. A day of respite.

The only item skewing from the norm was Dana's strange desire for water and how it coincided with Toni's trips past her office. Had her breakfast and lunch been overly salty? No. She hadn't eaten breakfast that morning and lunch had been a Cobb salad, with just a pinch of salt on the eggs. But every time Toni walked by her door, Dana felt like she'd just finished an hour on the treadmill without a drop of H_2O.

At three that afternoon, Toni skipped into her office and slid into the chair in front of Dana's desk. Dana held up her finger, grabbed the water bottle to her right, and took three huge gulps.

"Thirsty today?" Toni bobbed her head back and forth.

"Very. Don't ask why because I don't know."

"Gotta second?"

"Sure."

As Toni explained the promotion she wanted to do for the station in the fall, Dana continued to guzzle the water. Toni stopped turning the pages of her proposal, put her hands on her hips, and cocked her head. "Build an ark, baby. You're going to float away, girl."

"I know, it's weird. I don't know what's going on with me today."

As Dana set down the bottle, her vision blurred and a picture of a dried-out, dying sunflower filled her mind. The ground around the base of the flower was cracked and a trickle of water ran off to the side, too far away to bring moisture to the wilting plant. A man stood in the distance, arms folded, a scowl on his face. The picture faded and Toni's face came back into focus. The puzzle pieces snapped into place. The Lord had been speaking to her all day.

Dana turned and stared out her windows at the Space Needle and whispered to herself, "That's Toni, isn't it?"

"What did you say?"

She turned back to Toni. "Nothing."

"You said, 'That's Toni, isn't it?'"

Dana stared at her.

"What is me?"

"I, uh . . ."

"What's me, girl?"

Dana rose from her chair, went to her office door, and closed it. She smoothed her blouse and her skirt and eased back over to her desk and returned to her seat. *Here we go.*

"Are you okay, sweetie?"

"I'm really good." Dana hesitated, then leapt off the cliff. "But I don't think you are."

Toni frowned. "I'm great. What are you talking about?"

"You're not great. You're hurting inside."

"What have you been smoking?" Toni crossed her legs and squinted at Dana like she was crazy. "I'm fine."

"I don't think you are."

"Listen, if you have something you gotta say, spit it out."

"We've been friends for a long time, so the moment you tell me to stop talking about this, I will."

Toni bit her upper lip and folded her arms. "Go ahead."

Dana leaned forward and rested her elbows on her desk. "I think you're dying inside. You're this flower always full of sun and brightness for everyone around you, but you're drying up. The ground around is cracked but no one knows it."

Toni's eyes went wide and her head fell back. Then forward. And the dam broke. Tears came and didn't stop. From Toni, one of the strongest women Dana knew. Toni, whom she'd known for three years and had never seen cry. They sat in the tears and silence for at least five minutes till Toni's voice rose into the stillness like a sparrow taking evening flight.

"Where are you getting this stuff?"

"You wouldn't believe me." Dana leapt further. "You give so much to everyone around you. And most of all to your husband. But he never gives you water."

More tears. "I'll believe you."

"The Spirit of God told me—showed me."

"I don't believe you."

Dana laughed and Toni joined in with a mix of laughing and crying. Dana rose again, eased over, sat on the armrest of Toni's chair, and wrapped her arms around her friend's shoulders. And let her friend cry. After enough time had slid by for the sun to have moved beyond Dana's windows, Toni patted Dana's hand.

"I think I just moved from I don't believe in God to I might someday."

Dana hugged her friend and smiled. "I love you, Toni. And you'll get through it. We'll get through it."

Toni squeezed back and it wasn't Toni, it was God's hand, and soon Dana's tears joined those of her friend.

That night Dana sat in her study with an oil lamp providing a soft light as she studied the Gospels, seeing Jesus in a way she'd never seen him. Her emotions bounced from ones of wonder to determination to press further in, but in the end a sense of foreboding settled over her. Reece said the people on the front lines were the first ones shot at in any war. Today with Toni she'd definitely been on the front line. And she couldn't shake the feeling a sniper rifle was pointed at her head.

THIRTY

BRANDON'S CELL PHONE WENT OFF AT EIGHT O'CLOCK ON Monday morning, and it was exactly the person he wanted to talk to. Kevin. He wanted to tell his manager about Well Spring and how powerful it had been. He stumbled into his kitchen and turned on the coffee, trying to figure out a way he could talk about the retreat without sounding nuts.

What would he say? "How's it been going? Well, this Reece character believes he can beam all over the place like in *Star Trek*, dive into people's souls like they're swimming pools, make ourselves invisible, have modern-day visions, and see demons in church aisles. Other than that, it was your typical, boring Bible study."

He answered on the fourth ring, and as the smell of fresh-brewed coffee filled his nose, he agreed to meet Kevin at Tully's at ten thirty.

When Brandon walked through the door of Tully's and glanced around the coffee shop for Kevin, his gaze stopped for a moment on a guy at the back of the room where he and Kevin usually sat who looked vaguely familiar. The man was mammoth—probably played for the Seahawks. Brandon continued his sweep of the place, but no Kevin. He went to the front counter and ordered a cinnamon frappuccino. Still no Kevin by the time the drink was ready, so he sauntered toward the back to find seats.

As he scanned the room for an open spot, his feet stopped as if he'd stepped in instantly drying Super Glue. In the exact spot where the linebacker had just sat was Kevin. A moment later Brandon's drink slipped out of his hand and crashed to the floor. His heart pounded as he fumbled to pick up his coffee—thank goodness the lid had stayed on—and watched his friend transform from his five-foot-nine manager into Thor.

Brandon set his coffee down, mashed the palms of his hands into his eyes, and pressed hard. He looked up and it happened again. Kevin was Kevin, then he wasn't. His manager was changing back and forth like a holographic book cover where you tilt it one way and you see one picture, then you tilt it another way and the image morphs into something completely different.

"What is this, Lord?" Brandon whispered to himself.

There is so much more strength in him than what he shows you. And so much more talent than even he knows himself.

Reece said they would start seeing into the spiritual realm, but Brandon didn't think it meant seeing things like this. Kevin spotted him and waved him over. As Brandon walked to the back of the coffee shop, the transformations stopped. But his pulse kept pounding away like the pistons on a stock car.

After he settled into his seat, Kevin pulled out a calendar and a packet of photos. "I need to firm up our concert schedule for next season, and there are a couple of dates I wasn't sure about. Then I need you to take a look at the shots from the photo shoot we did a few weeks back, because one of them is going on the cover of your next CD. Then I'd like to hear about your time out in Colorado with Guru Reece and Dana and the physics dude."

Brandon stared at Kevin. Why had he never seen how strong his friend was?

"Okay." He took a drink of his frappuccino. "Choose a good shot of me. I know you will. Schedule the dates and the cities how you think it will be best for everyone. I know you'll do a better job than I could. And I had a great time in Colorado."

Brandon placed his palms on Kevin's papers and slid them to the side. "Now I want to talk about another issue. Something important."

"What?"

"You." Brandon stared at his friend till Kevin laughed. "What's going on with you?"

"What are you talking about?" Kevin shook his head. "I'm scheduling tour dates, picking photos, and hanging with my friend." He held his two forefingers up and swirled them in a circle. "We're rocking."

"I'm serious."

"You want to talk about what's going on with me?"

"Yeah. In your life."

"I'm missing what you're driving at."

"You're an amazing manager, Kevin. I would be dead without you, both literally and figuratively, so don't take this the wrong way, but what would you be doing if you weren't working for me?"

Kevin slumped back in his chair. "Why are you asking me this?"

"It's important."

His manager's perpetual smile vanished and his eyes grew distant. "I'm not sure what I'd be doing."

"Really? How long will it take you to get sure?" Brandon leaned forward, elbows on the table. "Let me put it this way. If thirty million dropped in your lap tomorrow, what would you do with your days and nights?"

"I love what I do. I love being your manager. Truly. So that's what I'd do during the day."

"But if I didn't exist and you had that money, what would you do? Find another musician to manage?"

Kevin slid his finger around the rim of his coffee cup three times before answering. "It's not something I'm ready to talk about."

"Sorry, I don't care. It's something you need to talk about."

Kevin glanced around him, then lowered his voice. "Is this part of your guru-guy training? To get people to talk about things they don't want to discuss?"

"The truth is always worth a discussion."

Kevin tilted his head back and as he did, the vision of him

pumped up as some kind of Norse god reappeared, then vanished. "I want to do what you do."

"What?" Brandon pushed back and slapped both hands on the table.

"Yes."

"Do you really? Write songs? Sing? Do concerts, the whole thing?" Brandon shook his head and laughed.

"Is that funny?"

"No. It's the coolest and most amazing thing I've heard in, well, I heard some amazing things up at Well Spring . . . Shut up, Brandon. Yes, I think that's crazy cool."

Kevin looked up from under his glasses. "You're serious."

"Very. You're the package. You have the look, you've got the personality." Brandon held up his fingers in a square and looked through them as if they were the frame of a TV camera. "Just one question. Do you have any musical ability?"

"I don't know. I've dabbled at songwriting since I was a kid. And I've been singing even longer. But I've always thought I'd be like one of those kids on *American Idol* who everyone knows can't sing except themselves."

"I don't get it. Why have you never told me this?"

"I didn't know how you'd react."

"What?" Brandon opened his arms. "You thought I'd laugh at you? Tell you it was stupid?"

"Now that you say it, no."

Brandon flipped over Kevin's notepad and pulled out a pen and made notes. "First, you're going to play a few of your songs for me. Second, we'll record them with the full band. And third, if I like what you've got, we're going to start writing songs together." He ripped off the piece of paper and handed it to Kevin. "And we're going to do it soon."

Kevin sat with his mouth slightly open, his eyes growing moist. "I don't know what to say."

"Freedom, baby. It's all about being set free for those with eyes to see."

THIRTY-ONE

DANA WALKED INTO THE STATION LOBBY ON TUESDAY morning hoping for an uneventful day but knowing she wouldn't get it. The dread from the night before still hung on her like a thirty-pound block of ice. After a department head meeting and a promotions meeting, she stepped into her office and unloaded her briefcase. Fifteen red-flagged e-mails took her attention till ten thirty. She didn't remember having her next meeting till lunch but pulled up her calendar to be sure.

Dana frowned as she stared at her calendar. ALEXIS SOLIA 10:45 A.M.–11:30 A.M.

"Who is Alexis Solia, Rebecca?" Dana called through her door. "I don't remember that being on my calendar."

Rebecca appeared at Dana's door a moment later. "I set it up last Thursday while you were in Colorado, but I forgot to put it on your calendar till this morning. I'm sorry."

"No worries. Who is she with?"

"TBWA/Chiat/Day out of LA." Rebecca eased over to Dana's desk.

"What's the appointment for?"

"I'm assuming to talk to you about their national accounts and spending money on the stations."

"I like that thought. We could use the revenue in a big way."

That was an understatement. No significant buys came in while she was in Colorado, which meant they were seven days closer to the end of the quarter and only pennies closer to meeting budget. *Let this lady be ready to spend, Lord.*

As Rebecca clipped out of her office, Dana warmed her hands on her cup of coffee and tried to push the heaviness from her mind. A quick prayer helped, but not much. It felt like her mind and body had been slowed down to three quarters of her normal pace, and nothing she could do would speed things up.

This was probably what Reece had warned them about last Wednesday night at Well Spring. That anytime significant break-through happened, there would be resistance and the enemy would throw oppression at them. She pushed back from her desk and prayed again. But the fog remained.

Ten minutes later Rebecca poked her head around the corner. "Your appointment is here. Are you ready?"

"Almost. I need a little, uh, me-time. Can you wait three, then go get her?"

"Of course." She smiled and pulled Dana's door almost closed.

Dana closed her eyes and prayed again. For strength. For clarity. For covering. Peace was starting to come just as a knock on her door frame startled her. Rebecca stood with the woman who must be her appointment.

"May we come in?" Rebecca asked.

Dana stood and motioned them forward with both hands. "Yes, yes, please come in."

Rebecca waved at her behind the woman's back. "I'm out for a few errands. I'll be back in an hour or so."

Dana mouthed, "Okay," and turned and studied the woman. Tall, pleasant looking, but not beautiful. Dark brown hair, trim figure— she guessed the woman's age at midthirties. But whatever her perfume was, she must have showered in it. It reminded Dana of the smell of cotton candy that used to make her stomach turn at the Puyallup Fair when she was little.

"It's fascinating to see you from this perspective." The woman extended her hand. "I'm Alexis Solia."

Fascinating to see her from this perspective? That was one of the more bizarre greetings she'd ever had. Dana blinked away the frown that tried to rise and forced out a smile. "It's nice to meet you."

"You have a lovely work space." The woman smiled back as she continued to glance around Dana's office, then pointed to the photos above Dana's couch. "And those pictures are quite catching. They remind me of Colorado. Are they?"

Something in the woman's voice irritated Dana, but she couldn't pinpoint the reason. And she didn't like the way the woman said "catching" about the pictures she'd taken at Well Spring. What was wrong with her? This woman could easily put a significant dent in her deflated budget sheets.

"Thank you." Dana motioned toward the two chairs in front of her windows. "Would you like to meet in the conference room or here?"

"No, it needs to be in your office."

Needs to be? For an instant Dana felt like she did fifteen years back when she was fired from a waitressing job. "All right."

"Do you mind if we close your door?" It wasn't a question.

This lady was odd. What were they smoking down in California these days? "No, that's fine."

Dana didn't like this woman.

"Welcome to Seattle. Have you been here before?"

She went to Dana's windows and gazed out over the Seattle skyline. "Your city has grown a great deal since the last time I was here."

"When was that?"

"A long, long time ago."

She turned, but not fast enough to hide the smirk on her face.

"I see." Dana motioned to the chair across the coffee table from her. "Would you like to sit?"

"Yes, I would. Thank you very much."

They settled into their chairs and Dana crossed her legs. "I'm the one who should be saying thank you very much. The business your agency has placed with our stations in the past three years is greatly appreciated."

"We would like to increase our spending this year."

"Wonderful."

"Do you mind?" Alexis held up her purse.

"Mind what?"

She pulled a bag of Hershey's Kisses out of her purse and shook a handful into her palm. "I love to suck on these in meetings. They help me get more creative and more focused."

Alexis popped one in her mouth. "Your station is an excellent choice for us. The music you play creates a very receptive audience. We like that. It makes our job easier. Thank you."

"Your job? You mean it's a good match for the products you're advertising?"

The woman continued as if Dana hadn't spoken. "For example, currently we believe television and movies are the most powerful ways to influence culture and change opinions and sway the viewers to our way of thinking. And this is not limited to the young. Although the mature adult mind is less pliable and takes longer to move, it most assuredly can be repositioned."

"You sound like more than an ad agency. You sound like you want to change the world."

"We already have changed the world. And we will continue to change it. When you own the airwaves, it offers a great deal of leverage."

Own the—? Realization swept over Dana like a wave. How could she have been so blind?

Alexis squished the tinfoil from her chocolate into a ball and tossed it on the carpet to her left. "Now to business. We're ready to exceed your current budgetary goals by 10 percent for this quarter— and the rest of the year—but I need you to do something in exchange for me."

Dana stared at the woman as her throat tightened. She tried not to admit what her spirit was screaming. Something she'd sensed from the moment Alexis walked into her office.

"How do you know what my budgets are?"

"There's very little that can stay hidden with a public corporation." The woman popped another Kiss into her mouth. "If you know how to dig."

"What do you need me to do for you?"

"Stay away from Reece Roth."

"Say that again?"

The temperature in the room seemed to rise .

"You heard me."

"How do you know—?"

"The details of how I know Reece and what you're doing with him matter not at all. The salient point is I can more than meet your budget, keep you from getting fired, and make everyone happy."

"I think how you know Reece matters a great deal." *Be here, Jesus.* "You're more than just an ad exec at Chiat/Day."

"Is that where they told you I was from?" The woman cocked her head and popped two more Kisses into her mouth. "Did I mention I love these things? I never even knew they existed until the late 1920s. Now I eat them all the time."

Dana silently prayed for ears to hear and eyes to see. Instantly a shimmer slid across the woman and Dana found herself staring at a man with average looks, thick brown hair, and pure black eyes. The memory of the man sitting at Tully's a few weeks back flashed through her mind. It was him. An instant later the woman was back.

"What do you want?"

"I've told you. Peace. The stress of your job lifted off of you for the rest of the year. Is there something else you want?"

Dana stood. "I want you to get out of my office."

"Here's the situation." The demon leaned forward and spoke in a mock whisper. "Your recent activities are starting to irritate us. Back off and things will be fine."

"Back off on what?"

"You're not as sharp as you seemed at Well Spring." The woman sat back and licked chocolate off her lips.

A chill shot down Dana's back. "You're demonic."

"That's your word, not mine."

"Get out of my office, now."

"We can make life easier on you and easier on me. Or we can make your life unbearable."

Dana glared at Alexis and pointed at her office door.

"See, the whole at-war thing isn't true." Alexis licked her fingers. "We don't want to be at war with God. We simply want to live in peace. We do our thing, you do yours, it's all good. The troubles start when people like your friend Reece whip up ordinary people like you and Marcus and Brandon into an uncontrollable frenzy and plant ideas in your heads that aren't right. Aren't true. He is not safe. People have died because of his out-of-control zeal."

Dana stared at the demon.

"It's quite true. Ask him."

She didn't need to. He'd admitted the fact at Well Spring. A second later a thought struck Dana like a steel hammer. What if Reece wasn't who he said he was? Maybe he was a demon himself, training them for his own twisted purposes. No! She shook off the insane thought.

Jesus.

"We are at war, and greater is the power inside me than anything you can throw my direction."

"Do you honestly believe that?"

"You made a deal with Tamera."

"Yes, but not as directly as we're doing with you. She needed only a little motivation, and we set up an opportunity for her. You're proving to be more stubborn."

"Get out." Dana jabbed her finger toward the door.

"You're not hearing me. We're not angry about what you've done. We're not upset about the training Reece has taken you through so far. We're not even worried about what Marcus saw at church. But at this point we'd like it all to stop."

Alexis stood. "And as a gesture of thanks, I'm willing to make sure you don't miss your budget for the next, oh, let's extend it to three years. And we'll include a nice promotion for you."

Dana's lips felt like lead, but she leaned forward and pushed out the only word left in her mind. "Jesus."

The woman's eyes snapped up and went dark. "Don't use that name."

"The Lord Jesus Christ and the power of his blood against you." The shimmer skittered over the woman again.

"I see." The woman stood, strode over to Dana, and lifted her by her neck an inch off the ground, then set her back down and ran a finger down her sleeve. "Let's get a few things abundantly clear. This is only a visit. But if I'm ordered to turn my full attention to you, I will make your job and your life miserable."

"Wait." The woman placed another Kiss on her tongue and pulled it slowly into her mouth. "Miserable is the wrong word. That doesn't sound dramatic enough. And 'make your life hell' is so cliché."

Alexis put her forefinger on her chin and cocked her head as if imitating some 1950s comedy. "Okay, I've got it. If you don't back off, I'll make it feel like someone ripped your brain out, dipped it in acid, and then stuffed it back inside your skull. Yes, that's better."

"Get out."

"No."

"Jesus is Lord and his blood covers me."

The demon sauntered to the door, then stopped in the doorway. "Oh, and if the dipped-in-acid description is too figurative for you, let me put it in practical terms. Back off from all this warrior activity"—the demon slid her finger across her neck—"or I will make sure you develop a case of arthritis so painful, putting a lid on a cup of coffee will become impossible."

"Jesus. His power. His fury. His blood. Against you now."

"You have no idea what kind of flamethrower you're dealing with." The woman's eyes flashed and instantly Dana's brain felt like it was on fire. No migraine had ever come close to the pain she felt.

"Jesus." Dana stepped toward the woman. "Jesus!" She threw it at the woman this time at the top of her voice. The pain in her head vanished and Alexis spun and strode through the door.

A moment later Clark, one of her salespeople, poked his head around her door frame and sauntered inside. "I'm guessing you didn't give that lady the rates she wanted?" He turned and looked down the hall. "Wow. I don't think I've ever heard you swear using that word before."

Dana blinked, steadied herself against her desk, and stared at Clark. "I wasn't swearing."

"From the look on that lady's face, I'd say you were. Her face was a little pale. See what the power of a well-placed swear word can do?"

Dana clutched the edge of her desk with both hands and tried to slow her breathing. That couldn't have been real. It wasn't possible. It didn't matter what Reece had told them. It didn't matter what Marcus had seen. That stuff happened in movies and books and nightmares. Not real life. Her hands shook and sweat broke out on her palms.

"Did you hear me, Dana?" Clark smiled and knocked on the air in front of him. "Hello? Whatever you said put some fright on her. You made her look like a ghost. You ought to think about using Jesus' name more often."

"Yeah. Okay." He had no idea how right he was.

He frowned. "Are you all right?"

"Sure." Dana sucked in a quick breath. "I'm good."

"No, you're not. Now you're looking pale."

"It was an intense meeting. That woman was . . ." She paused. "She stressed me out a bit."

"I guess. You want to talk about it?"

"No."

"You're sure you're okay?"

"Just a day of dealing with all those demons that keep coming at me." Dana gave a weak smile.

Clark laughed and turned to go. "I hear you. Sometimes it gets exhausting. See you later."

Dana nodded, then moved to the wall of her office and sank down, staring at the carpet. Her pulse didn't slow; it sped up. Then tears filled her eyes and she held herself as tight as she could. She hadn't signed up for this when she agreed to go to Well Spring. Going deeper spiritually and battling some thoughts tossed at her by the enemy was one thing. Going up against demons in human form was another.

Dana glanced at the phone on her desk. She needed to talk to Reece and tell him she was finished.

THIRTY-TWO ◉

DANA'S HANDS SHOOK AS SHE PICKED UP HER PHONE, dialed Reece's cell phone, went to her windows, and stared at the ripples moving across Lake Union. *Pick up.* She didn't want to leave a message. She wanted to get this over with.

"Hello?" Reece's baritone filled her ear.

"It's Dana. I need to . . . you have to . . . talk me through what just happened." She swallowed and grabbed her forehead. "I'm out of the group. I'm done for a while."

"Calm down, Dana. I'm here. Tell me what happened."

"I had a visitor in my office today. Just now." She went back to the window and stared down at the street below, waiting for the woman to walk out. But Dana suspected she wouldn't see Alexia, or whoever it was, leave the building. "I can't even say it."

"An unpleasant visitor?"

"Very." The emotion of the encounter fell heavy on her and tears came again.

"Demonic?"

She pressed her lips together for a moment before answering. "Yes."

"I'm sorry."

"You don't sound surprised."

"I'm not."

"What? You thought a psychopathic demonic woman might pay me a visit today?"

"I didn't know what was going to happen. But the Spirit told me to pray for you today. With intensity."

"She was a demon. And she stood right here in my office!"

"Tell me from the beginning."

"I thought she was an executive from an LA ad agency." Dana's legs went to rubber and she slumped onto her couch. "Jesus."

"Tell me what happened."

"I don't want to think about—"

"Your peace, Lord. We need it now." Reece's voice seemed to fill her head.

A hint of hope started deep in Dana's heart and slowly peace settled on her.

"More power, Lord. More comfort for my friend Dana."

His voice was a whisper but it surged through her like a thundering shout. The peace increased and Dana's breathing slowed.

"Tell me what happened."

"She told me she would destroy me if I didn't back off. Get out of the group, get back to the life I was living before Well Spring. She said my budgets would all be taken care of if I agreed."

"And what did you do?"

"I felt like I was drowning, my mouth was packed full of marshmallows, and all I could do was say 'Jesus.'"

"And what happened?"

"She came at me harder."

"And you?"

"Spoke his name again. I ended up shouting it."

"And she?"

"Left."

"Congratulations."

"I don't think you're understanding me. She said she would give me arthritis and get me fired, and—"

"Don't let the enemy steal what just happened away from you."

"Have Brandon or Marcus been hit like this?" Dana asked.

"Not that I've heard, but it wouldn't surprise me if they have."

"Why me? Why am I alone in this?"

"You're not alone. I'm right here. So is the Spirit. Tell me what happened."

"I don't understand what you're driving at. I told you what happened." Dana stood and walked to her window and watched the midday rain pound against her window. "The point is this demon had power over me that I couldn't fight against."

"No, she didn't. You're giving her way more credit than she deserves. She's likely only an underling. Not that powerful. Let me ask again. What happened when you fought back? What happened when you didn't agree to the temptation of her fixing your woes at work? Did anyone see the woman leave?"

Dana put her hand up to the window as if she could touch the rain. What had Clark said? His words rushed into her mind. *Whatever you said put some fright on her. You made her look like a ghost.* How had she forgotten that?

"One of my sales managers saw her. He said she looked pale. And in a hurry."

"That's interesting, no?"

The implications of what she'd done settled on her.

"Don't lose this, Dana. Right now the enemy is trying to convince you that you barely escaped. That's not true. One of the greatest lies he tries to make us swallow is his power is equal or even greater than ours. It's not even close. Think back to Marcus's vision. Consider the verse, 'Greater is he who is in you than he who is in the world.' You've heard that a million times so it's tempting to let it slide by. Greater is he that is *in* you. Inside your heart."

Shafts of sunlight were burning through the fog that had permeated Dana's brain since the demon walked through her door.

"A tank is always going to win against a Tonka toy. But if the tank just sits there while the Tonka truck launches miniature grenades on the tank, eventually the tank will be destroyed."

"I didn't do anything. I didn't fight well. All I did was speak his name."

"You did fight well, Dana. You acted in strength."

"I'm not joining you and Marcus tomorrow night."

"You can choose to do whatever you want to. But pray about it, okay?"

"Of course."

"Because I have a sense the Spirit is going to do something powerful for Brandon. But we'll need your help."

THIRTY-THREE

BRANDON STOOD ONSTAGE IN DALLAS ON WEDNESDAY afternoon, three hours before that night's concert, doing a routine sound check when he felt the Spirit say, *Get ready.*

"For what, Lord?" He took off his guitar and set it in its stand.

A moment later a kid with a *Brandon Scott* T-shirt thumped across the stage and stopped a few feet away.

"Can I help you?"

"I'm sorry to bother you, Mr. Scott, but I'm supposed to find out how many bottles of water you want for tonight's show."

"Do you work on the road crew?"

"Yeah, I'm new."

"Don't call me Mr. Scott." Brandon winked at him.

"Okay."

"Great to have you with us."

The kid glanced at the auditorium and smiled. "It's so wild to be here."

"Do you play?" Brandon motioned toward his guitar.

The kid nodded and as he did Brandon saw a flash around the roadie's body. When it faded there were dark purple and black splotches on the kid's face, neck, and arms. Across his forehead was stamped the word *WORTHLESS.* How ironic. Exactly what someone might find stamped on his own forehead if they could see it. *Physician, heal thyself.*

Brandon blinked and the bruises and word were gone. He

glanced at his watch, then at his sound crew who sat waiting at their board at the back of the auditorium, then back at the kid. There wasn't time for this. Yes, there was.

Brandon held a finger up to his sound crew and called out, "One minute! I have to take a quick break."

First Kevin, now this kid. These spiritual X-ray glasses were getting really, really weird. And really, really cool. *I need the right words, Jesus.*

"What's your name?"

"Toby."

"Good name. Stay here." Brandon jogged to the back of the stage and grabbed two folding chairs, brought them back, and offered one to Toby. "You follow Jesus?" Brandon asked as they sat.

"I'm trying. Some days are better than others."

"Me too. Can I tell you something? Something I feel about you? Something I think I'm ... uh ... sensing? I might be right and I might be wrong, so if it doesn't fit, no problem."

Shame covered Toby's face and he looked down.

"I get the feeling you've never thought you'd amount to much. Maybe you even think you're worthless. If that's true, I have to tell you that's a lie from the pit of hell. Don't believe it. Don't let it stay in your mind for one more second. I know what it's like to feel that way. I still feel that way sometimes."

Toby looked up. "You do?"

"I do."

"But you've made it, everyone loves you."

"Doesn't matter. I still feel it. Just like you. We've got to let it out. Let Jesus heal it."

The kid stared at Brandon for a few seconds, then started to weep. Through the tears he poured out the story of how when his grades slipped in junior high, his parents started ignoring him. "They're both teachers of the year and grades are everything, and I'm just not that smart and I embarrassed them so badly."

"Did they say that?"

"No, but they didn't have to. My sister, you know, she four pointed all through junior high and high school, and all their time went into her. When I dropped out after my junior year, they . . ." Toby stopped and rubbed his face. "They don't hate me, they're not mean, they're even polite, it's just—"

"Toby, look at me. They have missed out on you. You are so worth it."

A shimmer of hope appeared in Toby's eyes.

"So worth it and I'm so glad you're part of this team. And right now we're going to take some time to break the lie you've believed about yourself."

Fifteen minutes later, after more tears and a prayer for strength, Brandon stood and wrapped Toby in a huge hug.

"Thank you," Toby said as he turned to go. "I don't know what else to say."

"Thank you is perfect."

"I'll remember this day the rest of my life, Max."

"What?" Brandon squinted at Toby. "What did you call me?"

"I'm sorry."

"My name's Brandon." He frowned.

The kid smiled. "I know. They told me I should call you Mr. Scott or Brandon. I slipped."

"Slipped?"

"Yeah. Max is all they've called you. That's the name that popped into my mind—"

"Who calls me Max?"

"The crew." The kid waved his hands behind and to the side of him. "All of them. Well, most of them. I thought it was a nickname or a middle name or something."

"I've had most of this crew for two years. I've never heard them call me Max."

"I'm sorry, I'll call you Brandon or Mr. Scott."

"Like I said, never Mr. Scott, and don't be sorry." Brandon gave the kid a playful punch in his arm. "Why do they call me that?"

"I don't know."

Brandon held up his forefinger. "Hang on." He pulled out his phone and dialed Kevin's cell.

"Yeah, boss?"

"Do you have a few minutes?"

"Is there a problem?"

"Nothing. It's good. It's a minor thing, so if you're jamming we can talk about it later."

"I'm good. Are you doing a sound check?"

Brandon glanced at his sound crew, who looked like they were sleeping. "Kind of."

"I'm on my way."

Brandon turned back to Toby. "Go strong, my new friend, all right? Remember, don't listen to the lies. And let's talk again soon. Okay?"

Toby nodded and smiled, tears still wet on his face, and trotted back the way he'd come. As the kid clopped down the stairs stage left, Kevin passed him coming up, taking the stairs two at a time. He jogged over to Brandon and slid to a stop, arms up.

"Nice entrance."

"I try to please." Kevin straightened his Canali shirt and looked up at Brandon. "What's so urgent that you had to yank me away from an animated Facebook discussion with my cousin about the right amount of times to post in social media each day?"

"I want to know about this Max thing."

"What Max thing? You mean about the crew calling you Max?"

"Yeah. That Max thing."

"You don't know about that?" Kevin squished up his face in surprise. "It's been going on for at least a year. I thought we talked about it."

"No." Brandon cocked his head. "We didn't."

"You're positive."

"Yes."

"Stop looking at me like that." Kevin pulled his head back. "It's a good thing."

"Sure it is." Brandon smirked. "Roasting the boss when he's not there to hear it. Injects some humor into the crew. Makes me human, right? That's the good part?"

"What?"

"Just having a little fun with the guy who signs the checks, right? Who is Max? Someone's dog?"

"This is cracking me up." Kevin shook his head. "You honestly don't know what Max stands for? You have to know." He laughed. "I can't believe you haven't overheard one of them call you that."

"Kevin. I. Don't. Know."

"All right. I believe you." Kevin folded his arms and looked up at Brandon. "It comes from a movie."

"A movie?"

"Yep. Max is short for General Maximus Decimus Meridius."

Brandon balked. "From *Gladiator*?"

"Yes." Kevin shook his head, a thin smile on his lips. "You don't get it, do you?"

"Get what?"

"You don't see how much you inspire them."

Brandon shook his head, his mind in a daze.

"Think about it. Think about what's happened over the past fifteen years. You start out playing churches where the crowd is all of three people and you're one of the three. People tell you to give up, that you'll never conquer the music industry. But you put mufflers on your ears and ignored them.

"You work your way up to playing in front of crowds of college students, then finally get a shot at making an album and it doesn't sell. So you start your own record label, then sign with a major label, and now you're one of the biggest-selling Christian artists in the world.

"You never gave up, you fought the empire. You were true to your vision." Kevin tapped himself on the chest. "And you give people the courage to step into their dreams and fight for their own empire. Like you did with me just the other day."

Max was short for Maximus. From *Gladiator*. Brandon fumbled for the chair he'd sat in with Toby and sat down hard. He stared at Kevin, who grinned at him.

"You're a warrior. You're swinging the sword. Think about your fans. Do you realize the impact you've had on them? How you've set so many of them free? Do you ever let the words in their e-mails sink in?" Kevin pointed at Brandon's heart. "Into here?"

Brandon tilted his head back and closed his eyes. Unbelievable. He had his name. God had given it. Just like Reece said he would. Brandon leaned forward and smiled at Kevin. "Tonight let's slay some dragons."

THIRTY-FOUR

BRANDON WAS IN HIS DRESSING ROOM LEANING BACK on a tan couch, still on a high from God giving him a name, when Reece texted him a message that got him to his feet: YOU NEED TO BE CAREFUL TONIGHT. He dialed Reece's number.

"Hello?"

"I'm careful every night."

"I was praying for your concert just now and got two things."

"Tell me."

"I heard the Spirit say today would be good."

"It's already been that. And the other thing?"

"That you'd have a battle on your hands during the concert."

"What kind of battle?" Brandon strode from one side of the room to the other.

"I don't know, that's all I got. But I will say it feels serious. I know you have to go on soon, but what was the good?"

Brandon told him about his talk with Kevin and God revealing his new name.

"I'm thrilled for you, Brandon. Maximus is a powerful name. And it's interesting that you swung your sword just before you received it."

"I saw the shame and self-loathing all over Toby."

"Those with eyes to see."

Brandon smiled. "I almost blew the kid off."

"Now I know why the Spirit told me tonight is serious."

228

"Why?"

"The enemy can't be pleased that you got your name. Can't be pleased about what you did for Toby." Reece paused. "Dana and Marcus should be here soon. We'll war for you in the heavens tonight."

"I'll let you know what happens."

"I think your eyes are going to be opened."

Brandon rubbed his head and scuffed a light brown stain in the carpet with the toe of his shoe. "The last time you said that, Marcus saw demons."

"Yes, I know."

Brandon hung up the phone and stared at his guitar. That was his sword tonight. He would swing it well.

✦✦✦

Brandon glanced at Kevin as his manager strolled through the dressing room door. "Is everyone tanked up?" He put the last new string on his guitar and started tuning the Taylor six-string. If Reece was right—and he usually was—his team needed their spiritual radar to be finely calibrated.

"You have guitar techs who would install new strings for you." Kevin grabbed one of the folding chairs and sat backward, his arms resting on the back of the chair.

Brandon repeated his question. "Is everyone tanked up?"

"That question could be interpreted in a number of ways." Kevin laughed and mimicked taking a swig from a bottle. "Let me just say I strictly prohibit the band from getting drunk before they go onstage."

"I'm not kidding around, Kevin. Yes or no?"

"Why are you so worried if we've been praying?" Kevin gave Brandon an exasperated look. "We always pray before a show."

"Reece said something weird to me on the phone a few minutes ago."

"What?"

"That there would be some kind of spiritual battle at the concert tonight and that my eyes would be opened even more than they have been."

"Cool, you always play better when you can see."

Normally Brandon would appreciate Kevin's humor. But this time it fell flat. He'd felt a tingling at the back of his mind all day—which he'd ignored till now—but it seemed like it had grown exponentially in the last few minutes. He didn't know if the increase was the Spirit putting him on red alert or his own imaginings because of his conversation with Reece. It didn't matter. Either way Brandon needed to be ready.

An hour later Brandon strapped on his guitar and strode toward the stage. Kevin stood at the end of the hall, a Cheshire-cat grin on his face. When Brandon reached him, he gave a smile of his own in return.

"Someone is happy."

"Would you care to share in my joy?" Kevin made a mock bow.

"Speak."

"Sold out. We turned people away. And we've already sold the majority of the T-shirts. You are still loved, *mon frère*."

A thought streaked through Brandon's mind. He didn't care about sold-out crowds anymore. It didn't matter if one person came or one hundred thousand. This concert was about an audience of One. As Brandon took the stage, the crowd roared and he grinned and waved at them, which increased the volume of their greeting.

"Hello, Dallas." Brandon adjusted the mic clipped to his ear and gazed out over the crowd. "I love you! But God loves you more! And he wants to set you free!"

The crowd yelled its approval as Brandon turned to his band and gave a countdown. "One, two, three, four . . ."

They kicked into a sped-up version of his megahit from two years ago, "Flying Faster," and the crowd surged to their feet, arms raised, bodies moving in rhythm to the music.

Lord, this is for you. It's about making you more famous. Lead me tonight.

Brandon prayed that at the start of every concert, but this was the first time in ages he'd said it with his heart instead of his head. *Maximus.* The thought of his new name bypassed his mind and went straight to his heart. He gazed at the crowd. Tonight he would fight for them with all his strength.

Brandon turned and grinned at his band. This was right. He was at the center of the universe onstage. It hadn't been like this in so long. The music flowed out of him almost without effort.

"This is so cool, Jesus," Brandon whispered as his lead guitarist played a blistering solo.

The next forty minutes flashed by in what felt like seconds. In between songs he spoke out of his heart and the words flowed like the river at Well Spring.

After their eighth song, Anthony, his bass player, slid up to him. "Something is different tonight."

Brandon covered his mic with his fist. "You think? You're feeling it?" Brandon threw his other arm around Anthony's shoulder.

"What changed?"

"The Spirit. He's here and we're flowing in it again. Like the old days."

"You've had a wake-up call."

"I've been spending some time with a guy who's helped me get back on the sometimes straight and always narrow."

"That retreat you went on?"

"Yeah. I'll have to tell you more about it."

"I'd love it."

Brandon turned back to the audience and shouted, "Are you free tonight?"

The crowd roared.

"It's what he wants for you!"

The band kicked into their next song and Brandon soaked in the audience, the music—his head went light and he felt like he was floating. As the song finished Brandon glanced at the set sheet taped to the top of his guitar. Next up was "Water in the Wasteland." But a thought filled his heart: *Play "Free Me."*

Brandon glanced behind him at the band, then took a step toward the crowd. "We haven't played this next song in a while. But I think God is saying it's time to bring it out of hibernation. No vocals to this one, just music, so let the Spirit put whatever words to it he wants to."

Brandon glanced at his band members, asking with his eyes if they were good with the song. They all nodded. He turned back to the crowd and smiled. "On this song I don't do much more than play the opening chord, so when we're done, if you like the tune, be sure to give it up for my band."

As the crowd cheered, Brandon formed the opening chord high on the neck of his guitar and pulled his pick hard across the strings. An instant later the room went black. The only light he could see was a razor-thin sliver at the back of the auditorium. Faulty lighting? This had to be the attack of the enemy Reece had warned him about. But it didn't seem to faze his band.

Thirty seconds later the lights still hadn't come back on, but the song continued to ring out. That his band remembered the song well enough to keep playing in the dark surprised and pleased him. But it would be nice to be able to see.

Brandon fumbled his way over to Anthony and gripped his arm. "Any idea where the lights went?"

"What do you mean? You want the lights on over the audience?"

"Any lights would be nice at this point."

"So the ones in our eyes aren't enough?" His bass player laughed.

"What are you talking about? I can't see a thing."

"You have three spotlights on you right now. Are you blind?"

Brandon didn't answer because an instant later he could see again. But he didn't like the view. He knew he was the only one onstage who saw what was coming out of the chests of the audience. What was coming for him.

THIRTY-FIVE

MARCUS GLANCED FROM BETWEEN THE GPS ON HIS phone to the road as he tooled down Paradise Lake Road just north of Woodinville, trying to imagine what Reece's home would look like. According to the map on his phone, he'd know in a few minutes.

From what he knew about Reece, Marcus imagined it wouldn't be much to look at. But as soon as he started down the long gravel driveway lined with Douglas fir trees, his presumption was proven incorrect. Thirty seconds later Reece's house came into view and Marcus smiled.

It was a cabin, average in size, but striking. Dark beams protruded at the top of the steep-pitched roof and on the sides of the home. A massive picture window filled the front, a river-rock fireplace towered over the structure on the left side. It was a brother of the cabin at Well Spring.

Marcus got out of his car and strolled toward the front door. The landscaping around the home was impeccable. Lush grass, rich brown bark that looked like it had been laid yesterday, three large Japanese maples, and perfectly sculpted rhododendron bushes.

Even in the fading evening light, the colors made a stunning framework for the diminutive pond in the center of the yard. Apparently Reece wasn't down to his last dime.

A sign halfway to the front door said Around Back. When he reached the backyard the aroma of smoke filled his nostrils. A long gravel path—at least a hundred yards long—slalomed through the grass, ending at a fire pit that reminded him of the one at Well Spring. Of course it would. Reece probably based his fire pit on the one in Colorado.

Dana sat on the wooden bench surrounding the pit. Reece paced on the grass on the other side of it. When Reece saw him, the big man raised his arm and motioned him closer.

"Your home is spectacular." Marcus slid onto the circular bench across from Dana.

"Thank you." Reece glanced at his massive maple tree–lined backyard. "It's my slice of paradise."

"Our gathering spot won't be inside?"

"Nah. I never waste a sunny day or a cloudless night. They're too rare around here." Reece stopped pacing and sat down, but his knees continued to bounce and his hands gripped the edge of the wooden bench. Concern was etched into his craggy face.

"I'm glad you both came." He glanced at Dana. "The Spirit told me Brandon will be attacked tonight during his concert. And I'd rather not attempt to fight this battle alone." Reece massaged his fist with his other hand. "I need you two."

"Attacked? How?"

Reece shook his head at Marcus. "I'm not sure."

"Have you been given any clue as to what the assault will look like?" Marcus asked.

Reece stood and grabbed his ax and split kindling while he talked. "No. But I know we're needed and that's enough. So we're going to go to him right now. Stand next to him this evening."

"I thought he was in concert tonight." Dana frowned.

"Yes." Reece moved back to the bench and drummed his fingers on the redwood.

"A concert in Dallas that is four and a half hours away by plane."

"That's correct."

"So you mean we're going to pray the concert goes well, that he'll be protected, that God would do what he wants to do with the people there, etc.?"

"Not exactly." Reece leaned in and held his hands over the fire. "I mean, if you're willing, we'll travel there by unconventional means."

"Here we go again." Dana folded her hands across her stomach.

Reece rose again and paced, his face contorted as if he were trying to remember a long-forgotten code. "Our bodies are going to stay here. But our spirits will be onstage with Brandon."

Marcus flopped back in his chair. "My first thought is insane. My second is I've seen enough now to cast my hands in the air and say, 'Lead on.'"

Reece turned to Dana.

"Same."

Marcus glanced at his watch. "When do we go in?"

"Right now."

"Anything we need to know first?" Dana asked.

"Yes." Reece grabbed two pieces of maple and tossed them on the fire. "This is going to be strange for the two of you because it will feel like we're physically onstage with Brandon. We won't be. As I said, our spirits will be there but our bodies will be right here. I don't know if Brandon will be able to hear us. I don't even know if he'll see us."

"Have you done this kind of thing before?" Dana asked.

"Yes, but it's been awhile."

"Do you mind defining 'awhile'?"

"Just follow my lead and we'll be fine. But if either of you would like to stay here, just say the word."

Dana and Marcus shook their heads.

"You'll probably feel a rush and then we should be onstage. The Spirit will take us when he's ready. We might sit here for six minutes or six hours, but I think it will be right away."

"Six hours? That would be a pretty long concert."

"God is outside of time."

Dana glanced at Marcus. "Like you talked about at Well Spring." He nodded.

She rubbed her knees. "So when we are in the Spirit, he can take us forward or backward wherever and whenever he wants to."

"Exactly," Reece said. "Quantum physics and the Bible is something I want to talk to all of you about more—and, Marcus, I think it will take your teaching at the University of Washington in a new direction—but at the moment we don't have the time, no pun intended."

"That, I would enjoy taking part in. And I liked the pun, intended or not." Marcus smiled.

"Now close your eyes and focus on the Spirit."

Serenity settled on Marcus, mixed with a rush of adrenaline. His hands shook lightly in rhythm with waves of peace. It was intoxicating.

"Okay, here we go." Reece's voice sounded distant. "Take us in, Lord. With your strength, your power, your freedom."

The warmth of the fire swirled around him and the air seemed to grow thicker as if an extra molecule had been added to the O_2 surrounding them. It was the same sensation as when Marcus had dreamt of being underwater and being able to breathe. Then a sound like a thousand thundering waterfalls crashed against his ears.

A second later Marcus stood on a stage, music filling the arena in front of him. Brandon stood ten feet to his left, Dana and Reece beside him on his right. Unbelievable.

Marcus felt his arm. It was impossible to believe he wasn't standing onstage in the flesh. He shook the thought from his mind. No time—or inclination—to consider the physics of what was happening or how many supposed irrefutable laws of nature were being broken at the moment.

Reece pointed at the audience and Marcus turned to see what their leader's gaze was fixed on. At first he saw nothing unusual. A full house, people on their feet, swaying to the music—some with arms raised, some singing, some standing still with eyes closed.

Wait. Something moved down the bodies of the audience, thin lines slithering from their chests to their stomachs to their legs, like vines from a time-lapse movie, growing inches longer every second. What was happening? Then Marcus realized what he was seeing and gasped.

+ + +

Brandon stared in fascination and horror as thin, pale green vines emerged from the chests of hundreds in the audience. The vines ran down the people's stomachs and legs like liquid, then snaked along the floor into the aisles.

He glanced to his right and left. The tentacles from each aisle now slithered to the area in front of the seats and merged into one massive green vine that pulsed like it had a heartbeat. A moment later the front of the vine crept over the edge of the stage and a repulsive smell seeped into his nostrils. Rotting meat would be perfume compared to the stench. Brandon's feet felt welded to the floor and his breathing came in spurts.

"Can you see this?" Brandon turned to Anthony.

His bass player grinned. "Yeah, baby, it's awesome. We haven't had a crowd reaction like this for a while. They love us."

"I mean the vines!"

"Vines?" Anthony strutted over to him. "What do you mean, vines?"

Brandon stumbled back a step and pointed at the aisles and the edge of the stage where the front of the vine inched toward him.

"Yeah. Sure. And I can see Tarzan and Jane swinging off of them." He grinned. "What are you talking about?"

Spirit of God, I need you and your power here right now.

The vine stopped for a moment, then started to slither toward him again—more slowly—but it continued to creep forward. Brandon staggered another step backward as the vine, now as thick as a telephone pole, oozed toward him.

+ + +

Marcus tried to keep his breathing steady. "I'm skirting the edge here. Talk to me, Reece."

"Let's take this thing out." Reece turned to face the vine, fury on his face.

"With what?" Marcus said.

"Look at what you hold."

Marcus looked down to see a four-foot ax in his hands. Its weight was substantial, but he knew he had the strength to wield it.

"I'm with Marcus," Dana shouted. "This is freaking me out. That thing seems full of power, and not the good kind."

"Steady, Dana. Look at the blade of your ax. That's real power."

A razor-thin beam of light ran along the edge of her blade. Marcus glanced at his. Same thing.

Dana grinned at Reece and lifted the ax above her head. "Ready."

"Marcus?"

"Let's go."

+ + +

Brandon took two more steps back and glanced to his right and left. He had to move! But where? Then a flash of light to his right and Reece, Dana, and Marcus stood in front of him, between him and the vine, with some sort of axes in their hands. How could they be here?

In perfect unison the three swung their axes in a long arc down on the vine. Each of their blades bit into it and the vine shuddered. They raised their axes and swung again. This time their blades penetrated the surface of the vine and a dark, thick liquid spewed out. Two more blows and they hacked through the main vine, but the battle wasn't over.

From each side of the hacked-off vine, a new growth appeared, almost as thick as the original vine. They moved toward Brandon, faster this time, the two offshoots flanking him on his left and right. Another grew in a long circle around the stage and crept forward, directly in back of him. The vine on the left snaked over to Anthony and circled his foot, then ran up onto his foot and up his leg, up his torso toward his heart. *Move!*

Brandon leapt toward him and reached for the vine to tear it off his friend's chest. But his hand went right through the vine as if it were vapor, and in the next moment his hand felt like it had been dipped in dry ice. The vine circled Anthony's chest once, then disappeared through his shirt into the center of his heart.

Anthony didn't react, his fingers flowing over the frets of his bass, but the smile on his face grew wide. He turned and nodded at Brandon in rhythm with the music. "They love us, Brandon!"

How was he supposed to help fight this thing? He turned to Reece and the others. Reece shouted something to Marcus. He saw Reece's lips move but he couldn't hear the sound. Marcus leapt back and in two strides was behind Brandon, attacking the vine that had circled around behind him.

While Dana hacked away at the vine to his right, Reece pounced on the vine to his left that had entered Brandon's bass player. Reece turned and lasered his eyes on Brandon, opened his mouth, and shouted. Again Brandon couldn't hear Reece's words, but he could read the big man's lips as clear as if the words had been bellowed at 120 decibels.

"Sing. Now!" Reece turned and brought his blade down on the vine again with the speed of light. "Sing!"

Brandon turned to his band and slid his hand across his throat and the music came to a halt. He had no words to explain to his band or the audience why they'd stopped the song, so he didn't try. "I think God wants us all to sing this next song. Everyone in this room together. Let go. Surrender. Sing to him. Not to me. Not to the band. Him. Focus on God."

Brandon sang like he hadn't sung in forever. Not to the audience. Not for the band. Not for himself. He gazed at the sky and sang to the Spirit. There was no one else in the arena, and as the song filled the air, a sense of freedom flooded him.

A light exploded that was brighter and purer than any stage light he'd ever seen. There was no source for it and it seemed to move and shift as if it was thicker in the middle of the arena, then thicker on the sides, and soon the whole place shook as if the light would burst through the walls and rocket out through the entire city. The light swept over the stage, burying the vine like a giant wave.

The vine turned brown, then black, then gray as the light fell on it, then to dust, then it faded from sight. A moment later Reece, Marcus, and Dana vanished as well, but the light remained and only grew in intensity.

When the song ended, Brandon didn't cue his band as to what song would be next. He simply launched into "Untamed," another song he hadn't touched in years, trusting the band would follow his lead. They did and for a half hour there was no speaking, only the music and the light and God's presence like he'd never known.

Brandon closed his eyes, bowed his head, and prayed for the men and women in the audience. For their restoration, for their eyes to be opened, that they would be set free.

After a few minutes he opened his eyes and turned to Anthony. "Do you want to close?"

"Me?"

"Yes. Sing the final song."

"Which song?"

"One of yours."

His bass player stared at him with a stunned expression. "Are you serious?"

"Sing it from the deep part of your heart. Not for them. Not for you. For him."

His bass player shook his head and laughed.

"What?" Brandon asked.

"I . . . uh . . . this means the world."

"Then sing it as if the whole world is listening."

Anthony embraced him, then adjusted his microphone and played. After they finished the second encore, Brandon flipped off the wireless on his guitar and trotted offstage. Kevin was waiting for him at the bottom of the stage steps.

"Welcome back to earth."

"What does that mean?" Brandon unclipped his guitar strap and looked at three roadies who stood nearby. One of them was Toby. Brandon strode over to him and handed him the guitar. "Thanks for taking good care of her. I appreciate it."

"No problem." Toby cradled the guitar and smiled.

Kevin followed Brandon as he walked around the back of the stage. "I mean it in a good way. I haven't felt the presence of God like that at a Brandon Scott concert in a long time."

"You don't know the eighth of it."

"I think the expression is you don't know the half of it."

Brandon stopped behind the curtains separating them from the arena. "Believe me, in this case it's an eighth. Maybe a sixteenth."

"So what happened?"

"God showed up. So did Satan. And my eyes were opened just like Reece predicted they would be."

"You're starting to see things in the Spirit."

"Yeah. You could say that." Brandon grinned.

"Where are you going now?"

"Where I should have been going for the past three years." He pulled open the curtain and pointed toward the crowd still milling near the front of the stage. "To go be with them."

THİRTY-SİX

HAD IT REALLY HAPPENED? THAT NIGHT AT ELEVEN
forty-five Brandon sat alone in the corner of his Dallas hotel room,
the only light coming from the small lamp on the desk in front of the
mirror, the night flashing through his head, part of him wanting to
come down from the rush of what had happened, part of him wanting to live in it forever. Part of him freaked out by what he'd seen
and wanting to pretend it hadn't happened, part of him astonished
at the power of God.

His cell phone rang and he picked it up, willing it to be Reece.
He glanced at the caller ID. *Yes.* Brandon turned on his Bluetooth,
slipped it over his ear, and answered.

"How are you?"

"Freaked. Thrilled. Mind blown. Stunned by what the Spirit
did, and feeling everything else you can imagine."

"That was a wild ride."

"Actually, I'm a lot freaked." Brandon sat again and tapped his
foot on the carpet triple time as the images of the vine filled his mind.
"That . . . that . . . that thing . . ."

"Relax, bud."

"I am relaxed."

"Good. Talk to me."

Brandon scratched his head through his thick blond hair.
"When you said my eyes would be opened, I didn't think you meant
I was going to see so vividly."

"So you could see the vines?"

"Uh, *yeah*, I could see the vines."

"Could you see us?"

"Like the best holographs I've ever seen. Only better."

"Amazing," Reece said, more to himself than to Brandon. "So when I turned and yelled at you, you heard me?"

"I didn't hear you, but it wasn't hard to read your lips," Brandon said. "This night will be a turning point for me. I feel like I'm back and farther down the road than I've ever been."

Reece went silent.

"What aren't you telling me?"

"I'd love to say it's over for you. But it's not."

"You mean the vine? You destroyed it."

"That one. Yes. But there will be others. At every concert."

"What are you saying? That vine has attacked me before?"

"Many, many times. Just because you haven't been able to see it before now doesn't mean it doesn't exist."

"I think I'm going to barf. That thing has shot into me like it did into Anthony?"

"Think, Brandon, what was your bass player's reaction when it entered into him?"

Brandon replayed the scene in his mind and it made him sweat. "Pleasure. He liked it."

"Yes. Have you asked yourself why?"

"Not until now."

"It's a critical question."

"It gave him something. But it was evil."

"Think about where the vine started. Where did that vine come from?" Reece said.

"The people."

"Yes. Man was made to worship. And the enemy will twist that desire till the object of their adoration slides away from God and lands on someone they can more easily taste, touch, and feel. And there is a part of all of us that is hungry for that sort of admiration."

Brandon swallowed. So true. He'd often feasted from that table.

"You have to know who you are, Brandon. The enemy will constantly try to make you forget, which leads to the need for adoration and the praise of man."

"Who am I?"

"A king. An emperor. Unlike Maximus, you lived. And now you must live in who you are."

"Me. A king? No. Musician, yes, king, no."

"You are a king, Brandon. Your audience is your kingdom. Your band number among the ones you have been called to lead. You have been called to war for them. You must battle for them in the heavens. Now you know your name. But knowing your name is never enough. You have to learn to live in it."

Brandon listened to the hum of the phone as Reece's words seeped into his heart and he considered their implications. "I don't know if I'm ready for that."

"You don't have to be. Your training and healing and freedom are far from complete."

"What's next?"

"Can you be at my house this coming Sunday evening?"

"Sure. For what?"

"We're going after Marcus."

"What does that mean?"

"It means I've been seeking God on what's next, and I believe on Sunday night the Spirit wants to take us into the soul of the professor."

THIRTY-SEVEN

MURDERER.

No.

Because of you they perished.

"Get out!" Reece sat in front of the fire pit on Sunday evening and shook his head, grappling with the words being flung into his mind. He'd come out to pray before Dana and Brandon arrived but had been hammered from the moment he settled onto the bench. He had to be strong. Bold. Had to be ready to fight for Marcus's freedom.

Their blood will forever be on your hands.

Reece slumped forward onto his knees in front of the fire pit, the hiss of the light rain against the coals filling the air. "The belt of truth. The breastplate of righteousness. They are mine. The shield of faith. I raise it."

Stay on this path and we will take you down.

Reece massaged his head. It was true. If he hadn't been reckless, they wouldn't have died.

Stay on this path and we will take them *down.*

The buzz of his cell phone split into his thoughts and he yanked it out of his pocket and stared at the screen. Doug.

"Hello."

"How are you?"

Reece didn't answer.

"What is the truth, friend?"

Reece puffed out rapid breaths. "I don't know."

"What is happening tonight?"

"I killed them, Doug." He pulled his hat down over his face.

"You told me you're going into Marcus's soul tonight, yes? So you can't be surprised at this attack."

"I can't do it."

"Where does their power come from?"

"We're not going into your soul this time. It's different."

"Where does their power come from?"

Reece got back on the bench, the rain seeping through his jeans. "Deception."

"Where does their power come from?"

"Accusation."

"Where does their power come from?"

"Illusion."

"Do they have any claim over you? Any right?"

"No."

"Did the Spirit tell you to go after Marcus tonight?"

"Yes."

"Do you have any doubts about that?"

"No."

"As I said to you two weeks back, you must lead with a confidence you won't always feel, release the power that has long lain dormant, and live in the faith of the old days. You must be strong, friend. Let me seek the heavens for you right now."

As Doug prayed the fog clutching Reece's mind lifted and light flickered, then burst into full radiance. Three minutes later Reece strode back to his house, the words of his friend's prayer expanding in his heart, the vile thoughts held at bay—at least for the moment.

✦✦✦

As Dana stepped through the front door of Reece's house, her eyes were drawn to a baby grand piano sitting in the far right corner of the great room.

"You're the first to arrive," Reece said as he greeted her. "Make yourself at home, Dana, I'll be right back."

As Reece disappeared upstairs, Dana wandered over to the piano. Two framed photos sat on it. She picked up the first picture and studied the brunette woman in it. Her smile was bottled lightning. The woman didn't have the Hollywood-type beauty that was continually foisted on humanity but that deeper kind of beauty that made Dana instantly hope the person would like her.

Reece clomped back down the stairs and stopped at the bottom. "Who is the picture of?"

He didn't answer for several seconds. "My wife."

"She's stunning."

"Thank you."

"You're no longer together?"

"No." His eyes went dark.

"Divorced?"

"No longer together."

"I'm sorry. Do you want to talk about it?"

"I don't. But I appreciate the offer." Reece turned, walked toward the kitchen, and called out over his shoulder, "I'll just be three or four more minutes in here."

Dana set the photo of Reece's wife back on the piano in the spot clear of dust it had sat in, then looked at the next photo. In it was a little girl who looked to be in her tween years. Dana reached toward the picture but pulled her hand back before she touched it. She'd already pushed too deep into Reece's no-go zone, and something told her asking about this eleven- or-twelve-year-old girl who was likely Reece's daughter would be going too—

"My daughter."

Dana yanked her hand back from the top of the piano and knocked over the photo of his wife. "Sorry, you startled me. I thought you were still in the kitchen—"

"My fault." Reece rubbed his hands on his jeans. "I didn't mean to sneak up on you."

"You didn't." She moved away from the piano. "I shouldn't be looking at these pictures."

"It's okay, Dana." Reece eased past her and lifted both framed photos off the piano. "My wife was thirty-four when she died." He wiped the dust off the top of the frame, then held up the picture of his daughter. "She was ten."

"I'm sorry. How did they—?"

Reece shook his head and Dana stopped. Clearly the question was far beyond the off-limits border.

"Do you play?" Dana motioned toward the piano.

"No." Reece tossed the dish towel over his shoulder. "My wife did. But that's not the real question you wanted to ask, is it?"

"I wanted to know more about your wife and daughter. I'm sorry to pry."

"Someday I'll tell you that story. But not yet."

Reece stared at her as if daring her to ask to hear the story now. Just as she opened her mouth to speak, a sharp knock on the door filled the living room.

"That will be Brandon."

When Brandon and she had settled onto either end of Reece's couch, their mentor began.

"Thanks for coming. Tonight could be intense."

Intense? Should that be a surprise? Every night the four of them spent together was intense. It was still hard processing everything that had happened over the past two weeks and reconciling it with the uneventful type of Christianity she'd lived for the past ten years.

And now, showing up at the radio station, trying to go through the motions of a regular day—wondering when another demon might show up in her office and follow through on its threats—then at night delving into a spiritual world that had always been around her, but she'd never seen.

It was a kind of bizarre double life. But she didn't want to stop. The healing and freedom she saw exploding in her life and the others' lives made the battle worth it. And tonight they would fight to free Marcus from the regrets he lugged around like a steel drum full of concrete.

Reece struck a match and lit a dark blue candle, set it on the coffee table in front of him, and sat back in his oak chair. "Tonight we go into the professor's soul."

"And Marcus is okay with this?" Dana asked. "You know, the whole permission thing?"

"Without question. He and I spent a good chunk of the day together yesterday and he asked us to do this."

"Why isn't he here?"

"He said he'd rather not be." Reece steepled his fingers. "I didn't ask why."

"What if we need to ask him something?"

"Let's hope we don't have to." Reece stood and turned off the lights in the kitchen and living room.

"Is there anything else we need to know?"

"Yes." He pointed at Brandon and her. "I'm going to let you two lead us. You'll make the decisions. I'll be there if you need counsel, but I want you two running point."

He and Brandon closed their eyes and Dana did the same. "Here we go. Take us in by your Spirit, your power, your grace, your fire."

The almost familiar rush of air surrounded Dana and when she opened her eyes, the three of them stood in an unnaturally long hallway—at least one hundred yards long in each direction with doors spaced every ten or twelve feet along the corridor.

"I feel like I'm breaking and entering." Brandon spun a 360 on his heel. "It's one thing to be in the soul of a stranger. It's way different to be in the soul of an ally."

"Be on your guard. Watch your back. Watch each other's backs."

"I thought Marcus's soul would be vaster than just a hallway." Dana reached out and placed her palm on the wall. It was cool to her touch.

"We're only in one small part of it."

"Which way? Right or left?" she asked. A faint hospital smell was in the air.

"We should go left," Brandon said.

"How do you know? Did the Spirit tell you that?" Dana asked.

"No, but I have a fifty-fifty chance of being right."

"Left is fine," Reece said as they eased down the hall.

Every door looked exactly the same. The walls were off-white, the hallway floor off-white, and so were the doors.

"Marcus needs to get a decorator in here, bad." Brandon stopped and ran a finger along the wall to his right and held it up to his eyes. "At least he's keeping it clean."

"It makes sense." Dana stopped as well and glanced from ceiling to floor to the doors.

"Why?" Reece said.

"You already know why, don't you?"

"I do."

"It reflects his personality. He's precise. A scientist. He's ordered and it's reflected in his soul."

"Well said, Dana."

Brandon laughed. "I wonder what my soul looks like. I expect a full report once you guys go inside."

She knew exactly what it would look like. "I'm guessing it would be much more Gaudi-like or Salvador Dalí."

Brandon laughed again. "Probably true."

Reece motioned them with his fingers. "I don't mind you talking, but let's move at the same time."

"How do we know when we get to the right door?" Dana said.

"I'm guessing it will be pretty simple." Reece pointed at a door to his left. "Just look for the door that's open a crack. And look for light coming from underneath it."

They walked for thirty or forty yards without seeing an open door. And none had light spilling onto the floor in front of them.

"There." Dana pointed to a spot sixty feet ahead. "I see light."

"Where?" Brandon glanced back and forth between Dana and where she was pointing.

"Up ahead. Thirty yards or so. You can't see that?"

"No."

"You're blind then."

"He can't see it, Dana," Reece interjected. "Neither can I. You can. Extend grace. And if you don't understand the implication of his not seeing, then you're the one who's blind."

"The body of Christ. Needing each other," Dana responded.

"Exactly." Reece strode ahead of them and stopped when he reached the open door.

"Should we keep looking?"

"No, this is the door. Well done, Dana."

They pushed it open and walked in. The walls and ceiling were painted a muted blue. Thick gray carpet covered the floor except for the center of the room where a raised stage sat. It was made of a dark wood and round.

The space felt heavy, as if an unseen melancholy cloud permeated the room. And with every breath she took, the feeling intensified. The walls were lined with old-looking movie posters from floor to ceiling. As she looked more closely, Dana realized the people on the posters were Marcus, a woman, and two girls who looked like the photo Marcus had shown Dana at Well Spring. It had to be his wife, Kat, and his daughters, Abbie and Jayla.

It was macabre. Each poster had the feel of a 1960s horror film, but instead of promoting a movie, the images and headlines advertised the greatest regrets of the professor's life.

As Dana stared at a poster of Marcus hunched over a laptop while a birthday party went on in the background, the scene somehow came to life and the professor, his daughters, and Kat emerged from the poster and appeared on the stage in the center of the room acting out the scene.

Dana gasped and stepped back. It was so real. Kat's pleas for him to shut down the computer, the sadness on Abbie's face as she blew out seven yellow candles, him taking a quick photo, then going back to the computer.

"Marcus?" Dana reached her hand toward the stage even though she knew he wasn't really there.

She turned and looked at another poster of Marcus turning down a scuba-diving trip with some buddies. Ones of softball and soccer games where he sat in the stands with his face buried in books. One of him wanting to try out for a community play but backing out at the last second. Another of anniversaries where he called Kat from his office at school to say he wouldn't be home.

As Dana concentrated on the posters, each of them came alive and played out on the stage as if she were there when it happened.

Dana glanced at Brandon and Reece. "Are you guys seeing what I'm seeing?"

They nodded and she turned back—but not to look at the walls any longer. She was done looking at the posters. She'd seen enough. Dana gazed at the now-empty stage and tried to imagine the weight of Marcus's regrets. She started to ask Brandon what he wanted to do next when the stage, the room, the posters all vanished and Marcus appeared in front of them hunched over his laptop in an office, pounding on the keyboard, a cell phone scrunched between his cheek and his shoulder. A stack of thick, musty-looking books sat to his left, three more perched on his right.

"I'll be there. My arrival won't be as early as I desire, but I am coming."

Kat stood in the entryway of a home next to Abbie and Jayla.

"You're going to be late? She has the lead role," Kat said.

"She's in first grade, not on Broadway."

"She won't be six forever, Marcus."

The shorter of the two girls peered up at Kat.

"I realize this; however, if I'm to attain tenure I am compelled to finish this paper. And the sooner I get tenure, the sooner I'll be able to relax and spend more time with you and the girls. Who do you presume I'm doing this for?"

"Maybe part of this is about the girls and me, but I think more of it is about you."

He pulled the cell phone off his shoulder and squeezed it tight. "And maybe if you were raised with one meal a day and one set of clothes all the way up through junior high, you'd want to make sure when you achieved a family of your own, they were taken care of."

"There's a difference between wanting to provide for your family and wanting to gain the prestige and recognition you never had as—"

"Can we drop it? The longer we converse about this, the longer it will take me to get there." Marcus yanked one of the books to his right and pawed through it. "Your brother is taping the play, correct?"

"Yes."

"Good. I'll arrive in time to see the second half and watch the first half with Jayla, you, and Abbie when we all get home. It'll be like I was there the whole time."

"It's first grade. I don't think they'll have an intermission."

As the argument continued the scene faded, replaced by the site of a tiny gymnasium with a stage at one end crowded with grade-school children who lined the front of the stage and bowed as the small audience stood and clapped and hooted their praise. Kat, a man who resembled her, and Abbie scuffed toward the stage. The man—who had to be Kat's brother—clapped as they approached Jayla.

"You were so good, Jayla!" Kat grinned, bent down, hugged her daughter, and kissed her head. "Absolutely wonderful."

Jayla grinned and nodded.

"I agree." Kat's brother lifted the girl off the floor and gave her a quick spin through the air. "It was a stupendously stupendous performance!"

"What does that mean, Uncle Thomas?" Jayla tilted her head, her pink halo bobbing back and forth.

"It means your dad is going to be so incredibly proud of you when he sees the video because you were incredibly incredible." Kat's brother smiled and patted the video camera in his hand.

"Are you proud of me?"

"Of course I am!"

The scene shifted to Marcus as he half walked, half jogged through the school parking lot, through the doors to the gym. He pushed past parents and kids who flowed in the opposite direction. His gaze darted around the gym, then he strode toward the four of them. Jayla's back was to him, and Kat, her brother, and Abbie didn't see him approach.

Jayla's next statement stopped Marcus cold. He staggered to his left into the shadows of the bleachers.

"I'm glad you're proud of me 'cause you're like a daddy."

"Really? Am I like your daddy?" Kat's brother laughed.

"Uh-uh, you're not like him." She stared at him. "You come to my things." Jayla looked down and spun in a circle with her hands out. "He never does 'cause he's busy working a lot, he has stuffs to do, so he can't come, and that's why, you know?"

"Jayla—"

"I love you." She reached out and hugged Thomas.

"Thank you, but you love your daddy too."

"Uh-huh."

Marcus's face turned ashen. A second later there was a flash of light and the room and the posters materialized around the three of them again.

"He's the king of regret. Or maybe the emperor." Brandon put his hands on his hips.

"You would be too," Dana said.

"We need to destroy those posters. Any ideas how?"

"This one is yours to figure out." Reece took a step back and folded his arms.

"Do we get a clue?" Brandon said.

"What would you use if you were in the physical world?"

Brandon glanced around the room. "Ripping the posters to shreds wouldn't be enough. They need to burn. I'd toss them all in your fire pit."

"But since we don't have that at our disposal . . ."

Brandon held up his hands as if he held a bazooka. "A flame-thrower."

"Then make it happen."

Brandon smiled at Reece, then closed his eyes and held out his arms, palms up. A ball of flame appeared in each of Brandon's hands. "Yeah, now we're talking." He flung the balls of fire at the posters on the far wall. They struck the center of the wall and instantly exploded into flames.

"Yes!" Brandon gave a fist pump but a second later his arm went limp.

Once the flames died out, the posters and the frames were exactly the same as they had been. There was no damage.

"More power, Lord," Dana said. This had to work.

"Let's go again," Brandon said. This time the balls in his hand were half again as big and glowed with the intensity of a star. He heaved one of the fireballs at the screen and the explosion engulfed the entire wall. Seconds later the posters and frames caught fire and burned hot and bright.

"Strike one." Brandon transferred the ball of fire in his left hand to his right, wound up, and threw the second ball with the speed of lightning at the wall across from them with the same result as the first wall.

"Strike two."

The third ball of fire struck the wall to their left and within three minutes all that was left of the posters were a few charred pieces of framing and a bit of lingering smoke.

"Is it finished?" Reece asked.

"Strike three, game over." Brandon grinned. "Freedom for Marcus, baby."

"Is it time to go then?"

Dana stared at the smoldering hardware, a glitch gnawing at her mind.

Brandon danced. "We're outta here. Victory party is next. The professor is buying."

He and Reece walked out of the room and down the hall, and Dana followed a few steps behind. The door closed behind them on its own. The gnawing grew. After a few paces she stopped.

Reece spun. "Is something wrong, Dana?"

"I don't know." Dana jerked her thumb back toward the door they'd just stepped out of. "But something feels off. That was easy. Way too easy. And I didn't feel any peace in that room when we left. Only sorrow."

"I agree."

Brandon spun around and half walked, half hopped down the hall back to Dana, his Adidas sneakers squeaking on the floor of the hallway. "What are you talking about? We find the room, we call on God's power, he comes through with fire, everything burns, posters are destroyed, and you're saying it was too easy?"

"The resistance we had at first didn't slow us down for more than a minute."

"And that's a problem, why?"

Dana looked at Reece. "We didn't destroy anything, did we?"

"Hello." Brandon raised his arms. "We destroyed everything. Touchdown. Grand slam."

"There's an easy way to find out." Reece motioned toward the door. "Let's go back and make sure."

They clipped back over the twenty feet they'd just covered. Reece reached the door first and pushed it open. Dana stepped through the door and stared at the room. Even though part of her had expected it, it still felt strange. All the posters were back on the walls. The smell of smoke had vanished. There was no evidence they'd ever been inside the room.

"This is impossible." Brandon opened his palm and a ball of fire materialized instantly. "Fine. Let's go again."

"Let's not," Reece said.

Brandon set up like a major league pitcher standing on the mound for the World Series. "This time not even the room will stay standing."

"It won't do any good," Dana said.

Brandon ignored her comment and heaved the fireball at the center of the wall across from them. The posters along the entire wall were consumed in an instant. And an instant later the posters all returned.

He turned and stared at Reece. "Am I missing something here?"

"Yes."

"Don't you see, Brandon?" Dana asked. "Destroying the posters does nothing. That's like cutting off the top of a dandelion and expecting the root to die. We have to destroy the content." She paused and looked at Reece. "Where the content comes from."

"Exactly." Reece uncrossed his arms.

"Why didn't you tell us this at the start?" Brandon said.

"This is your mission, not mine."

"But you could have clued us in on what would happen in this room."

"Hearing is one way of learning. Experiencing is another. The latter is the more powerful of the two by far."

Brandon glanced around the room. "It has to be here somewhere."

"No. The content comes from somewhere else. Deeper. Hidden. Protected." Dana spun in a slow circle, gazing at every inch of the room. But where?

She circled the room, pausing at certain spots, touching the wall with her fingers. She didn't know what she was looking for, but if there was a time to start trusting the Spirit to tell her, it would be now. *Help me.*

As she circled the room a second time, she sensed something in the far wall. Wait. Not in the wall, it was at her feet. She stomped with her foot and a hollow muffled sound came back to her.

She motioned Brandon and Reece over. They peeled back the carpet, which revealed a small door. Dana opened it. A steep staircase descended far enough that the light from the room they kneeled in didn't show the bottom of the shaft. The walls were dark gray and the smell of thousand-year-old books wafted up at them.

"Who wants to go down the creepy, smelly staircase into God only knows what?" Brandon said.

"I'm going," Dana said.

"I'm with you." Reece stared at Brandon.

"Why not?" Brandon shrugged. "It's not like we have the chance of bumping into anything, say, demonic. Right?"

Dana scanned the top of the staircase for a light switch but there was none. She took a deep breath and descended as Brandon's voice called out behind her.

"Looks like our buddy Marcus has some pretty dark places in his soul."

"Like all of us," Reece muttered.

When she reached the bottom of the staircase, Dana found herself in an area the size of a cramped elevator shaft. The only door was to her right. She waited till Reece and Brandon stood beside her, then she pushed the door with her foot. It creaked open and bright light flooded them at the bottom of the staircase. In front of them was a tastefully furnished room about the size of a hotel lobby. Wood paneling covered the walls, and wall sconces were fixed every few feet.

A small fountain in the center of the room bubbled with liquid that looked almost transparent. A few men and women meandered through the room, entering and exiting from doors on either side. They smiled at the three as they passed.

"This is not what I was expecting to find." Dana glanced at the others.

"No kidding," Brandon said.

Dana glanced around the room. "See that door on the other side of the room? My guess is Marcus's content is coming from whatever is behind that door."

"How do you know that?" Brandon said. "The Spirit is talking to you again, huh?"

"No. Deductive reasoning, Sherlock. That's the only door with someone guarding it."

An elderly man stood in front of the door. He didn't have a beard, but he still looked like his December activity should be playing Santa at Macy's.

"I wouldn't call that guy a guard. Unless he takes a whack at you with a candy cane."

"Good. Then it shouldn't be difficult to get inside." But something told Dana it would not be easy. "Should we all go?" She glanced at Reece.

"Yes. Remember, stick together whenever possible."

Halfway across the room the man noticed them and looked up. He smiled and waved them closer. "Hello! Welcome. So good to see you. How may I help you on this fine day?"

They stopped a few feet from the man.

"We need to see what's behind that door." Dana pointed over his shoulder. From across the room it had looked like an innocuous six-paneled door that would be found in millions of homes across America. But close up it had changed. It was made of iron, triple bolted, and barred.

"This door?" The man turned and pointed behind him.

"Yes," Brandon said.

Santa shook his head like he was a bobblehead doll. "I don't think you mean this door. No, I don't." He smiled. "But if you'd like to have a look around the reception area, please feel free to do so. I'll be right here if you have any questions." He pointed to the floor at his feet and laughed and his belly shook.

"Yes, that's the door we mean." Reece took a step closer to the man.

Santa's smile grew bigger. "No, no. You mean some other door. I'm sure of it." He waved his hand and arm around the room. "Look at all the fine doors we have available. There are many others to choose from that I'm sure will suit you quite well."

"We need to get inside that room behind you," Reece said as he stepped forward.

"Yes, I'm sure you *think* you do, and golly, I sure wish I could let you in, but oh so regretfully, it simply cannot be allowed. No one has a key to get in except Marcus. Do you know Marcus? He's such a good friend. I would never do anything that might upset him."

Reece wagged his finger. "He won't be upset about us going inside."

"I believe it would upset him. I'm quite sure of that. Quite sure. Marcus and I have known each other for a long, long time, and I know how he feels about most things." The man clasped his hands over his ample stomach.

"No, I don't think you do. We need the key."

"That I have, of course. But I've promised him I won't open the door for anyone but him. But I sure don't mind telling him you stopped by. Can I do that for you? Very happy to do that."

"We're friends of his." Brandon forced a smile. "He said we could go in."

The man shook his head. "Oh no, he didn't. I'm sure of that."

"How can you be so sure?" Dana asked.

The smile vanished from the man's face. "Marcus doesn't tell anyone about this room. I make certain."

"He told us about it." Reece turned to Brandon and her and mouthed the word, "Pray."

The man stroked his chin and his smile returned. "I'm not going to be able to persuade you to leave, am I?"

"No," Dana said.

"I see." The man lifted his left hand in a flash and an invisible wall slammed into Dana's chest, and she flew backward halfway across the room. She pulled in a ragged breath and looked for Reece and Brandon. They lay next to her, both gasping for air, Brandon's eyes wide, Reece's narrow. Reece stood and helped Dana to her feet. She continued to pray but no solutions came.

Santa leaned against the wall next to the door. "Good-bye. You're going now, aren't you?"

She turned to Reece. "I know you're letting us lead this time, but I'm out of ideas and I'm not getting anything from the Spirit."

"Okay." Reece draped his arms around Brandon's and her shoulders and pulled them close. "Santa is the gatekeeper so you've assumed he has the keys to the door. But I think the door is an illusion. We don't need keys; we simply need to step through the door."

Brandon snorted. "Kris Kringle there isn't an illusion. His blasting us across the room isn't an illusion."

"True, but at least it means we don't have to worry about a key or about opening the door if it doesn't exist. We can concentrate on the guard."

"And how exactly will we get by Santa-man?"

Reece closed his eyes and opened them a moment later. "Hebrews chapter 1, verse 14."

"We're going to quote that to him?"

"No, we're going to do what the verse says."

Dana tried to recall what the chapter was about. "Tell us."

"'Isn't it obvious that all angels are sent to help out with those lined up to receive salvation?'"

"It's not obvious to me." Dana glanced toward the door. "So what's the verse?" She looked at Brandon's face, which told her he didn't know the Scripture either.

"That is the verse." Reece pulled them closer.

The floor shook and they glanced up to see Santa-man strolling toward them. "You couldn't take a hint, could you? I tried to be kind, I truly did, but kindness is gone now." He glanced at his wrist, which had no watch on it. "So you have about fifteen seconds before I demonstrate what real pain is."

His rubber shoes padded on the marble floor as he continued to amble toward them. Reece grabbed their hands like they were in a vise and yanked them back a step. "Pray with me!"

"We don't have time to pray—" Brandon yelled back.

Santa was within twenty feet, his arms reaching toward them, laughter chugging out of his mouth.

"Praying is all we have time for!"

They stumbled back another two steps.

"We summon your angels, Father, by the authority you've given us in Christ. Bring them now to war for us."

Light filled the room and the walls shook as two massive warriors appeared, their backs to the three of them, swords in their hands. Santa-man's eyes narrowed and in seconds his hair turned black and his body morphed to seven feet tall, thick muscles bulging from his neck and arms.

"You have no right to be here." The demon guarding the door raised a foot-long knife and spun it in his hand.

"We have every right."

"He's agreed with me on every regret I've planted. He's savored them. Meditated on them. They've seeped into the deepest parts of his soul. They'll live on with or without me."

The angel on the left took two steps forward. "Then destroying you might be a waste of time."

The demon stared at him, the light around him seemingly swallowed by his eyes.

"But"—the angel glanced at the other warrior to his right—"it is a chance we're willing to take."

The two blazing angels leapt at the demon, who screeched a guttural cry as his knife flashed toward the first angel's throat. The clash of blade on blade rang through the room for only seconds before the two angels straddled the still form of the demon on the ground, its head sliced from its body. The warrior on the right turned and gave Dana a slight nod. Then he, the other angel, and the demon vanished.

Dana shuddered and looked at the others. Reece had no expression but Brandon massaged the sides of his head with both hands. "Wow. Wow. Wow."

"No time to debrief. Sorry." Reece took two strides forward.

"We need to keep moving." He dragged them across the room and stopped in front of the door. "Ready?"

Dana stared at the door. It hadn't changed. The bars were still on it. An illusion? She didn't think so. Reece didn't hesitate and stepped through the closed door as if it didn't exist and he vanished. Brandon followed. Dana hesitated, then stepped through the door into the darkness.

THİRTY-EİGHT

As Dana crossed the threshold, bright sunshine flooded down on her and she found herself standing on a two-lane winding country road with birch trees lining both sides, the sun filtering through lime-green leaves. The air was fresh and crisp. Black-throated gray warblers perched on the branches. She turned to find the doorway behind her, but when she spun all she saw was the road curving off into the distance.

"I like this place muuuuuuch better." Brandon glanced at their surroundings. "Which way?"

"Forward," Reece said.

They strode down the road, the sun at their backs—warmth creeping back into her body. After a few paces, Dana stared at the curve in the road fifty yards ahead. Something gray seeped around the corner and swallowed the sunlight. As they rounded the bend, a thin fog swirled through their legs and up their bodies.

"On alert," Reece said.

Their pace slowed and Dana glanced back and forth to her right and her left. A minute later an old wooden bridge made of thick beams and cable supports appeared out of the mist. They stopped where the bridge and the road met, and Dana peered into the fog. There. Fifteen yards ahead. A man stood leaning over the bridge, his chest on the railing, arms hanging down, his body jerking as if something were trying to pull him up and over the edge. She jogged toward the figure and the others followed. It had to be the professor.

"Marcus?"

Yes—it was him.

The professor was at the center of the bridge, thin ropes slicing into his bare wrists and forearms. Attached to the ends of the ropes were weights of iron, thick rusted chains, and dark gray barbell plates.

"There's no way we can lift those," Dana said.

Marcus's body continued to shake and his speech came in stilted gasps.

"I don't know how . . . to let go."

"You don't need to," Brandon said. "Look."

On the railing just on the other side of Marcus lay a silver blade with an inlaid pearl handle that seemed to throw off light.

"I can never reach it," Marcus sputtered.

Brandon danced around the back of Marcus, plucked the blade off the railing, and didn't hesitate. In four swift motions he sliced through the ropes and the weights streaked into the chasm. Marcus pulled back from the edge and slumped to the wood planks at his feet.

"Thank you. Thank you." Marcus turned to Brandon, then stared at his arms and swiped at the cords still tied around his wrists and arms. The thin ropes fell off as if made of dust and floated to the wooden planks.

Dana didn't doubt the chasm they stood over was bottomless. Those insidious weights had vanished forever. But once again a niggling in her heart said it wasn't enough. There was more, but what?

Brandon set the knife down on the dark beam. "It's over."

But just as in the media room—it wasn't. Wispy strings grew around the professor's arms and thickened until they were as wide as before. They snaked over the railing, waving in the breeze coming up from the depths. Then tiny weights appeared at the end of the ropes, the size of lead weights used by fishermen. Within seconds they grew to the size of grapefruits, then watermelons. Their combined weight yanked Marcus back to the railing, his arms again over the side, his body straining to stay on the bridge.

"No!" Brandon snatched the knife off the railing and sliced through the ropes again. This time the weights came back faster. He turned, his face contorted in frustration.

"What are we supposed to do?"

Once again they were going after the symptom, not the cure. Dana turned to Reece, who had stood by with folded arms from the moment they'd spotted the professor. "Help us."

Reece nodded toward the end of the bridge. She sprinted to the end, then spun on her heel in a circle searching for clues. Dana scanned the trees along the steep slope that poked through the fog and spied a few caves that burrowed into the hills and thick rocks covered with jade moss that jutted out over the entrances. Something in the caves? No, that wasn't it. There was nothing here. What did Reece want her to find?

"What!" She screamed back the way she'd come, but the only answer was soft moans from Marcus.

"Show me, Jesus."

She did another slow spin and stopped as the faint edges of a huge sign nailed to the side of the bridge filled her vision. Of course.

"Let me see, Jesus."

The fog cleared around the sign and she gasped. On it were listed hundreds of Marcus's regrets. Every choice he wished he could make over. Every moment missed with his daughters. Every moment missed with his wife.

"Brandon!"

He reached her in seconds and she pointed to the sign. He scanned it and turned to her. "What are you thinking?"

"We burn it."

"No, that's not enough. Nature abhors a vacuum. We need to put something in its place. We need to cover this—erase it—remove the words and fill the sign with thoughts to take the place of these."

"Cover it?" Dana spun in a circle. With what? Dirt? Take a rock and scrape the writing off the sign? "How?"

"I don't know. Maybe we take it down and a new sign will

appear." Brandon reached up and grabbed the edge of the sign and yanked, but it didn't budge. He stepped back.

"Look!" Dana pointed to where Brandon's hands had been. Smudges of white in the shape of his fingers covered the sign.

She stepped forward, slapped her hands on the sign, and smeared them in sweeping circles. Brandon joined her and in seconds they stared at a white canvas.

"Now what?" Brandon said.

"Somehow we have to fill the vacuum."

"How?"

She stepped up, placed her forefinger on the sign, and drew it along the bottom. A bright crimson line appeared. Dana turned to Brandon and smiled. "Ready? You take that side, I'll take this."

"What do we write?"

"No time to think about it. Write whatever the Spirit brings to mind."

For the next ten minutes the only sound was the squeak of their fingers on the sign and the clomp of Reece's footsteps coming toward them. He stood to their right, his eyes bright, and offered a single nod in appraisement of their work. Dana reached the bottom of the sign with her words and stepped back. Brandon was already finished.

I am a child of the everlasting King.
I am forgiven.
I am a warrior.
I am cloaked in righteous armor.
I was made for adventure.
I was built for battle.
I am part of a larger story.
My true and lasting affirmation comes only from my King.
I am unique above all creation—planned and perfect in design.
I have been created for a glorious destiny.
All my ways are established by you, my King, and I walk in them.
My life and actions are real, authentic, and without compromise.

I am quickened and made alive through the power of your Spirit.
My whole life is before me.
I am a shining gift from God to this lost world.
I know my name, I understand my calling, and I am worthy to walk in it.
I am strong, brave, and courageous in the face of my enemies.
Whatever is good, whatever is pure, whatever is true, dwell on these things.
My sins are scattered as far as the east is from the west.
I am a good husband to my wife.
I am a good father to my daughters.
The past is over,
And the future glimmers with radiant light.
I will look to the new day,
The dawning of hope.
I will step forward with the truth before me and will no longer look on the day that is gone.
The past is over; the future has begun.

Brandon laughed and turned to Dana. "Where did those come from?"

"You know exactly where." She smiled back, then pointed toward Marcus. "Let's try cutting the cords one more time."

After the weights hurtled into the chasm, they waited. The professor's arms stayed free of the ropes and the wonder that filled his face seemed to burn into the light fog still hovering over the bridge. Then the fog lifted, shafts of sunlight cut through the dissipating mist, and Dana blinked and shut her eyes against the brilliance. When she opened them again, Brandon, Reece, and she were back at the fire pit—each of them breathing deep.

✦✦✦

Marcus sat on the back porch of his home in Seattle's Belvedere Terrace neighborhood, his eyes closed, praying for freedom. Praying for the others. He knew they were warring for him. Possibly even inside his soul at that moment. Going into areas he hadn't faced in years. Areas he didn't even know were there. But he felt nothing. He opened his eyes and glanced at his watch. Nine o'clock. At nine fifteen he'd go inside. He turned at the squeak of the screen door behind him.

"How are you doing?" Kat leaned against the wall to the right of the door in her dark sweats.

"I'm okay."

"If they're supposedly going into your soul, shouldn't you be feeling something by now?"

"I don't know. The data to draw from at this point is extremely limited."

"I'll keep praying." Kat smiled and opened the screen door. "I do think God is going to do something."

Why hadn't he felt anything? But as the screen door shut and the clop of Kat's shoes faded into the house, Marcus realized something had happened. Something felt different. As if a match had been lit deep in his soul and the light was growing. Over the next ten minutes the sensation intensified till his chest pulsed with an energy he'd never felt before. His cell phone rang and he squinted at the caller ID. Dana.

"How are you feeling?"

"As if my chest is about to explode. It's like I've swallowed a thousand gallons of light and have no power to keep it contained inside."

"I'm not surprised." She laughed, and the sound of it reverberated through his heart and the light inside grew even more. "I'd say we had a significant victory, but you have to take the final step."

"Whatever is required, tell me."

"I'm going to text you a series of statements. Read them, out loud if you can, and let them sink deep into your mind and heart and soul and spirit."

"Anything else?"

"You have to choose to believe them."

Marcus hung up and stared at his phone till Dana's text arrived. For the next twenty minutes Marcus read the list over and over again, and the light inside him exploded.

". . . the past is over; the future has begun." He finished the list for the seventh time and closed his eyes. So much weight had risen off his shoulders, he was surprised he wasn't floating up to the top of the Douglas fir trees in his backyard.

Freedom like he'd never known swirled about him and all he could say was, "Thank you."

The screen door squeaked again. "I'm sorry to interrupt, but the girls just went to bed if you want to come say good night."

Marcus waited for the words to fly across his mental screen—"You missed so many times of saying good night that will never come again!"—and lance him with guilt. But when they came, no pain came with them. No guilt. No regret.

His friends had made it inside—fought for him, set him free. He grinned at Kat as he reached out his arms and walked toward her. She stepped into his arms and he hugged her tight, then released her, took her hand, and stared up at the diamonds in the night sky. "I would love to come say good night."

"Your face tells me you've had quite an experience since I checked on you last time. Am I going to have to become a believer in your new wild and wonderful methods?"

He turned and looked deep into her eyes. "I've become a good father."

She stared at him for a long time, a smile growing on her face. "Yes, you have. A great father." Kat wrapped her arms around his waist and laid her head on his shoulder. "And a great husband."

That night Marcus dreamed of bridges and weights and sunlight and freedom, and he didn't want the dream to end.

THIRTY-NINE

MARCUS STROLLED TOWARD HIS FIRST CLASS ON Monday morning feeling like the poster boy for Clichés-R-Us. The air did seem cleaner. The songs from the birds in the oak trees were brighter. The color of the red square and Yoshino cherry trees in the quad seemed more vibrant than he'd ever seen them.

The battle of his regrets wasn't over. He realized there was more work to be done, more skirmishes ahead, and more rubble to be worked through. But his tower of regrets had been leveled and he would never allow it to be reconstructed.

When he stepped up to the podium to begin his class lecture, he felt the Spirit suggest a different topic than what he'd planned. He smiled at the idea and started in. "Today we'll be taking a slight detour from our current discussions to explore the intersection of what some would call the divine with quantum mechanics. Our beginning will be a review of Planck time."

Halfway through his lecture, a man of average height and build slipped into an aisle seat at the back of the room. Marcus had never seen him before, but he looked older than college age. Midthirties if he had to guess.

The man crossed his legs, a thin smile on his face, his dark eyes riveted on Marcus, his brown hair slicked back from his forehead. Probably a new grad student or TA dropping in on his class. It happened often. But there was something about this guy Marcus didn't like.

He continued to lecture but the feeling intensified. Maybe because the man continued to stare at him. He stopped lecturing and looked at the man. "Excuse me, can I assist you? Are you in the right class?"

As his students turned, the man rose from his seat and slipped through the door at the back of the lecture hall. Strange. Just before class ended, Marcus called to the student the man had sat next to. "Brodie, may I see you for a moment? The rest of you are dismissed."

Brodie shuffled up to the podium. Marcus stepped down and glanced around to make sure they were alone.

"Do you know of the individual who sat next to you about half-way through class? And if you don't, could you tell me if you felt anything strange about him? Or if he said anything to you that seemed off-kilter?"

"When, today?"

"Yes."

Brodie looked puzzled. "No one sat next to me today."

"I'm referring to the man who sat next to you for five minutes at most, at which point I said, 'Excuse me,' to him and he got up and left."

"No one sat next to me today, Prof." Brodie frowned.

"He sat right next to you. Brown hair, average size . . ."

Brodie grinned. "Are you working me for some example you're going to give in class later on? 'Cause if you are—"

Brodie was serious. He hadn't seen the man.

Marcus forced a smile. "You've discovered my subterfuge. Well done."

"Rock on, Prof. Can't wait to dive into alternate realities next quarter. Take care."

Brodie scooted down the aisle and pushed through the double doors at the back of the lecture hall.

Marcus lifted his laptop off the podium and shuffled to the door at the side of the room, turned his back, and pushed it open. Before he backed through he stared at the seat where the brown-haired man had sat. His new, finely tuned spiritual eyes were miraculous and disconcerting at the same time. Marcus pulled out his cell phone and called Reece.

Hopefully tonight he'd get to talk to Dana and Brandon about it as well when Reece took them to what he called a different kind of church.

FORTY

BRANDON STOOD WITH THE OTHERS ACROSS THE STREET from a two-story home in east Redmond on an unusually warm first day of summer as he tried to guess what the next few hours would hold.

"Thursday night should be powerful," Reece had told them a few days earlier. "I believe you'll gain a new appreciation for what prayer can do."

Casually dressed men and women in ones and twos and threes strolled up the lighted walkway, greeting one another with smiles and laughter.

"This is a church?" Brandon pointed at the house.

"Yes. A home church," Reece said. "Old friends of mine. Ready?"

They were greeted at the front door by a man in his late thirties or early forties who grabbed Reece by the shoulders. "Great to see you, Reece. It's been a few years."

"Too many, David." Reece stepped into the entryway and the rest of them followed. "Thanks for letting us drop by."

David grinned up at Reece, then turned to them. "Who are your friends?"

"They are the Warriors Riding. Come to see how your group prays for each other."

David waved them farther into his home. "Come, come then, we're just about to start."

He led them into a great room with chairs and couches strewn throughout the space on thick tan carpet. Forty or fifty people in

274

a wide range of ages were crammed in a large kitchen and dining area to the right, talking and laughing as they slugged down pop and coffee.

David clapped his hands and raised his voice. "Let's gather and see what Jesus has for us tonight."

After the people settled into the great room, a kid probably in his late teens picked up a guitar and threw furtive looks at Brandon as he tuned it. Did he know who Brandon was? It seemed like it. He flashed the kid a thumbs-up.

"Go with it, you'll be great," Brandon mouthed to the kid and the teenager smiled.

The teen didn't have a great voice, but it didn't matter as his passion and flawless guitar work took Brandon and the rest of the group deep into worship. Brandon got lost in the music, and peace settled on him like a dusting of snow.

Twenty minutes later David clasped his hands. "Does anyone have anything you want to tell us before we go after some hearts?"

A few people shared verses and how they impacted them, and another played a powerful clip on YouTube of a miraculous answer to prayer. When it was over, David stood and glanced around the group. "As always, we'll break up into circles of four or five and see where the Spirit wants to set people free."

Brandon studied the people in the room as they broke into groups. It was obvious this part of their time together was a regular activity.

David looked at Marcus, Dana, and him. "Each of you feel free to join any of the groups. You can take part as much or as little as you want to."

Brandon looked around the room and saw an open chair next to the guitar player. He walked over, slid into the seat, and shook the kid's hand. "Rock and roll."

"Are you really—?"

Brandon leaned close to the teen's ear. "Yeah, but let's keep that between you and me, okay?"

"Sure." The kid grinned at him.

"You did an awesome job up there."

"Really?" The kid's smile grew wider. "Thanks, man."

As the rest of the group settled in, Dana slipped into a seat directly across the circle from Brandon. Great. She couldn't have sat with one of the other groups?

A few minutes later a woman to his left raised her voice. "Is there anyone here who would like us to pray about something specific?" She patted her chest. "Did anyone feel that pounding in his or her chest during worship where you knew the Spirit was saying, 'Let's heal this tonight'?"

For a long time no one spoke. Then a man who looked like he was in his late twenties shifted in his chair. "Uh, yeah, but this might be a little awkward."

The woman who seemed to be the leader in the group smiled. "When does this ever get completely comfortable?"

"Yeah." The man glanced at her, then settled his eyes on Brandon. "It's just that we've never done it with someone their first time here." The man continued to stare at Brandon, then pointed his finger. "I think we're supposed to pray for you."

"I don't think it's me." Brandon frowned at the guy. "I'm fine."

"There is indeed a first time for everything." The woman glanced around at the others in the circle. "Let's pray for Brandon."

"No, really." Brandon held up a finger. "I'm fine."

"You don't want us to pray for you?"

Was she kidding? Of course he didn't. These people were strangers. What would he tell them to pray for? He glanced around the circle and his gaze locked onto Dana's. He knew that look and he knew she was right.

"Uh, yeah, I suppose it would be okay."

"Wonderful. Ready?" The woman bowed her head.

Brandon held up his finger again. "Since I'm brand new here, don't you want me to suggest something to pray for?"

She smiled. "No, we're going to ask the Holy Spirit what's going on."

"Okay." Brandon sat back. Wow. This really was Reece's kind of group.

After three or four minutes of silence, the man next to him put his hand on Brandon's shoulder. "You can open your eyes now, Brandon."

He glanced at the others in the circle. It was obvious from the looks on their faces they had been waiting for him to open his eyes. No one had said "Amen." No one spoke a word during the "prayer" time. How did they know when it was time to be done?

The woman glanced around the circle. "Did any of you sense anything or see anything?"

A teenage girl stared at her palms, then raised her gaze to Brandon. "I got the words *finish strong* and *push through*."

A middle-aged woman in a light blue blouse to Brandon's right nodded. "That's what I kind of got too. I kept seeing the word *incomplete* in big red letters."

To his left, an elderly gentleman with brown suspenders over a white dress shirt patted his cheek as he stared at Brandon. "I keep getting *discipline*, but not in a good way, as if that's a painful word."

"Is any of this making any sense?" The leader nodded to the man and turned to Brandon. "It's okay if it doesn't."

Brandon stared at them. How did they know? "Yeah, it's making sense."

As long as he could remember, finishing anything was a grind—an emotional marathon. Every song he wrote, every album he recorded took so much mental energy to get it right, that on some days he contemplated quitting music altogether. He'd prayed about the problem for years without any change. Even went to counseling at one time, but it hadn't helped. No one knew about the struggle—not even Kevin. Brandon always gutted through whatever the project was at the time, made it happen, completed the task, made it as good as possible, but it was like going through a strainer every time.

The part of him that couldn't settle for a mediocre recording or mediocre songs was bigger, but the part that fought against it, the part that didn't care how the song turned out, was almost as powerful and it seemed to be getting stronger.

"There's a part of me that wants things to be right, as perfect as possible. But there's another part that doesn't care. A part that says I'm not worth making it perfect or even just great. That I should settle for good enough. That part wears me out and I don't know how to fix it."

"Thanks for taking that risk." The woman nodded at Brandon. "I imagine it wasn't easy to open up to us like that." She turned and looked at Dana, who had a stunned look on her face and seemed to be staring through the group to the wall in back of him.

"How about you, Dana? Did you hear or see anything?"

"What?" She brought her attention back to the woman leading their small circle.

"Did the Spirit show you anything while we were listening?"

"Me? Um . . ." She blinked and gazed back and forth between the woman and Brandon.

"Do you want to tell us?"

"I'm not sure." Her face flushed as she glanced furtively at the people in the circle. "This whole way of praying is brand new to me. I don't even know what you're doing, so what I saw just now makes no sense. I didn't get a word like you three did"—she motioned to the two women and the man—"I got a picture."

"What did you see?" the leader asked.

Dana leaned forward and rested her elbows on her knees. "You're going to think I'm strange."

"Don't you think we're a little strange?" The leader smiled.

"Yes." Dana smiled back, then looked at Brandon as if to get his permission. He nodded and she began. "I saw a model airplane in a bedroom up on a windowsill. The sun was at an angle where it hit the wings just perfect, lighting them up. A little boy sat at a desk, staring at it. This kid was proud of that plane, his chin propped up on his hands like something out of a sappy holiday movie."

Brandon's body went numb. "What color was the plane?"

"Red with blue stripes, like the kind of plane Charlie Brown's dog flew in the comics."

Unbelievable. He hadn't thought about that plane for twenty years. Brandon slumped back in his chair, his eyes blinking back tears. "That was my plane. When I was eleven I wanted to make a model plane that was perfect. I decided on a Sopwith Camel because of Snoopy, because it's the kind of plane he flew when he battled the Red Baron. It took me three months working on it every night. When I finished it, I set it in my windowsill." Brandon stared at Dana. "Did I tell you about the plane?"

Dana shook her head.

"How did you know?"

She shrugged.

"What happened, Brandon?" their group leader said.

"When my stepmom came through the front door that evening, her scream pierced through my door like a sword. She yelled for me to come downstairs, so I did.

"There she stood, pointing at the dining room table and shouting how stupid I was. I'd put newspapers down, but some of the red paint still got on the table. I didn't know it till she showed me what I'd done.

"She asked what I was working on when I did it, and I told her my plane. She yanked me up the stairs and made me take my Sopwith Camel and set it in the middle of my room. She stood next to it and smiled at me, then raised her foot and smashed it down on the plane three times as hard as she could. She pointed at me and said, 'That will teach you to spill paint on my dining room table.' She made me sweep it up and dump it in the garbage can."

Their leader leaned forward. "Did you ever build another plane?"

Brandon stared at her for a moment before answering. "I never built another model of any kind." He dragged his fingers through his blond hair.

A man to Brandon's right who hadn't yet spoken got out of his chair, stepped around behind him, and put his hands on Brandon's shoulders. "You believed a lie that day. You made a vow you've had to fight against all your life. Do you know what it was?"

Brandon wiped his eyes and realization swept through him. It was so obvious and yet he'd never seen it. "I told myself I'd never make anything perfect again. That it wasn't worth it. Whatever I did or made or tried would just get destroyed, so why bother."

"Yes," the man behind him said. "What else?"

"That I wasn't worth it. I became that plane. Not worthy of flight."

"And how has that affected you?"

"I thought if I just forced myself through my projects, it would eventually get easier."

"But it's never worked, has it?" the man behind Brandon said.

"No."

"We are so good at treating the symptoms and so lacking in curing the disease."

Brandon nodded and tears rose to his eyes again. He'd always thought his deepest wound came from his stepmom calling him names. But this wound was even deeper. This wound and his mom walking out on him, then her not being interested in him as an adult, was a knockout combination.

"And what lie has the enemy told you all this time since the plane was destroyed?"

"That there's something wrong with me. And I'm not worthy of anything great."

"And yet the enemy is the one who set up the circumstances to make you believe that in the first place. First he gets us to make a vow, then beats us up when we continue to agree."

Brandon barely heard the words because a revelation sent him out of his chair and onto his knees. The vow had not only affected his music, it was a sledgehammer in his relationships. He hadn't told Dana the real reason he'd broken up with her. Yes, he wanted to protect himself—that was part of the reason—but there was a far deeper reason. He wasn't worthy of her. He wasn't worthy of a person as beautiful and kind and strong as she was. He wasn't worthy of anything truly wonderful.

Brandon stared at Dana as he spoke. "I'm not worthy of anything great, let alone perfect."

"We have to break the vow. You are so worth it, Brandon. Not because of your music or your concerts. But for you. Just you."

He shook his head no till strong hands came to rest on his shoulders and his head. For the next twenty minutes their circle prayed with Brandon and for Brandon and for each other. The freedom he felt when they finished was like breathing the freshest mountain air he'd ever breathed. He was worth it. He was worthy. He gazed at Dana. So beautiful, so true. Brandon thanked her with his eyes, then got up, walked over to her, took her hand, and thanked her with his words.

"You've set me free."

She didn't answer. She didn't need to.

Someday he would tell her the deeper reason. But not now, not until the time was right.

+ + +

As Reece, Marcus, Dana, and he walked toward their cars later that night, Reece said, "Thoughts before we call it a night?"

Marcus turned and looked at David's house. "I want to come back."

"I had no idea," Dana said.

"And you, Brandon?"

How could he describe what happened in just a few words? "Revelation. Healing. I feel like I just had a transfusion where superpowered blood was pumped into my veins. And Dana and the Holy Spirit and the others were the medical staff."

He told them what happened and Reece nodded throughout.

"If they'd let me say what I thought I needed prayer for, we would have missed the mind-blowing freedom the Spirit had for me."

"Exactly."

"I think from now on, my prayer is going to be more of a two-way conversation."

"Novel idea." Reece grasped his shoulder. "Well done, you just jumped off another cliff and built powerful wings."

Reece glanced over Brandon's shoulder and looked at each of them, an intense gleam in his eye. As if that was new. A concentrated gaze was his look 90 percent of the time, but his countenance as he studied their faces raised the intensity level past the red line.

"Friends, we need to talk about the days to come. This war continues to escalate." He described the visitor to Marcus's class and reminded them of the encounter in Dana's office and the incident on the soccer field with Marcus's daughter.

"We know Dana's visitor wasn't human." He looked at Marcus. "I don't believe the man you saw or the man Kat and your daughter saw were either."

A look passed over Marcus's face as though a truth he'd been trying to deny couldn't be held back any longer.

"I know." Marcus blew out a long breath. "And the action we need to take?"

Reece pointed to the home they'd just exited. "You've seen the power of listening prayer just now. The Spirit will speak. Take time to listen on your own. Then war in the heavens for the battle he reveals."

Marcus rubbed his temple.

Brandon turned to the professor. "You're getting something right now, aren't you?"

"There will be a battle tomorrow." Marcus's gaze flitted to all of them, then to the ground.

"With who?" Dana said.

"I don't know. But I know I need to pray."

Brandon grabbed his friend's elbow. "And we need to join you."

FORTY-ONE

"Come on, Mommy." Jayla yanked Kat's arm on Friday afternoon as they stood on the corner of 25th and 49th, just north of University Village, waiting to cross the street. "Let's go."

"Stop that, Jayla. We have to wait for the light to turn green."

"I know." Jayla bobbed her ten-year-old head back and forth. "But there's not any cars coming. So we should go. We gotta get Abbie from practice, right? Gotta be on time. You said. So I'm helping."

Kat laughed. "Yes, but we still have to wait." Jayla was always on the go, ready for the next adventure, always running everywhere she went.

The instant the sign said Walk, Jayla let go of Kat's hand and skipped out into the crosswalk. The roar of an engine being gunned filled the blue sky and time slowed. Kat turned to see a car come out of nowhere and streak toward Jayla—moving at least ninety.

"No!"

Jayla turned, her face toward the car about to end her life. Her complexion was the color of paste and her mouth opened a crack.

Kat stumbled into the street. It didn't matter there was little chance of making it in time. It didn't matter that they would both be killed. She had to try. But after one step something from behind yanked her back. Then a flash as a man darted around her and lunged toward Jayla, his feet digging into the asphalt like a sprinter.

Centimeters before impact, the man reached Jayla, snatched

her into his arms, and lifted her into the air. The car slammed into the man's hamstrings and launched him off the ground. Somehow he twisted his body while in the air so he landed with Jayla on top of him.

From behind her a voice shouted, "Get that guy's license plate! Did anyone see it?"

Kat staggered to her feet and stumbled over to Jayla and the man.

"Jayla!" Kat ran her hands up and down her daughter's sides. "Are you hurt?"

Jayla blinked, trying to hold back tears. "I'm okay, Mommy. I am." She glanced to her left. Kat spun toward the man, who raised himself to his knees and stared at her.

"How did you do that? How did you move so fast? You saved her life."

He nodded and brushed off his jacket. "She needed to be saved."

"He hit you. How bad are you hurt?"

"I'll be all right."

"Are you sure? You have to be injured after being hit at that speed."

"I'm sure, but I do appreciate the concern." The man got to his feet and eased over to Jayla and her.

As he did a woman approached them waving a white slip of paper. "I got his license plate."

The man kept his gaze fixed on Kat and shook his head. "They'll never find the man. That wasn't his car."

"He stole it?"

"Yes."

The way the man answered gave no room for doubt as to its truth.

"How do you know that?"

The man touched Jayla's shoulder. "Are you all right?"

She nodded.

"Good."

He turned back to Kat. "Will you do me a favor?"

"Of course. Anything."

"Pray for your children." The man's eyes grew more intense. "For yourself and for Marcus. There is power in prayer."

"Who are you?" Kat's body convulsed.

"A helper." The man leaned down and whispered in her ear, "Stay strong. The King is for you."

He stood and jogged through the gathering crowd. In seconds Kat lost sight of him and two thoughts raced through her mind in rhythm with the pounding of blood through her veins.

Jayla and she had just been rescued by an angel. Jayla and she had almost been murdered by a demon.

✦✦✦

Marcus set his cell phone down after a thirty-minute conversation with Kat and stared out the window of his office at the oak tree and the leaves jousting with the wind. A dull sensation crept through his body as he slumped into his chair as if he'd been misted with Novocain. They were all right. He kept repeating the mantra, but it didn't help the fear that pulsed through him. Kat was stronger than he'd imagined she could be. Told him it was okay. That God had protected them.

He stared at the *Blade Runner* poster on his office wall. He'd always imagined himself as the hero, Deckard, tracking down the replicants. But in this case he was the one being hunted. Marcus picked up his phone and dialed Reece.

"Hey, Professor."

His words sputtered. "The ice . . . this is . . . it's getting precariously thin, Reece."

"What do you mean?"

"Kat and Jayla . . ."

"Yes?"

"They were almost killed just now."

"What?"

Marcus spilled the story as he paced in front of his desk. "Do you understand what I'm saying? A demon came after them!"

"I understand and I can relate far more than you realize. I'm sorry."

"That is far from satisfactory." Marcus clenched his fist and pressed it against his lips. "He's targeting my daughters and you're sorry? How am I supposed to fight this?"

"You did fight it. You were warned last night and you stepped in and fought well. And there was victory today."

"I don't care. This has to come to a halt or I'm out."

"It did. You and Kat stopped it."

"So Kat and I will have to pray in the way we did last night and this morning all the time?"

"Not all the time. But at certain moments, without question. With her and on your own. You must fight for your family, Professor. Are you willing to?"

Yes, of course he would pray and bring the power of the Spirit against the attack. Yes, Kat and he would join together in the fight. Yes, he realized he'd signed up for a battle when he got on that plane for Well Spring. But he hadn't enlisted his family in this war.

"It's your choice to back down or not," Reece said.

"You make it sound like I'm a coward."

"That was not my intent. I know you are not a coward. You are a warrior riding strong. But that does not mean you are without choice."

"What about the prophecy?"

"All I can do is choose to step into or not step into what the Spirit has commissioned me to do and trust him with what happens. You must do the same, friend."

Marcus hung up and sat in his office till the sound of doors closing and shuffling feet in the hallway outside his office faded into the late afternoon. When he walked in his door at home half an hour later, the girls were slouched on the couch in front of the TV, and Kat was sitting at the kitchen table, her Bible open, a pen and pad of paper next to her. A hint of her perfume hung in the air, which seemed to bring a peace he shouldn't be feeling.

Marcus slid into the chair across from her and pulled her hands into his. "Are you all right?"

She answered by pulling one of her hands away and lifting a three-by-five card off the table. "Read this."

Marcus took the card and read Kat's impeccable cursive.

"You asked God for help and he gave you the victory. God is always on the alert, constantly on the lookout for people who are totally committed to him." 2 Chronicles 16:8–9

When he looked up, Kat leaned forward and clasped his hands. "It's time for you to make a choice."

"What choice?"

"Whether you trust God or not. Whether he is in this journey you're on with Reece and Dana and Brandon or not. Whether you want to be in this war God has invited you into, or look in the mirror with regret at the end of your life because you left the field of battle with things undone."

Marcus stared at Kat, a quiet fire of determination in her eyes. He folded the card with the verse on it and put it in his pocket. "I choose the life of no regrets."

At nine Marcus closed the door of his study, sank to his knees on his dark brown carpet, and entreated the Spirit to protect Kat, protect Abbie and Jayla, protect Brandon, Reece, and Dana. His sense of time seemed to melt and his pleas grew in their passion as he gripped the carpet with his hands and cried out to God. He didn't rise till the soft chime of his grandfather clock rang midnight.

FORTY-TWO

"I THINK IT'S DEFINITELY TIME, REECE." BRANDON pointed his stick at the big man and smiled.

Dana, Reece, Marcus, and he had sat around Reece's fire pit on Sunday evening for half an hour, hearing about the attack on the professor's wife and daughter, listening to the Spirit together, praying for protection, and learning a new song Brandon had written.

"Time for what?" Reece poked at the coals and a column of red sparks shot into the air. It reminded Brandon of Fourth of Julys when he was a little boy, and the parents and kids in the neighborhood would gather in the street and light off what he named Zippy Poppies.

"For you to speak to us of info you've been hanging on to for far too long."

Dana leaned back in her chair and crossed her legs. "I like this already."

"And what, pray tell, do you believe you deserve to hear about?" Brandon opened his arms. "Your name. Or names. Now that I have mine, the only one we're missing is yours. That conversation is long overdue, and I think my fellow warriors would agree with me."

"I concur," Marcus said.

"Great call, Brandon." Dana tapped Reece's leg with her foot. "You were going to do that ages ago."

"Nah, you guys don't want to hear about my names." Reece tossed the stick he'd stirred the coals with into the fire and sat back on the dark-stained cedar bench that circled the fire pit. "Let's stick to calling me Reece. Or OMT."

"OMT?" Dana said.

"Old Man Time."

They laughed.

"Nice try, boss," Brandon said.

"I'm not your boss; I'm your coach. But much more than that I'm your brother and I'm your friend. Like C. S. Lewis says, 'Friendship is born at that moment when one person says to another, "What! You too? I thought I was the only one."'" Reece glanced at each of them. "And that's what you've become to me during—"

"Whoa, cowboy! Let's get the horses back in the corral." Dana laughed. "While we appreciate the effort, going for the monologue-about-something-else-till-we forget-the-original-subject won't work, so you might as well save your breath."

Reece nodded and almost smiled. "I suppose I owe you that." He stared into the fire for a long time, the only sound the popping of the pitch inside the logs on the fire.

"God gave me a name thirty years back. And another one about six months ago."

"Interesting," Brandon said.

"The most recent first," Marcus said.

"Nah, first one first." Brandon picked up a stick off the pile of wood to his right. It reminded him of something. Something from Well Spring? Yes, that was it. It looked almost identical to the stick Dana had held when they walked the riverbank during their time at the ranch. As he studied it, the Spirit said, *Pay attention*. To a stick? Odd. He set it on his knees and turned to Dana.

"It looks like you're the tie-breaker vote, Dana. What order?"

"Chronological."

"All right, first name first." Reece leaned back in his chair and looked at the sky. "I was hiking the Pacific Crest Trail from California to Washington in the late seventies when I heard God say, *You're my Meriwether Lewis.*

"I had no idea who that was. But when I got home I looked up the name. He meant Meriwether Lewis of Lewis and Clark."

"He was saying you were a trailblazer in spiritual things," Dana said.

"Uh-huh." Reece's head fell forward and he stared at the fire. "True."

The big man went silent and an invisible weight seemed to settle on his shoulders. Brandon leaned forward and spoke softly. "And the second name?"

"I was on my Kawasaki Vulcan 1500 on a gorgeous early October afternoon almost to Leavenworth." Reece motioned with his right hand as if he were gunning the engine of his bike. "The leaves were this lemon-yellow color, the air was crisp, and the smell of fall was everywhere.

"When I hit Tumwater Canyon, I'm just drinking in God and talking to him about everything, when he says, *Stop the first chance you get and pull over. I want to tell you something.* So I pull off at this tiny picnic area, park my bike, and walk down to the river and step out on this boulder overlooking the Wenatchee River, the air just cool enough to make me keep my jacket on.

"It had rained the day before, so there is a decent amount of water running through the canyon for that time of the year. The view to the west makes me wish I had my camera, so I sit on the boulder and stare at the river to burn the image into my brain and wait for God to speak.

"After six or seven minutes a name fills my head: *Roy.*

"'God, is that you?' I ask, even though I know the Spirit is speaking to me.

"He says yes and that my name is Roy. This rush of peace fills me and I know the name fits, but I have no idea who Roy is or what the name means. Nothing else comes the rest of the day. But on my ride back to Seattle that night, just as I pass a small thundering waterfall next to the highway, another name comes to me and I know who Jesus is saying I am."

"What was the second name?" Marcus asked.

"Hobbs."

"Roy Hobbs? From *The Natural*?" Brandon said.

"Yes." Reece's eyes brightened.

Dana shook her head. "I don't know the movie."

Reece rubbed his knees. "It's the story of this baseball player from the early 1920s who is full of stunning natural talent. When he's younger he's one of the most amazing players ever. But he's targeted by this psychotic woman who has an obsession with killing the best player in every sport.

"When she discovers Roy Hobbs is the best in baseball, she comes after him and Roy makes the mistake of letting her into his life and she shoots him. It takes him out and he disappears for sixteen years before finally coming back to the game at an age when most players are long retired."

Reece stood and plucked a long, thin piece of wood off the pile next to Brandon and held it like a baseball bat. "I'm passing Zeke's Drive In on Highway 2 when the scene at the end of the movie where Roy hammers a home run to win the series lights up in my mind. I hear God's voice say, *Reece, you are my Roy Hobbs. This is your second chance. It's time to get back on the field and play again. It's time for the prophecy to be fulfilled.*"

He pointed to a spot above his home, then swung the stick in slow motion. "You three are my championship game."

"So what was the mistake you made, Roy? What took Meriwether off the path?"

Reece shook his head. "I do want to tell you about that, but the right time isn't quite here yet."

They sat in silence for two or three minutes and Brandon used the time to soak in the moment and study the faces around him. Marcus's countenance had changed. There was a peace on it the professor had never carried before their foray into his soul.

The perpetual unease on Reece's face had vanished, at least for the moment, and he guessed his own face was more relaxed than it had been in years. The Spirit had done amazing things over the past three weeks and every indication was that they would continue.

But the expression on Dana's face flitted back and forth from one of rest to one of distress. And her gaze kept darting to the stick Brandon had laid across his knees. Something was going on, and he asked the Spirit what it was.

Be there for her. Be strong. A few seconds later Dana stood and stuffed her hands into her coat pockets. "Will you excuse me for a few minutes?"

"What's going on, Dana?" Brandon said.

"I'll be right back." She took three strides away from the fire, then turned back to them. "I think God wants me to do something I don't want to do. So I'm going to go have a little wrestling match. I'll be back in a few and let you know who won."

She sliced through the tall grass leading to the edge of Reece's property and a few seconds later disappeared through the maple trees at the edge of his yard.

"Do you have any understanding of what it's about?" Marcus said.

"Yes," Brandon answered. "I think Dana's trying to decide if she'll invite us into her soul."

FORTY-THREE

"I CAN'T DO THIS, LORD." DANA STOOD ON THE OTHER SIDE
of a huge maple tree on the edge of Reece's property looking back
at the fire and the three men whom she would have to give permission to.

You can.

"I don't want to, with everything in me, I don't want to. Not
with Brandon here."

I know.

"Then why?"

For healing. For freedom.

"Can I do it later? Tomorrow?"

There is no tomorrow. The time is now. I am with you. You are not
alone.

A leaf floated down and landed on her shoulder. God's touch. She
ambled back to the fire, feeling like she was about to post her most
private journal entries on the Internet for the entire world to gawk at.

No, it's not like that. Be strong, dear one.

When she reached the fire pit she stopped on the outside of the
circular bench. *Deep breath. Here we go.*

"You don't have to do this." Reece stared at her with intense
eyes.

Dana shuffled over to Reece and sat, her chin resting on her
fists. "Yes, I do."

"Now?"

She nodded. If only Brandon were gone. Anyone else but him. But she didn't get to pick the actors in this movie.

✦✦✦

Brandon stared at Dana, wishing he could leave. She couldn't want him traipsing around her soul. But she didn't say anything and God had told him to be there for her. Words sputtered out of his mouth before he could stop them. "Do you want me to leave—?"

"Yes."

Brandon stood but as he did, Dana's head fell back and she gritted her teeth. "But you're not supposed to."

He eased back down and stared at the flames.

"Are you ready, Dana?" Reece asked.

She nodded and Reece turned to Marcus and Brandon.

"Ready?"

The professor nodded and Brandon did the same.

He glanced at Dana again, hoping to at least make eye contact before they went in, but her eyes stayed closed.

"Okay, let's do it."

Reece closed his eyes and Brandon followed his lead. A rush of wind and a sensation of falling struck Brandon and he held his breath. Seconds later they stood in a forest of redwood trees that towered above their heads. The sound of birds calling to one another across the canopy filled the air. Sun streamed through the trees, thin shafts of light warming their faces, and the rich scent of the forest swirled around them.

It felt like midmorning on a summer day. Patches of blue sky framed the branches three hundred feet above. Behind them a dark jade-green river flowed through the trees.

"My assessment is we're in the California redwoods," Marcus said. "This is reminiscent of places where I camped as a kid."

Reece gazed at their surroundings. "Dana must have done the same."

"Why?"

"People rarely create places in their souls they haven't experienced personally. So Dana must have been to a place or seen a place like this when she was growing up. A peaceful place. Beautiful. A place to escape. A place of safety."

"Any idea where we are?" Brandon asked.

"Dana's soul," Reece answered.

"Duh. I get that part. I mean, what area of her soul are we in? And what are we supposed to do?"

A beam of light flashed and a little girl stood before them. Dana? The girl smiled, but not at them. She spoke as if she were staring right through them—a lonely look in her eyes. "I'm so glad you're here. I know you can help me." She turned and waved her hand in front of the trees. "This is my forest. I hope you like it."

It was Dana's voice—younger and with a trace of sorrow—but there was no mistaking it was hers. She skipped in between the trees, disappeared behind one, then poked her head out from behind it. "I created it for myself. It took a long time to get it the way I wanted it to be."

"Dana?" Brandon called.

If she heard him she gave no indication.

"Take your time here." She came out from behind the tree and skipped along the border of the trees like she was playing hopscotch. "It's beautiful, don't you think? Sit by the river, or skip a rock, or just sit and listen to the birds."

"Dana!" Brandon called.

"I have to go now." A sad smile rose to her face as she again looked through them, then turned toward the forest. "I love having you here." Dana waved over her shoulder and skipped into the trees, where she vanished an instant later.

"Why couldn't she hear us?"

"That wasn't exactly her," Marcus said.

"You think?" Brandon said.

"What are you hearing from the Spirit?" Reece asked.

"That we follow her into the forest," Brandon said. And in his gut he heard the echoes of isolation. He knew they wouldn't find anyone else in the forest.

"Marcus?"

"I agree, although I didn't receive that from God. I'm simply flummoxed at what else we might attempt."

Reece stepped forward toward the forest. "Don't get separated in here. Things are never what they appear to be. Ten feet apart, max. Understood?"

Brandon and Marcus gave confirmation and the three stepped into the trees. The forest floor was covered in bark and needles. The birds had gone silent or had vanished. The only sound was the crunch of their feet on the ground as they wound through the massive redwood trees.

After fifty yards the trees grew closer together. After one hundred they were less than a foot apart and Brandon and the others had to turn sideways to slide in between them.

"If the trees get any closer together, this is going to be a problem," Reece said.

"No kidding." Brandon pushed through an opening, his front and back scraping against the trees.

Marcus pushed through the same opening, then pointed to a line of redwoods ten feet ahead that were less than a foot apart. "You mean like that?"

"Exactly."

"Interesting forest," Brandon said.

"And obvious." Marcus turned to watch Reece struggle through two trees behind them.

"Care to enlighten us?" Reece asked when he got through.

"She's built a forest to keep people out."

"Exactly."

Brandon glanced to his right and left. "If you're thinking what I'm thinking, and I am thinking you're thinking what I'm thinking, we could go back out to where the trees are thinner, circle this thing for eternity, and we wouldn't find an opening."

"You could be a songwriter with catchy lyrics like that," Reece said.

"The man who never smiles makes a joke." Brandon laughed. "Miracles still do happen."

"They do indeed." Reece motioned toward the trees. "Time is always against us when we're inside a soul, so let's figure out a solution."

"Why is time against us?" Marcus asked.

"The longer we stay in, the greater chance the enemy will notice our work to set someone free and send his soldiers through the gate to attack and thwart what we're doing."

"Then let's move." Brandon smacked the giant redwood in front of them. "Let's grab a chainsaw the size of the Space Needle and cut all the trees down."

"You're thinking in the physical realm. Here we are spirit and we're not bound by the same rules."

"What are you saying, we should fly over the tops of the trees?"

"That's an option."

"Are you kidding?"

"No. But I'm not sure you're quite ready for that," Reece said. "But you will be in time."

"Do you have another option in the meantime?"

"If we can't go around the trees, let's go through them."

"That makes perfect sense." Brandon nodded. "How?"

"Like Jesus did. He walked through walls. So we should be able to walk through trees." Reece held out his arms. "Grab my forearms and close your eyes."

Brandon reached out and grabbed Reece's arm with his left hand. Marcus did the same on the other side, then closed his eyes.

"Can you believe?" Reece flexed his forearms. "There is infinite space around every molecule in our bodies. All that has to happen is the empty space in those trees needs to line up with the empty space in our bodies."

Brandon cocked his head. "Of course, how could anything be simpler?"

Reece glanced at each of them. "Here we go."

It felt like he was walking through Jell-O, only the Jell-O was going through him as well as around him. Then a burst of wind and the sensation of the trees fading away. Brandon opened his eyes.

They stood on the edge of a massive meadow at least half a mile across. Lush wild grass wavered in the breeze. No birds sang here. A sense of peace and loneliness floated in the stillness.

"Take a look at what's in the middle of the field." Brandon pointed to the center of the meadow.

A person sat in a chair—it was too far away to see if it was a man or a woman—with their back turned toward them.

"Open our eyes, Lord," Reece said.

The range of Brandon's vision increased, and soon he saw light brown hair resting on the back of a woman dressed in jeans and a gray sweatshirt.

"I think we all know who that is," Brandon said.

"She's older than she was at the river." Marcus tore off a piece of grass and rubbed it between his fingers.

Reece extended his hand toward Dana. "Shall we go greet her?"

They waded through the knee-high waving grass. Dana sat so still that after a few minutes Brandon thought she might be a statue. But a few seconds later she turned and looked at them. Or looked at him. Even though he was much too far away to see her eyes, he couldn't shake the feeling she stared only at him and that the look on her face wasn't pleasant.

Emotions of rage and loneliness swirled inside him. Not his emotions. Hers. The feelings swept around him like a tornado, pushing out in wider circles till it felt as if he were the only being in the universe.

"Brandon," the professor called. "Are you feeling all right? Your face is gaunt."

Brandon stared at Marcus. "I know what she's feeling."

Reece stopped and turned to him. "So you know how to pray."

Brandon nodded and walked on. After what seemed like

fifteen minutes, he looked back. Something was wrong. The distance between them and the edge of the forest looked as far away as the distance between them and Dana when they'd first stepped out of the woods. They weren't getting any closer.

"Is my brain addled or does this field seem to keep getting bigger?"

"It's getting bigger." Reece marched on as if this wasn't a problem.

"So we just keep walking? Or do we do something about it?"

"I'm open to suggestions."

An instant later Brandon's head slammed into something hard, and he found himself knocked backward onto the ground as a feeling of simmering anger engulfed him.

"What in the world?" Marcus said, sprawled on the ground.

"Force field." Brandon rubbed his forehead and watched Reece and the professor do the same.

"She could have had the decency to put a sign up." Brandon staggered to his feet and reached out with his fingers. Two feet in front of him was an invisible wall. Hard. And ice cold.

"How do we penetrate this, Reece?" Marcus asked. He studied Reece's head. "You're bleeding."

"Yeah, I hit that wall pretty hard." Reece wiped his head. "I'll be fine."

Brandon stared at the cut on Reece's head. "Do you want to tell me if you'll carry that with you when we leave?"

"I will. What happens here becomes reality in the physical realm."

"That I don't understand." Marcus leaned in for a closer look. "But I'm sure you'll provide us the understanding at some point."

Reece nodded and reached up to feel the wall. "Spirit, break this by the blood of Jesus."

Nothing.

"Jesus, we need to get through to talk to Dana. By your power bring this wall down."

Again, nothing.

Reece turned to Marcus and him. "This resistance isn't from the enemy."

"Then where is it coming from?"

"Dana."

"What?" Brandon said.

"We need to get out of here and have a conversation with her. She's blocking us. We need to know why."

Their spirits slid back into their bodies and Brandon gasped. Having his spirit travel out of his body and back in would take getting used to. By the time the world stopped spinning, Reece was talking with Dana.

"Are you doing all right?"

"I'm fine." Dana glanced at each of them. "What are you guys seeing?"

Marcus described what they'd seen. Dana's eyes widened. "That's the field where I imagine myself being when I want to escape the world. I've done it since I was a little girl and camped in the redwoods in Northern California."

"We can't get to you," Reece said.

"What? Why not?"

"There's an invisible wall preventing us from getting close. We prayed against it and nothing happened. We're guessing it's not coming from the enemy."

"Then where is it coming from?" Her gaze darted from Marcus to Brandon, then stopped on Reece.

"I think you might know, Dana."

"I don't have any idea."

"This might be hard to hear, but it's the truth." Reece leaned forward and took Dana's hands in his. It was the first time Brandon had seen him display this amount of tenderness toward any of them. "You're the one blocking us."

Dana pulled free of Reece's grasp. "What? I'm not blocking anybody. I want this to happen."

"You are. The shield surrounding you isn't demonic resistance. It's you. It's the sin you've allowed to take root inside. You need to turn from it."

"Sin?" Dana put her hands on her hips. "How am I sinning?"

"Another way to define repentance is when we repent, we choose to think a different way. We renew our minds with the truth. We recognize the old thought patterns as sin, then step into the new way of thinking that leads to life."

"Where is my thinking off base?"

"You have believed it's okay to keep a shield around your heart. You've believed it's okay to protect yourself because you've been wounded. You've thought keeping a polite distance from others is appropriate because of your past. You're holding on to anger as well and feel you have a right to do so. None of these beliefs are true and they are keeping you from healing. You must renounce them as sin.

"And if you continue to walk in this sin, it will be impossible for you to walk fully in step with the greatest command Jesus gave."

"Which is?"

"Love one another."

As Brandon listened to the conversation, a truth exploded in his head like a hand grenade. How could he have been so stupid? When the Spirit said, "Be there for her," it didn't mean for him to be inside. It meant be warring in prayer while the other two were inside.

"I'm part of the problem as well." Brandon ground his teeth.

Reece turned to him. "What do you mean?"

"I mean it's me being here that's keeping us out. Dana doesn't want me getting that deep inside her soul. She didn't say it. She might not even know she's doing it. But she is. I don't blame her for a second."

Brandon stood. He should have been more sensitive. Thought things through. Prayed about it more. His gut ached. "I'm sorry, Dana. I should have figured that out the moment you talked about us going in." He backed up two steps. "Listen, I'm going to give you guys some space—I'll be in your house, Reece. I'll pray for this"— Brandon waved his hand—"from there."

Reece shook his head. "No, just the opposite. We'll stay out."

"What?" Brandon frowned.

Dana stared at Reece with a look of horror.

"It needs to be you, Brandon. You need to go in alone."

FORTY-FOUR

BRANDON STARED AT REECE. IT MADE NO SENSE. HIM? Go in alone? Crazy. He turned his gaze to Dana, who had an incredulous look on her face. He couldn't blame her.

"No!" Dana glared at Reece for a moment, then turned her back to the fire and looked up at the night sky splattered with stars.

"I don't think the Dana inside would like it any more than this Dana does," Brandon said.

"And what about rule number five?" Marcus said. "Avoid going in alone if at all possible?"

"This is a rare circumstance where it isn't possible. Dana and Brandon need to face this, just the two of them."

The only sound was the crackle of the wood. The silence stretched to thirty seconds, then a minute. Finally Dana said, "All right."

"All right?" Brandon said.

Dana sat back in her chair and tapped her feet on the concrete. "You're right. I don't want you in there. And she probably won't either. But Reece is right too. And I want to be free."

"Are you sure?" Reece said.

"Yes." She clasped her hands and fixed her gaze on the big man. A battle raged in her eyes. The part that wanted freedom against the part that would mean letting go of her protection—letting go of the pain she'd held up as a defense against him for the past three years. Letting go of the belief she had to keep people at a distance. Letting

303

go of the belief she was alone in this world. "What changed your mind? How do you know Reece is ri—?"

"I just know." Dana shoved her hands under her legs and glared at him. "Are we going to do this or not?"

Reece reached over and touched Dana's shoulder. "Seek truth. Choose to turn from the lie."

Dana nodded, leaned back, and closed her eyes. Brandon did the same and as he did, Reece and Marcus started praying for strength, for power, for love to cover Dana and him. Going in alone. Wow. The anxiety he felt when the idea was first suggested vanished, replaced by an unexpected confidence. He turned inward and the familiar feeling of his spirit rushing in upon itself swept him away, and the sound of Reece's and Marcus's prayers faded.

An instant later he found himself in the meadow again—Dana in the distance—her lilting song floating down on him. He jogged toward her, calling her name, "Dana!" But she either didn't hear him or chose not to respond.

When he reached the area where the invisible shield had stopped them, Brandon slowed his pace and held his hand in front of him. He didn't need another headache. It wasn't there. Hope rose inside him. He jogged on. In a few minutes Dana stood just twenty yards away, her back to him as last time, her hair in stark contrast to the long green grass waving in the breeze. Twenty yards to his left a river meandered through the meadow, gurgling out a smooth cadence.

Brandon stared at the water as it tumbled over stones and parts of trees fallen across the stream. Something about it seemed important.

At ten yards she turned. "Hello."

It was the Dana he'd met at Spirit 105.3 five years ago. The same short hair, the same favorite pair of American Eagle jeans.

"Hello, Dana."

"You know my name." She frowned.

"Yes."

"How?"

"We've known each other for a long time." He took tentative steps toward her, his feet sliding over the soft grass till he stood a few feet from her.

"Are we friends?"

Brandon hesitated. Truth. Only truth. "We used to be. And we're becoming friends again, I think." He held out his hand. "I hope."

"I see."

Dana frowned again and stared at him. She held an ornate stick in her hand. Not ornate because of stones or jewels embedded in it, but because of the intricate pattern of thin black lines that wove throughout its surface. The stick was around three feet long and a quarter inch thick and curved at one end, which made a perfect place for it to be held.

Brandon had seen that stick before, hadn't he? Or something very much like it. An image of Dana by the river at Well Spring flashed into his mind along with the stick he'd laid across his legs earlier that evening. Of course. Brandon stared at the stick, mesmerized by . . . by what? He shook his head as if to clear it. The surface of the stick shimmered as if covered with a high-gloss finish.

"Your walking stick is beautiful."

"It is now. It hasn't always been." She held it up and kissed the middle. "It's taken me a long time to get it this way."

"What is it for?"

She drew the end of the stick through the tall, thick grass at her feet. "I found it one day in the woods when its surface was dull, but I loved its shape and it looked like the perfect companion. And it has been. Over the years I've rubbed it and caressed it until the oils of my hands have brought out its natural beauty." She ran her fingers along its surface again. As she did a glaze seemed to pass over her eyes, then vanished. Brandon stared at the stick and called out to the Spirit. *Bring truth, Lord, in the innermost being.*

The stick turned jet black but an instant later it was back to normal. The transformation happened so fast, he couldn't be sure he'd seen it. Did he imagine that? *Show me again, Lord.* But the stick stayed the same.

"What do you use it for?" Brandon asked again.

"Protection." Dana grinned as if she were a little girl stealing cookies from her mom's pantry. "David said in Psalms that his shepherd's staff comforted him in the presence of his enemies. I understand that now."

She held the stick like a sword and sliced it through the air in front of him, missing his face by less than an inch. "If I didn't trust you, I could hurt you with my friend here." She set the end of the stick onto the ground and leaned against it. It seemed to quiver.

Run!

The thought streaked through his mind and a slice of fear rushed into his heart. No. It was a lie. "Can I hold the stick?"

"No." Her eyes narrowed. "Never."

"Why not?"

"It's mine." She slid it behind her back.

Brandon took a step closer to her, the grass under his feet now suddenly brittle. "I don't want to take it. I simply want to hold it. To see its beauty up close."

As he spoke the words, the stick moved in Dana's hands, then went rigid an instant later. Brandon took another step closer and pointed at the stick. "Did you feel that?"

She frowned at him. "Feel what?"

"The stick is evil, Dana."

"No." She took a step back. "This stick is my friend."

"It is not your friend. It is not a comfort. It's poison to your soul."

"It's my only comfort." She gazed over his shoulder into the redwoods at the edge of the meadow and then at the hills to her right and left. "It's often dangerous here. I have to have my stick to protect me."

"It needs to be destroyed."

Dana slowly backed up and held the stick to her chest, then rubbed it against her cheek. A shadow flitted across her face. She pointed at him and smiled—evil in her eyes. "You're the one who needs to be destroyed."

She turned as if to walk away but spun faster than Brandon thought possible and whipped the stick through the air at his head.

He threw his arm up as he dove for the ground, and the stick glanced off his forearm. Searing pain pierced his skin and radiated through his body. He stumbled and fell to his knees, the grass now rigid and sharp, and it tore into his kneecaps.

Dana strode to the stick, lifted it over her head with both hands, and brought it down hard.

Have to move! Brandon pretended to roll to his left, then rolled to his right, trying to ignore the pain that shot through his body as the grass pierced his clothes and needled into his side.

The effort of Dana's blow threw her off balance and she stumbled forward. Brandon leapt to his feet and backed ten yards away from her.

"Do you love Jesus?" Brandon asked.

"Yes."

"The Holy Spirit? Abba Father?"

"Yes, I do."

"Can you believe they've sent me here to help you?"

A shadow passed over her face. "No, they didn't send you. The enemy sent you."

Brandon reached down and yanked up a handful of grass and roots, the sides of the blades cutting into his hand like a razor. "What happened to the grass, Dana? Why isn't it green anymore?"

"I don't know."

"You do know. Seek the truth."

"I can't trust you." Dana shuddered. "Not anyone. Especially not you."

"You can." Brandon flung the grass and roots in his hand off to the side. "The grass is dying because this field, your forest, your stick, are all lies and can't stand against the truth I'm speaking."

Dana shook her head and her breathing grew ragged. "I can't give you my heart ever again."

"I'm not asking for that. I'm asking you to let go of the evil you hold in your hand. I'm asking you to break the vow you made to never let anyone inside your heart again." He glanced at the river. Yes. That was the answer.

"I'm alone. I need it." Dana shifted the stick back and forth in her hands. "I'll miss it."

"No, you won't. I promise." He stepped toward her. "Trust me."

"Stay away from me."

"You have to throw the stick in the river."

"No."

"Freedom, Dana. Freedom. The truth will set you free."

She shook her head and stumbled back another step.

"Throw it in the river." Brandon jabbed his finger toward the stream.

"Why?"

"So it is carried away. So it can be buried in the water and destroyed."

"I don't know."

Brandon pointed at the stick and shouted, "I bind you in the name of Jesus."

Blackness surged over the surface of the stick and Dana's face turned white. "It's not evil . . . it's not."

"You know the truth, Dana."

She held the stick in her hands and glanced up and down its length as she massaged it with her thumbs. "I don't know."

"You do."

She shuddered again. "Will you wait here with me while I decide?"

"Yes, as long as it takes."

Dana sank to her knees. Brandon prayed and did not stop. For courage for Dana. For truth to permeate the forest, the meadow, the depths of her soul. For the Holy Spirit to erupt with fire and burn away the lies the enemy had planted.

Seconds, or maybe days, later Dana stood and stared at him, her face stoic. Then, without speaking, she staggered toward the water, the stick hanging low in her hands as if she carried a mammoth bag of stones. When she reached the river she didn't hesitate. Dana tossed the stick into the air with both hands. It rotated twice, then struck the water, which exploded, sending spray in all directions. The river churned and foamed as if boiling, then settled as quickly as it had been stirred up.

Brandon's shoulders sagged. It was over. He trudged over to Dana, but she didn't look at him. Her gaze was fixed on the river, her face morphing from relief to horror. He whirled around and as his eyes took in the scene, he struggled for air.

The stick had transformed into a purple-black snake, its mouth open and hissing with the force of a blowtorch, its onyx eyes fixed on him. It swam toward the shore like lightning, and when it reached the bank, it reared up like a cobra, its fangs bared. Smoke poured off its hide as if it had been scorched by the river. Laughter seemed to come from the ground and the snake rocketed toward them.

"We have to get out of here!" Brandon grabbed Dana's arm and raced for . . . where? Nothing but open field. There was nowhere to go.

Twenty yards away a scream from the snake reverberated through the air. They sprinted, feet slipping in the soft soil. He glanced back. Fifteen yards.

"Come on!"

Another glance back. Ten.

Brandon spun to face the onslaught and shouted, "The blood of Jesus Christ and the power of his resurrection and ascension against you!"

The snake reared up three feet from them and circled to their right and hissed. Now closer. Brandon scoured the ground for a rock, anything to defend themselves. Nothing. The snake flicked its tongue and hissed—low and guttural this time. Closer.

Brandon stepped in front of Dana so she was at his back, his arms out to his sides. As he did a verse shot into his mind. *"I have given you authority to trample on snakes and scorpions and to overcome all the power of the enemy; nothing will harm you."* Yes. He spoke the verse and stepped forward. *No fear. No fear.*

"You have no power over us. I bind you in the name of Jesus." He spoke the name again, just above a whisper. "Jesus."

The snake quivered and veered to the right, the gaze of its black eyes darting back and forth between Dana and him.

"You have to finish it, Dana."

She leaned into his back and shuddered. "I don't know how."

"Yes, you do."

"You do it, please."

"I can't. It has to be your choice."

He felt her rapid breath on his neck. "I'm scared."

"You haven't been given a spirit of fear, but of power."

She took a labored breath. "I break you. I renounce the vow to protect my heart above all else. I renounce the agreement that I'll always be alone. I let go of my anger and I bring the blood of Jesus against you. Be gone by his power."

Instantly the snake froze, then shrank in size and thickness till it was the size of a piece of straw. Then it vanished without any evidence it had ever been.

✦✦✦

When Brandon's eyes shot open, Marcus sat next to him and Reece sat next to Dana, prayers pouring out of both their mouths. Dana's face was covered in sweat. Brandon raised his hand to his forehead and realized his face was the same. Her eyes fluttered open and widened as she stared at Brandon, tears spilling onto her cheeks.

"What happened in there? I feel . . ." She gazed at her shoulders, clutched them with both hands, and rubbed them slowly.

"Something has broken off or been . . ." She looked up and again stared into Brandon's eyes. "I can forgive you."

He nodded and tears filled his eyes. Reece put his arm around

Dana and pulled her close. She closed her eyes and plastered her head against his massive chest. He'd done it. She'd done it. The Spirit had set her free.

Dana raised her head, opened her eyes, and looked at Brandon a long time before speaking. Her gaze moved down to his hands. She lurched out of her seat and clutched Brandon's arms. "Tell me what happened in there!" She touched his palms with the tips of her fingers. "Where did these come from?"

He looked at his arms and hands. Thin cuts lined them. They weren't deep but they stung like alcohol had been poured into them. "There was a bit of a battle. It's okay." He smiled at her. "It was worth it. You're worth it."

For the next half hour Brandon explained what had happened inside her soul. Dana's face switched from amazement to deep gratitude to wonder and back again.

"This is a beginning, Dana. There is more work to be done. Complete healing rarely happens all at once. But it is a significant start."

After a few more minutes of conversation, Reece said, "An extraordinary night. I can't explain how proud I am of both of you." He spread the remaining coals of the fire, then stood. "It's late. Time for all of us to get some rest." He glanced at Dana. "Is there anything you want to say before we go?"

She shook her head. The peace radiating from her face said enough.

"Brandon? Marcus?"

Brandon shook his head and imagined his smile was as big as the one Marcus was displaying. As they sauntered over the hundred yards back to Reece's house, he said, "Can we get together again five nights from now? I have something special for each of you. A kind of graduation present."

"Are you saying we're done with our training?" Dana said.

"Almost."

"What's left?" Marcus asked.

Reece kicked at the grass, the toe of his boot sending up a small spray of night dew. "One final exercise." His countenance darkened.

"How involved?" Brandon said.

"I'm not sure." Reece sighed. "But I get the feeling it will be your most difficult path yet."

FORTY-FIVE

"WHEN DO YOU MEET WITH THEM AGAIN?"

Doug's voice was softer than usual. Reece sat on the front porch of his home on Friday afternoon, the western hemlock trees waving in the breeze. "Tonight."

"For what purpose?"

"To celebrate them. To tell them how proud I am."

"How are they holding up?"

"Strong. Each of them has had a breakthrough. They're seeing in the Spirit, they're starting to war for others . . ." Reece paused.

"But it's not over yet, is it?"

"I don't think so."

"What is Jesus telling you?"

"That they have one final challenge to go through. I don't know what it is, but I do know it will be difficult." Reece stood and sauntered down his wooden steps toward the pond in his front yard stocked with goldfish. "What about you? What are you hearing?"

"The same. And that your part in it will be different than what you expect."

"I see."

"How is your heart?"

"Weary and strong at the same time, if that makes sense."

"Yes, it does. Stay true, Reece. You are close to the end."

"Anything else?"

"What is the truth?"

Reece tilted his head back, closed his eyes, and let the Spirit speak to him. "That we have been seated with Christ in the heavens. That we have his authority, his power, his strength."

"Yes. What is the truth?"

"That the powers of darkness have been cast down and we are demolishing strongholds in every place."

"What is the truth?"

"'Blessed be the Lord, my rock, who trains my hands for war, and my fingers for battle.'" Reece heard the turning of pages through his phone.

"Contemplate those truths, friend, and this one as well: 'Pushed to the wall, I called to God; from the wide open spaces, he answered. God's now at my side and I'm not afraid; who would dare lay a hand on me? God's my strong champion; I flick off my enemies like flies.'"

Reece ended the call and looked at his watch. They would be here in two hours. He bent his head and began to meditate on the verses.

FORTY-SIX

ON FRIDAY NIGHT AN ELECTRICITY IN THE AIR—DANA couldn't tell if it was the Spirit or the rush of their victory—told her this evening would be special. She walked around the side of Reece's home, and by the time she reached the back corner of the house, the familiar glow of his fire pit beckoned her closer. Marcus and Brandon were already there. Brandon.

She smiled. The pain was gone. Was there a dull ache still lingering? Maybe. But if so, it was so minor she couldn't feel it. Certainly not tonight. The past month had changed her life forever. And this was just the beginning. Reece had said their training would last three months. Tonight might be graduation, but graduate school was coming and she could hardly wait.

After their greeting of each other settled down, Reece brought out four flute glasses and handed one to each of them. Then he pulled a bottle of Taittinger out of a bucket of ice sitting behind him and handed it to Marcus. "Will you prepare the champagne?"

"With certainty."

He looked at each of them and tapped the air with his glass. "Even though the taste of champagne isn't my favorite adult refreshment, I told myself I would toast you with it when you'd learned to go into each other's souls and fight for each other. To start the healing process. To set each other on the path of freedom. And you've done so. With brilliance.

"And now that you've learned how to do so, you will begin

to do it for others. You will enter into the souls of many. War for them. Begin the healing of *their* wounds. And show them the path of freedom."

Reece bowed, and as if choreographed, when their leader rose back up, the cork shot out of the bottle Marcus held. The professor poured each of them a glass, then filled his own. Reece put one foot on the bench surrounding the fire pit and lifted his glass.

"To you. For being willing to follow a crazy mystic to Colorado, for expanding your spiritual mind, for taking into your heart all God has for you, for embracing each other"—Reece tipped his glass toward Brandon and Dana—"even when it wasn't easy, and for jumping off cliffs and building your wings on the way down."

They raised their glasses and drank. A sense of peace settled on Dana, and from the looks in the eyes of the others, she wasn't the only one feeling it. She stared at the chaos of the dancing flames and marveled at how far she'd come. How far each of them had come. And now there was only one more lesson.

"Last Sunday you said there was one more part of our training we needed to complete before we were finished with this phase of our journey," Dana said.

"Yes, one final step." Reece leaned forward.

"What and when will that be?" Dana asked.

Reece's eyes darkened for a flash, then lifted. "This one is not mine to schedule. The Spirit will. When it comes, I'll know it. We'll all know it, I think."

"When will we gather together again?" Marcus said.

"I'm not sure. I feel the Spirit is saying wait. But tonight is not for trying to figure out the future or plan our next steps. It is for celebration. And as your glasses touch, look in each other's eyes. It's a moment to be savored. And it isn't truly a moment unless you gaze into the window of the other person's soul while you do it." He lifted his glass again. "To freedom."

As Dana's glass rang against Brandon's, she looked into his eyes and saw . . . what? Certainly acceptance. Friendship. It seemed so.

And she hoped he read in hers a confirmation of the forgiveness she'd offered five nights ago.

Reece tossed another log on the fire, then sat and grabbed a brown paper bag at his feet. "It's time for your gifts."

He reached into the bag and drew out three small leather-bound books and placed them on his leg. "I told you about the prophecy—how you were chosen when you were young. And that I was charged with training you. I've been friends with all of you for at least a few years, but I've been praying for you all your lives.

"I asked the Spirit what you were going through. And I recorded in these journals what I would have told you if I'd known you at each stage of your life.

"I've written down the things I've shown you over the past four weeks as well as many other things for us to study together and on your own."

He held the journals in the air. "And I recorded the things I have learned during forty-five years of exploring the deeper things of the Spirit. In other words, any wisdom. I didn't make a copy, so if you come to value them, guard them well."

"Come to value them?" Brandon said.

"They're gold." Dana scooted closer to him. "You're gold."

"Twenty-four karat," Marcus added.

Reece smiled.

"What?" Brandon leapt to his feet and pointed at Reece, then hopped over to Dana and Marcus. "Did you see that?"

"I saw it. It happened. The most amazing miracle we've seen. Ever. Reece Roth smiled." Marcus laughed and Brandon and she joined him.

"Stay true to each other. Fight for one another. Go after the hearts of others and set them free. Fulfill the prophecy. Be strong in his wild love for you, for that is where your strength comes from." Reece held out a journal to each of them.

"This is for you, Restorer." He handed the journal to the professor and kissed him on the top of his head.

"This is for you, Maximus." Reece laughed, sat next to Brandon, and threw his arm around the shoulder of the musician.

"And this is for you, Arwen." Reece held the journal out to her, but she stood, pushed it aside, and grabbed the big man in a hug as tight as she could give. When she pulled away, tears were in both their eyes. After he handed her the journal, Dana ran her fingers over the leather. Creamy soft. And embossed with two sets of gold letters: *Dana*. And underneath that, *Arwen*.

"These past four weeks with you have been the most significant of my life." Reece smiled again. "You've exceeded my expectations. You are truly Warriors Riding."

For the next hour they talked about the past month, and the conversation was full of laughter. Dana stared at Reece. His smile lit up the night and she wished the moment could last for eons. But soon Reece stood as he had two nights before and bid them farewell.

"You three go ahead. I'm going to stay by the fire for a while. I need some time alone with the Trinity."

✦✦✦

Reece watched the three shuffle off into the night. He had a feeling their final test would come soon. Sooner than he wanted it to. And sooner than they were ready for.

FORTY-SEVEN

As they left Reece at the fire pit and walked the hundred or so yards toward his home, Marcus saw what looked like a blanket made of iron settle onto Dana's shoulders. She shrugged as if to throw it off, but it only seeped deeper into her back. Her gait slowed and her body drooped.

"How are you feeling, Dana?"

"I'm fine, why?"

"Because I think I saw something that would indicate you are not fine."

Brandon and Dana stopped and turned to him.

"Just now?" Dana said.

Marcus hesitated. "This might sound incongruous given our jubilation tonight, but I saw a heavy blanket made of iron land on you."

Brandon rubbed his neck and looked at Dana. "So I'm not the only one seeing things."

"You too?" Dana stared at Brandon.

"I saw a blanket of dirty snow."

She blew out a slow breath. "It's true."

"An attack?" Marcus stopped next to the back corner of Reece's deck.

"No, it doesn't feel like that." Dana frowned and looked up to her left. Seconds later her gaze locked onto Marcus. "I think I know what it is. I think it's a message, and a warning. But it's not about me."

"Then who is it for?"

"Reece." Dana looked back toward the fire and then at them. "Do you think Michael Jordan ever had to battle doubts about his ability? Do you think Billy Graham ever needed to have friends tell him he was having an impact for God? Did Charles Dickens ever need anyone to come alongside him and offer encouragement?"

Brandon nodded as if he understood what she was driving at.

Marcus nodded as well. "In other words, Reece Roth needs friends and encouragement and people to believe in him just like everyone else."

"Exactly." Dana pointed at him. "But let's take it a step further. How much do you pray for Reece?" Dana turned to Brandon before Marcus could answer. "How 'bout you?"

Marcus shook his head and looked at Brandon, whose face was as blank as Marcus imagined his was.

"Obviously about as much as I do." Dana folded her arms. "He pours his life into us, and we're so focused on ourselves and each other, we miss the guy standing right in front of us with a gaping wound that needs to be healed."

"What's he carrying? What's his wound?" Brandon asked.

She glared at Brandon. "The death of his wife and daughter."

"You discussed this with him?" Marcus said.

"I didn't talk to him about it. That's the point. I've tried a few times and it's a subject he won't go into, and from the look of the pictures, it was ages ago. But he still can't let it go."

"Let what go?" Brandon said.

"I don't know. I can see it in his eyes. This deep regret. Guilt. Remorse. Sorrow. All of the above." She shifted on the lawn. "Don't you wonder what happened that made him Roy Hobbs? The thing that took him out of the game? Yes, we know it has to do with his family, but what happened?"

"I have wondered about that." Marcus glanced back at the fire pit, a soft red glow visible, and against it, Reece's silhouette.

"Can you say we've been so wrapped up in ourselves we've never realized he's not above it all? That he doesn't have this whole thing figured out? That he needs prayer and deliverance just like anyone?"

"So what should our actions be going forward?" Marcus said.

"We should go backward." Dana turned and pointed to Reece's home. "Right now. I think it's time to ask him for the full story."

"What if he's not in a sharing mood?" Brandon said.

"It doesn't matter. We obey the Spirit and leave the outcome up to him. Let's go."

Dana turned and strode back toward the fire pit and Brandon and Marcus followed.

✦✦✦

The low chatter of voices jerked Reece out of his meditation. Brandon, the professor, and Dana marched toward him, the light of the fire making their faces glow red. Not what he needed right now. He was drained. He'd poured much of himself into them tonight. It was a good celebration. It was rich being together, but now he wanted solitude. But their expressions said they had more than a quick question in mind.

"Didn't we already say good night?"

"We thought so," Dana said. "But the Spirit said otherwise."

"I see." Reece stared at the stoic looks on all their faces. "And did the Spirit tell you what we're supposed to do?"

Dana folded her arms. "He wants you to tell us your story."

Reece sighed as the three took seats around the fire. He'd known this time was coming, but right now wasn't right.

It should be later. But the truth was the timing would never be right. He stared at the fire and began. "I was cocky in those days. Thought I knew it all."

The memory swept over him. He'd stood on the vast lawn at

Green Lake on a Sunday afternoon decades back, near the four basketball courts filled with pickup games and the beige community center building with a banner promoting the annual milk-carton boat race.

An in-line skater in multicolored spandex rolled by on the path around the lake and "Thriller" blasted out of a gargantuan boom box sitting on a picnic blanket thirty yards to Reece's left. He paced in front of a semicircle of thirty of his followers, his voice ringing out with clarity over the distractions surrounding them.

"If we would believe what this book says is true, we would move mountains. We would walk on water, walk through walls, discover new dimensions all around us." He grinned and whapped the top of the Bible with the palm of his hand. "The magic is real. But we have to believe. But belief is not enough. We must act."

Reece continued to stride back and forth in front of the small gathering. "Who will join me?" He glanced at his wife and daughter, who sat to his right and smiled. His daughter raised her hand, but his wife pulled it down a second later.

Reece stopped and asked himself what the three others sitting at the fire with him would say when he told them the next part of the story. He stood and stirred the fire and breathed deep.

Dana whispered, "Did they? Join you?"

Reece nodded and closed his eyes as the events of the day after they'd been at Green Lake hit him like a flash flood.

"Why are you so against this?" Reece smacked the brown toaster on his kitchen counter with his palm. "I can't push the others to join me if you won't."

His wife tilted her head back and sighed. When she brought it forward again she glared at Reece. "Going into someone else's soul is dangerous. It's not child's play."

"We're not children."

His wife pointed to their daughter, who sat at the table, her brown eyes wide. "She is."

"She's ten years old." Reece walked around the table and took his wife by the shoulders. "Trust me. We'll be fine. You know I've been doing this successfully for six months. Please."

"I'm worried about her." His wife looked at their daughter, who glanced back and forth between them.

"She's more sensitive to the Spirit than anyone I've ever known. At any age."

"I agree, but that doesn't mean she's ready to go into someone else's soul."

"She can do it," Reece said.

"I'm not disputing if she can, but if she should."

"You and I will be right there with her."

"Have you prayed about this? God has told you to take her in?"

"I don't need to." Reece slumped into one of the chairs at the table. "I know this is right. How are we going to show the others they have to keep pressing deeper if we're not willing to go deeper ourselves?"

"Then go deeper. You go deeper. Not me. Not Willow." Olivia put her arms around their daughter and pulled her in close.

"Trust me, Olivia."

"I can do it, Mommy." She looked up at Reece. "I'm going to be safe, right, Daddy?"

"Very safe, honey." He took her hand in his. "I'll be there with you. So will Mommy. We're just going to do a little exploring. That's all. I want to show you what it's like."

"To be in the soul of another person?"

"Yes."

"How do we get inside?"

"You don't have to worry about that part."

"What are we going to do for them?"

"We're going to help them. When we see what's inside, we know how to pray for them. It's a way to pray for them on a deeper level."

"Shouldn't we ask to be there? Shouldn't we get permission?"

"No, I don't think we need to." Reece stroked her golden hair. "We'll go into the soul of a friend of mine. I know he'll be okay with it."

"I don't feel right about this, Reece. It would be nice if you asked him first," Olivia said.

"We'll be fine." Reece smiled and patted the chair next to him and Willow shuffled over to it and sat. "Hold hands." He grinned at his wife and daughter. "Here we go."

Reece, Olivia, and Willow stood in the center of a vast desert, with dark foothills on the far horizon. The last moments of day seeped away, but there was still enough light to see a man in the distance strolling toward them, his outline silhouetted against the sky.

"This isn't right." Reece pulled Olivia and Willow close. "We're not in the right soul."

An instant later the man appeared in front of them. Dark hair, a white dress shirt, and black slacks. He smiled as he stared at them. "What are you doing here?"

"Who are you?" Reece moved his wife and daughter behind him.

The man shook his head as his smile grew wider. "No, no, no. We need to focus on my question first. What are you doing here?"

"I'm here by the authority of God."

"That's where you're wrong." The man waved his finger at Reece. "You have no permission to be here. I suspect your education has not been thorough enough. In every system there are protocols that must be studied, understood, and implemented with precision. Your lack of adherence to these guidelines has landed you here."

"This is the soul of my friend."

"That's where you're wrong again." The man raised his arms and glanced at their surroundings. "You went through the wrong gate."

"This was the right gate."

"Did you know there are many ways to go through the gates? Wrong ways and right ways? This offers certain opportunities for influence when dealing with an enemy. Ah, I can see you don't know about that."

"You diverted us."

"Very good." The man grinned. "We've been watching you, of course, and I've commented to the others how bright you are."

"Who are you?"

"My name is Zennon." He bowed and pulled a gold coin out of his pocket and rolled it around his fingers so fast it blurred. "And I am going to prevent you from continuing to be a thorn in our sides."

"What are you going to do?"

"I'd worry more about what *you're* going to do."

"Explain that."

"If I were you, I'd make sure I used the next few seconds to say good-bye to her and the little one." Zennon pointed to Reece's wife and daughter. "They're about to go bye-bye." He stopped rolling the coin and flipped it into the air. "Heads you lose. Tails . . . you lose." Zennon snagged the coin as it fell and slapped it on his wrist. He lifted his hand half an inch and peeked underneath and shook his head. "I'm afraid you lose."

"You have no right and no authority over me."

Zennon laughed. "In here I do. You don't have permission to be here. Even God has no permission to be here. Not in this soul. He hasn't been invited in. So how could you? But I have permission. And in here, I have all the authority."

His smile faded and darkness flashed in Zennon's eyes as he waved his fingers at Olivia and Willow. They slumped to the brown dirt, their eyes wide, their mouths gasping for air.

Reece lunged at Zennon, who backhanded him to the ground. Reece struggled to his knees and crawled toward his wife and daughter, but Zennon flicked his finger and Reece was slammed onto his back. Pain flooded his eyes as if they were doused in acid as he stared at his wife and daughter, their outstretched arms growing limp.

Reece wrenched himself free from the memory and raised his head to the sky. "That's enough." He glanced at the others. "Now you know what happened, but that's as far as it's going to go. I'm not going to talk about it again. Good night."

He stood and folded his arms and stayed silent as the others took the hint and slowly walked off. When they rounded the corner of his home and disappeared from sight, he slumped onto a chair and stared at the fire. Reece wished he hadn't said anything. Reliving the memory was like a knife slicing across his mind and heart, and he didn't know how to stop the bleeding.

✦✦✦

Marcus sighed as he, Dana, and Brandon sat in his car. After leaving Reece's home, they'd driven to Maltby Community Park to decide what to do next, but after an hour and a half of discussion they still hadn't reached a consensus.

Marcus felt like a mule had planted its foot in his stomach with significant velocity. He clenched his steering wheel. "We have to help him even if his attitude would seem to preclude it."

"We all agree on that," Dana said. "It's time to move on to a specific plan of action."

"It explains everything." Brandon pressed a button on the passenger side door and his window lowered. Cool air swirled into the Jeep. "He's getting hammered all the time with that memory. He's learned to live with it, but does he have to?"

"If he were us, he'd say no." Dana sighed. "And I don't think he's learned to live with it."

"The cobbler with no shoes for his own children." Marcus fired up his engine.

"The answer is simple. Hard to do, which is why we've danced around it for the last ninety minutes, but it's obvious."

"War for him like we've warred for each other," Marcus said.

Brandon rolled the window up. "You're saying go into his soul."

"Yes." Dana sat up and glanced back and forth between the two men. "We go talk to him. Get permission to go through the gate. Free him from the chains. It's time to go to war. Marcus?"

"Agreed."

"Good." Dana nodded. "And something tells me the sand is running out of the hourglass."

Brandon tapped his chest right over his heart. "I'm getting the same thing."

"Tomorrow night? First thing tomorrow?" Marcus asked.

"I don't think so." Brandon rubbed his knuckles against his palm.

"Right now," Dana said. "I think we need to go in immediately."

Marcus glanced at his watch: 11:25. "He's probably asleep. Are we going to draw straws to see which one of us gets the honor of waking him up?"

They didn't answer and Marcus revved his car. "Do we want to meet there or drive together?"

"Stick together," Dana answered. "Hurry."

Marcus roared out of the parking lot. Whatever kind of urgency Dana and Brandon felt, he now felt as well.

"Can't you go faster?" Brandon said.

He glanced at his speedometer. "I'm already doing fifteen over."

Marcus propped his elbow on the door window and glanced in his mirror at the red taillights on the back of a car that zoomed past them traveling in the opposite direction. Were the three of them going the right way? Were they about to do something heroic or something foolish? Probably both. It didn't matter. He would do whatever it took to rescue Reece from whatever prison he was in. No regrets this time.

A splatter of rain pinged against the windshield, then grew into a downpour. Marcus switched his wipers to high to be able to see. *Give us eyes to see.*

✦✦✦

The man flipped his gold piece high into the air, the coin sending off flashes of light as it spun. On its way down he snatched the piece and slapped it onto the back of his wrist, his long fingers covering it from sight.

"Heads we take out Reece Roth now, tails we take out Reece Roth now."

"It is time," the other man standing next to him said.

"The self-proclaimed Roy Hobbs has hit his last home run."

"How soon do we leave?"

"Immediately." The man grinned and waved his hand, and a moment later they stood on the edge of Reece Roth's land.

FORTY-EIGHT

FOR A LONG TIME REECE STARED INTO HIS FIRE PIT—THE red coals starting to dim, the heat that had warmed the four of them starting to wane—and asked the Spirit what the three would be facing and what his part in it would be. But he heard nothing.

He pulled out his current journal and caressed the worn leather cover. So much gold on the pages inside. Yes, there were insights in the journals he'd given them, but there was more. When they were ready, he would take them further, usher them into worlds and realms they couldn't yet imagine.

They could do so much. The prophecy had been true. These three could change the world. They *would* change the world. Where Tamera fit into this, he didn't know. Maybe at some point she would join them. Reece set the journal beside him and gazed at the millions of stars that had gathered to watch him ponder his future. His phone vibrated and Reece glanced at his caller ID. Doug Lundeen.

"Hey, friend."

"Sorry to call you so late."

"It's not late." Reece glanced at his watch. Almost eleven thirty, which was almost twelve thirty in the morning for Doug. Yes, it was late.

"How did the celebration go tonight?"

"It went well."

"The four of the prophecy together."

"The three at least. I was just wondering how Tamera will fit in."

Doug chuckled. "I would have thought you'd have figured that out by now."

"Figured what out?"

"Who the fourth one of the prophecy is."

Realization swept over him. "No."

"Oh yes." Doug laughed again. "What do you love, Reece?"

"Taking pictures and hiking."

"What have I watched you do for forty years?"

"Climb a million mountains."

"You're in better shape than most men a quarter of your age. You drink on extremely rare occasions, you don't smoke, and a pinch of processed sugar passes your lips once a year, if that. Most assuredly, you are the temple, Reece."

Reece blinked and let the idea settle. "How long have you known?"

"A long time."

"But you let me think Tamera was the temple. Why?"

"You needed to bind your heart to the three without the pressure of being one of the four."

They talked another three minutes, but he didn't hear any of Doug's words. He was one of the four? Yes. He was one of the prophecy. Joy and peace he hadn't felt in decades settled on Reece and he soaked in every nuance of the sensation.

✦✦✦

An abrupt burst of wind sent a smattering of emerald maple leaves fluttering down on him, and one landed on the coals. For a few seconds the leaf stayed green, the moisture inside fending off the power in the coals. Then the leaf turned black and curled up against the onslaught of heat.

"That's you, Reece." The voice seemed to come from all directions at once.

Reece snapped his head up, his heart pounding. Three men in dark, long-sleeved T-shirts and dark slacks sat around the fire in the same spots Brandon, Marcus, and Dana had sat in nearly two hours ago. There had been no noise, no warning—and the pungent smell in the air confirmed what he already knew. These three were not human.

As Reece stared at them, he brushed his journal off the bench. It landed silently on the ground behind him. *Protect it, Lord.*

The man directly across from Reece smiled as he folded and unfolded his hands. "I had a feeling that visit at the beach we enjoyed together five or six weeks ago wasn't going to convince you."

He reached into the fire, pulled out a coal, held it between his thumb and forefinger, and watched the skin sizzle. "Fascinating." The smell of burning flesh filled the night.

"These bodies are so weak. But certainly useful in endeavors such as the one we're about to embark on." The man tossed the coal back into the fire and rubbed his fingers on his slacks. "Shall we get started?"

"Who are you?"

"Oh, come now. The great leader not knowing who sits before him? The teacher of spiritual mysteries forgotten or dismissed by most of the church can't discern who has come for a visit? Thirty years isn't that long, old friend." The man pulled a gold coin out of his pocket and rolled it around his fingers like lightning.

Reece's heart slammed against his chest, but his breathing was steady. The body might have changed, but the eyes hadn't. He knew those eyes.

"Zennon."

Zennon's smile widened. "I'm flattered. You remember me." He bowed.

"Jesus, come." Reece spoke the words as he stared directly into the demon's eyes.

"No, let's not be doing that, Reece." Zennon pressed the tips of his fingers and thumbs against each other till his hands shook. "It only serves to make me angry. My hope is we can convey what we need to and take the actions necessary without a lot of warring back and forth."

He motioned to the men on either side of him, and they circled around behind Reece to his sides and pinned him down with icy hands.

Reece strained against their grip. "Then your hope is in vain."

Zennon ignored the comment and smiled again. "We have to confess, you took your little band a great deal further than was expected. So in response we're going to take our retaliation further than you might have expected."

I need your power, Spirit.

Zennon waved his finger and a thin layer of smoke or fog appeared just outside the circle of chairs.

"It's home movie time, Reece. Movies from your life. What's really fun is when you watch them, they feel so real. As if you're standing right in the scene yourself."

Reece knew what was coming. He tried to close his eyes but invisible fingernails tore at the top and bottom of his eyelids, keeping them pried open. The scene started with Reece convincing his wife and daughter that the three of them should go into the soul of another.

Zennon pointed at the scene. "Do you recognize this man?"

Reece watched himself sitting at his kitchen table with his wife and daughter. Watched them go into an unknown soul. Watched the soundless scream on the faces of his wife and daughter as they were slain.

He'd played it over and over in his mind a thousand, ten thousand times over the past thirty years, but seeing it this way was like living it again for the first time. He struggled to break free but the demons' grips were iron.

"Let's play it again. But this time, let's get some sound going. How would that be?" Zennon stepped around the fire pit and ran his finger down the side of Reece's neck, sending ice into his body and a rush of pain into his mind.

"Some say sound is more powerful than sight, that hearing

affects us to a greater degree than seeing. I believe that's true. Did you know the area of a human's brain that collects sound is bigger than the area that collects images?

"Think about it from your practical experience. What makes a scary movie scary? It's the sound!" Zennon stood and motioned like a conductor presiding over a hundred-piece orchestra. "Watch a scary movie without the sound and it's just not that moving an occurrence. But turn up the sound and it seems to come alive. So let's do that for you with the day you slayed your wife and daughter and see if it makes a difference."

Reece struggled again and jerked his arm hard. Pain shot through his right shoulder as if it had popped out of its socket. "Jesus!"

"Tsk-tsk. Stop that." Zennon waved his finger. "I don't like it. Now we're all out of popcorn, but I'm guessing you'll enjoy the scene just as much without it."

The scene started again and the sound pounded into his mind as if he were surrounded by a circular wall of speakers pumping out noise at 120 decibels. He strained once again to break free of the demons clutching his arms, but he might as well have been trying to break free of a suit of concrete. Tentacles of panic pressed into Reece's mind. *Resist.*

He tried to call out to the Spirit—and speak Jesus' name again—but as the words were about to escape his lips, a steel-like hand clamped over his mouth and drove his lips into his teeth.

"Let's not say that name for a few minutes, okay?" Zennon stood above him. He leaned down and poked his knife-like finger into Reece's chin, lifting Reece's head till the pressure on the back of his neck sent a sliver of pain down his spine. "It makes me uncomfortable."

Jesus.

He screamed the thought in his mind as loud as he could, but the word turned to dust and floated away.

"Now let's play the scene one more time. But this time let's do something truly special." Zennon leaned down and whispered in Reece's ear, "You are going to love this. I promise."

Immediately his wife and daughter stood before Reece, as solid and substantial as if they were alive again. Tears streaked both their faces. He couldn't watch them die again. Not like this, not this life-like. To see them go through that pain again . . .

It's not real! But the thought was swallowed up by emotion as he watched them die again. And again.

"Stop!" he screamed through the hand grinding into his face and mouth. "I'll do—"

"Anything?" Zennon waved his hand and Reece's wife and daughter froze. "You'll do anything to stop it? Wonderful. If you swear on your life and the life of the Jew that you will stop training the three, I will leave immediately."

Zennon placed his finger under Reece's chin and yanked it up. "But if you do keep training them, I promise, I will finish what I started with Marcus's daughters, and the blood of two more inno-cent girls will be on your hands."

Reece strained against the vise-like grips holding him down. An impossible choice. He believed Zennon. If he didn't stop, Marcus's daughters would die, just like Willow had. But if he did stop, he'd be stepping back into the shadows, denying what Jesus had commanded him to do and halting what the three could bring to the world.

His head fell forward, his body went limp, and his remaining resolve seeped out of him. No. It couldn't end like this. But it was about to. *Lord, speak to your servant.* A barely discernible breeze stirred the tendrils of smoke that rose from the fire pit.

You have to jump off cliffs all the time . . . and raise the shield of faith on the way down.

Reece rose up straight and nodded.

"Are you agreeing to give me your word you'll back off?"

He nodded again.

Zennon tilted his head toward the demon to Reece's right. The demon released his grip over Reece's mouth.

"Speak, Reece Roth," Zennon whispered. "Let me hear your vow with clarity."

Reece sucked in a breath and shouted, "The blood of Jesus Christ—"

The demon's hand mashed into Reece's mouth again.

"I didn't think so." Zennon waved his hand and pain scorched across Reece's head.

Protect me, Jesus.

"Let's get back to the show."

His wife and daughter were on their knees, then on their sides, dying. His wife turned to him, her eyes wide with fear. "Why? Why did you murder us? Why, Reece? Why, Reece? Why, Reece?" Each time she asked, her voice grew till she screamed the question.

He knew it wasn't her but it didn't help. Then Olivia's eyes rolled back in her head and her head crashed to the gound. Something snapped inside Reece's mind and the images around him blurred as if he were looking at them through water.

Zennon and the other two laughed, but the sound faded as the sensation of falling washed over Reece and he held out his arms behind him to brace his fall. But the ground didn't meet him and he kept falling. His shoulder didn't hurt anymore. The pain in his head vanished and he couldn't tell if the demon on his right still covered his mouth. He couldn't feel anything.

The red glow of the coals turned into a pinprick, the men turned to vapor, and Reece was floating or lying on something soft. The sides of his vision faded and he was in a tunnel with a faint glow a light-year away. Then the light was snuffed out and the blackness rushed at him, then into him, and he gasped for air.

"First you, then the others." Zennon's voice sounded thin. "It's time for you to go."

Jesus. The name echoed in his mind as if from a great distance.

"Good-bye, Reece Roth."

For an instant he saw a flicker of light. Then the darkness swallowed him.

FORTY-NINE

MARCUS SCREECHED INTO REECE'S DRIVEWAY AND BRANDON and Dana already had their doors open before he skidded to a stop. He jammed the gear shift into Park, opened his door, and raced after Brandon and Dana, who were already sprinting toward Reece's front door. By the time he reached them, Brandon had pounded out ten knocks on Reece's door.

"Do either of you have a key?"

Brandon and Dana shook their heads.

"Try it."

Dana turned the knob. Unlocked. They strode into the darkness of Reece's house and Dana shivered. It was colder in here than outside.

"Reece!" Marcus turned on the lamp next to the twenty-inch computer monitor and it pushed back the darkness. "Talk to us, Reece, are you home?"

Marcus pointed down the hall. "Brandon, you check his bedroom and the bathroom. Dana, please take the kitchen, I'll look in the garage and see if his car is here."

Twenty seconds later they gathered in the front room.

"I'm not liking this." Brandon counted on his fingers. "Not in the bedroom. Not in the bathroom. Kitchen. Garage. Den. And I don't think he went out for any salsa at this hour."

Marcus glanced over Dana's shoulder at the door leading to Reece's backyard. "What about outside?"

"It's close to midnight. What would he be doing outside at this hour?"

"When we left he indicated he would be spending time at the fire pit before coming inside."

Brandon strode to the sliding glass door, opened it, and took three steps onto the redwood deck. "Reece!" He cupped his hands around his eyes and looked toward the fire pit.

"Can you see anything?" He and Dana joined Brandon on the deck.

"Nothing, and we'd see a glow even at a hundred yards. You'd think there'd be a fire if he was at the pit."

Marcus eased past him. "I think it wise to look there anyway." He half walked, half jogged toward the fire pit, Dana and Brandon at his side, as the churning feeling he'd had in his stomach in his car on the way over turned into a full-out rugby match. His feet slipped on the dew-laden grass but he only increased his speed. Halfway there he spotted a dark clump lying by the circular stones and he picked up his pace.

A few seconds later he reached Reece, who lay on his side in a fetal position, hands over his face. Marcus dropped down, his knees slamming into the ground, and grabbed Reece's shoulder. "Reece, can you hear us?"

Nothing. He gently turned the big man's head and stared into eyes that no longer carried their color, let alone the fiery spark the three of them had come to cherish. Marcus waved his hands in front of Reece's eyes. No reaction.

"Is he breathing?"

"Don't say that," Brandon sputtered.

Dana put her ear up to Reece's mouth. "I can't tell. I think so."

"Check his pulse," Marcus said.

She fumbled to pull back his coat and laid two fingers on his carotid artery.

"Does he have a pulse?" Marcus shouted.

"Hang on." Dana focused on her fingers. "It's there. It's steady and strong; it seems fine."

"Brandon, call 911."

Three minutes later the air was filled with the wail of sirens. In five an ambulance with Reece inside screeched away.

"I can't believe this." Dana rubbed her lips, tears forming in her eyes.

"I assume we're going to follow him to the hospital?" Brandon said.

"Correct assumption. Let's go," Dana said.

They ran to Marcus's car and raced back down the street.

"Are we going straight there?" Brandon asked. "Or are we going to stop and get our cars?"

"We stick together," Dana said from the backseat.

"No." Marcus shook his head. "Since we live in opposite directions, the more prudent decision would be to meet there."

"If we're together we can be warring for him on the way to the hospital," Dana said.

"We can still do that in separate cars."

"Fine." Brandon flashed a thumbs-up. "Let's just get there."

✦✦✦

After Marcus dropped them off, Brandon turned to Dana. "Do you want to ride together? You're only fifteen minutes from my place. I can drop you at home when we're done, and I'll bring you back here tomorrow to grab your car."

As she stared at him it felt like a tennis match was going on inside her mind. At the end of the rally, the score must somehow still have been tied Love-Love because she said, "I'm not sure I want to, but yes."

The part of Dana that had resisted riding with Brandon melted away thirty seconds down the road. It wasn't because of any latent feelings toward him now that she'd been freed. It was because she didn't want to be alone as the thoughts of what she'd just witnessed assaulted her. She'd believed Reece was dead, and as she fumbled in finding a pulse the thought of losing him had consumed her. It couldn't happen. Her life had just begun and it was because of him.

She checked her own pulse. Back to normal. Adrenaline and fear had pushed it to its limit, but now that she admitted there was nothing she could do at the moment, and probably nothing she could do even when they got to the hospital, her body allowed itself to relax. Sort of.

And in the midst of a moment where her mind should be on nothing but Reece, she couldn't ignore the realization that she did want Brandon's friendship.

"I'm glad I'm not headed there alo—by myself."

Brandon glanced over at her, blinking. Was he holding back tears?

"You okay?"

"Reece can't be dead, Dana." He popped the steering wheel with a balled-up hand. "Can he?"

"No." For the second time in the past minute she shoved her own tears deep down and swallowed hard. "He's going to be okay." She stopped, then added under her breath, "He has to be, Jesus. Please."

"I heard that." Brandon peeled around a corner, pressing her into the truck's passenger door.

Dana glanced at Brandon's speedometer. Twenty-five miles an hour over. He glanced at her, then the speedometer and tapped on his brakes. "You're right. Getting pulled over on the way to the hospital would definitely slow us down."

"I should have ridden with him in the ambulance."

"Why?"

"I could have prayed for him." She rested her head on her fist.

"We can do that now."

When they finished Brandon softly said, "That brought back some memories."

"Of what?"

"Of us praying together." He glanced at her.

No. She wouldn't allow herself to think of those days. Not out of pain, but out of . . . She shook the memory from her brain.

But it wouldn't stay buried and her mind was flooded with the times they had spent together walking along the Edmonds waterfront, taking excursions up into the San Juan Islands, and skiing together at Stevens Pass. She admitted it. Whatever she felt now, there was a time when she loved him and that part of her had never completely died.

"Hey, you want some seeds?" Brandon held out his ever-present bag of sunflower seeds.

She hesitated, then held out her hand. "Sure."

They rode for the next three or four minutes in silence, the slice of Brandon's tires through the wet road providing the sound track for their late-night drive.

As a sign for Evergreen Hospital flashed by them, Dana found words spilling out of her mouth. "I didn't get that much of a chance to thank you for what you did. Thanks for coming after me. For freeing me from the lies . . ."

He didn't speak for probably a minute. When he did his voice caught and he didn't start again for another thirty seconds. "You're welcome." He glanced at her, eyes moist. "Your forgiving me was . . . it was incredibly freeing."

She reached for his hand and squeezed it and he squeezed back. No feelings surfaced, no urge to play the squeeze game they played in another life, just warmth and peace shared with a friend.

Then the realization of where they were going and why they were going there swept back through her and Dana's stomach tightened. "What if he dies?"

"He won't die. He's Superman and the Incredible Hulk and Billy Graham all rolled into one. He's going to live forever like he said at Well Spring."

Marcus was waiting for them in the hospital lobby, and for the next forty minutes they sat doing nothing. Not exactly nothing. Brandon tried to wear a path in the carpet.

"The tedium is about to send you over the edge, isn't it?" Marcus asked.

Brandon stopped, bent down, and stared at the tropical fish as they skittered back and forth in the fifty-gallon aquarium next to him. "I've never been great at doing absolutely nothing while a person I'd give my life for is lying somewhere above me and no one wants to tell us what's going on."

An hour crawled by like snails sprinting. Then two. Brandon stood. "That's it. I'm going to get some answers."

"They said they'd come tell us when they knew anything," Dana said.

"They have to know something by now."

But before Brandon could get two steps, a doctor shuffled up to them who didn't look a second over twenty. Dana couldn't tell if the doctor was tired or had bad news for them.

"Are you the friends of Reece Roth?" she asked, a clipboard in her hand.

Brandon folded his arms. "The look on your face isn't instilling me with a lot of confidence."

The doctor waved her hand. "No, no. That's not it. It's just that we can't find a reason for him to be in this coma. His vitals are strong. His pulse is fine, his breathing is good, his blood pressure is right where it should be. If I was looking at his chart and hadn't seen him, I'd swear he was sleeping, not buried in a coma. I've never seen one like this."

"Which means . . . ," Marcus said.

"That he could be in it for another ten minutes or another ten years."

"There's nothing else unusual going on?"

"Actually, there is." The doctor lifted the top paper on her clipboard and studied the one underneath. "His brain patterns have been in REM since he got here." The doctor looked at her watch. "That's going on three hours. Highly unusual."

"Rapid Eye Movement. The state your mind resides in when you're dreaming." Marcus glanced over her shoulder at her clipboard. She saw him and snatched the clipboard to her chest.

"Isn't it dangerous for him to be in a continual state of REM sleep?" the professor said.

"We think so. We're talking to a sleep specialist right now."

"But you have no idea why he's in a coma?" Dana said.

The doctor shook her head.

"When will you know?" Brandon tapped his foot on the maroon carpet.

The doctor smiled. "I'm sorry. Everyone thinks medicine is a science. And it is. But it's also an art. And right now we can't see the whole painting. So we're going to paint a few more of the numbers with the best brushes we have and see what we can see. But that will take some time. I wish I could tell you more, but that's all we have for the moment."

"Is there anything else?" Marcus put on his coat.

"Yes. I don't mean to be insensitive, but since you are his friends, I have to ask about medical coverage. Reece didn't have any ID on him or medical insurance cards." She glanced at each of them. "Do you happen to know if he has a medical plan?"

Should she tell? Dana wasn't sure, but at this point her exhaustion put her in a position of not caring who knew. Besides, it might make them take better care of him. "If he doesn't have coverage, he's good for the money."

"How do you know that?" The doctor folded her arms, the clipboard pressed against her chest.

"He's got millions."

Brandon and Marcus stared at her.

"He's got what?" Brandon said.

Dana waved her hand. "It's a long story."

Brandon opened his palms. "I have time."

"Not now." She turned to the doctor. "He's good for it. Trust me. Can we see him?"

The doctor shook her head. "Not yet. Tomorrow, yes. I'm guessing the best thing for the three of you would be to get some sleep. Don't worry. He's in good hands here."

✦✦✦

As Marcus drove away, he bounced his fist on his steering wheel. "God, I need some light. Reveal what is going on below the surface."

Instantly a picture of Reece lying in a hospital room with a dark cloud seeming to be holding him down flashed into Marcus's mind. "What are you showing me, Jesus?"

After a mile farther, Marcus slapped his knee with an open palm. "That's it!"

He grabbed his cell phone and dialed Brandon.

"Hey, Marcus."

"Is Dana still with you?"

"Yeah."

"Put me on speaker, please."

"You're on."

The noise of Brandon's truck filled Marcus's Bluetooth. "I don't think Reece's situation has anything to do with his body or his mind."

"What's left?"

"His spirit. His coma is not a medical condition. It's spiritual."

"Comas are not caused by spiritual dysfunction," Brandon said.

"This one is."

"Why do you think so?"

Marcus hesitated. "God told me."

"God told you? Hmm."

"Is that not one of the points of our training? That we will hear the voice of the Spirit? Well, I heard from him. The doctors can't explain it because there's nothing on the physical level to explain."

"Let's say you're right. What do we do?" Brandon asked.

"We enter in and free him from whatever has him held captive."

"Go in? What do you mean, go in?"

"Precisely the same battle we fought inside Dana and inside me. We must discover a way through the gate and into Reece's soul and neutralize whatever is holding him hostage." Marcus rubbed his head. "Strike that. Not neutralize. Destroy it."

Dana's voice floated through his cell phone. "I appreciate your passion, Marcus. Really. Brandon and I love the guy too. But if what you're saying is true, we don't have the experience to do something like that."

"What about the admonition to jump off cliffs and build our wings on the way down? We've already entered into souls."

"That's the point, we've done it with Reece." Dana sighed. "Not on our own."

"At some point we have to grow up."

"I agree, but people don't go from a yellow belt to a double black belt," Dana said. "There're orange belts, green belts, purple belts, brown belts, and other belts along the way."

"That's inconsequential. I cannot allow myself to let him lie there knowing what I now know. Will you join me or not?" Marcus smacked the back of his fist into the side window.

"No offense, Marcus," Brandon said. "But you heard the Spirit speak this. We didn't. And—"

"I'm in," Dana said.

"Thank you." Relief coursed through Marcus. "Brandon?"

He could imagine the look on the musician's face.

"All right, I'm in too."

"Do either of you have a suggestion where we might gather for this attempt?" Marcus asked. "Reece's fire pit?"

"No," Brandon said. "Too wet, too great a chance of being disturbed."

The line went silent for a moment. Then Dana spoke with confidence. "I know exactly where we should go in from."

"Where?"

"I'll tell you when we get to the park. See you there in a few minutes."

Marcus stared at the hint of dawn in the rain-soaked sky. Wherever Dana had in mind, he hoped it was close. His heart told him they were running out of time.

+ + +

Dana and Brandon arrived at the park first. He pounded out a quick rhythm on his steering wheel as they waited for the professor to arrive. Where did she think they should go in from? There wasn't anywhere nearby that he'd choose.

"You want to tell me the place while we wait?" He turned to her.

She pointed out the windshield. "He's here."

After Marcus's car skidded into the parking lot, he shut off his engine, stepped out of his Jeep, and joined them in Brandon's truck. The second the door shut, the professor zeroed in on Dana. "Where is this perfect place?"

"A place where we know we won't be disturbed. A place that has a prayer covering over it. A place where the curtain between us and the spiritual realm is thinner, which will make it easier."

A look of disbelief passed over Marcus's features. Brandon scowled. She couldn't mean—

"You're talking about Well Spring," Marcus said.

"Yes."

"Great idea." Brandon pointed at Dana and winked. "I'm sure we can be there in about twelve hours."

She raised her eyebrows and he realized what she was suggesting.

"You want to try that? Reece's beam-me-up technique? Sure. Oh yeah, perfect time to test it."

Marcus scrubbed the top of his head with his fingers. "Maybe it is. Maybe it's time to find out what we believe. Maybe it's cliff-jumping time."

"You two are crazy." Brandon tapped his temple.

"So was Peter. So was Paul. So was Elijah. So was—"

"Okay, I get it," Brandon said. "Sure, it might work. But what happens if we show up there and the owners are hanging out at the listening post or grilling up a few steaks on the barbecue out back?"

Marcus glanced at his watch. "If they are there, they'll probably be asleep. Unless they're early risers."

"The owner won't be there," Dana said.

"How do you know?"

"He's not there. I promise you." She closed her eyes and massaged her forehead. "And he won't be showing up for at least a few days, if he ever shows up again."

"How can you be certain of that?" Brandon asked.

Dana sighed. "Because at this moment the owner is lying in a hospital bed at Evergreen Hospital in Kirkland, Washington."

FIFTY

"Reece owns Well Spring?" Brandon twisted in his seat and stared at Dana. "You're kidding."

"Yes. And no, I'm not kidding."

"It makes sense." Marcus shook his head and let out a soft laugh. "I'm flabbergasted we missed it."

"How does it make sense?" Brandon asked.

"It was obvious. Consider his demeanor surrounding Well Spring. The way he described it to me when he was inviting me to come, the way he talked about it when he gave us the tour, his countenance when he strolled around the main cabin. And didn't you ever see him standing out back gazing at the cabin or the bunkhouses? Like they were made of gold."

Sure, Brandon had seen that, but it didn't mean Reece owned the place. He turned to Dana. "When were you going to share this nugget with us?"

"He asked me not to."

"Why?"

"He didn't say."

"What does one guy need with a ranch that size?" Marcus said.

"Training center, probably," Brandon said. "Do you—?"

"Guys!" Dana popped them both in their shoulders. "Time to stop talking about how Well Spring came to be and get moving."

"You're right," Brandon said. "Where should we try this ludicrous idea?"

Dana patted her leather seat. "Right here in the car. I don't think the location has anything to do with it working or not working."

Marcus and he nodded.

"I agree." Marcus held out his palms. "Join hands."

Brandon stared at the determination on Dana's face. "You believe this will work?"

"I don't know. That's why it's called faith."

Brandon nodded. "Reece had you memorize the special words he uses, right?"

Dana smiled. "I thought he told you."

Marcus shifted in his seat. "Have you considered the actuality that we have no idea how to make this occur?"

"I have, and I admit that could be a problem." Dana held tighter. "But I'm not going to worry about it."

"I believe." Brandon looked into Marcus's eyes, then Dana's. "Help my unbelief."

"Amen." Dana glanced at Marcus. "Do you want to lead this thing?"

"Sure. Is everybody ready?"

Dana shook her head once and then nodded.

"Rock and roll." Brandon grinned at him.

"Then let's proceed." Marcus sucked in a deep breath and held it as long as he could, then slowly released it. "Jesus, if this is you leading us—"

Instantly the air around them swirled and a flash of brilliant light made Brandon slam his eyes shut. He felt weightless, more than weightless—as if his body no longer existed, only his spirit. Ecstasy erupted out of his heart and he felt like Dorothy caught up in the middle of a tornado—only this one was a tornado of indescribable joy.

The sensation of time vanished. It was like swimming in an ocean of utter bliss and unquenchable love. If he was given a choice to stay in this forever, he would have agreed in an instant. He still felt Marcus's and Dana's hands in his, and when he squeezed tighter they returned the pressure. Another flash of brilliance, then the light enveloping him dimmed and Brandon opened his eyes. He wiggled his toes. Terra firma. He looked down to make sure his shoes were standing on real earth. They were. The three of them stood just above the main cabin of Well Spring Ranch.

"Did you two just experience—?"

"If that's the Spirit of God, I want more," Marcus puffed out.

"I think that's just a taste," Dana said.

"What a rush! Have you ever felt God's love like that before?" Brandon patted the air with both palms. "Definitely some song-writing material in that experience."

The sun had just crested the ridge to their left and it lit up Dana's hair like gold.

"Unbelievable." Brandon released the professor's and Dana's hands and spun in a slow circle. "Simply utterly unbelievable."

He was stunned. It had worked. They'd done it. He shook his head and smiled. Not true. They'd done nothing. The Spirit had done it all.

"Not to rush past this moment, but we need to rush past this moment and go after Reece." Dana started down the slope toward the cabin, her shoes sinking in the soft soil. Marcus and he followed and when they reached the front door they found it open. They walked in and stood in the center of the living room.

"Where should we try this from?"

"Try there is no. Only do." Brandon attempted to imitate Yoda's voice.

Marcus laughed. "A worthy attempt, Master Jedi. However, it's 'Try not. Do or do not. There is no try.'"

"Thanks, Professor Trivia."

Dana gazed toward the nine-foot-tall sliding glass door. "At the listening post of course."

They walked through the door onto the pathway and to the end of the patio where they would take a crack at entering Reece's soul. Brandon's heart pounded. He guessed Marcus and Dana had thundering going on in their chests as well. They'd gone quantum in their learning in the past five weeks, but going into Reece's soul without Reece there—that was quantum learning with nitro afterburners.

They sat and joined hands. "All right, let's go," Brandon said softly. He waited till Marcus and Dana closed their eyes before closing his. Then he focused his spirit inward and waited for the Spirit to take them. The by-now-familiar sensation closed in on him and—

"Stop!" Dana said.

Brandon jerked his eyes open and rocked forward in his chair. "What's wrong?"

Dana opened her palms. "We can't do this."

"Why not?" Marcus frowned.

"What is the second rule of going into a person's soul?"

Brandon let go of their hands. "Uh . . ."

Dana tapped her forefingers together. "You do not go in without explicit permission."

Marcus pulled off his glasses. "And I quote, 'There is never an exception to rule number two. Never. Are we abundantly, exceedingly clear on that point?'"

"Explicit permission. We don't have it, do we?" Dana said. "Let alone implicit."

Brandon looked at her. She was right. The scene from the movie screen in Reece's memories flashed through his mind. "We try to go into his soul without permission and we could wind up going through a gate into a soul that isn't that of our fearless leader."

"Precisely." Marcus shifted in his chair. "And it is a virtual impossibility to get permission from Reece with him in a coma."

Brandon reached out and took their hands again. "I say we go anyway."

"And if you're wrong?" Dana said. "And we go through the wrong gate?"

The image of Reece's wife and daughter pounded through his mind. *No.* He wouldn't allow fear to machine gun his belief. Why would the Spirit have brought them to Well Spring if he didn't want them to go inside Reece's soul? Then again, what if Dana was right?

Brandon glanced back and forth between them as sweat dripped down his back. "If we go through the wrong gate? We might die. But I don't care anymore. Really. Yes, I'm terrified. But I'm more terrified of what will happen to my heart if I don't go in. I'm not going to carry around that kind of regret the rest of my life. I'm ready to jump off the cliff for Reece. Because he would do it for me."

Dana propped her elbow on her knee and buried her face in her hand. "Marcus?"

The professor glanced at Brandon. "When you present it that way . . ."

Brandon held out his shaking hands to Dana and Marcus. "Let's go."

They sat in silence. No one moved. But at seven seconds Marcus offered his hand. At ten Dana slid her palm against his. "Lead on."

Brandon took a deep breath as he gazed down at the river, then let it out slowly. "Jesus, if it's not right, block us. Keep us out. Show us another way to save Reece. But if this is you, take us in now—"

Well Spring vanished. There was no sensation of movement, no sensation of time. One moment he sat at the listening post, the next they stood on a tiny island—two acres or less in size—in the middle of a vast ocean, its gentle waves spreading out as far as he could see in every direction.

The air was sweet, too sweet, and a light wind swirled the fragrance around his head like circling flies. Brandon raised his hand against the midday sun and glanced at the others. "You both good?"

"Yes," Marcus said. "Fine."

Dana nodded and pointed to something dark in the middle of the island on top of sparse green vegetation. They eased toward it. It looked like a person lying on his back, head tilted to the side, with one arm splayed out as if reaching for something.

"Reece?" Dana said.

Brandon broke into a jog; Marcus and Dana did the same. After twenty-five yards it was clear Dana was right. When he got within five feet, Brandon slowed and stared. A blood-red flower drooped over Reece's chest and every few seconds a drop of what looked like yellow-tainted light dripped off the end of the lowest petal and disappeared into his chest.

"I'm not thinking that flower is a good thing," Brandon said.

"We have to obliterate it." Marcus stepped forward. As he did, a light red mist swirled around Reece's body, forming a ring that extended three feet in every direction. Sporadic bursts of long, thin streams of red light shot out of it toward them. They stumbled back as if one.

"I don't think we want to get touched by one of those," Dana said.

Marcus circled the mist, his hand out as if gauging its power. "If we have the power of the Spirit, fear is not a consideration we need to dwell on."

As the professor reached the halfway point, one of the tendrils shot out at his hand and latched onto the tips of his fingers. He cried out in pain. "Jesus!" The tendril pulled back and a sizzling sound filled the air.

"Marcus!"

"I'm okay." He held his fingers. "It stings but nothing more."

"Look." Dana pointed at Reece, who stirred and whose head flopped from side to side. "He's trying to speak."

His voice was a whisper and sounded like he spoke through a phone from the 1920s. "It's my fault. My fault. I murdered them."

As he spoke a thick, gray smoke oozed out of his mouth and joined with the red mist. In seconds the mixture became a cloud too thick for them to see through and Reece faded from sight. Brandon forced himself to breathe steady. The Spirit had brought them here. There had to be something they could do. *Show us, Jesus.*

"How do we fight this?" Dana said.

"It's obvious." Marcus rubbed the end of his chin between his thumb and forefinger. "Truth must prevail. He believes the lie. He's accepted it so we must war against it."

Dana knelt in front of the mist—now almost black—and spoke with more power than Brandon had ever heard from her. "We come against the lie that Reece Roth killed his daughter. That he killed his wife. By the blood of Jesus and the power of his crucifixion, the power of his resurrection and the power of his ascension, we break that agreement, we break its oppression, we break any power it holds over Reece."

Blazing sparks of light appeared over the cloud, swirling like a gyroscope. Then they dropped like bullets into the black-red mist, which turned to red to pink to yellow to a flash of brilliance so bright Brandon covered his eyes.

When he opened them the flower was gone, the ground charred in the spot from which it grew. Reece was up—on his knees—gasping for air. A few seconds later his breathing slowed and he glanced at the sun, then turned his squinting eyes to where they stood.

Confusion was carved into his face and he frowned as he studied each of them. Reece put his head down and pawed at the grass and sand as if to dig a trench to hide in, then stopped and stared up at them again.

"I need to sleep. What do you want? Who are you?"

+ + +

Dana stepped forward, her gaze locked on Reece. It was a lie. She felt it in her spirit. He knew exactly who they were but the enemy had him wrapped in deception. *Bring truth, Lord.*

There! A shimmer of light. For a flash she saw the true Reece under the muddled countenance in front of them. She took another step forward. "You're one of us. We are the Warriors Riding. And the four of us are one in Christ Jesus. His power and Spirit live in your heart."

"I met you in a dream, yes?" Reece sat back and wrapped his arms around his knees.

Good. The lie was cracking. "No. In life. We are your intimate allies." She turned to the others. "Pray."

As Marcus and Brandon prayed silently, she held out her hand. "Come out, Reece. Breathe the air of freedom."

Another flash of the real Reece, then he closed his eyes and shook his head. "No, I don't know you. And I killed them." He got to his knees and stared at the black circle in the ground where the flower had grown from. "I have to go back."

A green shoot seeped out of the ground and snaked toward Reece, waving in the velvety island breeze. Reece reached out trembling fingers to touch the flower but before he could, a ball of fire slammed into the flower and consumed it in an instant.

Reece fell back and slumped to the ground, the light from the fireball swirling around him for a moment before fading into the sky. Surprise filled the professor's face as he spun toward Brandon. "Where did you learn that?"

"Inside your soul, bro." Brandon winked. "I'll teach you how someday."

Dana knelt in front of Reece and took his hands. His eyes were clear. The fire had worked. At least for a moment. "Reece, are you with us?"

"Yes."

"Do you know who I am?"

"Dana."

"Are you all right?"

"No." Reece shuddered. "I can feel the pull of the poison even now." Sweat dripped down his forehead and his hands shook. "I don't know how to hold out."

"Ideas?" She turned to Marcus and Brandon but did not let go of Reece's hands. "Quick."

"Yes." Marcus squatted beside her as Brandon did the same. "The student must instruct the master."

She instantly knew what the professor meant and jerked on Reece's hands. "Look at me, Reece. Now!"

The big man's head weaved but he didn't break eye contact.

"You must repent and turn. You've embraced the lie. You must change your thinking. What is the truth?"

Reece's lips quivered and beads of perspiration dropped from his graying eyebrows. "The truth is . . . that I . . . I killed—"

"No! What is the truth?"

He stared at her, a war raging in his eyes, their color shifting from blue to black back to blue. Ages later Reece grasped her hands and his words sputtered out one at a time as if weights were on his lips. "He. Has. Forgiven. Me."

"What is the truth? Again!" Marcus and Brandon rocked forward onto their knees on either side of her and each grabbed one of Reece's arms.

"I am forgiven." Reece blinked.

She whispered the words, "Once more."

"I am forgiven." His hands went limp and the last hint of darkness vanished from his eyes.

Reece's head fell back and Dana released his hands. He raised his arms to the sky and shouted the words, "I am forgiven."

As the words echoed through Reece's soul he brought his head forward and stared at them. The brilliance of his blue eyes was mesmerizing. Dana smiled and looked at Marcus and Brandon, who returned her grin. They'd done it.

"I'm free." Reece glanced at each of them. "I'm finally free." He leaned back and laughter—deep, from-the-gut laughter—poured out of him. "You came for me. And you set me free."

"It's over," Brandon said, a smile continuing to light up his face.

"I'm sorry, my dear friends." Reece's smile vanished and he shook his head. "Even though I most certainly would have given my permission to enter if you had asked, the fact remains that I didn't give it. Consequently, I don't believe this battle is yet finished."

FIFTY-ONE

THE MOMENT THE LAST OF REECE'S WORDS ESCAPED HIS mouth, the sea around them vanished. In its place appeared hills of rock and sand that rose on every side. They were in a bowl the size of a small arena and heat radiated off the sand as if they stood in an oven cranked up to 450.

A hard wind blew from behind and peppered the back of Brandon's neck. The sky in the distance swirled and dark gray clouds streaked toward them. The smell of strong ammonia assaulted his nose. As he stared at the horizon where the hill met the sky, the air shimmered and eight men appeared on the ridge. He glanced behind them to the ridge on the other side of the bowl. Five more. All held swords.

"Steady, friends." Reece's strong voice rang out over the shriek of the wind. "Look in your hands."

Brandon stared at the sword that had appeared in his hand and glanced at the ones now in the hands of Dana, Marcus, and Reece.

"You can leave, you know," Reece said. "This isn't your battle."

Brandon wasn't going anywhere. He knew Marcus and Dana wouldn't be either. "We're staying."

The men on the hills above them sprinted down the slope, dirt and sand spraying up behind them like a curtain.

"Form a circle, backs to each other. Stay together. Don't let them separate you." Reece shouted instructions as the men rushed toward them. "Their greatest weapon is fear—and we have nothing to fear. God is for us. Our lives are in his hands."

Grins burst out on their attackers' faces and Brandon shivered—an icy blast cut through his skin and raced through his body as if trying to penetrate his mind. He staggered and dug his feet into the ground. "I don't know how to use a sword, Reece!"

Reece shouted back against the wind, "You do, Brandon! Fight with the sword of the Spirit. It's not you alone wielding that sword; it's you and the Spirit of power."

Brandon's mind went blank. Sword of the Spirit? The men racing down the slope were only twenty yards away. It hit him when one of the demons was five feet from him, his dark blade lifted high above his head, ready to flash down like lightning into Brandon's neck.

God's words. His truth. So razor sharp it could separate soul and spirit. Brandon braced himself and shouted into the screaming wind, "'In My name they will cast out demons.' He gave his own the power and authority over all demons. No weapon formed against us will prevail. Jesus, come!"

As the words erupted out of his mouth, Brandon raised his sword and it sliced through the air, parrying the sword of the demon in front of him. The demon roared, its hot breath scalding Brandon's face. Another flash of the demon's sword. Another parry, the clash of metal ringing through the air and joining the sound of the others' as they each battled their own demon.

Another attack came from the demon in front of him, this time at Brandon's legs. As he jumped he thrust his sword into the demon's exposed chest. The demon's eyes widened, then narrowed as Brandon thrust the sword deeper.

As the demon crumpled to the ground, Brandon shouted, "'Through You we will push back our adversaries; through Your name we will trample down those who rise up against us. For You have guided me with strength for battle; You have subdued under me those who rose up against me.'"

Brandon held up his sword and lasered his eyes on another demon five yards in front of him. This one didn't charge but side-stepped to his left, his gaze riveted on Brandon, a thin smile at the corner of his mouth.

Worthless. That is your true name. You know this to be true. No psychobabble pack of lies from your guru and others is ever going to change that.

The thought smashed into Brandon's mind and he gasped. Then an image of his stepmom screaming at him flashed through his brain and his grip on his sword loosened.

Yes. Embrace the truth. You are nothing. Worthless.

The demon continued to circle, the radius growing tighter.

And you can pretend you've come back to God, but it's only emo-tions. The truth is, the only thing you care about is Brandon Scott. The vine of praise has taken root in you and is growing. And you like it. Confess the truth and this battle will end. You will save your friends. You will save yourself.

Brandon sank to his knees. "No."

Yes, surrender and save them. It's your only hope.

Brandon's breaths grew shallow. The demon closed his circle tighter.

Save them, Brandon.

The sword slipped from his hand and thumped into the sand and time slowed. The demon leapt forward and its sword flashed toward him. No chance to move. But as it streaked to Brandon's throat a blade flashed out of the corner of his eye to block the strike. The demon's steel glanced off the other blade but it wasn't enough.

It tore through Brandon's shirt at his shoulder, slicing through his skin. "Arrrgh!"

Then a cry above him and a piercing scream from the demon that had almost ended his life. Brandon staggered to his feet. The professor stood in front of him holding Brandon's sword, but he was staring at something to the right. Brandon turned. Three more demons twenty yards away warily approached, spreading out on their left and right. Brandon held out his hand for his sword, but Marcus didn't give it to him.

"I think now would be an excellent time to give me back my sword."

"You don't need it."

"Are you crazy?"

"It's time to live from your strength, to fight from your glory, to battle from the core of your gifting."

Brandon glanced at the demons, now fifteen yards away, then stepped toward Marcus. "No, I need my sword."

"You wield the sword well, but you wield something else with even more power." The professor pointed at Brandon's mouth. "You are the song. Step into it now without holding back, with all faith in the Spirit."

An image of himself singing on top of a snow-covered peak as a morning sun crested a far range of mountains flashed into his mind, then vanished. Yes. Brandon blinked and leveled his gaze on the demons. He opened his mouth and a song poured out he'd never heard. The sound of it thundered throughout the battleground and grew still louder—the melody soaring to the sky and shaking the ground.

As he continued to sing, Brandon advanced toward the demons, whose eyes widened as they staggered backward. Brandon closed his eyes and ten seconds later the song was over. He opened his eyes and where the demons had been a moment earlier only gray dust remained.

He spun toward Marcus. "Did you see that?"

"You are indeed the song."

"And you most certainly are the teacher."

The professor smiled.

"Thank you." Brandon embraced Marcus, then took his sword and glanced around the bowl. None of the demons were left unless they had regrouped behind the massive boulders the size of a small building to his left. "Did you see where Reece and Dana went?"

"I was too engaged with other activities."

"Same here." Brandon pointed to the pile of boulders. "You circle from the left, I'll come in from the right. It's the only place they could be."

Marcus nodded and in a less than a minute they reached the boulders and split in either direction. After six paces he found Dana leaning against the rock wall, her chest heaving as she sucked in breaths and glanced rapidly side to side. She slumped forward when she spotted him. Splattered blood covered her left side and her hair looked like she'd been in a wind tunnel.

"Are you all right?"

She nodded and let the tip of her sword drop to the ground. "Better now. And you?"

"I'm okay." He pointed over her shoulder. "Marcus went that way to find Reece. Let's go find them and get out of here."

They jogged around the circumference of the boulder, but after only ten strides a piercing wail filled the air and they stumbled to a halt. "We need to keep going." He glanced at Dana's wide eyes. "What's wrong?"

She pointed to the top of the bowl. At least forty demons were climbing down from the ridge toward them. An instant later another wave appeared behind them and followed them down. Then another wave behind those.

"Where are they coming from?"

"Remember what Reece said? I'm guessing too much time has passed since we came inside. The gate has been open too long and the enemy is sending reinforcements."

"We have to get out now." He grabbed her hands.

"No. We have to all be together."

She was right. Reece had said if they didn't leave together, some of them could get stuck inside. Brandon turned to the demons sprinting toward them, swords raised, guttural cries pouring out of their dark maws. He opened his mouth to sing but this time no song came. Not good. He raised his sword and braced for impact. "We have a problem."

Dana didn't answer and sank to her knees.

"What are you doing? There's no time for prayer."

She didn't answer.

"Dana! Get your sword up!"

"Trust me, Brandon, as I trusted you." He barely heard her response against the wind and the shrieks of the demons. "Join me."

"You're calling for angels."

"No, something more powerful. Trust me."

The demons would reach them in twenty heartbeats at most. But multiple times since coming to Well Spring he'd seen her sense things in the spiritual realm he hadn't. In her soul he'd asked her to trust him. And she had.

Brandon knelt and closed his eyes, ready for his head to leave his shoulders at any second. The screech of the demons' voices sliced through the air and images of death filled his mind.

"You are a consuming fire, Lord. Consume us now, and bring the power of your light."

"So be it." Brandon opened his eyes to a wall of demons closing in on them. Three seconds. He grabbed Dana's hand and wrapped his other arm around her in a futile attempt to block her from the onslaught.

As he did, a razor-thin column of light appeared between them and the demons and grew till it was as thick as one of the redwoods inside Dana's soul. Then it exploded into bits of light the size of snowflakes, filling the air around them. Then each snowflake of light exploded and Brandon covered his eyes and fell flat on the ground. A sound like thunder rushed overhead and then there was silence.

Brandon pushed himself to his knees and pulled in a breath. The air was cool, the heat had vanished, and thin blades of grass pushed their way up through the barren soil. Hundreds of demons lay motionless on the sand and as he stared at their bodies they turned from black to gray to the color of the soil. A moment later they sank into the ground and were gone. He raised his face to the now-blue sky and continued to take in huge draws of air. This time it was over.

Blood seeped out of the wound on Brandon's left shoulder and the right leg of his pants was ripped and smeared with blood, but he couldn't feel it. All he felt was freedom. After a minute he glanced up at the field of battle. Dana breathed deep and opened her eyes.

"Are you okay?"

She nodded but didn't speak, her eyes bright.

He pulled her to her feet. "Let's go find Reece and the professor."

When they rounded the far corner they spotted Marcus on the ground fifty yards away. Marcus knelt with his back to them, gulping air into his lungs—but where was Reece? Oh no. Reece lay on the other side of Marcus—motionless—the ground in front of him stained with blood. Brandon and Dana staggered over to them and thudded to their knees.

"No." Brandon pressed his hand on Reece's chest where blood seeped out of a long gash.

The big man laid one palm over the top of Brandon's hand, the other covering his eyes, and smiled.

"We've got to get you out of here now."

"Yes, it's time to go, but don't worry, Maximus. The cut is not deep, the wound not mortal. I'll be all right and I will have a nice scar on my physical body to remind me of this battle."

Brandon sat back on his heels. Not a mortal wound. Relief surged through him.

Reece coughed. "Remember me talking about your final lesson? The one I couldn't tell you when it would happen? This was it. And you have all passed with soaring colors. Well done."

"Defeating the enemy and setting you free," Brandon said.

"No, that's not the lesson. Maybe you haven't passed." He squeezed Brandon's hand. The grip was strong. Reece would be all right.

"The final lesson is learning to love. The lesson is discovering that within you lies the willingness to lay down your life for others. That is love. That is what you have done. All of you."

Brandon's breathing slowed as he glanced at Marcus. The professor's face was gaunt and full of pain.

"What's wrong?" He followed Marcus's gaze to Reece, who slid his hand away from covering his eyes. No. It couldn't be. His eye sockets were seared as if a white-hot piece of iron had been shoved into each of them. Blood around the outside of the sockets had already dried, and nothing remained of Reece's eyes but two black-charred orbs.

"Reece, I don't understand . . ." He had no words. Brandon looked at the others and the despair on their faces told him they didn't either.

"I don't understand why the darkness either."

He didn't know? How could he not know what had happened? Was he in too much shock to realize?

Reece tried to sit up and collapsed back on the sand. "Time to get out of here. I'll see you three on the other side. Take hands."

An instant later the sand, the sky, Reece—all vanished. The chair Brandon sat on at Well Spring seemed to push up into his legs, telling him they were back in the real world . . . no, not the real world, the physical world. Brandon grabbed the edges of his chair to steady himself as a cool breeze floated up from the river and pressed into his sweat-soaked T-shirt. Dana sat forward in her chair, blinking, breathing slowly through narrowed lips, tears welling up.

"Did you see his eyes? They're gone!" Brandon stared over the river into the mountains, his face warm, disbelief pounding against him. "We have to get to the hospital."

"Why?"

"To make sure he's come out of the coma." Brandon stood and walked to the edge of the patio, then spun back toward them. "To see if he still has his sight."

"He doesn't, Brandon," Marcus said.

"Just because he lost his sight inside his soul doesn't mean the same thing happened in the physical world."

Dana stood and shuffled toward him. "That's exactly what it means."

"How do you know?"

She stared at him. "Brandon, think what happened to your arms when you went into my soul and rescued me." She pointed down. "Look at your arms and legs right now."

He scraped at the blood hardening on his pants and shirt.

"We don't know for sure." Brandon paced back and forth across the limestone and stopped on the edge overlooking the river.

Marcus joined them on the edge of the listening post. "Then let's get cleaned up and return to Seattle and find out—one way or another."

+++

They arrived at the hospital at three o'clock Saturday afternoon. Dana sat on the sofa in the lobby praying for Brandon, for Marcus, for herself. As the doctor ambled out of the elevator she spotted the three of them and clipped over, her face a mixture of puzzlement and concern.

"What's his condition?"

"He came out of the coma this morning and we thought things were fine. He talked to us briefly, then almost immediately went into a deep sleep, which is not uncommon."

She pressed her lips together and pulled her chart tight into her chest. "Then he started thrashing about in his sleep. We gave him a mild sedative that calmed him down until . . ." She trailed off, the bewildered look surfacing again on her face.

"What happened?" Brandon leaned in toward her.

"There's no explanation for it." She glanced at each of them. "I'm afraid your friend has been blinded."

Dana closed her eyes as her chin drooped to her chest. Unbelievable. But why was she surprised? She'd told Brandon this would happen. But she'd held on to the sliver of hope that this time would be different. That because it was Reece Roth, he would be okay.

"How?" Marcus said.

The doctor rubbed the edge of her pen along the top of her clipboard. "We don't understand it. One moment he was sleeping, his breathing steady, the next he's screaming and clutching his eyes. When we pulled his hands away it was as if—"

"A branding iron had been shoved into each eye." Dana stared out the window and watched a stiff wind bending the fir trees outside the hospital.

"Yes." She frowned at her. "That's exactly what it was like. We've run every test we could think of and even called in an ophthalmologist, and he is as baffled as we are as to what happened."

"Can we see him?"

"Tomorrow, yes. We are keeping him under close observation."

"When will he be able to leave?"

The doctor stared at Dana, then looked at Marcus and Brandon. "Physically he'll be able to leave as early as tomorrow night, but on a practical level his life is going to be radically different—a life that will take months to adjust to. At some point he might be able to live alone again, but there's no telling how long that will take. I'm sorry."

As they left the hospital, Brandon scrubbed the back of his head. "I'm sure you two are struggling with this as much as I am. Since we've been up for thirty-two hours I should be exhausted, but with Reece on my mind sleep will elude me for a few more."

"I feel the same," the professor said. "Shall we gather at the fire pit? Dana?"

Dana nodded. Something told her it was a good idea to stay together a little longer.

FIFTY-TWO⊙

Marcus stood with Brandon and Dana and stared at the growing flames as more of the wood in Reece's fire pit was engulfed, the aroma of smoke spreading over the backyard. A fine mist dropped out of the slate-gray sky and covered the grass and trees in moisture and silence. No birds sang. No wind caressed their faces as the reality of the battle sank in.

A great victory. At a terrible price. Each of them said a few words. They didn't need to say more. There was comfort in the quiet. Where would they go from here? What would happen to their training? What would this do to Reece?

Marcus looked up at the ring of maple trees along the back edge of Reece's land. A fitting cathedral for questions that couldn't be answered. The only sounds were Dana's soft sobs and the ripping of his own heart.

"How is he going to lead us now?" Brandon asked.

"Maybe we're supposed to lead him," Dana said.

Brandon kicked at the stones surrounding the fire pit. "I don't think that's the way it works."

A squiggle of rain wound its way down Marcus's neck. He didn't bother to brush it away. It was a kiss. Of pain. Of life. Of grief. Of hope. A tear from the eye of God. Living water.

I am in this.

How could God be in this? Marcus waited for the Spirit to tell him, but no answer came. Brandon tilted his head back and sang, his voice just above a whisper. It looked like his eyes were closed. The haunting melody stirred peace and sorrow in equal measure and Marcus soaked it deep into his soul.

> *A warrior riding, a warrior broken,*
> *Wounds are healed and freedom spoken,*
> *The price of battle, so high a cost,*
> *Dreams are born, and dreams are lost,*
> *Ever onward, no more in hiding,*
> *We are four, the Warriors Riding.*

By the time Brandon had repeated it twice, tears slid down Marcus's cheeks. It didn't make sense to be this torn up inside. It wasn't like the man was dead. But Reece Roth without his piercing blue eyes? Him not being able to gaze on the mountains of Well Spring, to see the sun fire the river full of diamonds on early summer mornings?

"I ache for him. I . . ." Dana's voice caught and she didn't finish.

No one responded. No one needed to. The three stood for another . . . Marcus didn't know how long. A minute? An hour? He was about to suggest moving inside when something dark flashed in his peripheral vision far to the left. Marcus whipped his head up. A man stood on the edge of the woods seventy yards away. "Nine o'clock, friends. On point."

They turned as one and Marcus took a step ahead of Brandon and Dana. "Speak to me. What are you seeing?"

"Darkness. All around him." Brandon stepped forward to Marcus's side. "Not thinking this party crasher is human."

"My assessment is the same." Marcus turned to Dana. "What are you sensing?"

"He's clearly demonic."

The man strolled toward them as if he were walking through Bothell's Blythe Park on a lazy Sunday afternoon, a placid smile on his face. He twirled a varnished walking stick in a wide arc, then pointed it at them when he was twenty yards away.

"Hello, my lovely friends."

His hair was dark, parted on the side; average features, average height, average build. He could be a thousand men. One hundred thousand. He seemed familiar. It was in the eyes. Three images flashed through Marcus's mind. The usher at the church service. The man who had slipped into the back of his class unseen. The man who was in Reece's memory when the three of them watched the killing of his wife and daughter. Anger surged in Marcus's chest. And a sense of power far greater than he'd ever felt.

He glanced at Dana and Brandon. The expression on both their faces said they recognized the man as well. It was Zennon. The demon stopped ten yards away and opened his arms—his smile even wider. "Good evening. At least it will be for seven more hours." He pulled back his jacket sleeve and the navy blue shirt underneath, revealing a thin white watch. "Ah, I was wrong. Six hours and thirty-nine minutes. I enjoy this human penchant for keeping track of the seconds."

The man lowered his arms and stabbed the point of the walking stick into the grass at his feet. "Do you mind terribly if I join you?"

"All indicators say you already have." Marcus took a step forward, as did Dana and Brandon.

"This is true." The man laughed and slid his hands into the pockets of his coat. "Look at you. My, my. The three of the prophecy, singing songs, enjoying the exquisite evening together."

"What do you want?" Marcus said.

"Why, isn't it obvious?" He motioned to his right toward Reece's home. "To offer my condolences on the tragic disfigurement of your meddlesome mentor."

"We know what you are, Zennon," Brandon said.

"Or should we call you Alexis?" Dana said.

"I have no name. Not really." The man gave them a mock frown. "I think you've realized this, no?" Zennon took a step to the right and gazed up at the maples. "I must convey my congratulations on your victory." He turned and gave a slight bow. "We didn't anticipate you being as strong as you turned out to be."

Zennon stepped back to the left, lifted his head, and fixed his black eyes on them one at a time, then reached into his pocket and pulled out a gold coin. He placed it on the back of his hand and rolled it across his fingers, then flicked it into the air. He caught it in his other hand and squeezed it till his hand turned white.

"But now you have our attention. Full attention. And not just mine." The demon pointed at each of them, then made a circle in the air above his head with his forefinger. "You are now known at higher echelons of our organization." Zennon raised his hand and fingers toward them as if to attack.

A chill washed over Marcus but he batted it aside. Not anymore. He glanced at Brandon and Dana. "Are you thinking what I'm thinking?"

They both nodded. He turned back to Zennon and pointed his finger at the demon as he took another step forward. "Go, in the name of Jesus and by his blood and his authority. You are cast down, defeated, and have no power over us."

Zennon shuddered and stumbled back—but a moment later confidence and contempt filled his face. "You have no idea what you're dealing with."

Brandon's voice filled the air to Marcus's left as the musician joined him stride for stride. "Jesus Christ is Lord. He is King. He is the Morning Star, His eyes are full of fire and a sword is in his hand. All rule in heaven and on earth has been given to him and we claim that power against you now."

Zennon staggered back another few steps as Dana called out from Marcus's right.

"He is the Alpha and Omega, the beginning and end of all things. There is lightning in his hands and he is crushing his enemies. We bind you in the name of Christ. Leave us!"

Frustration and fear flitted across Zennon's face as he slowly backed away. "Do you really want to bring this on yourselves? Do you really want to take on this battle? Do you truly realize what you're about to set in motion? It's not over."

A voice behind them called out, clear and powerful. "No more lies, Zennon. It *is* over. Go now or we will destroy you."

Zennon glanced behind them and rage filled his face.

"Go!"

As the word rang out, Zennon vanished and Marcus and the others spun around.

Reece stood twenty yards behind them, sunglasses covering his eyes, his hand on the shoulder of another man. Dana sprinted to him and wrapped her arms around the big man and pressed her head into his chest. Marcus and Brandon jogged over and joined her.

"What are you doing here?" Marcus said.

He grinned. "You didn't think I'd let you three have all the fun, did you?"

Brandon pointed south. "But the hospital . . . we thought they weren't going to let you out till tomorrow night at the earliest."

Reece smiled again. "I convinced them otherwise."

"How are you . . . ?" Marcus didn't know how to finish the sentence.

"I'm free." Reece adjusted his glasses, then turned to the short silver-haired man beside him. "I'd like you to meet Doug Lundeen, whom you've met previously, but not in the conventional way."

Marcus smiled. It felt strange to shake the hand of a man he'd been inside the soul of, but at the same time it felt like the most natural thing in the world. After greeting Doug they all ambled over to Reece's deck and sat in a circle.

Silence lingered for a few moments till Reece patted his legs. "Go ahead, ask the question, I know you want to."

Dana leaned forward. "Your eyes . . . how will you—?"

"It's okay, Dana." Reece patted Dana's hands. "Doug will be staying with me for a while and help me do some rearranging inside the house. And he'll coach me on how to get around the place without taking out my kneecaps and forehead till I get used to my new condition. Blind people live alone all over the world."

Dana glanced at the others. "No, what I meant was—"

"I know what you meant." He patted her hand again. "We'll talk about that more when the time is right. It's okay. In the meantime, do you remember what the prophecy says? 'And for one, their vision will grow clear . . .' I am going to assume that means me."

"Grow clear?" Dana said. "Meaning your blindness will be healed?"

"That's my hope, but I don't know. But it is an assurance to me that he is utterly and completely in this."

"Wait a second." Brandon frowned. "Throw that train in reverse. You just applied the prophecy to yourself. Tamera isn't the temple? Are you saying you're one of the four?"

Reece pulled back his hat, then opened his arms. "That's exactly what I'm saying. You're stuck with me for the long run."

Joy spilled over Marcus and he saw it on the faces of Brandon and Dana as well. For the next hour they told Doug the story of being inside Reece's soul, celebrated that their leader was one of the four, and thanked the Spirit for all he had brought them through together.

Finally Reece clasped his hands and took a deep breath. "Friends, the spirit is willing but the flesh is weak. I would enjoy going on for many more hours, but my body has been through a bit of trauma and it's telling me to rest. I must obey. But before we part, I'd like to get a final thought from Doug. He's been a spiritual mentor to me for many years and he has much wisdom to offer."

Doug stared at the wood decking for a few moments, then raised his head and looked at each of them. "Are you beginning to believe? Are you starting to accept who you are?" He didn't wait for an answer and pointed at Dana. "You are the leader."

Dana shook her head. "I still don't see—"

Brandon's laughter stopped her. "Are you kidding? You're the one who took the lead in getting us back to the fire pit to hear Reece's story, then you led us into his soul, led in his healing, then led in bringing God's fire down as I floundered about what to do. Don't you see it?" He motioned to the others. "We all do."

Marcus grinned as acceptance and wonder flashed on Dana's face. Brandon was so right. She was the leader. Just as Reece was the temple, bringing healing to Dana's, Brandon's, and his heart in a way he could never have imagined when this journey began.

Doug smiled at Brandon. "And I would surmise that when Marcus demonstrated to you that he is indeed the teacher, you came to a full understanding that you are indeed the song."

"This is true." Brandon grinned.

"You all must know who you are." Doug's face grew serious and he pointed to his heart. "In here. The wolf has risen, and your battle comes quickly."

Brandon glanced at Reece, then back to Doug. "So is now the time we get to know about who the wolf is and what we have to do?"

"Soon we will speak to you of it in detail." His somber countenance vanished and was replaced with one of joy. "But for now let us rejoice in that which he has bestowed on the four of you."

Doug clasped his hands together. "One final question. Have each of you found gratification in what has been placed upon your plate since going to Well Spring?"

"Most assuredly," Marcus said.

Dana closed her eyes, smiled, and nodded. "Oh yes."

"Brandon?" Doug said.

"Are you kidding? My world's been totally rocked with revelation and revolution. It'll never be the same now that we've traveled the path of freedom."

"Traveled?" Doug wagged a thin finger in the air. "Nay. You speak of your journey as if it has already happened. There is no accuracy in your use of the past tense. The path of joy and freedom has not yet been traveled. It has only just begun."

Doug smiled at each of them. "Yes, you've had a taste of freedom, but only a taste. There is a banquet awaiting you. And you've all been invited to the head of the table."

BONUS CHAPTER

FIFTY-THREE

BRANDON ROLLED OUT OF BED ON SUNDAY, TAPPED HIS cell phone, and looked at the time. *Wow.* Three in the afternoon. He'd slept for sixteen hours but felt like he could go another eight.

His mind spun at the events of the past forty-eight hours. Reece's rescue. The loss of Reece's sight. Meeting Doug Lundeen, and his hinting about the wolf rising, but also about more freedom coming. Realizing he and Marcus and Dana and Reece, and maybe now Doug, would be together awhile longer. The reality of spiritual battle. He shook his head as if it could stop the onslaught of thoughts and emotions and stumbled into his kitchen. Too much. The thoughts invigorated and overwhelmed him at the same time. He needed a distraction.

As Brandon headed for the kitchen, his cell phone chimed. It was a text message from Kevin. Perfect timing. YOU AROUND?

After brewing strong black coffee and downing two cups as he buzzed through his e-mail, Brandon dialed his manager.

"I'm around."

"You have plans this afternoon?"

"Hanging with you and not talking about the past few days." Brandon rubbed his eyes and glanced down the hallway toward his bedroom. "The other option is going back to bed."

"Quite the adventure, huh?"

"It'll rock you, I promise. We'll yak about it, but right now I just want a little escape."

"Excellent. I was hoping to play you one of my songs," Kevin said.

Yes! Brandon tapped his feet in rhythm with his hand pounding against his thigh and grinned as he looked through the windows at the sun streaming through his backyard. Kevin was going cliff jumping. "That is so sweet. You're totally ready for me to hear it?"

"I wouldn't say I'm—"

"Kevin Kaison in concert. Rock on." He tried to imagine what kind of song Kevin had written. Rock? Pop? Folk? It didn't matter. It didn't even matter if it was any good. So many people talked about dreams but never tried to live them. But Kevin had taken their talk about the strength Brandon had seen in him and turned it into action. And he would do everything he could to help launch Kevin's musical rocket ship into the heavens.

"Where do you want to go?"

"I'm thinking outside. The sun is shining, and do we Seattleites ever waste a sunny day?" Kevin said.

"Name the place."

"What do you think about meeting at Gas Works Park?"

"Gas Works? Not much."

"How long has it been since you were there?" Kevin asked.

"I've never been there."

"Are you kidding? It's been used for movies and reality TV shows and people say it's the strangest park in Seattle, and probably ranks among the strangest in the world."

"I know, I know, I've actually read a lot about the place—just haven't gotten around to checking it out." He had been meaning to get there ever since he moved to Seattle fourteen years ago, but he'd been meaning to see a lot of things he hadn't gotten around to seeing. Why was it the tourists often did more interesting things in cities than the residents ever had?

"You live too far from downtown."

Brandon laughed. "You live too close."

✦✦✦

An hour and twenty minutes later Brandon pulled into the lot next to the park, got out of his car, and stared at the remnants of the last remaining coal gasification plant in the US.

The old boiler house had been converted into a picnic shelter and the former exhauster-compressor building was now a children's play barn, with a maze of painted machines.

Kevin pulled up a few minutes later and they strolled through the park, his manager searching for the right spot to unveil his song.

"Did you know that hill was built specifically for flying kites?" Brandon pointed at the mound to their right.

"I did."

He pointed to their left. "Did you know they've shot fireworks off on the Fourth here for years?"

"Yes." Kevin smiled.

"Did you know the Peace Concerts they do in Seattle every summer used to be exclusively held at Gas Works?"

"No." Kevin laughed and shifted his guitar to his other hand. "Explain this to me. You've got all this trivia locked away about the park, but you've never been here?"

"History has a habit of frequently snagging my rapt attention."

"Now I'm finding out things about you I never knew."

They eased down to the edge of the park where it met up with Lake Union. Two women and a man paddled by in yellow and red kayaks, the man on the verge of rolling over, the other two laughing at him.

Kevin stopped and pointed to a bench. "This is a good spot. There's no one else around unless more kayaks come by."

"I have to warn you, if you're serious about music, someday you'll have to start playing for more people than just me."

"Someday isn't today. And not when I'm playing a new song for the first time."

As Kevin tuned his guitar, Brandon gazed at the Seattle skyline and watched a group of kids fly navy blue and bright yellow and red kites. A young couple tossed a Frisbee near the south end of the park.

The sound of Kevin's tuning stopped and Brandon turned back toward him. "Ready?"

"The song's rough."

"Oh really? I can't relate." Brandon grinned. "My songs are never, ever rough when I first play them for you."

Kevin nodded. "Point taken." He slid his hand up the neck of the guitar near the fifth fret, laid his fingers on the strings, and strummed a chord that sounded like an A. Then he launched into a quickly shifting series of chords up and down the neck from the twelfth fret to the first with a fluidity that tweaked Brandon's brain. Kevin didn't miss a note and the chord progression wasn't simple. He'd told Brandon he dabbled in playing guitar. This wasn't dabbling. Brandon didn't know many musicians who could make a guitar sing like this.

Amazing. The image of Kevin as Thor flashed into his mind. His friend was a guitar god. For a moment Brandon considered interrupting Kevin, then decided against it. This was too good to ruin by wondering how he'd gotten this skilled and why he'd kept it a secret for so long.

Brandon folded his arms and smiled as his manager closed his eyes, lost in the music, his hand gliding over the fret board like the river flowed over the rocks at Well Spring. A few minutes later the instrumental piece ended and he glanced up at Brandon.

"It was okay?"

"It was more than okay, bro." Brandon grabbed Kevin around the neck. "Wanna tell me why you've been holding out on me about the rock-star talent?"

"No reason."

"Liar."

"I'll tell you someday." Kevin rubbed the body of his guitar with his palm. "Not quite yet."

Brandon stood and stepped back to watch Kevin from the front. "If that was the warm-up, I can't wait to hear your song."

Kevin adjusted his glasses and nodded. The opening chord this time was a D, to an A-minor, to a G. Nothing fancy, but then he kicked it into a higher gear again, moving up the fret board with ease and utilizing a series of more exotic chords and fingerings.

When he started singing, Brandon was surprised for the second time. Kevin's voice was almost as good as his guitar playing. A high baritone with a depth to it that suggested a natural talent combined with years of training.

> Needing, reaching, wanting more of this to follow,
> Feeling, hoping, seeing dreams that fade and turn so hollow,
> See me, lead me, can I truly lay it down,
> My life a vapor, casting off my crown,
> Time for living, time for dying, one breath left to take,
> In this moment, leaping, flying, a destiny to make.
>
> And our lives are gone in an instant,
> But they echo on forever,
> And our lives are poured out for a moment,
> But they ripple out everlasting.

The Spirit rushed through Brandon and he stopped analyzing the tune as a musician. He let the power of the words and the rest of the music and lyrics bury him simply as a person who needed to hear this song. When Kevin finished, Brandon said nothing for well over thirty seconds. When he did speak, it was almost a whisper.

"Unbelievable."

Kevin's eyes asked if Brandon meant it.

"Thirty-seven thousand feet. That's how high you've blown me out of the water. If you have eight more songs like that one, you're getting a record deal in about ten seconds. And next concert you're playing that song."

"I don't kno—"

"I do." Brandon stood for a moment longer grinning at his friend. Kevin had a gift. And as much more than a guitar god. He was a warrior of song.

"I think you've just got your first fan." Brandon hitched his thumb toward a woman with shoulder-length brown hair sitting twenty yards to the left who looked their direction, then back toward the park. She wore sunglasses, khaki shorts, a blue sleeveless shirt, and white running shoes. One hand held a phone, the other a black leather leash attached to a young-looking golden retriever.

Kevin glanced at her, then turned back to Brandon. "Wow. Brain fry."

"What?"

A confused look passed over Kevin's face.

"Why the weird look?"

"You're going to think I'm out there beyond Jupiter."

"Try me."

Kevin lowered his voice. "I saw her before I started playing. Way before. I saw that exact woman this morning as I was making breakfast."

"You what?"

"I was frying eggs for a sausage, bagel, and egg sandwich when this scene goes off in my head like I'm watching a movie." Kevin stopped. "Why are you smiling?"

"Nothing. Keep going."

"She was standing with one foot on the wood decking of a small sailboat and her other foot on a gray dock. The boat wasn't tied up and it was inching away from the dock, and she's still straddling the dock and the boat. It was obvious she would have to choose one to step onto in a few seconds at most or she'd end up taking a bath. She was glancing back and forth between the boat and the dock when the picture faded."

"I think that might have been God."

"Really?"

"Now here's where you're going to think I'm strange." Brandon planted his foot on the bench. "I think you should go talk to her."

"Yeah, right."

"Yeah. Right. Step into it, bro. Follow the Wild Goose."

Kevin frowned. "The Wild—?"

"The Holy Spirit."

As it turned out, Kevin didn't need to.

"Excuse me."

They turned to the woman, who was now a few yards away and strolling toward them.

"What's the name of the song you just played?"

Kevin raised his hand to block the sun as he looked up at her. "It doesn't have a name yet."

She only nodded in response.

"It's new."

"So you haven't recorded it?"

Kevin glanced at Brandon and smiled. "Not yet."

"People need to hear it."

"You liked it?"

The woman nodded. "I think your song just gave me an answer." She extended her hand. "Jane Love."

"My pleasure." Kevin stood and shook her hand. "I'm Kevin Kaison and this is Brandon Scott."

She turned to Brandon. "The singer."

Brandon nodded at Kevin. "We're both singers."

"I can hear that."

Kevin set his guitar lightly against the bench. "You said the song answered a question?"

Jane took off her sunglasses to reveal bright, intelligent eyes. "I own a small publishing company here in Seattle. Business has been surprisingly good and I'm at the point where I need to either stay small and keep turning down opportunities to grow or bite the proverbial bullet and expand. Which means reaching more people with our books."

She tapped her head. "But it also means more headaches, more stress, and less freedom. The pressure of societal expectations—friends and family and authors—versus the tranquility that comes with a lower speed setting on life's treadmill. I didn't know what I was going to do till just now."

A look of surprise splashed across Kevin's face. "I know what you're going to do."

"Is that so?"

Kevin nodded.

"In other words, among your list of accomplishments is the ability to read minds? But even if you didn't have that skill, you'd still have a 50 percent chance of being right."

Kevin rubbed his fingers against his lips as his gaze bounced from the ground to Brandon and back to the ground. "Uh, I had a . . . I saw you in my mind this morning."

Jane didn't respond so Kevin continued and told her about his vision.

Her face went blank and she blinked. "How do you know that? How do you know about that dream?" She took half a step back and her dog barked twice.

"I don't. I just—"

"That's been my recurring dream for the past two months. How did you do that? Who are you?"

"Just a guy." Kevin gestured toward Brandon with his thumb. "His manager. A wannabe musician. Someone trying to get closer to God and get better at hearing his voice. Happily married. Now you know everything about me."

"I have a suspicion there's much more to you than what you've just described." She bent down, patted her dog, and whispered something in its ear.

Brandon nodded. "Um, sorry to freak you out like that. Things like this have been happening a lot lately and—"

"No, no." Jane stood and held up her free hand. "Your insight did set me back for a moment, yes, but there's no apology necessary.

I think God speaks as well, but I've never had something like this happen to me directly."

She put her sunglasses back on, pulled two business cards out of her pocket, and handed one to each of them. "If you ever have a notion to do a book on these experiences of yours, call me. It could be a fascinating read. And thank you."

As Jane sauntered off, Brandon called after her, "Are you going to expand or stay small?"

Jane spun, smiled, and pointed at Kevin. "Ask him."

Brandon laughed and turned to Kevin. "I like her. She's going to stay small and avoid the insanity, don't you think?"

"I thought you were the one who heard from God." Kevin winked. "She's going to grow."

"How do you kn—?" Brandon stopped himself and smiled. "Welcome to the new world of the Spirit, bro."

BONUS CHAPTER

FÍFTY-FOUR

DANA WOKE UP EARLY SUNDAY AFTERNOON KNOWING she had to do two things: e-mail the station to let them know she wouldn't be showing up in the morning, and e-mail Perry to see if he'd be willing to get together and have a brief conversation. The first made sense—she needed at least a little time to process everything that had happened over the past few days without the pressure of business pounding down on her. But getting together with Perry? Was that idea the Spirit's or some crazy idea left of left field?

She sighed as she made herself a latte with an extra shot. The idea wasn't out of left field. It was right. The thought had floated at the back of her mind ever since Brandon went into her soul and set her on the path of healing. And now was the time to take action. She needed restitution, or resolution, or to make amends. It didn't matter what she called it—it was time to apologize.

When her drink was finished, she topped it with chocolate sprinkles, carried it over to her kitchen table, and turned on her laptop. As it booted up she tried to form the right words in her mind. Nothing came.

After sitting and staring at her laptop screen for three minutes, she made it simple:

Hi, Perry,

I'd like to have a short talk with you. It has nothing to do with getting back together. There are just a few things I need to say. I'd prefer it was in person, sometime this week if possible.

Thanks for considering it,

Dana

After a long, near-scalding bath that made her relax more than she had in a week, Dana fixed herself another latte and meandered over to the built-in bookshelves on both sides of her fireplace. Getting lost in a classic film from the thirties or forties was the perfect antidote to two days of severe overstimulation of her emotional, physical, and spiritual resources.

After four minutes of browsing she finally settled on *Holiday*, with Katharine Hepburn and Cary Grant. Before starting she refreshed her e-mail and was surprised to see a response already from Perry.

Dana,

That's interesting that you'd like to meet. I would too. I've wanted to say something to you as well. So, yes, I'd like to get together. I know it's short notice, but if you're not busy, how about this evening? If you are, I'm open pretty much all week. Name the time.

Perry

Dana looked at the clock above her fireplace. Three o'clock. Sure. Why not? The Great Kate and Cary could wait.

✦✦✦

The day was beautiful so they agreed to meet at Kirkland's Marina Park. Perry's dark curly hair was ruffled by a breeze out of the south, just cool enough to make the mocha in her hands a welcome treat. Her third latte of the day. She wouldn't get to sleep till midnight.

They walked to the end of the pier and watched the boats march back and forth across their vision on a choppy Lake Washington. They chatted about plans for the summer and what they'd been reading and how work was going for each of them. Their banter was natural and frequent laughter added a nice flavor to the conversation.

She smiled as she watched Perry talk as much with his hands as his mouth, his dark brown eyes growing wide, then narrowing as he talked. She still liked this guy.

"Can I go first?" Perry said.

"Sure."

He adjusted his Disneyland baseball cap and shifted his weight. "I was the definition of cad and scoundrel for breaking up with you on the phone. It's bothered me for a month now, so when I saw your e-mail, well, when I said I think you're an amazing person I meant it. I like you. And you don't do that to amazing, likable people. So I'm really sorry."

"Thanks, and apology accepted, but it's really okay."

Three boats passed in front of them before Dana spoke again. "My turn." She looked at Perry, then turned back to the water. "You were right. I wouldn't open up. I couldn't. But still . . ." She trailed off, searching for the right words.

"It's okay—"

"No, it isn't and it wasn't. I strung you along, promising to go deeper than a centimeter under the surface, and I never did. You hung in there and were very gentle, trying to draw me out, and all I did was fight it. I'm really sorry. Forgive me?"

Perry scuffed the wood at his feet. "There's no reason to apologize. You had every right to be however you wanted to be."

"Yes, but I told you I'd be something different and I didn't do it."

"I forgive you then."

Dana smiled. "Thanks."

"You're welcome."

She wanted that to be it, but Dana needed to say one more thing. "God has been healing me. I don't know if you remember that retreat I told you I was going to in Colorado, but it was powerful. I have a ways to go, but there's hope for me. And someday I'll be ready for a relationship. One that has depth to it. I'm not afraid anymore."

"God is a spectacular physician. You might be ready faster than you think." Perry smiled and held her gaze.

Dana stared into his eyes. Whoops. Perry was receiving a signal she hadn't sent.

"I think I'll be ready slower than you think." There was a part of her that wanted to jump into Perry's arms right then and have him wrap her up in his huge arms and not only pick up where they'd left off but go deeper immediately. But it wasn't right. It wasn't time yet, and she wasn't going to let her emotions carry her off somewhere she wasn't ready to go.

Perry didn't speak but didn't drop his gaze. Finally he smiled. "Okay."

Dana turned and they made their way back to the park. As they reached their cars, Perry offered to take her empty coffee cup. He held his up and looked at it.

"I'd like another shot." He held up hers. "What about you?"

She tried to keep her smile inside but lost the battle. "You're a little too obvious."

He tossed the cups into a trash can. "What if you and I were to connect up again, and instead of watching the boats, we get out on mine next weekend? Out on the Sound? Just as friends."

"Just friends?" She squinted at him.

"Yes. Nothing more."

"Okay. That might work." She pulled her hair back over her ear. "Let me think about it. I'll call you."

That night as Dana watched Hepburn and Grant on-screen, she imagined a man sitting beside her, his arm around her, her pushing in tight, then pushing some popcorn with extra butter into his mouth. She could almost feel the warmth radiating off his body, almost smell his freshly showered man-smell, and almost hear his laughter—but his face was nothing but a blur.

BONUS CHAPTER
FİFTY-FİVE

THE CLINK OF SILVERWARE WAS THE ONLY SOUND AS Marcus and Abbie ate dinner at the top of the Space Needle on Friday night. It was supposed to be a special evening of talking and celebrating. But he'd exhausted his small talk in the car on the way here, and nothing witty to say was coming to mind. And Abbie wouldn't be providing scintillating dinner conversation. He didn't expect her to. The seeds of neglect he'd planted long ago were still growing strong.

"Thanks for coming to dinner."

"Yeah. No one could do anything tonight, so why not?"

Marcus didn't know what he'd expected. Not that winning a battle over his regrets would instantly heal his relationship with Abbie, but he'd hoped it would at least start the thawing process. Kat had suggested this dinner. He wished he'd thought of it.

"I was so inattentive to you girls for so—"

"Let's stay off that trail, okay, Dad? We've been over this a million times. You're sorry, you've changed, it's okay. I forgive you. Done deal, okay?"

No, it wasn't okay, but she was right. The horse was not only dead, but buried so deep there was nothing left to beat. The familiar voice of guilt rose up from his gut, its thin limbs wrapping around his mind. *No, not this time. Hold every thought captive.* He knew it wouldn't be easy becoming a real part of her world. It would probably take the rest of his life. And that was okay.

"Have you been up here before?" He should know whether she had or not, but he didn't.

"Mom brought Jayla and me up here three years ago." Abbie poked at her fettuccine. "But not to the restaurant."

Marcus looked down on Puget Sound and Queen Anne Hill and an orange sunset spreading over the water. "The views are spectacular and the way the restaurant spins, we get to see every view without ever having to move."

"Yeah."

"So is there anything you're particularly looking forward to doing during your summer hiatus?"

Abbie set her fork on the white tablecloth and looked him in the eyes for the first time since they'd arrived at the restaurant. "You know, I appreciate the attempt at doing the whole small-talk thing and asking about me and being interested and I feel like a complete jerk for saying this, and I totally don't want to say this, but here goes . . . You don't have to go to all this effort and try so hard. We're good. Really, truly, totally, okay?" She slumped back in her seat and stared out the huge glass windows.

Marcus swallowed hard. Yes, he knew it wouldn't be easy, but downright brutal?

"My motive for making conversation is not false." Marcus leaned forward. "And I am inter—"

"I know. I just . . ." Abbie picked up her fork and stirred her food.

"I simply thought this would be a fun father-daughter birthday dinner. A chance to spend some time just the two of us."

"My birthday isn't for another three weeks."

"It's an early celebration."

"Uh-huh."

Their waiter arrived a moment later with a refill of bread to Marcus's relief and probably Abbie's as well. When he left, Marcus pulled out an 8 x 10 piece of heavy stock paper. At the top in bold blue-and-green letters he'd written HAPPY BIRTHDAY, ABBIE!

and underneath in smaller letters, Want to Send My Beautiful Daughter a Birthday Wish?

"I won't take any offense if you think this is stupid."

"What are you going to do?"

Marcus showed her the card, then pointed to the windowsill. "We're moving, but this ledge and the windowsill are not. So if I put this card here along with a pen, when we return to this spot in forty-seven minutes or so, I predict many birthday wishes will have been bestowed on you."

Abbie snorted. "Okay."

During the next forty-five minutes there was abundant silence but also conversation as Marcus continued to ask questions that Abbie answered—sometimes with abbreviated answers, sometimes with longer explanations. Behind the hard exterior he could still see the little girl he'd hurt for too many years. No guilt. Instead he would use it to fuel a growing determination to do whatever it took to win back his daughter's heart.

Abbie looked over his shoulder and a smile grew on her face. Marcus turned. They'd come full rotation and the birthday card inched toward them. It was full of writing. He leaned back over his seat, lifted it off the windowsill, and handed it to her.

Her eyes lit up and she laughed as she read through the messages. "Listen to this one, Dad. 'Happy Birthday. Don't kiss boys, they're smelly. But when they get older, they're way better. Wait till they're way better.' Or get this one: 'Birthday wishes and abundant joy, visiting from Germany, your new friends, Aaron and Karoline Kuhn.' They're a long way from home."

After reading three more of the messages, Abbie looked up and gave him the first genuine smile he'd seen in . . . too long. "This was a cool idea."

"You're welcome." Marcus let the ember of hope burn deep inside. "May I see it?"

Marcus laughed as much as Abbie had as he read the notes. At the bottom of the card he stopped and pulled the paper closer.

Get fit, get strong, happy birthday, and hope you live long. Happy Day, Abbie! There was a sketch of a woman lifting a small dumbbell and it was signed *Tamera*. No. Could it be? Marcus looked up and scanned the tables in front and then behind them. Yes, it was her, three tables back.

A second later Tamera spotted him looking at her and a confused look passed over her face. She pointed at him, her expression asking if she knew him. Then she smiled, excused herself from two other ladies, and scooted toward them.

When she reached the table she pointed at Marcus. "I know you!"

"Marcus Amber, we met at Snoqualmie Falls—"

"Oh my gosh, yes! With Reece. I can't believe I didn't realize it immediately. Out of context, you know? How wild to bump into you up here. I've been thinking about you guys."

"Tamera, I'd like you to meet my daughter Abbie."

She pointed both hands at Abbie and leaned back. "The one I just signed the card for. That is too cool. I love, love, love it." She put a hand on the table and leaned in. "You are beautiful."

"Thanks. It's a pleasure to meet you. And thanks also for signing my card. Your drawing is really good."

Tamera laughed. "No, it's not, but you're kind to say so." She spun back to Marcus. "So explain this to me: I've texted Reece four or five times and I've never heard back."

"It's been an intense time, and he recently entered into one of the more challenging moments of his life."

"You going to explain that to me, or do you want me to guess?"

Marcus smiled. "Neither."

"Oh, come on."

"I believe it would be best if he illuminates it for you."

"Okaaaay." Tamera swung her head as if trying to get rid of a crick in her neck. "Are you allowed to tell me how the whole Well Spring getaway thingamabob went?"

Marcus leaned back and opened his palms. "It was an astounding time. Very rich spiritually, very healing for all of us."

"That's so good to hear." Tamera nodded but the expression on her face didn't match her words. "I really wanted to be there. And I still want to be part of what you guys have going on. Are you getting together often?"

"We've been meeting together, yes. We saw each other last Sunday, and I believe we'll convene again sometime next week."

"I like it." Tamera played with her sliver hoop earring. "I'm going to be there."

Marcus stared at her. She didn't say it with even the hint of a question in her mind.

"Reece would be the best one to chat with regarding that."

"You're saying I'm not invited?" She grinned.

"I'm saying I'm not the inviter, only an invitee." Marcus didn't remember Tamera being this assertive at Snoqualmie Falls, but then again, the meeting was brief. Well Spring would have been quite different if Tamera had come. And not necessarily in a good way.

"And you? How is the progression on the TV show going? Reece said you had a meeting with some folks in LA."

She curled her arm slowly. "Better than anyone expected. God is behind the show in a major kick-booty way. It's locked, loaded, and moving forward like a peregrine falcon."

"I see."

They chatted for a few more minutes after which Tamera excused herself. Marcus and Abbie indulged in the Space Needle's famous Lunar Orbiter dessert, complete with billowing clouds of dry ice, served there since the 1962 World's Fair.

On the way home Abbie asked the question Marcus had been wondering himself. "So is that Tamera lady going to be part of this group thing you have going?"

"I don't know." He pulled onto I-5 and glanced at Abbie. "What did you think of her?"

"Not much."

Marcus laughed and his daughter offered her second authentic smile of the evening.

WRITING NOVELS AND LIVING YOUR DREAM

THE OTHER DAY A FRIEND SAID, "YOUR FOURTH BOOK [*Soul's Gate*] comes out this fall? Wow, that is so cool. How long have you dreamed of writing novels?"

"Not that long," I responded with a playful smile. "Only since seventh grade."

He laughed and suggested the desire was built into my DNA the moment God formed me. Yep. Exactly. I believe the dream has been there my whole life—even before I could voice it. And when I read the Chronicles of Narnia at age eleven (thanks, Mom!), I knew I wanted to try to do for others what C. S. Lewis had done for me—take me away to other worlds and immerse me in a story of wonder and fantastical ideas.

But when I tried out for the school paper in eigth grade and was rejected, I constructed a huge sign that said YOU CAN'T WRITE and pasted it on the wall of my mind. I stared at the sign often and I believed. How I believed.

Even with my sign at the forefront of my brain, the dream wouldn't leave. So I dabbled in short stories throughout my teens. I took a creative writing class in high school. I subscribed to *Writer's Digest* magazine. I even went to a few one-day writing seminars in my twenties. I studied books on the craft but rarely—if ever—told anyone about my dream. I never showed anyone my writing and never took any real action to try to make the dream come true.

Because what happens when you launch yourself off the cliff, grasp for your dream, and it slips through your fingers? What do you have then? What do you live for after the biggest vision for your life crashes and burns? As long as I never tried, the dream could stay alive.

In 2002, due to a number of divine circumstances and the unbelievable support of my wife, I started peeling the sign off the wall of my mind and I jumped off the cliff. And in 2010, my first novel, *Rooms*, was published.

Now that the dream has come true, I realize reaching the dream isn't the treasure. The treasure is stepping into something bigger than yourself. It's stepping into the larger story God has created for you. In that moment, when we make that choice, life isn't about you and me anymore, it's about him and living in his story, and his story is so much more than ours could ever be.

Yes, I hope *Soul's Gate* has an impact on your life, but even more I hope you choose to jump off your cliff—whatever it is—and build your wings on the way down. Because a life without risk is one lived in the shadow lands, and I believe we were made to live in the glory of the sun.

AUTHOR'S NOTE

ON THE WRITING OF *SOUL'S GATE*

ONE OF THE MOST FREQUENT QUESTIONS AN AUTHOR GETS is, "How do you come up with your ideas?" The answer is, myriad ways. For *Soul's Gate*, the story came from a friend and me sitting in our shorts around a fire, brainstorming ideas. Once we got going, the story came in a flash. The basic premise was laid out in under half an hour.

And the place we brainstormed? Well Spring. Yes, the ranch is real. I took some liberties and embellished in a few areas, but since the foundation of the story was formed there, my friend and I both thought it would be intriguing for Well Spring to play a large role in the novel.

Soul's Gate didn't start out as a book about the spiritual battle that ebbs and flows all around us—and I still don't think of it in those terms. I see the book as a novel about freedom—which is the reason Christ set us free (Gal. 5:1). Freedom is the aspect of Jesus I love to explore and dwell on the most; that he desires us to be everything we've been designed to be. That he longs for us to be free of our fears, to be free to love with abandon, to be free to step into our destinies with confidence and abundant expectation.

But in writing a story about healing and freedom, there isn't a way to avoid writing about spiritual warfare as well, given the fact we have an enemy whose goal is to steal and destroy that freedom. And writing a story about freedom isn't entered into without resistance.

This novel was my most difficult to write yet by far. That shouldn't have surprised me. While *Rooms* addressed spiritual warfare, *Soul's Gate* takes it up a notch. A few notches.

The enemy of our souls has done a brilliant job of making Western man believe he only exists on TV shows and in movies or in churches that have plunged off the deep end. He doesn't want followers of Jesus to believe demons are real and that they can wreak real havoc in believers' lives. But the enemy *is* real and has a specific goal for your life: destruction, whether you believe in him or not (see 1 Peter 5:8; John 10:10). And much of what followers of Jesus accept as "that's just life" is a calculated attack on their thought life, emotions, and circumstances.

A novel like *Soul's Gate* does not assist the enemy's wish of keeping his deception quiet, so I was hit hard. I've experienced spiritual warfare over the past twenty-five years—in some cases in a very direct way—but I've never had it go on as long and as intensely as during the time I wrote this novel. Which I take as good news. To me this means *Soul's Gate* will likely bring freedom to readers, and that is an exhilarating thought.

But as I've already said, the point isn't the war. The point of *Soul's Gate* is the freedom available if we're willing to fight, and my hope is you'll come away from reading this novel with more freedom than when you started.

Also, I'd be remiss to leave you with the idea that writing this novel was drudgery. It wasn't. There were many moments of pure joy: When scenes popped into my mind fully fleshed out and all I had to do was write them down. When one of the characters would do something I wasn't expecting and I got the chance to watch his actions unfold. (Yes, it's true, novelists are simply scribes more than you know.) When my editors or publisher would throw out an idea and I instantly knew it would improve the novel.

My guess is some of you are wondering if I believe the ideas presented in the novel can really happen, so I'll answer that briefly. Yes, I believe they can. In fact, a number of the incidents in the story come from true-life experiences—some from my life and some from friends of mine. I'll allow you to decide which ones really happened and which ones sprang from my sometimes fertile imagination.

With regard to our spirits traveling inside the souls of others, no, I don't believe that's possible. But then again, I am only a man and I haven't quite figured God out yet—I'm assuming you haven't either—so maybe we should say it is possible in one form or another. I do know we can pray more intensely and more deeply for each other than we often do.

In the end I hope the story entertained you, made you press deeper into Jesus, and gave you a glimpse into the vastness of his love.

To your freedom and his glory,
James L. Rubart, Spring 2012

ACKNOWLEDGMENTS

TO MY BRO, DR. HARRY LEE KRAUS, FOR KEEPING ME inside the lines with regard to medical accuracy.

To my smartest friend, Dr. Randall Ingermanson, for pointing out the shaky spots in my physics and giving me grace to stray into gray areas when I chose to.

To Ruth Voetmann, for your wonderful way with brainstorming.

To my prayer team, for carrying me through the warfare that came in the course of writing this novel.

To my team at Thomas Nelson, for your skill, hearts full of passion, and friendship.

To my editors, Amanda Bostic and Julee Schwarzburg, I want to be as amazingly talented as you someday.

To my publisher and forever friend, Allen Arnold, the playground was better than I imagined.

To Darci, Taylor, and Micah, for seeing me through the journey of writing another novel.

To Jesus, I love this ride you have me on.

READING GROUP GUIDE

1. What are the themes you saw in *Soul's Gate*?

2. Which character could you most relate to? Why is that?

3. Because Reece was taken out by the enemy when he was younger, he doesn't live out of his true strength for many years. Have you done the same during a period of your life? If so, explain.

4. Marcus's heaviest burden is regret. Do you have regrets in your life with which you're letting the enemy weigh you down? If yes, how do you deal with that?

5. Because of Brandon's childhood, he's felt worthless most of his life. Can you relate? If yes, has God helped you combat that lie by telling you how worthwhile you are? How did it happen?

6. Dana has felt abandoned and alone since she was a little girl. Have you ever felt like that? Why? Has anything helped you overcome those feelings?

7. During their time at Well Spring, God gives Dana and Marcus a new name and Brandon gets a name a bit later. Has God ever given you a new name? What is it? What does it mean to you?

8. In chapter 22, Reece implies it might be possible for demons to be inside Christians. Do you think this can happen? Why or why not?

9. During the scene in the church, Marcus sees how the spirit of religion can weigh people down, even though the pastor of that church is a good man. Have you ever experienced anything like this in your own life?

10. Throughout the book, Reece introduces ideas that might seem beyond far-fetched, among them, instant teleportation and God making a person unseen by others. Do you feel these things are possible today? If so, why? Have you experienced or heard of these types of things happening? If you don't think they're possible, why not? They happened in the Bible, so could they still be happening today?

11. Spiritual warfare is one of the central themes in *Soul's Gate*. Have you experienced spiritual warfare? Do you believe it's real?

12. It's obvious the deeper Reece, Marcus, Dana, and Brandon step into freedom, the greater the attack of the enemy. Have you seen this play out in your own life?

13. In chapter 40, Brandon is prayed for in a way not commonly seen. They listened first for the Holy Spirit to speak. Have you ever prayed this way? What happened? Is it something you'd like to try?

14. Our hope is *Soul's Gate* will draw you deep into the freedom that is in Jesus Christ and show you new ways to pursue the life that is in him. If that has happened, what are one or two things you're going to do or explore further going forward?

Don't miss the next
Well Spring Novel:

Memory's Door

CONNECT WITH
JAMES RUBART

WWW.JIMRUBART.COM

 James L. Rubart

 @jimrubart

ABOUT
THE AUTHOR

Author photo by Christophoto, Bothell, WA

JAMES L. RUBART IS A PROFESSIONAL MARKETER, SPEAKER, and writer. He lives with his wife and sons in the Pacific Northwest and still believes he's young enough to water-ski like a madman.